Praise for Rene Gutteridge's Novels

"Got two days? That's all you'll need! Once you start *My Life as a Doormat (in Three Acts)* you'll forget your kids, husband, bills, and need for food or sleep. The only thing you'll wish you had is enough pages for day number three!"

—Denise Hildreth, author of *Savannah from Savannah* and *Savannah Comes Undone*

". . . so enjoyable are Gutteridge's offbeat characterizations and her sense of mischievous delight in the story."

— *Publishers Weekly* review of *Boo Who*

"Gutteridge has a fantastic wit and a firm understanding of what makes everyday life funny."

—Christian Fiction Reviewer

"Gutteridge's characters are believably eccentric."

—American Library Association

"Highly recommended."

—Christian Fiction Review for *Boo, Boo Who,* and *Boo Hiss*

"Rene Gutteridge is a truly gifted comic writer. Her drama background enables her to put sparkling dialogue into her characters' mouths, generating hilarity and turning seemingly mundane incidents into high comedy."

—*The Romance Readers Connection*

"Gutteridge's ability to create down-to-earth characters will cause you to wonder if she's writing about your family."

—www.myshelf.com review of *Troubled Waters*

"The unique and hilarious plot of Rene Gutteridge's latest offering will hold the reader's attention from start to finish."

—www.romantictimes.com review of *Boo*

My Life as a Doormat

(in Three Acts)

Other Books by Rene Gutteridge

Boo

Boo Who

Boo Hiss

The Splitting Storm

Storm Gathering

Storm Surge

Ghost Writer

Troubled Waters

My Life as a Doormat

(IN THREE ACTS)

a romantic comedy

by Rene Gutteridge

WESTBOW
PRESS
A Division of Thomas Nelson Publishers
Since 1798

visit us at www.westbowpress.com

Published in Nashville, Tennessee, by WestBow Press, a division of Thomas Nelson, Inc.

WestBow Press books may be purchased in bulk for educational, business, fund-raising, or sales promotional use. For information, please e-mail SpecialMarkets@ThomasNelson.com.

Library of Congress Cataloging-in-Publication Data

Gutteridge, Rene.
My life as a doormat (in three acts) : a romantic comedy / by Rene Gutteridge.
p. cm.
ISBN 1-59554-084-9 (trade paper)
I. Title.
PS3557.U887M9 2006
813'.6—dc22 2005029656

Printed in the United States of America
06 07 08 09 10 RRD 6 5 4 3

To anyone who has ever
felt stepped on.

Chapter 1

[She glances over the menu.]

I'm practical. Practical people can be romantics. I don't think the two contradict each other. Sure, I cringe when an insane amount of money is spent on a dozen roses, and as I watch them die their slow deaths despite the Evian and the aspirin tablet, I can't help but wonder what better use there was for forty dollars. Can the feeling of holding roses really match saving the starving children of the world? I simply pose the question.

I'm getting sidetracked. The fact of the matter is that I just see romance differently. I see it in defined spaces, with reason and structure attached. Romance doesn't necessarily need spontaneity either. Scheduled romance is certainly a viable option for busy people. There's no reason why a bottle of wine can't be sought out days ahead of time, why a horse-drawn carriage can't be ridden in the off-season to save ten dollars. Practicality is a simple frame of mind that in all honesty offers more perks and functionality than such frivolousness.

Jodie Bellarusa wanted more head time. She was on quite a roll up there, and I didn't want to stop her stream of consciousness, but it was 7:03 p.m. The workday was over, and it was Edward's time to arrive. You could set your watch by his schedule. Every Thursday night we meet at this French restaurant for dinner, and every

Thursday night he arrived at 7:03 p.m., claiming to be on time because, he reminded me, "It's not fair to factor in parking and the distance it takes to walk to the front door."

Secretly, I wanted him to arrive just once at 7:10 p.m. Or even 7:30 p.m., rushing in with a frantic look on his face, finding me in the crowd, relieved I was still there, and with exhaustion and anxiety in his eyes, approach the table cautiously, reverently, hoping I wasn't mad. He'd apologize and wait to see if I would accept. And then I would smile and tell him that of course I would accept.

But Edward was never late. Edward never looked frantic. And now Edward was doing the same thing he always did at the front door, which was removing his scarf, folding it three times, and instructing the maître d' on how to hang his coat, which was the same coat he wore every single spring.

As I watched him, my mind wandered back to my character of Jodie Bellarusa. For now she would have to wait. But soon enough, I'd be able to bring her back alive on the pages of my computer. I was still in the first act, and Jodie had yet to meet Timothy, her eccentric opposite. Four or five scenes down the road, they would meet and hate each other. But like all good romances, love would blossom, despite Jodie's preference for practicality.

I watched Edward make his way around the tables that stood between us. He could maneuver them blindfolded. We'd been eating at this restaurant for two years. I'd once suggested we try a window seat. Edward gave his best to be compliant, but I was forced to watch him eye our "regular" table all night like it was another woman.

And just like two years ago, we still loved each other's company.

He sat down without making eye contact, found his napkin, placed it on his lap, and then looked directly across the table at me. Smiling warmly, he said, "Good evening, Leah."

He'd never had a pet name for me, and I guess I never wanted one. I used to hate when I'd go out with couple friends and they'd call each other the weirdest things that would be offensive in any other context. But as the months passed, I started wishing for a pet name, something whispered in public, in my ear, like a private joke. But it was always Leah, pronounced with preciseness but not lacking delight.

"Hi." I smiled back.

He took my hand from across the table. His were cold, and he apologized by explaining he'd left his gloves at the office.

He glanced around for our waiter, who would be Joel on this evening, because it was the second Thursday of the month, and Joel always took Curtis's shift, because Curtis played in a band or something like that. "How was your day?" he asked, obviously still monitoring Joel's response time.

Something held my tongue and it surprised me. Normally I would say "fine" and provide some highlights if he looked in the mood for details. But today was not fine. My agent had explained my desperate need for a new and dynamic script, reminding me that despite my first success, the last two plays had been "utter flops" and that my career was hanging in the balance of hell and heaven, as if all of eternity rested on my ability to move dialogue along. She'd said this as though I might be unaware that my last two plays had been disasters. But I was very much aware. A bright One-Hit Wonder sign hung itself on the dark side of my eyelids every night when I went to sleep.

"Where is Joel tonight?" asked Edward. "I really don't like him as well as Curtis."

"He'll be here. Just gives us more time to talk, right?"

His honey-colored eyes, the ones that I fell in love with more than two years ago at a banquet, studied me like I was a formula written out across an expansive chalkboard.

"Sure, of course."

"Good evening," Joel said, sliding toward the table out of nowhere. "How are you two this evening?"

"Fine, Joel," Edward said. Edward then proceeded to order. I had to hand it to him. We didn't eat the same dish every Thursday. He liked to throw in a few surprises. This evening, he requested a pasta dish that I couldn't pronounce.

But just as he finished speaking, the words "crêpes suzette" flew from my mouth. I think I gasped as they escaped. Edward looked up at me. Joel glanced my way, too, as if he was surprised I could actually speak, since Edward had always ordered for us. But the fact was, I didn't feel like pasta tonight.

Edward frowned at me. "Those flaming French pancakes? So everyone can observe what we're eating?" It was true. The waiters would bring the dish out with fire encircling the mushroom crepes. It was one of the restaurant's specialties, and they liked to brag by way of dangerous combustion. I'd once observed a man order it for his wife, then watch with pleasure as all attention shifted to her when they delivered it to their table.

"It sounds kind of good to me. I'm not really in the mood for pasta."

Edward was leaning toward me, examining me with intense eyes. "Why not fish?"

"I don't know, fish just doesn't—"

Edward turned to Joel and said something that sounded like *kah bee yoh ehn pee puh rahd*. Joel smiled and turned to me. "We have a wonderful baked cod in a Piperade sauce. We use serrano peppers, blended with bell peppers, plum tomatoes, and garlic, simmered to perfection . . ."

I was nodding and acting interested, but my attention focused on a strange stirring inside me. It was nothing I could identify, and it could just as easily be related to nerves about the new play I was attempting. But some kind of restlessness was provoking bizarre behavior, like ordering flaming pancakes.

"Sure," I finally said, noticing Joel's mouth had stopped moving and both men seemed to be waiting for an answer. "The baked cod sounds lovely."

Edward leaned back in his chair and smiled. The smile stretched into a grin. "So, I've been working on my speech all day."

It was a speech he was to give five months from now, but Edward had a long and distinguished history of speech phobias. To nearly everyone but me, he was Dr. Edward Crowse, professor of physics at Boston University. I still did not understand what exactly the speech was for or to whom he was giving it, but I knew it was important. Edward had been talking about it nonstop for five weeks.

"Yes. I think I've finally got the perfect opening joke." He rubbed his hands together with anticipation.

"Well, let me hear it." I grinned.

"Okay. There's this farmer, who is having a great deal of problems with his chickens. They're quite sick, and he has no idea what to do about them."

"Uh-huh."

"And so after trying all conventional means to find why his chickens are sick, he decides to call a biologist, a chemist, and a physicist to see if they can help figure out why the chickens are sick."

"Okay."

"So the biologist takes a look at the chickens, handles them a bit, and looks them over. But he cannot figure out what's wrong with the roosters."

"I thought they were chickens."

"Right. Yes. Chickens."

"Okay, go ahead."

"Well, then the chemist takes some tests and makes some measurements, but he cannot come to any conclusions about the chickens either."

"Interesting."

"So the physicist tries. He stands there for the longest time looking at the chickens. Not touching them. Just looking at them. Then, all of a sudden, he starts scribbling away in his notebook! The farmer rushes to his side, wondering if he's figured it out. After several lengthy calculations, he suddenly states, 'I've got it! But it only works for spherical chickens in a vacuum!'"

Edward leaned toward me, his eyes wide with expectation.

"In a vacuum. That's funny."

"Do you get it?"

"Sure. That's good."

Edward leaned back in his chair, scratching his chin. Then, flopping a lock of moppy golden hair to its proper side, he said, "I don't know."

"Well, joke-telling is really all about the timing—"

"Maybe it's too long."

"How long do you have?"

"Forty-five minutes, but I have to make some introductions and things like that. What about this one? Two atoms accidentally bump into each other. One atom says, 'I think I lost an electron.' The other asks, 'Are you sure?' to which he replies, 'I'm positive.'"

"Too obvious."

"Yes, I guess you're right." Edward sighed, and the conversation continued about his day until Joel returned with our meals.

I stared down at my baked cod then looked up at Joel. "Would you mind lighting this on fire just for kicks?"

The startled expression covered Joel's face again and Edward's fork dangled from his long fingers as he stared across the table.

"I'm kidding." I laughed, a warm blush crawling up my neck. I liked to call it a blush sometimes, as if that single word would somehow add a femininity and attractiveness to what was really just splotching. "I'm sorry," I said to Edward after Joel left. "I don't know what's gotten into me."

Edward shook his head. "That's okay. The cod does look a little dull, doesn't it?"

"It's okay. Fish is better for me than mushroom-and-cream-filled crepes, right?"

Edward went on to a new joke. "Two pheromones walk into a bar. One orders a drink. The other says, 'I'll have what he's having.'"

"I don't get it."

Edward was looking dejected. "I suppose I do have to worry about the wives and girlfriends in attendance. I have to tell something universally funny."

I tried again. "Edward, telling a joke successfully is all about the timing and delivery. For instance, remember that joke you told me last week at the party? About the superconductor in Alaska?"

"I don't remember."

"Sure you do."

Edward shook his head.

"Come on. You told it to Tom, and then to Jeff, and I think later to Mr. and Mrs. Lavonte. About the researchers in Fairbanks?"

"What researchers?"

"In the joke."

"Oh, I know. About the fish."

"No. About the superconductor. How the researchers in Fairbanks, Alaska, had discovered a superconductor that would operate at room temperature."

Edward blinked, his eyes dimmed for a moment of thought, and then he raised his fork, indicating he did remember.

"Well," I said, holding back a sigh, "that right there is a great example of how not to tell a joke."

Edward didn't get what a remarkable display of bad timing that was. Instead, he suddenly seemed interested in his pasta, poking around in it with his fork.

"There's an odd spice in here. I can't quite identify it. It's not

French, I can tell you that. Strange. It definitely doesn't belong in this dish."

"Hmm. Maybe the chef is trying something new."

"Maybe. But he should be careful. A spice this strong can really wreck the medley of flavors a dish such as this is supposed to have." He moved the pasta around some more. "Maybe you could come over tonight. Help me out. This is, after all, your area of expertise." He managed a smile and a glance at me in the midst of his search for the mysterious spice.

"Don't you have chess club tonight?"

"Didn't I mention it? They're changing it to Wednesdays on the third week of every month. What is this spice? It's nearly overwhelming the entire platter."

I found myself staring at the cod, flaking its flesh with my fork tines, realizing that in a strange way Edward had put into words what I was feeling. There was an odd spice inside me. Something that was bold and strong and distinct, yet misplaced. It was interrupting all the flavors that were important to my daily life. Tiny and unidentifiable, yet there, nevertheless.

What was it? And on what dish in my life did it belong? Was it there intentionally or had it been put there by mistake?

"I think I'm going to call for the chef," Edward said.

"Edward."

He looked up. "Yes?"

I gazed at his delicate face, his amazingly beautiful eyes, his blond, curly hair. How could I tell him all that I was feeling? How could I explain that once in a while I wanted to have dinner on Wednesday and eat hot dogs at the park? Could this simply be about food?

"Leah, are you okay?" He set down his fork. "Is something wrong? You've been acting strangely all night."

"It's just that . . ."

His eyebrows rose, his lips pursed in an expectant manner.

"What?"

"Well, it's about . . ."

"Yes, Leah? What is it?"

I sighed. Who was I kidding? "I think I taste that spice in my food too."

He beckoned Joel.

Chapter 2

[She turns, examining herself.]

I met Elisabeth Bates six years ago. She lived in the apartment across from mine, and we instantly hit it off. We spent hours together watching movies, decorating each other's walls, shopping, and complaining about other tenants.

Then she met Henry Jameson. Now she has three children under the age of six. She's always called herself a forward thinker, refusing Henry's last name, wearing her wedding ring on her left middle finger (which somehow was supposed to represent balance), and naming all of her children after people she's forgiven in her life, two of them being former boyfriends. She swears it never creates an awkward moment. Maybe not for her.

So, what with her being a forward thinker, I always considered it amusing that she had a bad habit of referring to her nondeceased mother in the past tense. She told me it helped her say nice things. For the longest time I actually thought her mother was dead.

And Elisabeth is one of those mothers who doesn't understand how important the basics of parenting are. Conventional mothering—things like discipline and social instruction—aren't relevant today, she claims. But in my view Danny, Cedric, and little Amelia are the reason more and more parents are deciding to homeschool their children.

My apartment door opened as I hid my last piece of valuable decor. Elisabeth never, ever knocked. I greeted her with a hug, looking behind her. No trailing children. "Where are the kids?"

"At my neighbor's," she said, throwing her bag on my couch and looking around. "Leah, your place is so dull. It wouldn't kill you to have a nice crystal vase sitting around, you know. And I'm not a knickknack person, but in your case, I'd go for it."

I laughed. I didn't want to, but it was one of those crazy, instant reactions, like gagging or swatting at a fly around your face. "Have a seat," I said.

"Thanks." She sat on the end of the couch and looked at me. "You look good. Vibrant. Life is treating you well?"

"It is." I took a seat in my oversized leather chair, just catty-corner to Elisabeth, pushing the ottoman to the side.

Four weeks had passed since I'd talked to Elisabeth. I never could quite understand what it was that still drew me to her after all these years, but I'd finally decided it must be the familiarity of the older days. I hadn't seen those days in a long while, but they were vivid in my memory, and maybe I always hoped they would be back.

"How are the kids?"

I expected the usual answer, which consisted of detailed descriptions of each of their latest and greatest accomplishments, such as wiping their own bottoms or graduating from bottle to sippy cup. I waited, but then I realized she wasn't answering. She was staring. At my carpet. Then I expected a quip about how I should add more color to the living room and get rid of the grays. But she was still staring. I stared too. Was there a stain? A crumb? A faux pas of some other sort?

"We're all fine." Dullness filled her voice, a tone that suggested exhaustion. And as I studied her, I found other signs. Dark circles that hadn't seen the light of day since her last child was a newborn. The top of her hair pulled back unevenly with a rubber band. Top-lip fuzz that could've used some bleaching cream. Though her children usually looked like extras in the cast of *Annie,* Elisabeth had always taken pride in appearing polished.

"Are you sure?"

"I read a review of your last play."

I cringed.

"It wasn't bad."

"It couldn't have been good."

"Critics. What do they know?"

"The best way to make a playwright suicidal."

"She actually said something good about it."

I looked up. "Really?"

"She said had the dialogue been any more predictable, she might've signed up to be a psychic."

I blinked. "That's not a compliment."

"It's not?"

"Dialogue is not supposed to be predictable."

Elisabeth frowned, staring at the carpet again. But then she raised a finger. "Wait. I know she said something good about it, because she used a word like *clinched.* It was clinching dialogue. That's good, right?"

"Are you sure she didn't say clichéd?"

Elisabeth looked blank.

"Was there an accent over the *e*?"

"Yes, but I thought she was just trying to be fancy. I could've sworn I saw an *n* in that word."

Maybe the critic did say clinched, describing the way her jaw was set while she was watching it. I didn't ask, but I knew the woman was probably Dora Mendez, otherwise known around the theater community as Dora the Exploder. She had a tendency to take out her frustrations with her personal life on anything that came with a playbill.

"So what are you working on now?" Elisabeth asked. That was

unusual. She was hardly ever interested in my plays. She would come to see them, more out of obligation than interest. That was actually one of the things that had drawn me to her in the first place. She was a nice vacation away from the relentlessly aesthetic theater world that I seemed to live in 24/7.

"It's a romantic comedy."

"Oh! Like a Meg Ryan/Tom Hanks kind of thing?"

Well, no. In fact, it was really more an antiromantic comedy. I was calling it a "romanti comedy," leaving off the *c* in order to form the word *anti*. I thought this descriptor very clever until I discovered that it took a good ten minutes to explain it to everyone. And even then I'd get vague nods and hear whispering as people walked off.

In all actuality, Jodie Bellarusa, the main character, was about as close to a Meg Ryan type as Cher. She wasn't perky. She wasn't blonde. And she didn't like men who continued to be in romantic comedies long after they were considered adorable.

You're going to do it, aren't you? You're actually going to nod your head. Meg Ryan/Tom Hanks—repulsive and completely unrealistic. Look, you know I respect you. You created me, after all, and who wouldn't respect their Creator? But I have to question this relationship sometimes. I mean, I've been in some unhealthy relationships, thanks to you. But what good is a relationship when you can't be real? That's what I've been preaching since I came into existence! Forget the romance. Forget the flowers. Let's all be real here! Be real!

"Sure. Wouldn't I be lucky to get Meg Ryan?" I lied.

"I'd kill for her curls. And her body. And her money."

"Speaking of no curls, no body and, well, no money, I need your help. Your fashion help."

That perked her up. "Oh?"

"I've got to go to this *thing* with Edward tonight. It's a semiformal outdoor dinner party, but the real challenge is the company I'll be keeping. Physicists. And some other scientist-types."

"So that low-plunging number won't do." Elisabeth was being facetious. By low-plunging, she was referring to a scoop-neck dress I wore to one of her parties. For me, it was risky, because I didn't like my neck exposed.

She followed me into my bedroom where I opened my small closet. She let out a laugh. I did too. Again, a regrettable fly-swatting moment, and I could sense Jodie Bellarusa's disapproval.

"How do you get by?" Elisabeth lamented. "And why is everything black?"

"It's an artist thing." It wasn't. It was actually an insecurity-about-color-and-the-attention-it-drew thing, but I kept mum.

"None of these will do," she finally said after scooting every hanger contemptuously down the line. "We have to get you a new dress."

"New? In case you haven't heard, playwriting isn't the lucrative business it used to be for me."

"Come on. I know where to find all the bargains."

How ridiculous. I didn't need a new dress. Any of these would suffice. "Okay."

Glavier had a deceivingly fancy name. Inside it looked more like a warehouse that had potential for conversion but hadn't been converted. The dressing room, I noticed immediately, was a sheet strung from one empty clothes rack to another.

"Don't worry," Elisabeth said. "I know it looks a little scary, but I'm telling you, one of these days you'll hear about Glavier in all the best fashion magazines. Kitty has a real vision for what's in style."

"Kitty?"

"She owns the place."

In place of a meow, the petite, middle-aged woman came around the corner and greeted us with an exquisite politeness. Elisabeth got busy explaining my desperate need for a new dress. But Kitty seemed more interested in me.

"Is this outdoor or indoor?"

"Outdoor," I said.

"How nice. Evenings in the spring are usually very cool, but it's been unusually warm this year, and it's going to be warm tonight." She took me by the hand and guided me toward a collection of dresses. I didn't see anything black. I was seeing a lot of pastels. She pulled me along, and with her free hand gathered four dresses and then took me to the suspended sheet.

She pulled it to one side and hung the dresses on what looked like a meat hook attached to the wall. "Here you are."

"They, um, they have spaghetti straps."

"Yes."

"Unfortunately I'm on a low-carb diet." Kitty didn't get my joke. She was staring at my waistline.

I looked at the dresses. Not one resembled anything I would ever dream of wearing. But as she pulled the sheet again in an attempt to create a place for some modesty, I realized that I was lying to myself. These *were* the kinds of dresses I'd dreamed of wearing. Many times. I fingered my way through each one, feeling the fabric, trying to imagine myself by Edward's side. Trying to imagine the looks on the other professors' faces.

I pushed the sheet aside and stepped out, only to be greeted by two eager faces.

"I'm sorry, these aren't going to work."

"Leah, you didn't even try them on!" Elisabeth said.

"How do you know?"

"We can see through the sheet."

I knew my instincts were right. It was time to leave. But each woman grabbed one of my arms and swung me back in front of the dressing sheet.

"Just try them on," Kitty said. "There's no pressure. Just see how you feel about them."

"I can already tell you how I feel about them. They're not really me."

"How do you know," asked Elisabeth, "without trying them on?"

"If you didn't notice, I don't have anything mint or pink in my closet."

Both of their faces indicated they might die of sorrow if I didn't give this a shot, so with a sigh I went back in, yanked the translucent sheet behind me, and tried on mint #1.

"Kitty went to get you some shoes."

"Oh. Good." Mint #1 had some cleavage issues. Actually, I had some cleavage issues, but nevertheless, mint #1 went back on the hanger.

"I've been thinking about your plays," Elisabeth said, filling the silence.

This was startling. It actually sent a chill down my spine. My friend who hadn't been to the theater before she met me had been pondering my plays. Not that I was desperate for approval and attention, even from nonpeers, but I was curious.

Oh, who are you kidding? You're desperate.

I believed Jodie had retreated, but since she hadn't, I forcibly tucked her away and, in the most casual voice I could manage, considering the topic and the current outfit, mint #2, asked, "What do you mean?"

"I haven't been sleeping well lately," Elisabeth began, which should've prompted a *why not?* but artists can be gracious and loving people until there's an opportunity to talk about their work, and then they become the equivalent of a pushy first-time mother showing off a baby. That my baby, according to critics, happened to have acne and red splotches, was irrelevant. "And I was thinking of all of your three plays."

The Twilight T-Zone, my masterpiece that gave me the title "Most Promising Young Playwright" by Dora the Exploder herself, was about the cosmetics industry, and gave a nice message about our perception of beauty. It was an instant hit, and how I met Jillian Rose Thompson, otherwise known as J. R., the famed agent.

My next effort, a political satire called *Spint,* wasn't as well received. In fact, I believe it was called an "attempt." I never thought "attempt" was very well defined. Attempt at satire? Attempt at plot? Attempt at character? Maybe they were being nice about it because they really meant all of the above.

Whatever the case, my third play put the satire to shame. It was called *A Day in the Lie,* and despite its corny title, I truly thought it would be a sensational drama. It was about the wife of a famous basketball player. Turned out nobody wanted to know what it's like to be married to a famous athlete. Who knew?

Elisabeth wasn't offering up further information, so I asked, "What about them?"

"Maybe it's a coincidence, I don't know, but it seems like something out of all three of your plays has come true."

I pondered this while nearly throwing out my back trying to reach the zipper of mint #2.

"Like a prophet. Think about it. In *The Twilight T-Zone,* you have a cosmetics company go bankrupt. Just last year Lyla went out of business. Then in *Spint,* doesn't the vice president have an affair with his secretary?"

Yes, and it was dogged for being too unrealistic. Everyone shut up after the Clinton scandal.

"Okay," I said. I could see where she was going.

"The third one, two words: Kobe Bryant."

I flung uncooperative mint #2 to the ground, then returned it to the hanger. Pink #1 was next, and I could already tell the Lycra was going to be a problem.

"See what I mean?" Elisabeth said. "It's like you're a prophet."

Or a victim of pop culture, but she did have a point. I hadn't really thought of it like that. I had certainly never thought of myself as a prophet, though I was beginning to predict Edward with an accuracy that only a scientist could appreciate.

Elisabeth went on, presumably to distract me from the fact that this dress was fitting tighter than my skin.

"Doesn't it freak you out that everything you write comes true?"

"What's freaking me out is that I feel like I need to be in an aerobics class to wear all this Lycra." And flab.

"You have one more, don't you?"

I pulled pink #2 on. It was just above knee length and, all straps considered, fairly modest. The neckline was square and high, and the back didn't even reveal a shoulder blade, to my surprising disappointment.

I stepped out. Elisabeth gasped. Kitty, a pair of heels in hand, smiled with pleasure. But so far I hadn't seen a mirror. Kitty rectified that situation by turning me to the right. I gasped too.

Elisabeth pulled my hair up and out of my face, and Kitty slipped me into a pair of strappy silver heels. I began to understand that Kitty was quite talented because so far I hadn't revealed a single one of my sizes.

"Leah! You look amazing! I never knew you could wear pink."

"Me either," I said, looking myself up and down.

"It looks like it was made for you," Kitty said.

The dress put a particular innocence on me and took about ten years off my age. I found myself grinning and spinning and imagining Edward gushing at the sight. It wasn't exactly pastel, but it stopped short of being hot pink.

After a few moments, Elisabeth asked, "How much is it?"

"Three hundred and forty dollars," Kitty said.

"Whoa," Elisabeth said. "Oh well. Listen, Leah, surely we can find something similar that will fit your budget. Kitty has a lot of different dresses and styles and—"

"I'll take it."

"You will?" they both asked.

"And the shoes too."

Elisabeth's mouth was hanging open.

I turned to Kitty. "I'm going to need a handbag."

Chapter 3

[Walking beside her, he doesn't notice.]

Each of my hands cupped the opposite shoulder, my arms creating a large X across my body. I sat in the passenger's seat of Edward's Volvo station wagon, waiting for him to walk around the back end to get into the driver's side. He always went around the front. Today he went around the back.

I'd spent two hours getting ready. I actually curled my hair and wore it up. The last time I tried that was at prom. I carefully applied makeup and chose a dark pink lipstick that coordinated perfectly with the dress. I wore earrings that dangled past my jaw and a pink-jeweled bracelet I'd borrowed from Elisabeth.

The last fifteen minutes before Edward arrived I spent pacing my apartment, walking in front of mirrors and anything else that would supply a reflection. I turned on some music to see if there was a chance I could dance in heels.

Edward was right on time, and my body trembled when he knocked. I opened the door as wide as the grin on my face. I was prepared for the shocked look. I knew Edward would've been expecting my black blouse with the black-and-gray skirt. I'd worn it to several events, only changing the brooch. And Edward always wore the same suit, only changing the tie.

His steady smile, the one he could generate even during a gallstone, held its own against the display in front of him. I stood still, with my hands clasped at my lower back, and let him look. His smile couldn't hide the fear that flashed in his eyes, though. And soon enough that dependable smile faded.

"What's going on?" he asked.

I'd imagined, *Leah, you look amazing.* But then I realized that was asking too much of him, so then I'd imagined, *Leah, I've never seen you wear something like this before. But I like it.* Again, that was probably giving him a lot of credit in the spontaneity category, so my mind had settled for *Leah, I'm . . . speechless.*

But he wasn't speechless. And *What's going on?* hadn't crossed my mind as a possibility, so I didn't have a ready response.

"I did say this was the department party, didn't I?" He was staring at my shoes. And frowning.

"Yes." I couldn't help notice how my bright, flashy pink didn't go very well with the dull gray ensemble he called a suit. Even his tie was gray.

I felt the splotching begin. The dress had a fairly high neckline, but that would do no good once the splotches crawled up my neck. They always started at my chest and defied gravity in a most impressive way. Soon enough my ears would be matching my dress.

"It said semiformal." I did my best to gather my composure as I waited for him to get into the Volvo. This *was* a semiformal dress. This was perfectly acceptable. It wasn't like I was wearing a snowsuit.

Edward opened the driver's-side door and got in. He didn't look at me. He just started the car, looked in his rearview mirror before pulling out, and off we went.

Five minutes of complete silence were interrupted by Edward's asking, "Did you print out those directions?"

I pulled the paper out of my new silver clutch, which matched my shoes perfectly, but who was going to notice?

He tried to drive and read at the same time. Then he said, "Why didn't you use MapPoint?"

"I like MapQuest."

"I told you Microsoft MapPoint is better." He studied the map at a stoplight. "Why is it taking us through all the construction? MapPoint is more accurate."

"The construction went up this week, Edward."

Edward's eyes cut to me, then to my dress, then back to the paper. He slowed down as a construction worker pointed in the direction of a detour. Edward's sigh could've defogged a window.

"What's the hurry? It's a party. It's not like you're late for a lecture."

His eyebrows popped up. Edward was surprised. A minor miracle.

"You know I always use MapPoint."

"Why not change things up a bit every now and then?"

Edward looked at me, then looked back at the road, swerving in order not to hit the curb. I grabbed the door handle, but that's not why my heart was beating fast. Edward and I were having an argument. A real, live argument. It was our first. In our two and a half years of dating, it was our first.

"That's sort of the theme of the night, isn't it?" he asked, his attention back on my dress. "What kind of statement are you trying to make with that dress?"

"I'm not wearing it to make a statement. I'm wearing it for you."

"Me?" He laughed. "That's funny."

"I thought you'd like it."

"Why would you think that?"

I felt tears in my eyes, but I didn't let them fall. "Because I feel beautiful in it."

Edward didn't respond. Of course not. This was all in my head—a dramatic buildup in an unstable evening with an undetermined climax. And I wasn't sure what I wanted—him to tell me that I looked horrible or to say nothing at all. The nothing at all was ripping my heart out. But a real-life argument was as far-fetched as my imagination.

After weaving through the backstreets of a neighborhood and finding the correct street again, we arrived at the home of Dr. Glyndell, the department chair and Edward's idol. Dr. Glyndell and his wife, Margaret, had purchased this colonial-style home last year, and this was the first time we'd visited. As we parked, I marveled at its beauty. It was a dream home for sure.

Edward hardly seemed to notice. He was standing outside the car now, adjusting his tie and messing with something on his shirt. My fingers reached for the door handle to get out, but then something stopped me and my fingers slid back down onto my lap. My shaking fingers, I should add.

I waited. It seemed like an hour, but it was merely a few seconds before Edward realized I wasn't standing beside him. He peered into the car, I suppose to see if I was really still sitting there. I was. I looked at him and tried to smile. I didn't have one of those gallstone smiles, mind you. I was known to have trouble smiling even when happy. I most likely looked like one of those sock puppets who, though grinning with full teeth, still manages to look creepy.

Finally he walked around to my side and opened the door. I stepped out and he closed the door.

"This is a beautiful house," I said.

He looked up and mumbled something. We walked together toward the front door, and as my heels clicked against the white, manicured concrete, I knew what a terrible mistake I'd made. This evening was going to rank right up there with the stomach flu. What was I thinking? Why did I do this to myself? I could've worn black and functioned as I normally do at these events. My throat swelled with regret. I wanted to cling to Edward for support, but I had a feeling he wouldn't want to be standing by me tonight.

The door opened, and Margaret Glyndell greeted us. Her eyes flicked over my dress immediately, yet she only said, "Welcome, Edward! Hello, Leah. I'm so glad to have you both to our new home!" She ushered us in. "We're out back. The weather is so lovely, and we have the gardens and pool. Come with me."

She guided us outdoors to a large deck surrounded by a perfectly groomed lawn and flowers that released the most amazing fragrance. Small, quaint candles were lit around the deck and the gardens, and the pool reflected their light. Several tables of food and drinks offered a nice selection—or diversion, whatever the case may be.

"Mrs. Glyndell, it's beautiful," I said.

"Please, call me Margaret. And thank you." She smiled. At me. Like the dress didn't matter. I held my head a little higher. "Please, help yourself to some refreshments. Most everyone is here, I think. Geoff is down there somewhere, talking about who knows what. Probably gravity. You know how he is about gravity."

Edward laughed and headed toward the crowd of his peers. I followed along behind him, but when I noticed he was a few paces in front of me, I decided to head off toward the drinks. I wasn't even sure he would care. In fact, he would probably be relieved not to have to acknowledge my presence.

At the drink table I noticed Andrea, the wife of Beau, a former professor at Boston University and now a postdoctoral student at Stanford. She was wearing a red pantsuit. I was never so glad to see red in my life. I thought if we stood next to each other we might look like a Valentine's Day card, but I didn't care.

Andrea noticed me approach. "Hi, Leah. My goodness, that dress is fabulous."

I looked down as if it were the last thing on my mind. "You think so?"

"I've never seen you wear pink. It's a good color for you."

"It's not too fancy for this occasion?"

"Too fancy? No way. Did you see Margaret's sequins?"

I hadn't noticed. I was too busy worrying about my own outfit. I glanced up toward the house, and sure enough, there she stood, reflecting light like a disco ball.

"I'm not sure I've ever seen you in an actual dress."

"Sure you have."

"When?"

"At Professor Jones's funeral."

She thought for a moment. "That's right. The black number."

I nodded and glanced around. I was the only one in pink, but not the only one in color. And I realized I didn't stand out as much as I'd imagined.

Andrea was holding two drinks in her hand. "You coming?" She nodded toward the crowd where her husband and Edward were.

"In a bit." I smiled and pretended to be interested in what drink I would choose. I strolled alongside the table, listening to the professors talk and laugh and crack jokes most people would never understand.

From what I could tell, the group was talking about chess, which was no surprise since Dr. Glyndell was a big chess fanatic. Rumor had it that he owned more than a hundred different chessboards (another reason for Edward to look up to him) and that he once claimed to be playing the ghost of his great-grandfather. Somehow, because he could discuss string theory with such casualness, that particular personality flaw (his fondness for ghosts) was dismissed. I once teased with Edward that Dr. Glyndell was one proton away from being Bobby Fischer's strange half brother. Edward had looked like I'd personally insulted him.

The slight breeze carried the voices and laughter toward me, and I could hear Edward's distinguished lilt, the one he used only in the presence of colleagues and students. "Thought that leads nowhere, mathematics that add up to nothing, art without an end product, architecture without substance." Another professor said, "That's Zweig from *The Royal Game*."

That's what they liked to do. Quote and be quoted. Edward had a photographic memory, so he often stunned the crowd by his ability to quote nearly everything he'd read. It was an endearing trait, especially when he quoted my work. Sometimes when we'd be in a heavy discussion about philosophy or religion or something of that nature, he would defend his position by quoting one of my plays. It always made me laugh. How could I argue against myself?

I ladled myself a glass of what looked like freshly squeezed pink lemonade and decided to walk through the gardens. I wasn't sure Edward had missed me yet. He didn't seem to care anyway. Every time I looked his way, I felt myself wanting to cry, and what better place for a pink standout like myself to hide than in the flower gardens?

I followed a cobbled pathway a few yards out and wandered around, smelling each type of flower and wondering how many groundskeepers were needed to maintain all this. I didn't have to think long, because soon what appeared to be a groundskeeper came walking toward me.

"Hi," he said. He wore jeans, a denim shirt, and near-perfect features.

"Hi. I was just admiring the flowers."

"Are you part of the party?"

"Yes."

He looked in that direction and then back at me. Then he smiled. My heart fluttered. I begged myself not to splotch. "Do you keep the gardens?"

He held out his hand. "I'm Robby. Geoff and Margaret's son."

"Oh, sorry," I said, and shook his hand. "Not about being their son. About thinking you were the groundskeeper."

"No need to apologize. And it is a sad story, really, being Dr.

Glyndell's son. I don't play chess, after all." He laughed. If this man had any more charm about him, he'd be a bracelet. "Who are you?"

"Leah. Townsend."

"Nice to meet you. And you're here with . . . ?"

"Edward Crowse. Dr. Edward Crowse."

"Is there anyone here without a doctorate?"

"Me."

"Me too." He smiled. "What do you do?"

"I'm a playwright."

"Really?"

"Really. What do you do?"

"I'm a landscaper." He swept his hand over the tulips.

"You did this?"

"Some of it. The landscaping was here when my parents bought the house, but it was in need of a lot of attention. I spent most of last year getting it together." He looked at me, and the look said a lot of things, the least of which was that he approved of my dress.

I flattened my hand against the side of it, smoothing out non-existent wrinkles, and sipped my lemonade. I was blushing. Not splotching. Real-life blushing.

"Leah?"

I turned to find Edward walking toward us. Robby cleared his throat and took a step away from me.

"Hi," I said. Edward gave me and then Robby equally polite smiles. "Have you met the Glyndells' son Robby before?"

They shook hands. "I think I've met you before," Edward said.

"Robby is a landscaper. I was just admiring his work." I looked at the flowers for something to do other than stare at these two men staring at each other.

"I thought you'd gone to fetch us some drinks," Edward said, glancing at the drink in my hand.

"It's serve yourself tonight," Robby said, startling me as much as Edward. Robby admired me one more time with a stare that defied Edward's presence, then excused himself and started toward the house. Edward was watching Robby like a science experiment that had just stood up and walked away.

Edward then turned to me. "I wasn't implying you should get us drinks. I just thought that's what you went to do."

His defensiveness was nothing short of satisfying, but instead of relishing the moment, I said, "I know. I didn't take it that way."

"Good." He chewed his lip. "So do you want to join me up there?"

"What's going on?"

"I think Dr. Glyndell's going to show us some pictures of his trip to Egypt."

"Are you sure the glare from my dress won't be too distracting?"

Edward flopped his head to the side. "Is that what this is all about? Your dress? I didn't say enough about your dress?"

"You didn't say anything about my dress."

He glanced behind him, as if to see whether anyone was in earshot. "It's different, okay? You're usually not this loud."

Loud. Now, that was an unusual description for a man who would be able to prove mathematically that colors do not have sound. He looked at my dress again, as if trying his best to give it a second chance. He gave his mouth a good rubbing. He threw out his hands like a few gestures might help him find a simple word like *nice*.

"Look," I said, breaking the silence, "I'm sorry, okay? I got a little carried away. I was with Elisabeth, and we went shopping, and it seemed like a good idea at the time. I see now that it wasn't. I've embarrassed you."

A smile returned to his lips and he took my hands. "You don't need any of this fancy stuff, okay? That's not who you are. You're Leah Townsend, not Julia Roberts."

"I know." I returned his smile and let him lead me toward the others. The tension was gone and everything returned to normal. At least outwardly. I walked beside him now, and as we entered the house through the French doors off the patio, I mumbled, "Right. For tonight only, I'll answer to Miss Cotton Candy." But I don't think he heard me.

Chapter 4

[Shocked, she opens the envelope.]

I really need more zest. You're putting too much of yourself in me. This isn't an autobiography, okay? And don't get me wrong. You have some really good zingers, some one-liners that could knock a person on their back if they ever made it past that roadblock called your tongue. But I'm not you. I'm Jodie Bellarusa, and I have no problem with my tongue. You're going to have to let me soar. Stop reining me in.

Jodie was right. I was inhibiting her. She was sassy, strong, and satisfied without a man. I stared at the cursor on my screen. It blinked monotonously, as if tracking the time ticking away this morning as I struggled to write.

My play didn't have a title yet. Titling was not my gift. But if I was honest, my play also seemed to lack direction, and even a theme. All I knew was that I had this fabulous character named Jodie Bellarusa who thought she was ready to make her public appearance on the stage. I had to remind her she was barely ready to make her appearance on the white page.

Jodie had been around for about three years. She first appeared the night an actor named James stood me up. I'd sat in a little café for an hour after our scheduled date, believing that he would come.

I kept feeding myself all the excuses I wanted to hear, from the idea that we got our times mixed up to the hopeful possibility that he was in a horrible car crash on the way to see me and was in a hospital somewhere unconscious and unaware that he'd never arrived.

Suddenly this woman appeared. It wasn't kooky, like she was sitting across from me as a ghost. It was all in my head. Maybe that sounds kooky too. Anyway, she was the one that talked me out of the whole thing. She explained that there was no misunderstanding and no tragic accident. He just didn't come.

I named her after the waiter, Jodie, a guy who seemed genuinely distraught as each minute ticked by. He bought me a drink and told me the guy was an idiot. And Bellarusa came from the name of the café.

Jodie Bellarusa was born that day. She hasn't left me alone since, and last year she became a little headstrong, wanting an entire story built around her.

Writing a story with Jodie at the center wasn't hard. She was an easy character to develop. She was a die-hard antiromantic who was certain love would never be for her. She turned off the guys she met, challenging them to break down the thick wall of sarcasm she'd built around herself. They all failed. But she had yet to meet Timothy, the handsome dentist who lived next door.

I could admit that, yes, Jodie was the anti-Leah. We were polar opposites, but she didn't represent everything I wanted to be. *That* would make for a very boring character. Jodie was full of flaws and drama, and I was banking on her to be my Next Big Thing.

But unlike most days, this Monday morning brought nothing new and extraordinary to the page. In fact, the entire story seemed to have stalled out. I couldn't type a thing, and so Jodie sat mid-sentence, her mouth hanging wide open as she quipped to her friend, "I couldn't be happier that . . ." This was where it all stopped. Poor Jodie was suspended between happiness and complete failure. It was up to me to fill in the blank.

And I went blank.

In the kitchen I poured another cup of coffee, feeling fatigued from the weekend. Although it had brought a bit of unexpected drama, Saturday night had ended as it always did. Edward dropped me off at my apartment, gave me a quick kiss, and said we'd see each other the next day at church, and off I went. I changed out of my pink dress, which would be mentioned no more for the rest of the night and probably the rest of our lives, and hung it in the back of my closet, toying with the idea of trying to put the tag back on it. I knew that dress would never see the light of day again.

Edward and I parted peacefully, and he seemed content and satisfied that all was resolved. But for me, there was a lot more emotion to work through. As I tossed and turned Saturday night, I hoped my sleeplessness would work it out.

But Sunday I really felt no better, even after picking my favorite and most dependable black dress for church. It was a great find, because it was sleeveless and featured my favorite accessory: a turtleneck. In it, I could splotch all the way up to my chin and still look somewhat elegant. Edward made a comment about it, and that I can remember, it was the first time he'd complimented me on my attire in the last year. But I felt cold and isolated, even with him sitting next to me. And instead of going to lunch afterward like we had since the beginning of our relationship, I excused myself and went home.

I napped then, only to be awoken by the phone ringing. It was Edward. We talked briefly, and I pretended to be fine. Afterward, I ordered pizza, watched *Footloose,* and lost myself in the evening.

So Monday morning arrived with the living room light lifting me off the couch. I knocked over the pizza box as I stumbled into consciousness. I showered and got dressed, which was something my mother had insisted on every morning I'd lived under her roof. She would be shocked to learn that I spend most mornings in my pajamas in front of the computer.

I did realize my mother's insistence on a shower, and clothing in the morning was a positive and healthy step in fighting off depression. Like many people, I found it easier when I didn't care about the world to stop caring about myself too. But for me, being a little grimy helped pull out the subtle and not-so-subtle flaws I needed for each of my characters. Subtle required the simple oversight of brushing my teeth. Not-so-subtle, and you'd usually find me on day three without a shower.

But Jodie Bellarusa's flaws were already fully developed. They didn't need any help from me.

I took one look in the mirror this morning and knew a shower was in order, if not for personal hygiene then at least for personal respect. So I was fully dressed, fully fed, and had all my bills paid. That was a perfect recipe for success. Yet it had been an hour and I still couldn't get the exact right words for Jodie Bellarusa. Jodie was claiming she wasn't tough enough, but I felt it was something different. It was vague and hard to pinpoint.

I believed at some point the blinking cursor would give it up, but so far it was holding its own.

The phone on my desk rang and my caller ID announced it was a private caller, which was usually code for my agent. I squeezed my eyes shut. I wasn't sure J. R. was a good person to talk to right now. But on the other hand, she did have a knack for motivating me.

"Hello?"

"Leah, it's J. R." She had a deep, scratchy voice that matched her personality but not her looks. If you ever saw her approaching, she'd remind you of your favorite grandmother, complete with a cane and pin curls. But then she would open her mouth. And not even pin curls could save her then. The woman roared, and not in a majestic, lioness sort of way. "I'm wondering how the play is coming along. The one you can't seem to find a title for."

"It's coming along fine. I think this one is going to be great." The blinking cursor mocked my every word.

"Oh, Leah, darling, don't curse yourself like that. I believe those were your exact words right before *A Day in the Lie* opened."

There was something prestigious about having J. R. Thompson as your agent. It was like the difference between the Cub Scouts and the marines. We were few. They were proud. And after J. R. was finished with them, they were lethal. Having her name attached to anything you did gave you a legitimacy that only she could create. And admittedly, it was her name that had carried me through the last two disasters.

J.R. was known to represent some of the most up-and-coming writers in Boston and New York. She was known to scout talent and snag the future superstars. But nobody's perfect, as I apparently remind her every time we speak.

"You're still sure about this romantic comedy?"

"Antiromantic comedy."

"That's hard to say. It doesn't roll off the tongue."

"That's what's funny about it."

She paused. I could hear her sucking in the smoke from her cigarette. "Okay, well, whatever the case, how's it coming?"

"Really well. It's flowing like . . . crazy." I turned away from my computer.

"Peter's been asking about you." She was referring to Peter Deutsch, the director and producer who had believed in *The Twilight T-Zone* and had helped make it such a hit. He was a rare find in that he was interested only in scripts that had never been produced. He'd skipped on my last two.

"How is Peter?" I asked casually.

"He's fine. He's been having a lot of success, but he's always interested in what you're working on. And in fact called me Friday to ask specifically about you. I had to explain you were writing a three-act, and of course Peter said what I said, which is nobody does three acts anymore."

"I'm a few weeks from being finished, but Peter is welcome to take a look then."

"I came across as nondesperate as possible, Leah, but as you know, there is a lot riding on this play. Not to mention, rumor has it that Kelly Gundy is getting ready to shop a new two-act. You know how fond Peter is of Kelly."

Kelly Gundy. She was a top-notch playwright from New York whose father was a famous Broadway actor and whose mother was a stage manager. It seemed everything Kelly touched turned to gold.

"I didn't realize that Kelly was working on something new."

"Leah, I have never personally doubted your talent. The first time I saw *The Twilight T-Zone* I knew that you were going to go places."

"Thank you."

"And it's also not completely uncommon to have a second show that doesn't do as well as the first. It's almost inevitable. You've been put on such a high platform. Everyone is looking to knock you off."

"Yes." J. R. had given me this speech about four times. But I pretended each time that it was fresh advice.

"The third time is usually a charm, but in your case it was a bad-luck charm. We're just going to move on past that like it never happened. I don't even mention it when I'm talking about you. It's like that strange cousin we all have who is 'accidentally' left out of all the photos. You know what I mean."

"Sure."

"I shouldn't keep you. You have a lot of work to do. Just wanted to tell you about Peter. I took it as a good sign that he actually called me."

"That is a good sign."

"All right. I have to be in New York this evening so I better run, but I'll check in with you soon."

You can't run, you old fogey. You have a cane. "Good talking with you, J. R." I hung up the phone just as my doorbell rang.

Thankful I'd decided to get dressed, I cautiously approached. I hardly ever had visitors during the day, or anytime for that matter. The security door downstairs had been broken for three weeks now, so people, like Elisabeth, could just come on up, unannounced. I peeked through the hole and saw a bouquet of flowers.

"Flowers?" I swung the door open with no regard for personal safety.

The man behind the flowers said, "For Leah Townsend?" He pronounced my first name wrong, like I had two buns on either side of my head and was fond of Jedi masters and men with furry side-kicks. "Lee-ah," I corrected.

He handed me the clipboard and I signed. I took the bouquet inside, more than a little curious about its sender. I couldn't remember the last time I was sent flowers. Maybe two years ago on my birthday when my parents were out of town and not here to celebrate.

The carnations were bright pink and in full bloom, nearly dripping with moisture. And they smelled wonderful. I set them on the table, forgetting to close the front door, and snatched the card. Who were they from? Elisabeth, congratulating me on my fun night out? (I'd led her to believe the night went well, because I didn't want to hurt her feelings.) Peter, wanting to let me know in a more personal way that he wanted my next play? I lifted the flap. Maybe Robby, the understated son of the Glyndells? I pulled out the card.

Edward?

I want you to know that all is well on my end. But I think the situation regarding the contention on Saturday needs to be addressed to maintain a healthy and organic relationship. We can't do that if you're angry. With love, Edward.

I didn't exactly understand what he meant, and if there was a more sterile way to send a love note, I couldn't think of it. Then I noticed there was something else sticking out of the envelope. I reached in and pulled it out. It was a flimsy square piece of paper, a little slick and colorful, with a sticky note in Edward's handwriting attached.

> *It is the person with the most character who admits when she needs help. I want to make "us" work. Everything is paid in full. I know you want to make it work too. XO*

What was he talking about? I flipped over the small square I was holding, and to my surprise it looked like a coupon with dashed lines framing the black and blue lettering. I wasn't sure I was reading it right, and in fact was pretty sure there was some sort of mistake.

20% off
Conflict Resolution Class
This month only!

It gave a phone number and address and instructions to call before it filled up.

Learn to deal with difficulties
in a proactive, life-enhancing way!

"How ridiculous!" What was Edward thinking? A *conflict resolution* class? He was the one who had a problem with the dress. "How stupid!" He wanted us to attend a conflict resolution class together? Like therapy?

Therapy?

Even Jodie was nearly speechless. I'd never once known her to repeat what I said. I stared at the fine print, underlined by Edward's pen: *Starts this Tuesday at 7 p.m.* I crushed the small piece of paper between my fingers and threw it in the garbage. Plopping myself into my desk chair, I glanced at the bright pink carnations sitting on the table, ironically—or maybe not—the same color as the dress I'd worn Saturday night.

I glimpsed the phone from the corner of my eye. No. *Block it out,* I instructed myself. *You've got a play to write.* But no matter how hard I tried, I couldn't get Jodie to finish her sentence. After ten more minutes of padlocking my mind to my computer screen, I finally had to stand up and remove the flowers from my line of sight. Jodie Bellarusa hated flowers.

And with that out of the way, I skipped over the sentence I couldn't finish, telling myself I could fill in the blanks later, and let Jodie rant about flowers. It felt good, as good as any recreational drug could make me feel, I was sure.

I sat back, threaded my fingers together behind my head, popped my knuckles with one swift *crack,* and smiled. I'd not only salvaged the scene, but I'd salvaged what had the potential to be a very, very rotten day.

But then the phone rang.

It was Mother.

Chapter 5

[The conversation lulls, briefly.]

The dining table stretched from one end of the room to the other, with twelve expensively upholstered chairs lining either side and the two ends. Their tall, erect backs created the uninviting sense that even the slightest slump would not be tolerated.

The upholstery had changed over the years, now to a lavish gold color, but the sentiment was still the same. I hated these chairs. We ate dinner at this table every evening that Dad was home, and as a child, all I could think about was how I wished all those empty chairs were filled with people, so that the conversation might revolve around something other than my father's work.

My mother knew guilt worked well with me, and even though I had plainly spelled out over the phone that I had a lot of work to do and that I'd not had a good day, I somehow found myself over at their house for dinner. It must've been that key phrase: *you know I don't ask much of you.*

With my napkin properly in my lap and my back straining in the awkward position called good posture, I watched Lola, my parents' housekeeper and cook for the last twenty years, bring in a roasted chicken. Mother, across the table, busied herself by arranging trivets and candles. It was remarkable to me how important family dinners were to my parents, yet how little conversation took place. In fact, at the moment, Dad was in the other room on a phone call, which in these postsenatorial days consisted of heavy political conversations with other ex-senators, usually ending with an important discussion about tee times.

"Lola, the chicken looks wonderful," I said as Mother took her seat.

"Thank you, Leah." Over the years, Lola had become less talkative, as if she was out of practice. She smiled at me and went back to the kitchen.

"So, how was your day?" I asked.

Mother glanced up at me with a startled expression, as if I'd just asked her to detail her mammogram. I knew Mother wasn't one for light chitchat, but she also wasn't one for deep, substantive conversations. So I was never sure exactly where the middle could be found.

"Fine," she said. Then she smiled. Just like Lola.

"That's good." *And how was your day, Leah? Oh, fine. Thanks for asking.*

Dad walked into the room. His face lit up when he saw me.

"Hi there," he said, his strong authoritative voice taking on that kind, warm tone that he used only for his daughter. I had vivid memories of watching my dad give speeches, hearing the certain inflections in his voice that caused thousands of people to sit silently and listen.

Dad was never one for affection. His hugs were rare, and usually reserved for photo ops, but I knew that nobody else heard the voice I got to hear. As a child, it made me grin. And I still found myself grinning.

"Hi," I said.

"I'm glad you're here for dinner." He sat at the head of the table. "Where's your sister?"

If I'd heard that once, I'd heard it a thousand times. Katherine

Elaine, known as Kate, or even better known as "I can't believe she did that," was late as usual. If ever there was a prodigal daughter, Kate was it. My little sister made Patti Davis look like a saint. And had the tattoos to prove it. We were distinct in so many ways, including how we addressed our matriarch. I called her Mother, which is what she had always wanted to be called, because she thought it would sound nice if she somehow found herself in the White House. Kate always refused and just called her Mom or, if she wanted to be really sassy, Mommy.

In more recent years, Kate had settled into the idea that she was an adult, and no matter how many ways she chose to rebel, her family wasn't going to ditch her. So though she still wasn't the model politician's daughter, her rebellion was much more subdued, and she attended most family gatherings.

We were all thankful that her hair was fully grown back—even if we weren't fond of the current color. She had shaved it off completely four years ago to protest hair products being tested on animals, which I found ironic since she never fed or watered any of our pets growing up.

We all heard the front door open as Lola brought in the final dish. I could see relief in my mother's features. As uptight as ever, she always seemed to be waiting for the other shoe to drop.

"Hurry up, Kate, dinner is served," Dad called.

Kate breezed into the dining room and flung herself into the seat next to Mother. Her hair, highlighted in four different colors that would never be seen together on wallpaper, looked windblown, but was actually the result of her latest protest against blow-dryers. She didn't wear a stitch of makeup anymore either, due to an embarrassing allergy outbreak during her goth years. But she didn't need it. She was really a natural beauty.

She was now into bohemian. And as naturally beautiful as she was, she could never quite pull it off as well as the Olsen sisters.

Mother pretended not to notice Kate's appearance. Dad shot me that look, the same one he'd given me many times through the years. It was a smile, a wink, and a reassuring nod, telling me he was grateful for my khakis.

Several minutes passed as we scooted platters around to one another and pretended to be interested in cutting our chicken or seasoning our vegetables. I stole glances at Kate, who seemed exceptionally happy. There was a sparkle in her eyes, and she was smiling at the saltshaker. My parents didn't seem to notice, though.

Suddenly my sister's announcement broke the silence: "I've found the man of my dreams."

Dad stopped chewing. Mother tried to smile through the perpetual frown that left deep creases between her eyes. Kate glanced at me, realized I was somehow smiling, and smiled back.

Understandably, my parents were nervous. The last love of Kate's life was a biker named Joey, who came complete with the chains, the leather, and a motorcycle that cost more than my car. We all thought it was a phase, but the relationship lasted more than two years. We thought there was even a possibility of marriage.

But then Joey was in a motorcycle accident. He survived but lost his left arm. Shortly thereafter, Kate broke up with him, citing her need for a man with two arms.

Watching my parents in this situation was amusing, because although they were desperate to get rid of Joey, there was a certain amount of embarrassment attached to the fact that Joey was being dumped because Kate couldn't live with a one-armed man.

I watched Mother's practiced expression feign interest and delight. She'd mastered this over the years as a politician's wife. "Oh? How wonderful. Tell us more."

"His name is Dillan," Kate gushed, "and he's an attorney."

All of our eyebrows popped up in unison, and Mother's smile looked real. "A lawyer; how wonderful," she said.

"He's with Swadderly-Wade." Kate looked at Dad.

"That's impressive," Dad said with a nod.

"He's not only really successful, but he's very nice too," Kate said. "His family is from South Carolina, and he's got the *best* Southern accent. He's tall, dark-headed. So handsome."

I knew that would really get my parents. We were Southern, even though we'd made our final home in the anti-South. All of us still had an accent, and Mother and Dad still owned a vacation home in Charlotte, just to prove they still loved the South.

I was trying my best to smile again. Feign a smile. Just like Mother. But inside I was becoming distressed. The thing that had been so reliable about Kate all these years was the fact that she was a continuous disappointment to my parents. It made my life so much easier. Impressing my parents took little work. All I had to do was wear proper clothing and keep my hair a basic color.

I looked across the table at my father, who'd set his fork down and was now giving his full attention to Kate. Mother's mouth had spread into an eager grin coaxing for more information. On the tip of my tongue sat many less-than-appropriate questions, but they all drowned waiting in the saliva. I managed to choke out a few basics.

"How old is he?"

"Thirty-four, never married."

"How'd you meet?" Surely Kate's answer would hint to my parents that there was something dysfunctional going on here.

"At church," she said innocently, as though the statement held no surprise.

I snorted. That triggered a cough, then a sneeze. Everyone was looking at me. "Excuse me," I said through another cough. "Something went down the windpipe." Like reality. My sister hadn't been to church in ages. The last time I'd invited her, about four years ago, she laughed at me and told me that if I was ever going to meet a man, I would have to look elsewhere. "The men there remind me of white bread, Leah. There's nothing exciting. Reliable, sure. But where is the focaccia?"

I had wanted to point out that the invitation to come to church was for spiritual purposes, but I realized it would do no good. Kate wasn't interested and viewed my life as boring and pathetic. So I'd not mentioned it again.

"So is this the focaccia you've been waiting for your whole life?" I asked. Only after I said these words out loud did I realize that apart from the context of my head, they formed a very weird statement. Mother cast a sharp look in my direction, a warning that any further word from me could completely destroy any chances for her second daughter to turn out halfway normal.

"What does this have to do with bread?" my dad asked.

"I want you to meet him," Kate said, unfazed by my comment. "I'd like to have you all over for dinner, maybe next week."

"That would be lovely," Mother said, like it was typical for Kate to invite us for dinner. Nobody had been to her apartment in more than two years.

"I'll have to check with Dillan on the date. He has a very busy schedule."

"That's fine, dear; we can work around his schedule. And I know Leah can come anytime. Right, Leah?" Mother asked.

Of course I can come anytime. I have no life. I have no schedule. Nothing I do is important; therefore, I can be at your beck and call. "Sure." I had to admit, I was curious to meet the new focaccia named Dillan. There had to be something abnormal going on with him, like a third eye or webbed feet.

Kate detailed Dillan's life for another ten minutes, including his Harvard education, his wealthy parents, his twin brother, his weekly visits to his elderly grandmother, and his fondness for children. He sounded perfectly preppy, and I had to wonder what impression Kate would make on his parents.

Finally she seemed to run out of good things to say about Dillan, and as I pushed my plate away she asked, "So, Leah, how's Edward?"

Ordinarily, this would be an easy question to answer. But my gut didn't want to say nice things about Edward right now. For crying out loud, he'd signed us up for therapy. He'd embarrassed me for embarrassing him, all over a color choice. And I was starting to see him as a fortified piece of wheat bread.

"He's fine; thanks for asking." I smiled, and all three of my family members smiled back.

Then Mother said, "Kate, why don't you help me in the kitchen? Let's see what Lola made for dessert, and maybe you can tell me a little bit more about Dillan."

The two rose and carried their plates into the kitchen together. Dad sighed and stretched his arms outward, signifying that a perfectly satisfying meal and conversation had just been consumed.

"Dillan sounds just about perfect, doesn't he?" I asked Dad.

"Let's just hope he's a democrat," my dad said, then excused himself to the study.

I sat there at the table alone, listening to the vague chatter of my mom and sister in the kitchen, wondering if the day would ever come when I would have the courage to tell my dad I was a republican.

Chapter 6

[She cowers in her seat.]

I'd never been to therapy of any sort. Therapy signified everything I was against, which was the fact that sometimes things go wrong in life. On one hand, I couldn't think of anything more mortifying. Yet, on the other hand, I had to acknowledge that because I had a lot of hang-ups about this, maybe I wasn't seeing that this was Edward's way of showing his love for me. Maybe he cared too much about our relationship to let a pink dress stand in the way.

I tried to leave it at that as I worked on my play throughout the day. Tuesdays were notoriously bad writing days for me. Mondays were always met with a lot of creativity and enthusiasm for the project. Tuesday was known as the Question Mark Day. On that day I questioned everything: what I wrote, why I'm writing, where my career's going, whose going to read it anyway, when will I ever get it done. I figured out that I consume three times as much caffeine on Tuesdays than any other day of the week. If I were a smoker, it'd be a three-pack day. If were a drinker, I'd be dead.

But on this particular Tuesday, I was trying to sort out a new set of problems that had crept into my day. First, there was the therapy ordeal. I'd worked through it a little bit by giving Jodie Bellarusa a few good lines. She was also against therapy, and that subject worked in nicely since I could give her family background at the same time.

Second, I couldn't figure out how my sister had suddenly risen to the top of the stock like fat boiling from a chicken. Except fat is really easy to skim off. Kate, with her unseasonal fur boots and ensemble of clothing that shouldn't be worn together, had "come home," in a sense. Except in the prodigal story in the Bible, the prodigal does a little groveling, a little insinuating that he's no better than pigs. My sister somehow managed to skip that part. Our parents gave her the fattened calf because of her association with a Harvard graduate who likes children and the elderly.

The Big Bad Wolf liked pigs, children, and the elderly, and look how that turned out.

Third, Elisabeth's words continued to ring in my ears. The more I gave it thought, the more I realized that what she was saying about my ability to predict the future did seem slightly plausible. After all, in her own words, something had come true in all three of the plays I'd written.

So as I stared at the taunting cursor, I had to wonder what exactly I was predicting in this next masterpiece. (Yes, I call all of my plays masterpieces. It helps my self-esteem.) Every word I wrote could be someone else's demise.

Or your own.

Jodie pointed that out, citing the remarkable similarities between the two of us. Outwardly, we were very opposite. But Jodie knew a secret nobody else knew. Inwardly, I was one heck of an Italian. But most of it stayed in my head.

In a way, the possibility that I might be predicting events made the play a bit more tantalizing, like I had some special power to control the universe with a few select keystrokes. But Jodie kept reminding me that the universe I was writing about was my own. Sure, it was cleverly disguised with anti-Leah characters and exotic locations like Detroit. But at the end of the day, I knew the truth.

The hours ticked by. I'd expected Edward to call to confirm our therapy appointment. I was surprised when he didn't, and it made me wonder if the relationship was in more jeopardy than I thought. Maybe this was a do-or-die situation and I hadn't realized it. If I didn't go to therapy, was Edward going to call it all off?

My imagination took me back to the impending dinner Kate had referred to, where she would introduce Tall, Dark, and Handsome while I explained that ever-reliable Edward had dumped me because of a pink dress.

I looked at the clock. It was six. I had half an hour to decide. I snatched up the phone and dialed Edward's home number. This was ridiculous. I wasn't going to stand for it.

I was greeted by his voice mail. A sweaty tingle pricked my skin. Edward was always home at six on Tuesdays. Where would he be? I hung up and redialed. Again, his voice announced he wasn't home.

I dialed his cell phone. I'd only dialed it once, when I had a flat on the interstate. Edward made it clear that his cell phone was for emergencies only. I think he purchased a total of twenty-five minutes every month.

He didn't answer that either.

My chest felt tight as I hung up the phone. I staggered to the window in my apartment, which I lifted with a hefty shove. Sticking my head out, I tried to breathe in some fresh air, a near impossibility in the city. Then I heard the phone ring.

After bumping my head, I hurried over to the phone and snatched it up. "Where are you?"

"Leah?"

"Mother?" My heart thumped in my chest. I smoothed down my breeze-blown hair as if she had the power to see me standing in my living room with this shocked look on my face. "Hi there. How are you?"

"What's the matter?"

"Why?" I asked innocently.

"You sound frazzled." A favorite of her words, *frazzled* had so many different meanings and intentions. Here it meant that I was doing a poor job of hiding my irritability at a situation that she wasn't privy to. Yet.

"Sorry, I thought you were . . . Edward." Why lie? Maybe it was time to spread the news about my sudden concerns for our relationship. Maybe Mother could help me through my feelings.

I could hear her breathing.

"We're running late for something, and I don't know where he is."

"I was calling about Dillan. Aren't you thrilled? Kate has finally found someone worthy of her."

My eyeballs rolled as far back in my head as they could without rendering me unconscious. "We haven't even met him yet. He could be a jerk."

"Did you see the way she talked about him? I've never seen Kate that passionate."

I didn't know what else to say. Why was Mother calling anyway? She never called to simply chat. Small talk was a waste of time in her world. I looked at my watch. I would have to leave in five minutes if I was going to make it on time.

But then again, this could be a good excuse not to go.

I waited for Mother to continue.

"I just want Kate to be happy," she finally said. There was something strange in her voice. Emotion. Huh.

"We all want Kate to be happy," I said. But I knew Mother was really trying to say she wanted Kate to be normal.

Mother's voice reverted to tidy and polite. "Well, I just wanted to see what you thought about the situation."

The part of me that admitted I'd been snappy when I thought the caller was Edward also wanted me to confess my hesitations about Kate's relationship. But my mother sounded so happy . . . so hopeful that Dillan might be the answer to her deepest longings—that one day soon the formal family portrait she'd always dreamed of might become a reality.

Admittedly, I was curious about Dillan myself. What about Kate was he attracted to? What made him think that bringing her home would fulfill his mother's dream? Maybe his parents were dead. That was a reasonable explanation. Or maybe in an insane asylum. There were too many possibilities to consider at this point.

I realized Mother was waiting for me to agree with her. "I think it's great," I said. That's what she wanted to hear. In my mind's eye I could see that thin smile of satisfaction spread over her lips.

"Well, we'll see." Always the diplomat.

I looked at my watch. "Mother, I'd better go. Like I said, I'm meeting Edward."

"Something fun, I hope?"

"As fun as it can get with a physicist," I said jokingly. I almost said psychiatrist. Wouldn't that have been something.

"Well, have a good time. We'll talk soon."

I hung up the phone and grabbed my handbag, checking to make sure I'd put the paper with the directions in it. I stopped at the door of my apartment, keys in hand, and stared at my watch. How could I agree to do this? How could he ask me to go to therapy with him by way of a flower bouquet and a coupon? This wasn't even insanely expensive therapy. This was discount therapy!

My hands were actually trembling. A sick feeling washed over my stomach. Maybe Edward would take a hint if I didn't show up. Maybe he would see what a moron he was for how he reacted to the pink dress.

But that was just a fantasy. I couldn't bear the prospect of harming our relationship. So how could I not go? The sickness slowly faded. My stomach started rumbling with hunger instead. I hadn't eaten much all day, but there was no time to eat now. I closed my eyes and stepped outside, shutting the door behind me.

Waiting for the elevator, I had a sudden craving for focaccia.

I wasn't a fan of public transportation. I liked to drive. It was the Southerner in me. Edward thought I was insane. He took the T everywhere. But I liked my car. As I drove the short distance toward downtown Boston, fighting the mad and rushed crowd of cars on this Tuesday evening, I couldn't help the memories that flooded my mind. I recalled the first time I'd brought Edward home to meet my parents. I had been nervous, wanting him to make a good impression, wanting my parents to approve. Edward, whose excitement level could be measured by how far up his eyebrows rose on his forehead, even looked more anxious than normal. We held hands and walked up the long sidewalk and steep steps that led to the gigantic wooden door of my parents' five-thousand-square-foot manor. Dad had worked years and years in Washington so they could live peacefully in a house too big for them and too formal for any grandchildren they might someday expect. I'd always hoped they would move back to the South, where our Southern accents could really shine. Mother had opened the door, a pleasant and inviting smile on her lips. She shook Edward's hand and she invited us in. Dad came down the spiral staircase, stoic and mannerly, his tall shadow leading the way.

We enjoyed a pleasant dinner, filled with predictable and easy conversation. Edward's long and impressive credentials took us through the first two courses. Dad's carried us through the third and fourth. The fifth course included a short explanation about the sister I hadn't mentioned. Over dessert we discussed favorite movies.

And that was it. That was the evening. Back then it seemed

perfect. Everything had gone as planned. But as I drove now, something recurred in my mind. It was Mother's expression. There hadn't been a bit of surprise in her face when she met Edward. It was as if he was everything she'd ever expected me to bring home. Why was that bothering me now? Was it because over the phone I'd heard a hint of tantalized excitement in her voice when she was talking about Dillan?

I focused on the road, realizing I was getting close to the address I was looking for. I had folded the piece of paper neatly three times and stuck it between my fingers like a cigarette. I reread the address, the only line showing between the folds.

I found the building and drove around trying to find a parking spot, questioning my decision not to use the T. Finally I spotted a car leaving. I took its place and got out, dumping quarters into the meter. It only allowed an hour. That would be a good excuse to leave.

I walked two blocks toward the building, old and tall and imposing with dusty ornate windows and faded brick. It looked to be important once. It reminded me of Dad. I double-checked the address. This was it.

I opened one of the front doors and stepped through. Elevators waited lifelessly against the back wall. The lobby was clean but didn't look to impress. I moved to the elevators and pushed the up arrow. One slid open, its doors rattling and revealing its age. Inside, I punched the third-floor button. The elevator didn't even give me the courtesy of a *ding*. It just hoisted me up and slid its doors open again. I walked out, surprised to find a large, empty, unfinished area waiting for me. A group of people clustered near the windows, their chairs situated in a small circle. Nobody turned to watch me. I looked around. The floor was cement. Sheetrock stood where walls should be. New wood paneling was unpainted. The ceiling's electrical, venting, and plumbing showed. Maybe I had the wrong place. I had imagined a more intimate setting, like an office with plush leather and expensive wood desks and elaborate bookcases. And also, far fewer people. Like three . . . me, him, and the therapist.

I looked at the small crowd, trying to find Edward's curly golden hair. I glanced back down at the piece of paper in my hand. According to it, I had the right place. I reread the coupon. *Conflict Resolution Class.* The word *class* did seem to signify we weren't going to be alone. That cheap man! Couldn't he have at least paid for private therapy?

I was about to turn around and punch the elevator button when the doors whooshed open. I stepped aside, hoping to see Edward's face emerge. But instead a shorter man with dark hair and intense eyes stepped off. He looked at me, didn't offer a smile, then looked at the rest of the people standing by the windows.

"Is this the conflict resolution class?" he asked me.

"I think so," I said with a shrug.

With a heavy sigh he walked toward the group. The elevator doors clamped shut before I could step back on.

Where was Edward? How could he be on time for everything in the world except this? I turned back to watch the crowd, squeezing my handbag strap until my knuckles were white. Then one of the women in the group turned my direction. Her gaze startled me, and I felt my face distort into something I intended as a smile but may have been a grimace. With a clipboard held against her chest, she walked toward me, her sandals tapping against the concrete. She extended a hand while still several feet out, which made the situation more awkward. Finally she arrived, her hand still extended. I shook it quickly.

"Hi there. I'm Marilyn Hawkins. I'm the instructor."

"Hi."

"What is your name?

"Edward Crowse." I looked up at her. "I mean, we may be under that name."

"Are you preregistered?"

"Yes." I resisted the urge to slap my coupon down for the discount. Edward would do that, just to be doubly sure we were getting our bargain.

She scanned the messy top page of the clipboard, which looked to be filled with names and crossed-out names. Then she lifted that sheet of paper and scanned the next page. Finally she went back to the first page. "I'm sorry, I don't have that name here."

"What about Leah. Townsend."

"Right here!" She took her pencil and gave my name a charismatic check mark. "Glad to have you with us. We're about to begin, so if you want to join us—"

"What about Edward? Edward Crowse?"

She looked at her clipboard again. "I'm sorry, I don't have that name down."

"Probably an oversight. He was the one that signed us up, so he should be there."

She studied the paper. "Looks like you're already paid in full. But I'm sorry, I don't have another name here."

I looked at the crowd of people, who had now taken seats in the circle. About five chairs were empty. "He'll be here. He's probably just running . . . late." The word felt heavy on my tongue. I'd never used *late* and *Edward* in the same sentence.

Marilyn put a hand on my back. I felt myself stiffen. "Why don't you go ahead and join us. As soon as he gets here, he's welcome to come on in."

I could hardly swallow. Marilyn urged me on, like it was what she was best at, and with leaden steps I walked toward the circle of people. Marilyn paused to look at something on her clipboard, but momentum apparently kept me going. Some people were chatting. Others sat and watched me decide which chair to take. I aimed for a grouping of three that had a view of the elevator, plopping myself down on the one in the center. I put my handbag on the one to my right. My neck felt hot, and I placed a hand around my throat to try to hide whatever red color was making its appearance.

A couple of seats to my left sat the guy who'd come off the elevator after I did. He was observing me with careful eyes. "Don't strangle yourself yet," he said softly. "You never know, you might like it."

"I'm not strangling myself," I said with a frown. But I dropped my hand into my lap.

"I was joking." His brown eyes smiled at me, though his lips held an even line. He stretched a hand across the space between us. "Cinco."

I reached out to shake it. "Cinco. Odd name."

"I'm the fifth in a long line of people who think they're important enough to name someone after them."

"I see. Well, nice to meet you."

"This is the point where you would normally introduce yourself."

I eyed him. "Sorry. I'm not feeling very friendly. This isn't what I was expecting," I said, glancing at the circle of people around me.

"What were you expecting?"

Luckily I didn't have a chance to explain. Marilyn, a throwback to the eighties with her blue leggings, stiff-collared polo shirt, and inflexible bangs, sat down between me and Cinco and brought the meeting to order.

I looked behind her toward the elevator, listening intently for any sign of movement from the old mechanical box. But the doors were quiet and tightly shut.

"As you're aware, this class is called Conflict Resolution, and as the title indicates, we're about learning to resolve conflict. I know most of you don't want to be here, but that just means I'm going to have to work harder to win you over." She grinned. A nervous fellow across from me chuckled, and that satisfied Marilyn enough to release the hold she had on her smile. My gaze wound around the room as Marilyn's words *you don't want to be here* echoed in my ears.

Nobody looked like they wanted to be here. And only the nervous fellow was attempting to do anything but scowl at her.

"Every day," she began after another award-winning smile, "we are faced with conflict. Sometimes small, sometimes big. Sometimes it's on the job, sometimes it's with people we love, sometimes it's with a neighbor or even a stranger. But conflict is all around us. You're here today to learn better ways not only to face conflict, but to resolve it. Everyone has a choice when faced with conflict. The one true thing about conflict is that you *will* handle it in some way. It's impossible not to. But sometimes how we handle it can lead to more and more conflict. I'm here to teach you how to handle it in a way that will resolve it." She gave a definitive nod and then continued, "All right. I want you to all feel like family for the next seven weeks. You'll be working closely together, so I want you to know one another well. We're going to begin by going around and introducing ourselves. But before we do that, let me add just a couple of housekeeping notes: First, we are normally in the conference room on the first floor, but they're renovating, so, unfortunately, for the duration of this class, we're going to be in this unfinished room. But nobody is here for the scenery, right? Also, this class meets Tuesdays and Thursdays. If you are here by court order, you must attend every class in order to fulfill the court's requirement."

Her words punched me in the stomach. A tiny grunt escaped. Nervous fellow and I had the same stunned expression on our faces, so I tried to meld mine with a pleasant, nondubious semismile while willing the elevator doors to open. Where was Edward? And why were people here by court order? Were these people *criminals*?

"Your name and why you're here," she said, and looked to her left, thankfully.

My left hand found the empty chair and plopped itself down, as if it were expecting Edward's lap to be there. It only hit my handbag.

The man who had introduced himself as Cinco was laughing,

his arms crossed over his chest, chuckling like St. Nick. It took me a few seconds to realize he was chuckling at me. I wanted to ask what was so funny, but instead I tried to act as if I was in on the joke, whatever that was. Cinco had seemed to connect with the man across from him, who looked like he should be working as a bouncer at a nightclub. They were both laughing and looking at each other, then at me.

"Go ahead," Marilyn said to Cinco.

"I'm Cinco Dublin, and I'm a recovering conflict causer," he said with a wry grin. A few people laughed. "But the guy I slugged isn't recovering as well." More laughs. I was laughing too, but not for reasons of amusement. It was just keeping me from crying.

"I can see I'm going to have my hands full with you, Cinco," Marilyn said, seeming to take it all in stride. She winked, and I wondered how a woman so stuck in one decade could be that confident. I shriveled in my seat as I watched her. "And Cinco, may I add for the record that I'm a fan of your show."

I looked at Cinco. He didn't look familiar. But there was something about his . . . voice! He was the radio guy! The Cinco Dublin show. He hosted a conservative talk-radio show that loved to ruffle people's feathers. I'd listened to him a couple of times, but I could never get past all the arguing that went on. I always felt so badly for the guest. Cinco could size them up and then throw them down with just a few swift sentences. Though I agreed with some of his views, I never could enjoy listening. Instead, I'd usually switch to the classical station with the monotone host who came on once an hour. The only chance Milbert Connelly had to stir controversy was to attribute a song to the wrong composer. And not once, in the twenty years he'd been hosting the classical station, had he ever done that. I had only once heard an inflection in his voice, on 9/11, when he reported that his listeners should get to their nearest television. It was only a slight inflection but enough to make me feel the sky was falling. For the rest of the day, Milbert Connelly played classical patriotic music.

"Thank you, Marilyn. I hope to make myself a fan of yours soon too."

Marilyn laughed and a few other people chuckled. "I can't imagine why you're here. You? Causing conflict?"

Cinco's smile faded a little. "Lost my temper and let a few fly on a reporter in front of my home. I'm one of your beloved court-ordereds."

"Good to have you, Cinco," Marilyn said. "Next."

Next to Cinco sat a woman with Merle Norman´eyes and a drawn mouth. Her face was shiny with either overdone moisturizer or one too many cosmetic procedures. With penciled-in eyebrows and ratted blonde hair that looked like it'd been cooked over high heat, she was the quintessential sixty-year-old trying for forty. Her practiced smile greeted the group and then she focused on Marilyn.

"I'm Glenda. I'd prefer not to use my last name. You can't be too careful these days."

I glanced at Cinco, who looked like he was willing himself not to zing her with some sarcastic challenge.

"I'm court-ordered as well, but it wasn't really my fault. The police officer that pulled me over was a complete jerk and an imbecile. And if you can't protect yourself against the police, how can you protect yourself at all?"

Cinco couldn't keep quiet. "What'd you do?"

Her head lifted with superiority. "It's nobody's business, but let's just say the police will think twice about pulling me over in a school zone again." She blinked and looked at everyone. "And listen, if you believe the newspaper article about how those kindergartners were traumatized by the event, you're a moron. Their screams were no doubt a result of some high-sugar snack they were fed that day. And just for the record, any police officer who gets knocked down by a purse is a ninny anyway."

Marilyn's mouth was hanging open, and I realized mine was too. "Next," she said.

"Next" was the biggest guy I'd ever seen. His muscles rippled under his shirt, his head was smooth and bald, his skin tan, and his eyes green and mean looking. He sat with both feet firmly planted on the ground and his large arms entwined across his large chest.

"I'm Robert Goden. I'm a police officer."

My whole body flushed with heat, and I looked at the ground instead of all the shocked expressions I knew were making their way around the group. And, to my horror, I felt the first signs of my most dreaded weakness . . . my hives. They were simply uncontrollable, and the most I could hope to do about them was avoid uncomfortable situations. But I knew that soon enough the itching would begin. Large welts would climb up my chest, and people would start asking me if I was okay. My hand nonchalantly crept up my shirt to feel my neckline. Fairly high, thankfully. If I took a few deep breaths and tried to calm myself, I had a chance of slowing them down at least, and with some careful maneuvering of my hair around my neck, I could possibly hide it all, including my beet-red ears.

I stared at the concrete below my feet and tried not to listen, but it was impossible. Robert was saying, "I'm here under court order. The anger management class was full." I glanced up, and Robert was staring at Glenda. I quickly glanced back down. Robert continued. "And lady, if you'd like to try to swing your purse at me, go right ahead. Just make sure it's not one of your favorites."

I could hear Cinco laughing. He was the only one. By the way feet moved back and forth slightly, I could tell everyone else was squirming in their seats. The hives were at my collarbone. I carefully moved one side of my hair and wrapped it across my neck nonchalantly, willing myself not to scratch. I glanced up once and noticed Cinco watching me. I tried my best not to appear startled. I wasn't sure if I pulled it off. So instead, I looked at the next fellow in this torturous line. He was the nervous one.

Maybe. But does he have hives?

"I'm Ernest. Ernest Jones. Reverend Ernest Jones." Why it took three attempts to get his name out was unclear, but his face opened up with an eager smile and bright eyes. "I'm here because I would like to learn more about resolving conflict. I feel it's one area of my life that could really use some attention. God wants all of us to try to live in peace with one another, and so I'm here to try to find a way to do that while addressing the problems my church faces."

"What kind of problems?" Cinco asked, as if completely unaware that Marilyn was the group leader. Marilyn looked curious too. And it seemed my hives had stopped spreading long enough for me to focus.

Reverend Jones glanced around the circle, then with a humble slump stated, "There's been a hostile takeover."

"What do you mean?" Marilyn asked.

"At my church. My committee has taken over."

Only silence answered the poor reverend. He looked up from staring at his feet and shrugged, a small smile acknowledging he felt it a bit absurd too. "It all started with the choir robes," he continued. "After forty years of maroon, some of us thought it might be time for a color change. Things just got out of control after that."

"Reverend, I'm glad you're here," Marilyn interjected quickly, halting Cinco as he opened his mouth to add what I supposed would be some commentary on the situation. "Sounds like you're in the right place."

Next up was a small woman I'd hardly noticed before. She was sitting on the other side of my handbag, and I hadn't even been sure what she looked like up until now. I studied her face. She had small features, including a tiny nose that tipped a bit upward toward narrow, plain brown eyes. Her hair was fastened to the nape of her neck with bobby pins, and she wore an out-of-date skirt and glasses that looked like they could swallow her head. She was smiling, laughing almost, through her obvious insecurity. I worried that at a moment's notice she might burst into tears. I knew the feeling. Through a tight grin she managed to state her name, Carol. But after that, nobody could hear anything, including me, and I was practically sitting right next to her.

"Carol, nobody can hear you. Could you speak up?" Marilyn asked.

Carol nodded but still couldn't be heard on her second attempt. Marilyn looked to me for what I guessed was an interpretation. I heard every fourth or fifth word of the third attempt, but was unable to gather enough. "Carol is hoping to be more assertive in her life," I said, glancing at Carol, who smiled broadly at me. Then she looked at Marilyn and nodded.

"Glad to have you, Carol. By the end of this class, you'll have no problem with that." Then Marilyn turned to me. "Leah, why are you here?"

My fingers clawed through my tangled hair, and I smoothed it around the exposed side of my neck. I tried to smile, but my lips quivered and I felt the heat return. In the best way I knew how, inspired by my new friend Carol, I lifted my head and met Marilyn's eyes.

That was the million-dollar question. Or, with a coupon, the eight-hundred-thousand-dollar question.

Chapter 7

[She shivers.]

That was priceless. Really. I knew you were creative, but that, my friend, took you to an entirely new level. And to say it with such conviction. Maybe you missed your calling as an actor.

Rain poured. The wipers swiping back and forth across my windshield weren't loud enough to drown out Jodie's voice, even with the squeak. So I let her continue. A good berating helped me unleash my guilt sometimes. And I had enough anger going right now that I wasn't paying too much attention to the guilt anyway.

I do hope Edward never shows up, because I doubt he could pass for your brother. But what a heartwarming story you told. My goodness. Had it been true, you might've landed yourself in People *magazine.*

My windshield fogged over. I quickly swiped my hand across the glass to make a circle I could see through, then fumbled to turn the defrost on full blast. I tried to stop replaying the scene in my head, but it looped over and over again, taunting me to pick through it with a fine-tooth comb.

My plan would've been completely successful had it not been for

Marilyn's unfortunate mention of Edward and Cinco's curious mouth working me over. I'd simply mentioned I was here to learn more about dealing with conflict. That was good enough, wasn't it? But then Marilyn had to ask whether or not the Edward fellow would be coming. Too ashamed to admit my boyfriend had stood me up for therapy, somehow I casually made him out to be my brother. It was a little white lie that could've stayed perfectly pristine had Cinco not been so stubborn about it all. He seemed to sense my story wasn't true and kept asking me detailed questions. By the end of their interrogation, my brother Edward hadn't shown up because of complications from a kidney transplant, for which I'd been the donor, which was my explanation for why I was suddenly splotching and reevaluating life and attending classes that would help me become the best person I could be.

Despite driving full speed ahead in the pouring rain, I squeezed my eyes shut for a moment, trying to block the painful realization of what a pansy I was. Well, for every measure of pansy, I was certainly going to make up for it now. I looked at my clock. It was three minutes after nine. I accelerated. Edward was always in bed by nine.

Turning onto the street of his apartment, I prayed for a parking spot at the curb. But the cars were squeezed together like sardines. After five minutes, I found a semilegal spot three blocks away. I turned off the car and stared out at the black night and white rain.

With eyes closed, I built my resolve. After all, I'd been wronged, and I had every right to be mad. I made sure I wasn't being irrational. Irrationality never won an argument. I played through the entire incident, and as far as I could tell, I wasn't wrong in the least bit.

Opening the car door, I willed myself out of the warmth and into the cold rain. I'd already been caught off guard by the storm when I left the therapy session. But not even a record-breaking blizzard could've kept me from escaping that humiliating gathering. Hunching my shoulders and wrapping my arms around my body, I jogged toward Edward's apartment, scurrying underneath overhangs as I could. The urban streets were mostly empty, though a few restaurants were still open for customers. The few people who were out didn't seem to notice I was walking in the rain without a coat or an umbrella. But in this city, people kept their noticing to themselves.

By the time I reached Edward's brick apartment building, I was soaked through. It was fine with me. Looking pathetic and cold would only help my cause. I checked the doors but felt no surprise that they were locked for the night. The keypad glowed against the brick wall. I reached for the numbers, but paused with the tip of my index finger only centimeters away from the six. I looked at my watch. It was almost twenty past nine.

Edward was sure to be in bed.

All the better, right? An argument always goes better when the accused is woken out of a dead sleep.

Jodie taunted me, but I tried to ignore her. I wasn't here to stir up trouble. I just wanted an explanation. His complete and total absence from the day was a sure sign that things were not as they should be in our relationship. After all, we were a very tidy couple, always tying up loose ends. Edward was the most thorough of the two of us. The Battle of Hastings wasn't as well planned as the one and only road trip we took together a year ago. Edward had brought enough food for six days in case "something happened."

I pushed the six. Then the three. Then the four. The electronic sound of the phone ringing made my heart pound against my chest. After the fourth ring, I almost decided to stop the call. I could sneak away, and he would never have to know it was me. But right as I reached for the End Call button, Edward's voice crackled through the speaker.

"Hello? Who is this?" he said groggily.

I swallowed. It wasn't too late to run. But hadn't I suffered enough humiliation for one night? Edward was the cause of all of it. He should at least have to answer for it.

"Hello?" His voice had an edge to it now.

"It's me," I said.

"Who?"

"*Me.* Leah." I threw the wet hair out of my eyes.

I could hear him breathing. Or maybe that was me. Somebody was breathing hard.

"Hello?" I said, moving my lips closer to the speaker box.

"I heard you. It's after nine."

"I know that."

"What's the matter?"

"It's raining out here. I'm freezing. Can you unlock the door?"

"Hold on."

I heard the door click. I opened it and approached the creaky excuse for an elevator. A well-dressed couple got off as the doors split. I avoided eye contact and hurried in, jamming my thumb into the Close Door button. Six floors up, the doors opened again and I walked to Edward's apartment. I'd expected him to be waiting for me at his door, but it was closed and quiet.

I knocked.

Shuffling feet could be heard, then the two clicks of both his deadbolts. He opened the door. Behind him his apartment was dark, and he squinted at the hallway lights. After the shock of the glare, he looked at me like he'd just discovered the Loch Ness Monster.

"Are you okay?" he asked, but I didn't detect much sympathy in his voice.

"I could use a towel." I walked past him into his apartment and went to the bathroom. I grabbed a clean towel, neatly folded in the cabinet, and squeezed it around my hair. After I blotted my face dry, I found Edward in the living room, a single lamp clicked on. He was sitting down, watching me.

"What's going on?" he asked.

"I'm here to ask you that same question." I tried to make my voice bold, but it quivered. I chalked it up to being cold.

"Leah, I'm not following, and frankly, it's late and I need the sleep."

Late? That's hilarious. It's nine. Maybe you should offer to warm some milk for him.

"You have no clue why I'm here?" I asked.

He blinked. He really looked confused, but I tried not to let that distract me.

"You stood me up tonight."

He blinked again. A worried expression flickered across his features.

I threw up my hands. "For therapy."

"Therapy? What therapy?"

"The therapy you suggested we go to?" My voice was climbing like I might attempt a high-range opera song. And admittedly, I did end the sentence with a question in my voice, so Edward looked unsure whether he was supposed to answer or listen. I rolled my eyes.

"The conflict resolution class," I finally said.

"That?" He opened his hands.

"Yes." Of course that! What do you mean, *that*? "Why didn't you come?"

Edward stood, his hands sliding down the front of his purple silk pajamas. "That was for you, not me."

"What do you mean?"

"I wanted you to attend."

"Not the both of us?" The soprano in me was preparing for the finale.

"I thought it might do you some good and therefore benefit both of us."

"Me? Why me?"

He cocked his head to the side. "Leah, the thing is, you don't handle conflict very well."

"What does that mean?"

"It's just an observation I've made throughout our relationship. And this weekend was a perfect example. At the party, you were practically hiding in the garden!"

"I was *strolling.*"

"I just thought the class might help you. I saw it advertised in the paper."

"You don't even know what this class is!" Edward took a step back. I was a little stunned myself. "It's for criminals!"

"That's not what the coupon said."

"They send everyone over to this class when the anger management class is full!" I willed myself to calm down or face the prospect of another coupon.

"I called about it, Leah. She said nothing about criminals. The lady was very nice. She just said that it helps people learn to deal with conflict the right way." Edward spoke like we were discussing a dinner menu. Why was he so calm?

"You never intended on coming?"

"I didn't realize I gave that impression."

"This is humiliating."

He gently took my shoulders into his hands. "Leah, this was just meant to help you. That's all."

"I called you at six and you weren't home. Where were you?"

"I stopped to help an old lady who was in a car accident."

I turned and tried to catch my breath. Was he telling the truth? Little old lady stories are about as easy to concoct as organ transplant stories.

"I didn't think it would be this big of a deal," Edward finally said, exhaustion in his voice. "I didn't mean to hurt you. Did you get the flowers?"

I turned and watched him lower himself back onto his couch. He seemed sincere. And he really did look tired. His bloodshot eyes glowed against his shadowy face. Surely this could've waited until morning.

"I've got a big presentation tomorrow," he said, punctuated by a large yawn.

"I'm sorry," I replied, shaking my wet head. I folded the towel and went to drape it across the tub in the bathroom. When I came back, Edward was standing again, facing the hallway to his bedroom as if counting down the seconds to when he could crawl back into bed. I was feeling tired too.

"Look, if the class is that horrible, don't go. It doesn't matter, okay?" He took a step down the hallway.

I nodded and walked to the door.

"I'll call you tomorrow," he said, his voice distant as he turned into his bedroom.

The elevator dinged open as soon as I punched the button, and the descending ride embodied the spiral down which I felt myself sliding. Stiffening my lower eyelids to hold in the tears, I dragged myself three blocks to my car, not caring that I was already too wet to worry that I was being drenched.

It was a hard thing to shake. Edward thought I needed help with conflict. This was just another sign that this relationship was not what it should be.

It was nearly ten by the time I got to my apartment building. Puddles of water trailed behind me in the hallway. I pulled off one sock and tried to wipe them up as I walked to the elevator. I didn't need to be responsible for someone falling and breaking their neck tonight. Though that would be how I would expect this day to end.

Thankful for the carpeting in the elevator, I went quickly to my apartment and turned the key to unlock the door, except the bolt didn't click. The door was already unlocked. I pulled my key out, trying to remember whether I'd locked it before leaving for the class. I couldn't deny I'd been flustered.

My thoughts suddenly turned to every serial-killer movie I'd ever seen. But then I laughed at myself. Was this what Edward was talking about? Did I overreact to simple things like my door being unlocked?

Gripping the key in my hand, I pretended to continue to laugh and turned the knob. I left in a tizzy. Of course, I'd forgotten to lock the door. Naturally. I shoved the door inward and stared at my dark apartment, a smile pasted on as I eyed the dark, shadowy corners of the room.

I started in, making haste toward the lamp at the end of the couch. A little light would quickly diffuse this situation. But when I got halfway there, a dark figure emerged suddenly from the hallway.

I screamed. And screamed again. My body wiggled with the electrocution of sheer terror. Then I realized something astonishing. I wasn't the one screaming. With my mouth open but with no sound coming out, I stared through the darkness and realized the person hopping up and down in the hallway looked remarkably like Elisabeth.

She finally stopped screaming. I switched on the light by the couch. "Elisabeth! What are you doing?"

Grasping her T-shirt at chest level, she managed to say, "You scared me to death!"

"How did I do that? You're sneaking around my apartment in the dark!"

Her nostrils flared. "I'm not *sneaking*. I just got here and I was using the bathroom. I do have a key, if you remember."

I glanced down the hallway and saw a small slice of light glowing from the bathroom. "What are you doing here?"

"Looking for you. I called twice and you didn't answer."

"Did it occur to you I might be out?"

"You're never out on Tuesdays, especially after nine."

Her words stung. Was I that predictable?

"I was worried," she added, but not convincingly. "Looks like I should've been. Heard of an umbrella?"

I sighed. "I need to go change." I walked past her and into my bedroom, where I dried off, wrapped my hair in a towel, and changed into a T-shirt and sweatpants. In the kitchen, Elisabeth was fixing us both tea, which meant only one thing. She needed to talk.

I didn't feel like listening to her problems. Not tonight. I had enough to deal with. I noticed she was fixing chai. This was not a good sign. It didn't just mean conversation. It meant a heavy conversation. I walked straight to the living room and sat down.

After a few minutes, she joined me. "Here you go." She smiled, handing me a large mug.

"Elisabeth," I started. All I wanted to do was fall into bed and cry myself into a deep sleep. She turned, waiting for me to finish.

"What is it?"

I could see trouble in her eyes. "Need more sugar."

She plopped another cube into my mug, then made herself comfortable on the couch.

I switched on the lamp, my body aching with the weight of so much worry. Elisabeth didn't notice. She was now furiously stirring her tea and looked like she was about to cry.

I sat down next to her, and as soon as I put my arm around her shoulder, she burst into tears. I held her, my heart aching for her unknown sorrow. I'd never seen her this upset in all our years of friendship.

Soon enough, though, she calmed down and I went in search of tissues. When I returned, she set her cup down and said, "I've decided to have an affair."

Chapter 8

[Fumbling her words, she becomes silent.]

Rain was coming down again, the damp environment a constant reminder of the new low I found myself in. I drove cautiously, both hands gripping the steering wheel, my bloodshot eyes stinging and scared to blink for fear it would turn into a short snooze at the wheel.

I'd spent yesterday deleting scene after scene from my play, punching the Delete key in rapid succession to try to get that same feeling I used to have when I actually ripped up pieces of paper. It wasn't quite the same. But close. Especially when my Delete key jammed up.

But in reality, it wasn't my play that was frustrating me. In fact I'd made some progress today, though the idea that I had in my possession some sort of prophetic talents still made me shiver. No, my mind was plagued by my friend Elisabeth's dilemma.

Was it really a dilemma?

Somehow it had turned into a dilemma, and somehow I had let her walk out the door of my home remaining confident that this was what she had to do.

"This" was named Creyton, described by Elisabeth as the ideal man she'd written about in her diary when she was twenty.

"He's everything I've ever wanted in a man," she'd told me, without the slightest hint of embarrassment at her cliché or conviction at her more-than-obvious moral quagmire. She explained that Creyton was her neighbor, but what she didn't explain was why an out-of-work mechanic with two grown children was on her list of wants in her twenties.

I'd posed the question of how a mechanic could possibly be out of work since there seemed to be an unending supply of broken mechanical things, but Elisabeth brushed past it and began a long and detailed oratory in which she corrected my apparent misconception that she had a happy life.

I learned during our two hours over chai that motherhood was taking its toll, and with her husband Henry's travel schedule, Elisabeth was feeling lonely and burdened.

I listened intently. My friend was clearly in an emotional and mental crisis, and frankly it made all my problems seem small.

"Have you talked with Henry about your feelings?" I asked as she rose for more tea.

"How can I talk to Henry? Henry is the problem."

"But maybe he doesn't know he's the problem."

"Are you saying maybe I'm the problem?"

I paused. Hadn't I only said maybe he didn't know he was the problem?

"You're taking Henry's side."

"I'm not taking his side. I'm just trying to help."

"Believe me, I've tried everything. There's no hope."

"So you want a divorce?"

"No, I can't divorce Henry. What would I do? Where would I go?" She dropped sugar cubes into her mug as fast as I was trying to drop hints, but I could see this conversation was dissolving as fast as the cubes. "I'm a permanent fixture on the wall of disgruntled mother-figures. That's Henry's problem too. He wanted a big family. It's a trap. Men know that once you leave the workforce and have small children, it's impossible to do anything else."

"Elisabeth, maybe you could try getting a part-time job. Maybe that would help. Get a nanny."

Her eyes turned fierce. "I don't need a job, Leah. I need a passion. A reason to get up in the morning. You should see how Creyton treats me. In all the years I've known Henry, he's never made me feel this way."

"Maybe it's not Creyton. Maybe it's the idea of having something that is forbidden." I shrugged at her scowl. "I mean, I'm just thinking out loud here."

"I realize it's hard for you to be rational in this situation because you haven't met Creyton so you don't know what kind of amazing man he is."

"How am I being irrational? I'm trying to help you." That wasn't what I wanted to say at all. But that's what came out of my mouth, which was like a double-edged sword except one edge was too dull to cut through baloney, and the other edge was really just there for appearances.

"Leah, your definition of help is to push your high-and-mighty ideas about what is right and wrong onto other people. You see your fly-by-the-seat-of-her-pants friend pursuing a lurid, hypocritical affair because she's bored with her life. What you don't see is that this just may be my ticket to salvation."

"But Elisabeth, don't you see that—"

"Don't I see what? The world through your eyes? No, Leah, I don't." She slammed her mug onto the counter. "I don't know why I came over here. I'm in a crisis, and I don't need lectures from you!"

She swept past me and grabbed her handbag.

"Elisabeth, wait. Please." I rushed after her and she waited for me at the front door, arms twisted around each other and handbag pushed hard against her chest. "I'm sorry."

She eyed me, letting her arms fall slowly to her sides.

"I don't want you to leave angry. I wasn't trying to upset you."

"You did upset me."

I chose my words carefully. "I guess I don't fully understand your situation, and I shouldn't . . ."

"Judge me?" She gave me a tight squeeze. "I'm going to need you to get through this. Whatever happens."

"What do you think is going to happen?"

She smiled a little. "I think I'm going to find happiness again."

I blinked and the scene faded as I continued driving through the rain. I turned the corner, and the sight of an empty parking spot against the curb in front of the building just about sent me into tears. I parked the car and sat quietly, listening to the rain.

Why was I here again? I glanced up at the gloomy building, washed in rain but still looking dirty. I pulled my yellow rain-slicker hood over my head, but couldn't get myself to get out of the car. I was so stunned I'd come back, and not against my own will. Edward had given me an out. Yet here I was, using the darkness and rain as cover, returning to my biggest nightmare.

There was one irony I couldn't escape. I wasn't having dinner with Edward on Thursday. I couldn't remember the last time that was true.

I looked up at the building. It was absurd to think that I didn't handle conflict well. And maybe that's why I was here, to prove him and myself wrong. My gaze dropped down to my car clock. In three minutes, I could be late. Or in three minutes, I could just start the car again and go back home.

A fist pounded against my passenger-side window. I screamed and shuddered, making sure my doors were still locked. Then I looked at the face staring at me through the rain, the nose nearly pressed against the glass like a little boy's.

Cinco?

I rolled down the window.

"What are you doing?" he shouted over the racket of the storm.

"What are you doing?" I shouted back.

"Wondering if you needed to use my umbrella."

"No, I've got my raincoat."

A clap of thunder filled in the pause.

"Are you coming?" he finally shouted.

I sighed and pulled the keys out of the ignition. No turning back now. I opened the car door and closed my coat, ducking into the rain. I hastened toward the building, and he followed me with his umbrella. Inside, I wiped the wetness off my face. He shook out his umbrella.

The humiliation of being there obliterated my social skills, and I walked toward the elevator without him. The doors dinged open and I stepped inside, but his hand reached for the closing door. Soon enough he joined me, but not without a suspicious look. I tried to ignore it.

The elevator lifted us and I stared forward.

"How's your brother?" he asked.

"He's fine," I replied, not even hesitating to perpetuate my white lie. I felt Cinco staring at me. I felt the splotching begin. I prayed for those doors to open quickly, and they did. I actually said "Thank you" to the elevator.

Marilyn was gathering the group into the circle. I took off my coat and shook the water off, laying it on a steel bar near the elevator to dry, pretending not to hear Cinco's offer to take it. I walked forward, trying to shake off the shakes and look as confident as Marilyn did wearing leggings and a wide-necked purple sweatshirt.

"Hi, Leah. Hi, Cinco, come sit down. We're just about to begin." I took a seat next to Carol again, the woman who'd been unable to raise her voice above a whisper.

I was pretty sure she said hi when I sat down.

"Hi," I said back.

Cinco took a seat next to Robert. I was trying to decide whether an attempt at small talk was worth it with Carol when Marilyn began the meeting.

"Before we begin," she said, flipping through the paper on her clipboard, "there are a few minor housekeeping notes I'd like to go over quickly. First of all, I'd like everybody to be on time. We don't have a lot of sessions to cover a great deal of material, so let's make the most of it. Second, Robert, I have a note here from the court that says you've refused to pay the fee for this class."

Robert's gloomy face jerked up. "What? What are you talking about?"

"It says here you are unwilling to pay the court fees that include this class."

"That's absurd," his voice boomed. "I paid them the day I was in court."

She flipped through her notes. "No . . . sorry, I don't have any record here except what the court clerk said."

"What'd she say?" he asked.

"It's hard to read her handwriting, but it looks like she called you . . . oh, um, never mind."

"What?"

Marilyn glanced up and attempted a smile. "What's important here, Robert, is that you pay this fee. They can actually put you in jail for not paying it."

"I paid it!"

"Not according to the court clerk."

"The court clerk looked half-drunk the day I was there," Robert said with a frightful laugh. He glanced at Carol, and Carol complied by laughing with him, except nobody could hear her but me.

Marilyn wasn't laughing. "Robert, they tend to keep very good records at the court. But this can all be resolved if you can produce the receipt."

Robert's joyless smile faded, and he reached for his wallet. He thumbed through it rapidly, then thumbed through it again.

Marilyn glanced around the room with a reassuring smile, but nobody but me saw her because everyone else was watching Robert, who was grumbling louder and louder.

Marilyn said, "Well, folks, this is a good object lesson about keeping receipts, isn't it?"

"I paid the fee!" Robert shouted, and the room fell silent to his bulging eyes and beet-red face. He went back to thumbing through his wallet. I looked at Marilyn, who was watching him with careful but fearless eyes. I noticed Carol was trembling beside me. The pastor's lips moved like he was praying silently. And Cinco looked amused. Glenda mumbled something about how all cops are alike.

That broke the mammoth's back. Robert's large frame flew out of the chair and he threw his wallet to the ground. His large, muscular arm shot out like an arrow straight at Glenda, and his index finger flipped toward her with perfect precision. "Marilyn, you better shut this woman up before I do."

My heart felt like it was sliding down my small intestine, and at that particular moment I didn't care how or where my hives showed up. I wondered if Marilyn kept a stun gun nearby. But she was grinning. She stood quietly and approached Robert as if he weren't a foot taller.

"Robert, you can sit down. I'm done with my illustration."

Robert was frowning, still pointing his sharp finger over at Glenda, whose coloring had been reduced to two pink powder-blush circles on her cheeks. "What are you talking about?"

"This class is about conflict, and I'm going to be using a lot of illustrations, so you all should get used to it. Robert, there's no court problem. I made it up." She swiveled to make eye contact with the rest of us. "But this was a perfect illustration that conflict will almost always take us by surprise. So it's not something that you can plan on dealing with or avoid dealing with; it's something that you have to condition yourself to accept and address. Accept and address. That's going to be a big part of your success in this class."

I tried to listen to Marilyn, but Robert was still standing there fuming, and he didn't look pleased to be a part of her trick.

Marilyn looked at Robert again. "Okay, thanks, Robert. You can sit down."

But Robert didn't sit down. Instead, he drew air through his nostrils at such speed they sucked shut and made the most terrifying squeaky noise. Everyone gasped, probably because we had geared ourselves up for Robert shouting at the top of his lungs, but that short squeaky noise was just as surprising.

His head rotated slowly toward Glenda, but his eyeballs kept turning, eying me, Carol, and the pastor. None of us said a word. I noticed, however, that I was very, very damp.

He then looked back at Glenda. "I am going to deal with you in a minute," Robert said, "but Marilyn, I have to say, I don't like being the butt of anybody's joke. *Ever.*" The two-syllable word stretched into four. I looked at Marilyn. She seemed slightly worried, but kept a good poker face.

"I'm sorry, Robert. But again, conflict catches us by surprise. And among other things, we're each going to learn to be the butt of a joke, with class and style."

I watched Robert's hands ball up, and then he looked at Glenda. "Lady, if I were you, I'd make sure you kept a good distance from me if you want to make it out of this class with your handbag intact."

Glenda was still pale, but she said, "Are you threatening me?"

Robert started to march over to Glenda, but Cinco hopped up and took Robert's arm. I expected Cinco to be thrown back into his chair with one swift move, but instead Robert stopped.

"Dude, let's just sit down," Cinco said. "It's not worth taking this class over again, is it?" There was humor in Cinco's voice, and Robert turned and looked at him, then let go of a smile.

Then he smiled at Marilyn. Then at the rest of us. I felt myself smiling, but I didn't know why, because Robert's swing to the lighter side was making me equally as nervous. Now he was chuckling and all I could think was, *We're all going to die.*

"If you're paying attention, this is a good example of how layered conflict can be. It's not just a problem that gets solved. Conflict is often complicated because of people's emotions." Marilyn suddenly stood, clipboard in hand, and patted Robert on the arm. "Thanks, Robert. You can sit down."

Robert sat down.

"Robert was in on this from the beginning," Marilyn announced with a smile. Cinco was still standing in the middle of our circle and Marilyn said to him, "Cinco, you did a great job diffusing the situation."

"Robert wasn't really mad?" Glenda asked.

"No. He was with me from the beginning, even on the court case. I wanted to do this to show you all how to deal with conflict." She looked at each of us as Cinco took his seat. "How did you deal with what just happened? From the start when I told Robert about the court problem, to when I told Robert I was just using him as an example, how did you feel? What was your first reaction? What about when Robert got angry? How did you feel then?"

Marilyn looked at each of us, and I looked down. I tried to sort through it all, wanting to be a good student of the class. After getting over the initial shock that this was all a setup, twice, I tried to remember what I was feeling.

Nothing. I'd gone into shock.

Marilyn let silence go by as she took her seat. She let us all dwell on our wretched shortcomings. Then she spoke with a great deal of authority.

"Cinco, I was impressed with your ability and courage to stand up and stop Robert when you felt he was going to attack Glenda.

That's a good attribute, but if not reined in, it can be a hindrance too. Some conflict can't be quickly 'fixed,' and takes time and patience. Just remember that. Glenda, it's obvious to me that you take conflict by the horns, so to speak. You're a tough woman and don't take things lying down. But sometimes that strength can fuel conflict that's already in motion. Ernest, while I can appreciate your faith, as I am a woman of faith, remember that God uses conflict to stretch and mold us, and oftentimes he won't deliver us out of the fire. Instead, he wants us to walk through it. You can pray all you want, but sometimes, conflict is just going to happen. Carol, I saw complete and utter fear in your eyes at the situation that was unfolding. You felt helpless and weak. By the end of this class, you're going to feel empowered. And Leah, the expression on your face was priceless. You looked like you were watching an animal die a slow death. I'm certain you would choose root-canal surgery over dealing with conflict. Am I right?"

Well, once I'd had an ingrown toenail removed because my mother thought it was ghastly. The procedure didn't bother me all that much. I nodded very slightly.

"I'm glad you're all here. You're going to make this a dynamic and diverse group."

As soon as all eyes were off me, I let myself breathe and inventory the splotching. Everything about me felt hot, so it was hard to know whether the splotches had made their way up my neck or had completely taken over my entire body. But at this point, I didn't really care, because just sixty seconds ago I thought I was going to see death by handbag.

I took a moment and tried to calm myself with the thought that at least tonight I could breathe easier. The worst part was over, thank the good Lord.

Then Marilyn said, "And now, we're going to rip each other's hearts out."

Chapter 9

[She eyes the exit longingly.]

"Tonight, we're going to let other people tell us what they think is fake about us."

Splotching usually stopped at midneck for me, but this was sure to send it up to my nose.

Beside me, Carol was mumbling, but I couldn't hear anything except hissing sounds every time she said something with an *s* in it.

A little comfort came my way when I realized nobody liked the idea. And then another comforting thought floated by. How much could people really know about us? This was only the second class.

Marilyn said, "One of the most conflict-causing situations in the universe stems from people feeling they've been insulted. Today we are going to focus on handling ourselves when we are insulted. Now, I am going to break you off into pairs." I actually reached out and grabbed Carol's arm. She clung to me. We would be perfect for each other. But Marilyn said, "I am going to pair you with your complete opposite."

Carol's clinging turned to clawing. I tried to pat her arm, but my hand was shaking so badly I missed and patted my own arm. I suddenly noticed that all the while, I was smiling pleasantly. Well, this was an impressive trick I never knew I had. Smiling pleasantly. Huh.

Maybe that would be a distraction from the large welts that were surely engulfing my face by now.

"Another point of this exercise is to learn to be forthright, which is actually an attribute when done with the right attitude and in the right circumstances. So you're going to be given permission to tell someone what you think is fake about their personality. For some of you, this may be harder than receiving the criticism. For others, it will be as easy as chewing gum. Let's begin." She glanced down at her clipboard. "I'm going to pair Glenda and Carol, Cinco and Ernest, and Robert and Leah." I looked over at Robert. Then glanced at Cinco. I was actually relieved not to be with him, but I wasn't sure why. Cinco caught my eye and smiled. I didn't have to smile back, because I was already pleasantly smiling.

"You'll stay where you are. No need to sit by the person, because we're going to be doing this in front of the class."

I knew I was in even more trouble when a lump formed in my throat. Was it the lack of sleep? The emotional evening I'd had with Elisabeth? The fact that Edward thought I should be here?

The idea someone might think I was fake? Faking what? The fact that I didn't want to be here?

"Cinco, we're going to start with you. Why don't you tell Ernest what you think is fake about him."

Cinco stared at the ground for a moment. He didn't appear to relish the task. After all, Ernest was a pastor. In the Old Testament, bad things could happen to those who insulted a man of God. But Cinco also didn't look nervous, even though everyone was staring at him, waiting for him to start.

Ernest was surprisingly calm, like this was the most natural thing in the world. I had the sudden urge to go to the bathroom, but then that would probably be seen as an attempt to escape. And it would be. But I sat still and crossed my legs. In the short time Cinco required to think through his answer, I planned on escaping by other means: urgent cell phone call, smelling smoke, or gagging on my pen and making myself throw up.

Cinco looked up at Ernest with a gentle, apologetic look on his face. Then he said, "Ernest, I think that you're not as peaceful on the inside as you look on the outside. I think in reality you're really angry."

Ernest's docile eyes flickered as we all watched his reaction. He met Cinco's gaze for a moment, then looked down at his feet. His hands were clasped together like he might be praying, but then he looked up and said, "Thank you, Cinco. And I think your on-air persona is a bunch of bull." Everyone's heads rotated back to Cinco, who stared right at Ernest. Cinco maintained steady, expressionless eyes. There was a cold silence except for a strange noise I couldn't at first identify. I suddenly realized it was my grinding teeth, and I stopped immediately.

After the rest of us finished gawking at the two, we looked to Marilyn for continued guidance. She had the luxury of focusing on her notepad while jotting notes. I thought maybe I should jot down some notes.

Finally she looked up and smiled. "Good. Both of you. I sensed some tension, which isn't unexpected. But let me assure you that when you're in that kind of situation, the tension is noticeable. You may be talking in a normal, nonthreatening voice. You may be making normal eye contact. You may even be smiling, like Leah's illustrating so perfectly." The smile dropped off my face. "But when there's tension, there's tension. There's nothing wrong with tension, let me clarify, but let me also say that nobody is fooled by practiced body language. If you're going to resolve the conflict, you're going to have to be genuine about your resolve, or else there will still be underlying tension, which can be just as damaging as conflict itself." She looked at Carol. "Carol, why don't you go ahead."

Carol whimpered. She looked at me. Her eyes actually brimmed with tears, magnified by her gigantic glasses. Carol couldn't even manage to look at Glenda. She was fumbling around with her words, making slight gestures with her hands, which wasn't helping in the translation. This went on for a good minute and a half, and Marilyn looked content to wait patiently, but Glenda suddenly shouted, "Carol, for crying out loud, get it out! I don't want to sit here any longer than I have to!"

I gasped, Carol gasped, and the other faces froze with shock. Glenda looked around the circle. "What? This class is obviously going to take some guts. I'm not sure Carol is cut out for this kind of thing."

I looked at Carol, and a big tear rolled down her left cheek. Now I could hear apologies rolling out of her mouth. I looked at Marilyn, but she was jotting down notes again. I was about ready to go over and snatch them out of her hands.

"Well?" Glenda said, folding her arms and staring hard at Carol. "What's it going to be?"

Carol tried to control her tears. She swiped at them and after a deep breath, looked right at Glenda and spoke. But nobody, including me, could hear her. Marilyn looked up and said, "Carol, you're going to have to talk a little louder."

And to her credit, each of the three attempts was louder than the previous one, but still inaudible to the rest of the class.

Except me.

I swallowed and watched Glenda, who was becoming more and more irritated by the minute. Carol tried again, in the best voice she knew how, but it sounded like a morning breeze, and that was it.

"Come on, Carol! Let's get this over with!" Glenda tapped her foot against the concrete. "What are you waiting for? Speak up! Don't be such a mouse!"

Carol probably wished she was a mouse. She still couldn't make her voice any stronger. But what I'd heard her say was, "You're nicer than you seem." I looked at Carol, whose lips were trembling as she watched Glenda's fuming expression. She was nicer than she seemed? Surely Carol could come up with something better than that. But as I watched Carol, I realized that was quite possibly the best she could do.

Glenda threw up her hands like a mad cook on a wild cooking show and aimed a frozen expression of disgust right at Carol. I looked at Glenda and, without further hesitation, said, "Carol said she thinks you wear your makeup heavy to hide the fact that you look older than you are." My pleasant smile returned. I couldn't will it away.

I patted Carol's knee. Her eyes were so wide they were almost bulging. We both looked at Glenda for a reaction.

Glenda's mouth was clamped shut, but her lips were doing a little wiggle across her face. Then she said. "Yeah? Well I don't think there's anything fake about you, Carol. I just think you're pathetic."

I felt my heart freeze. I took Carol's hand and stared hard at Glenda. Words were forming in my mouth, at the tip of my tongue, and ready to be unleashed, but Marilyn said, "Okay, Robert, Leah, it's your turn. Robert, go first."

My anger toward Glenda shifted to my fear of Robert. I'd already seen Robert get mad, twice, and I wasn't so sure the second time was really acting. How could a person get his face to turn that red while acting?

Robert wasn't looking at me. He was looking at the ground. I wanted to look at the ground, but I suddenly felt myself paralyzed. Except for one hand, which managed to climb to my neckline and feel for splotching. My gaze came to a rest on Cinco. To my surprise, he gave me a reassuring nod and a wink. I didn't want to wink and I didn't want to nod, so I think what I gave in return was a scowl. He looked away.

Robert said, "Okay, look, Leah, I think you choose to be around people who are completely safe."

Strangely, the anger lifted. Mostly because I wasn't even sure what Robert meant. I was contemplating that when Marilyn said, "Leah, your turn."

My turn. My time to hurl the insult. My chance at a small piece of justice. I focused on Robert, but what came out of my mouth stunned me. "I think you're the one with the conflict problem and that your silly outfits and your calm, collected, caring voice are just a front for the fact that you're unable to stand up for what is right. Your hairstyle is unflattering too." I blinked. That didn't even sound like my voice. I looked at Robert, and he looked a bit puzzled. He was smoothing his hand over his bald head.

I glanced around the group and everyone was staring at Robert's hair . . . or the lack thereof. But Marilyn said, "Good, Leah, but you're actually supposed to be talking to Robert, not me."

Had I said that to Marilyn? I rewound my brain and played back my exact words. I realized that while I'd meant to address Robert, every hateful thought I was having about Marilyn came out instead. I began to feel light-headed.

Marilyn smiled. "It's okay, Leah. Don't worry. In a couple of weeks we'll be discussing misplaced anger."

Sitting on my wooden apartment balcony that was barely big enough to hold both a chair and a plant, I couldn't stop thinking about the evening. I'd made myself a hot cup of Sleepytime Tea, made more sleepytime by the two Tylenol P.M. I plopped in and stirred to dissolve. I wasn't fond of using sleep aids, but Elisabeth swore by them, and if ever there was a night that sleep might elude me, this was it. I was comfortably warm in my pajamas, and I had a nonmagnificent view of the Boston skyline twinkling against the black sky. I could see about two inches of it, because another building blocked the way. But I could see a bright, illuminating halo hanging above, and as I sat there I thought I might look like a casual observer who was at peace with the world.

On the contrary. I was distressed to the point that my organs were hurting. I had managed to horrify myself beyond my usual expectations, which were pretty lofty to begin with. No matter how many times I played events over in my head, I couldn't understand how I'd gotten so confused and insulted Marilyn instead of Robert.

Worse, my splotching had eventually become evident to everyone by the time Glenda handed me two Benadryl and I had to explain I wasn't having an allergic reaction. If I'd taken the Benadryl, it would've rendered me unconscious, which, looking back, might not have been a bad option.

I was certainly having a hard time losing consciousness now. I gulped my tea and stared into the night.

Marilyn had ended the evening talking to us about conflict. She asked us to identify the parts of our lives with the most conflict in them and write them down. Thankfully, she didn't want us to share this information with anybody, because I couldn't identify anything in my life that caused conflict. Besides the incident with Edward and maybe the recent conversation with Elisabeth, I couldn't even remember the last time I'd had a fight with anyone, which began to confirm my suspicions that I shouldn't be going to this class in the first place.

I could only consider conflict in a theatrical manner, the thing that drives the story arc and the character arc.

I thought about how I'd been avoiding Edward. I'd left him a message on his answering machine at home, knowing full well he was at his yearly chess tournament. I'd acted casual, making up something about a busy schedule this week but suggested we connect over the weekend.

I finished my tea and used my fingers to scoop up the leftover Tylenol granules. I wasn't feeling a bit sleepy and started to get aggravated. What was so special about this medicine, anyway? Licking my fingers, I decided to go inside. If I wasn't going to sleep, then I would have to work.

As I sat down in front of my computer, I glanced at the clock. It was after ten. I pulled up my play and stared at my slim beginnings to Act Two. If sleep wouldn't come, maybe something creative would.

Act Two is the most daunting of all the acts. Act One is exposition, which is difficult to write in that you have to make a whole bunch of facts and backstory sound interesting and entertaining. But Act Two, that is where most people bail on their story. It's the hardest to get through because you must write your character into a corner that seems impossible to climb out of.

If ever I felt more in a corner, it was tonight. And I knew there was no graceful way out of it. I had managed to escape after class was over without further embarrassment. I sensed Cinco wanted to talk with me, but I excused myself to the bathroom and then down the dark, creepy stairwell that was worth every heart-pounding moment as long as I didn't have to face anybody.

This ending to the night wasn't exactly a worthy resolution for any hero I would write in a story. And in fact, it had its very own playwriting term. *Reversal.* That's when a character achieves the exact opposite of his or her intention, causing the plot to change either for the better or for the worse.

For the worse, I would say.

Jodie Bellarusa was itching to offer her own insight into this evening's events, but instead I put her to work in the world in which she was supposed to be living. And I fully intended to flesh out the details of how she might survive the dreaded "reversal."

Chapter 10

[She blinks, confused.]

The first indication of something being wrong was the feeling that my lips were smashed against my right nostril, causing a restriction of airflow. Then, as I turned my face, I felt a sticky wet sensation on my cheek, which generated another red flag, because I knew my pillow always did a good job of soaking up any unforeseen drool that might leak during the night.

I opened my eyes and saw a mouse. I screamed and lifted my head. Staring back at me was my computer screen, with rows and rows and rows of the letter *L*. Three hundred and two pages, to be exact. I'd apparently fallen asleep on top of my keyboard and, at some point during the night, had turned my head to where my nose was pushing the letter *L* down. Grabbing the mouse, I scrolled to the last page I'd been working on, checked to make sure my changes were still in place, and deleted the rest of the pages. Then I wiped off the slimy keys.

I cranked my mind backward. At some point the Tylenol P.M. must've kicked in, but I had no recollection of even becoming sleepy. The last thing I remembered was typing out a hysterical diatribe by Jodie on the functionality (not to mention ethical) issues in the movie *Pretty Woman*.

I felt disoriented at my own desk, so I decided to go get some coffee, thankful for my automatic coffeemaker. In the kitchen, the pot sat completely full, beckoning me. I fumbled through the cabinet until I found a large mug, then poured so fast that coffee splashed onto the counter. I skipped the sugar and cream for the moment. I needed a boost first. After that I would enjoy the coffee for its flavor.

"Ack!" I spit the cool liquid into the sink. The timer indicated that the two-hour heating countdown had expired. What time was it?

I looked at the microwave. "What?" I gasped. That couldn't be right. Maybe there was a power surge sometime last night. I went to my bedroom, but the battery-powered clock confirmed my fear.

I'd slept until one in the afternoon. The crick in my neck confirmed that I had also slept in a really awkward position. In fact, I noticed I couldn't move my neck far to the left or the right.

Slapping my cheeks, I tried to jostle some sense into my mind, which was currently as chaotic as Elisabeth's children's bedrooms. Then my heart skipped a beat as I remembered why, in fact, I'd drugged myself last night. The conflict resolution class.

I plodded back to the kitchen where I stuck my mug of coffee into the microwave, willing those thoughts to leave. And surprisingly, they did. But what replaced them confused me even more. It was the sound of J. R.'s raspy voice, asking me if I was okay. Was I imagining that? Then I heard her tell me thank you, and that she would get back to me with her thoughts.

"Her thoughts on what?" I whispered at my coffee.

I rushed to my computer screen and checked my e-mail, but there was nothing from J. R. Where were these thoughts coming from? I could hear myself forcing a laugh at one of her stupid literary jokes.

I snatched up my phone and looked at the caller ID.

"Oh, no . . ." There was her name, recorded at 8:12 a.m. We'd talked? This morning? What in the world did I say? Why had she called? What had I agreed to?

I squeezed my eyes shut, poured the now-scalding coffee down my throat, and tried to think. My eyes flew open.

"Yeah, J. R., it's ready for you to take a peek. I'm halfway finished, and so far I think it's a beauty." That's what I'd said. *I called it a beauty?* That was practically a curse all by itself.

I scrambled back to my computer and clicked on my Sent folder in e-mail. There it was! I'd sent her the half-written play in an attachment! Squinting, I tried to focus on the time it was sent: 8:14 a.m. Falling into my desk chair, I pinched the bridge of my nose, knowing that the play was in absolutely no condition for anyone to look at. It was a little over halfway finished, at least as far as word count was concerned, but I still had a long way to go.

The phone rang, startling me to a degree I wasn't aware existed. The caller ID announced it was J. R. My fingers hovered and twitched over the receiver. She was calling to tell me I'd lost my mind, for which I actually had a good explanation. Okay, well, not a good explanation. And truthfully, not an explanation I could explain in less than five minutes.

On the fourth ring I snatched it up. "Hello?"

"Leah, hello. It's J. R."

I inserted surprise into my voice. "Hi, J. R. How are you?"

"How do you think I am? I've just spent an entire lunch hour and more reading the first half of your play."

I grimaced while sounding pleasantly serene. "Oh?"

"Leah . . . this is . . . well, there's no other way to say it. This is good."

"Good?"

"Darling, this Jodie Bellarusa that you've come up with is a character like none other. I don't know whether to love her or hate her. She just pops off the page. Most definitely your best character ever, Leah. Really. Very impressive. Peter will love it."

My hand was clasped over my chest, the way I might look observing a newborn that was actually adorable.

"And I must say, you've really engaged me with this new technique you're using."

"New technique?"

"Well, yes. I mean, I'm on page thirty-eight, and as engaging as Jodie is, I'm still shocked that we haven't even seen a hint of conflict yet."

"No?"

"Maybe I'm missing it, but it doesn't appear to be there."

"Well . . . yeah, that's a new . . . you know, a new technique I'm playing with," I lied. I had no idea what she was talking about. I pulled up the play on my screen and paged down.

"I have to say it's interesting, but I'm not sure it's going to hold for much longer. At some point, I want Jodie to have to face *something.* As romantically challenged as she is, perhaps what she must face is a romantic date."

"Right. Yeah."

"Anyway, I have to run, but I just wanted to tell you how much I'm enjoying this character. I'll put in a good word to Peter. Keep up the hasty work, and I'll be in touch. Oh, and have a good time tonight."

"Tonight? What's tonight?"

J.R. paused. "This morning you told me you were going to meet your sister's new boyfriend."

"Ooookay, thanks. Bye." I hung up the phone. Going to meet my sister's boyfriend? What was she talking about? It was as if I'd lived an entire other life while unconscious by way of Tylenol P.M.

I turned the phone over and checked the caller ID. There was J. R.'s number twice, and then, at 10:40 p.m. last night, my sister's number.

My sister hardly ever called me. And when she did call me, it usually ended with my apologizing for something I could never identify. I pressed the backs of my hands into my eye sockets and tried to push out a sliver of the conversation we'd had last night. Nothing rang a bell. So with great trepidation, I dialed her number.

It wasn't surprising that she picked up. Her work hours at the new restaurant started at five, according to my mom.

"Kate, it's Leah."

"Oh." She sounded disappointed. How could I have disappointed her this early in the conversation? Anger simmered beneath my skin. "You're backing out, aren't you?"

"Backing out?"

"You were so agreeable last night about it all. It was weird, but I fell for it."

"Noooo, no, no," I said, trying to resist the urge to clear my throat. "I'm just . . . just wanted the details, that's all."

"What details?"

"I must've forgotten to write down the time."

"Six. At Dillan's place; 631 Westchester. Suite 1209."

Westchester? That was a nice stretch of real estate.

"Is he . . . cooking?"

A sigh filled my ear. "You're acting like we didn't even talk. What are you, on drugs? Yes, he's cooking. I told you he's a wonderful cook. Mom and Dad are coming too, in case you forgot that little detail."

"Sounds serious."

"You said that last night too, and yes, it's serious. Dillan's a wonderful man. I just hope my family doesn't screw up this relationship."

"How could we screw it up?"

"Just please, try to make a good impression, will you? I'll see you two tonight."

"Two?"

A pause. "Edward, Leah. He is coming, isn't he? I told Dillan he's coming."

"Yes . . . yes, of course. We'll be there."

Kate hung up the phone. I checked the time. One o'clock.

Edward would be in class. I would have no way of getting a hold of him until five when he left, as his department was horrible about getting messages to him.

As I slid my feet toward the bathroom, my mind toyed with a few good excuses to get out of this thing. Had it not been for that stupid Tylenol P.M., I would've been able to come up with an excuse on the spot.

You could always tell her tonight's dinner conflicts with your conflict class.

I could only be so lucky that something good like that would come from that despicable class. Unfortunately, tonight I was free. And I had no plans with Edward. As I stared at my face, still bright red with the imprint of my keyboard, I decided I must take the higher road. Kate had a chance to turn her life around, find someone who might motivate her in some good way. I couldn't stand in the way of it. Not once had Kate ever wanted her family to meet one of the men in her life. The only one I'd met in the last six years was Jinx, when I went to bail Kate out of jail after a bar brawl. That relationship fizzled when Jinx took a deal from the DA and tried to blame the entire incident on Kate. Luckily, her lawyer was able to prove that a woman of her weight couldn't turn over an entire pool table by herself.

I got dressed, braided my hair to avoid the frizzies, and decided I would have to try to catch Edward at the university. He wasn't one for surprises, but there was nothing like coming home from work to find you were due to arrive at a dinner party in an hour.

I decided to take my car. I could use the drive, or rather the "slow crawl toward insanity," as the town liked to refer to it. I ignored the growl and scowl of the traffic. Instead, I turned on my radio and tried to relax. In the middle of the madness of the last twenty-four hours, I did, after all, get the good news that J. R. liked my play.

I switched through the stations, trying to find something that would soothe and inspire. Nothing was doing the job. Then I heard a frightful noise coming through my radio.

"You're being a wimp. You can't stand up for what you believe in. Come on, you're going to sit there and try to convince me that this is for the good of people you love? Everybody knows that's not true, and the only person you're fooling is you."

My heart stopped and I stared at my radio. It sounded just like . . . Cinco? I reached to turn it off, but another voice came on.

"Look, Cinco, you're one of the most pompous people I've ever had the curse of knowing. Yes, I happen to think that abortion is helping this nation. I think women are choosing what's best for them, and their lives are better for it. But neither of us really knows, since neither of us is a woman."

"But both of us came from a woman, and I thank God that my mom decided not to choose what was 'best' for her. If she had, neither I nor any of my eight brothers and sisters would be around, now, would we?"

"This isn't about convenience. It's about their right to their own bodies."

"So the child inside has no rights?"

My heart restarted and fell into a slightly accelerated rhythm as I listened to the two men go back and forth. I finally switched to my favorite classical station, hoping to hear Milbert's unexcitable voice.

My mind drifted to thoughts of Cinco and the class that I'd decided I would never again attend. Strangely, I felt a little remorse, and guilt, for not going back. But who would know, really? Edward said it didn't matter to him, and the chances of running into one of those people again were scarce to none.

Why the apprehension?

I chalked it up to another one of the bizarre side effects of the sleep medication and pulled my car onto the campus of Boston University. I drove around the visitors' parking lot for ten minutes waiting for a space to open up. Thankfully, the visitors' lot was near Edward's building.

I parked, got out, and started walking along the pristine sidewalk, lined by a thin strip of perfectly manicured grass. Boston University was considerably beautiful and, for an urban university, had the look of a sprawling Midwestern campus. It seemed like forever since I'd been a college student. I felt out of place with my comfortable jeans and white, properly fitting T-shirt.

I turned toward Edward's building and immediately noticed commotion ahead. A white tent erected in the middle of the grass drew a small crowd of about thirty students, almost all of them with backpacks swung over their shoulders.

Approaching, I tried to stand on my tiptoes to see what was under the tent. A physicist doing stand-up? Now, that would be something to watch. I couldn't see much, so I leaned toward the guy next to me.

"What's going on?" I whispered.

"He's doing a live broadcast from the campus today."

"Who?"

"Cinco Dublin."

I'd always dreamed of my knees going weak for a man, but not in this way. I think I swayed and the guy next to me stepped away instead of grabbing my elbow. I managed to recover myself while simultaneously offering that everything's-perfectly-lovely smile. I had to stop doing that.

I shimmied between people until I could see Cinco. Over one woman's left shoulder I finally got a glimpse. He had headphones on, and there was a man sitting next to him. Both had microphones. My ears finally tuned in to his voice, which was coming from a small speaker set on the ground in front of the table. A couple of radio-station people, evident by the way they proudly wore their identical T-shirts, milled around behind him.

"We're going to take a short break, and we'll be back with you in just a few minutes. Stay tuned as we broadcast live from Boston University!"

Cinco took off his headphones and glanced toward the crowd. I ducked and managed to bow out semigracefully. A stream of students came through the front doors of the science building, which was opposite Cinco's tent, so I headed that way, trying not to look behind me when I walked up the steps. I begged whoever was listening inside my head not to let him recognize me.

I made it inside safely and took the stairs to the third floor. The physics department, on the west side, proudly displayed famous scientists' pictures in the glass case next to the office door. Apparently this week was "Discover a New Formula" week. The cardboard letters hanging from the shelf behind the glass said so.

I opened the door, a little unfamiliar with my setting. I'd only been up here to see Edward two or three times. It wasn't like the English department, that was for sure. There was laughter in the physics department, but it was rigid and so high-brow that it was useless for the average person to try to figure out the joke.

A skinny, sulky woman at the desk looked up and plainly couldn't manage words, so she just stared at me.

"I'm looking for Edward."

"Dr. Crowse is probably still in his classroom."

I waited for more, but she was already back to her reading.

"Which classroom is that?"

"38-E."

I walked out of the office and followed the corridor around until I found it. The door was shut so I peeked inside the small window. The classroom was mostly empty except for two students still gathering their things and a scholarly looking woman standing near Edward, talking to him.

I wanted to walk in, but I didn't want to disturb them, so I watched a moment, and soon discovered that I should've barged in. Unfortunately for Edward and Scholar Girl, I speak fluent body language.

She fingered her glasses for no reason, pushed one hip out in an apparent attempt to look casual, and laughed on cue. Even though I couldn't hear what Edward was saying, his expression made it clear he thought he was being very witty. Edward wasn't witty, was he? I mean, he was stale. Not stale in a bad way. Stale like . . . like a crouton. It's what you expect from a crouton, and if a crouton was stale, it could really damage a salad. "Hi, babe," I said, pushing the door open. I'd never called him "babe" once in our relationship. I'm not even sure I could describe with words the look on his face. He slid away from the woman and tried to smile, then let out a laugh that sounded more like a whimper.

"Hi . . . Leah. What are you doing here?" He asked the question while looking at Scholar Girl. I was looking at her too. She noticed us both and excused herself to walk stiffly out the door, hips in their proper place.

"Surprise." I grinned. He didn't grin back.

"I've got class," he said, his previous witty expression apparently out the door as well.

"Looks like class is out," I said.

He eyed me. "Why are you here?"

I sighed and dropped the shtick. "I found out this morning that Kate is having a dinner party for the family to meet her new boyfriend. She really wants us to come."

"Kate your sister?"

"That's the one."

Edward gathered his things. "I'm not in the mood to be social."

"It's important to her. And to me."

"Since when has hanging out with your sister been important?" He walked past me, and I followed him out the door.

"What's the hurry?" I demanded.

He whipped around, his eyes harsh. "You can't just drop by, Leah. This is my place of business. It's where I'm respected, okay?"

My hands found my hips. Hips made quite a statement today. "And what does that have to do with me?"

He stepped closer to me. "I don't discuss my personal life with anyone here, okay?"

"So I'm a secret?"

"Look, I'll call you later this afternoon, all right? I don't know about tonight. I'm going to have to think about it."

"What is there to think about? I'm asking you to come. After all, I spent last weekend at your stupid colleague party."

His eyes lit at the word *stupid,* and I immediately regretted it.

"Edward, I'm sorry, it's just that—"

"I'm not going to do this now. I'll call you later." He turned and walked off. A student nearby came alongside him, and I watched them talk until they rounded the corner.

I took the elevator down and walked out the front doors. *Great. What a way to spend an afternoon.* Why was Edward acting this way? Because of Scholar Girl? Was there something going on? I'd never, ever worried about Edward cheating on me. Truthfully, I wasn't sure he was someone girls would swoon after. He had dashing good looks, but his science-stricken personality seemed an undesirable second. Then again, I wasn't a scientist. Maybe his jokes were funny.

I'd fallen for Edward for many reasons. We had a lot in common, despite the fact that we were on opposite ends of the career spectrum. His intelligence was a huge draw for me in the beginning. I could've listened to him talk about supernovas for hours.

But who was I kidding now? Every conversation we had seemed

to suck me into a black hole. I was bored to death. Right? Wasn't that what I was feeling? Boredom? Scholar Girl didn't look bored.

I angrily unzipped my bag and pulled out my keys. Not only would I have to spend the evening with my family and most likely without Edward, but I would have to explain where Edward was.

"Leah?"

I looked up. Oh, no. "Uh . . . hi, Cinco."

I heard a thud. No, I was still standing. I looked down. I'd dropped my bag. I smiled and tried to pretend that was on purpose, but there was really nothing more that I could do except stoop to pick it up.

"Let me get that for you," he said, and grabbed it before I could do anything. He handed it to me.

"Thanks. Well, good to see you." I turned to go.

"Wait, what are you doing here? Are you a student?"

"Oh, um . . . no. Just came to . . ." My mind wasn't cooperating. My strength was imagination, but so far I couldn't come up with anything convincing. "Brother."

"Brother?"

"To see him."

"You came to see your brother."

"Yes." I glanced toward the tent I'd passed earlier. "I noticed you were doing your broadcast out here."

"Yeah. We try to get around some, get out and meet people, show them I'm not nearly as scary as I sound." He laughed.

I laughed too. No idea why. I really wanted to cry. No idea why. "Well, I should probably let you get back to it."

"I've got a thirty-minute break while they do the news. Then we're back on."

"Oh."

"So, how are you liking the class?"

"It's fun," I said. I was pretty sure that wasn't the least bit convincing, but I tried to smile anyway. He was scrutinizing the daylights out of me.

"Huh."

I quickly added, "But I won't be able to come back."

"Why?"

"Just . . . life, you know. Really busy. I'm finishing up a play that is in high demand, and . . . well, things like that."

Cinco looked disappointed. "That's too bad. Since you were having so much fun, I mean."

I looked at the watch on my arm, hoping I'd indeed put it on. Thankfully, it was there. "I have to go; I've got a dinner party tonight."

"Now, that sounds fun."

"Not really. Meeting my sister's new boyfriend that we'll surely disapprove of in some way."

He smiled as if he'd met my sister. "I guess, then, it's good-bye." He held out his hand for me to shake.

I looked at it for a moment, like I was a foreigner unsure what the gesture meant. But he continued to hold it out, so I slipped my hand into his. A warming sensation crawled through my arm and into my body, where a euphoric tickle made me giggle. He squeezed my hand, a few seconds longer than necessary, and our eyes engaged.

I felt like I should be arrested. I pulled my hand from his and backed away a few steps. "I should let you go. Good luck engaging combat with the city."

"Thanks," he said, and I could feel him watch me walk away. And there's nothing like being aware of how you walk to increase your chances of a stumble. You've walked nearly your whole life, but when you start paying attention to it, your legs feel wobbly and suddenly your hips don't seem to work in sync. Thankfully, I managed only to drag a toe against the concrete. I ducked into my car and tried to calm myself before facing the city traffic again.

As I pulled out, I willed myself not to look. But I did. Cinco was standing on the grass with two other men. He glanced up from their conversation and waved when he saw me.

I couldn't help myself. I waved back. And even smiled. What was wrong with me?

Then I heard a crunch.

Chapter 11

[She avoids the balcony.]

After my third attempt to put on mascara by way of shaking hand, I decided to get by without it. I wasn't a big makeup wearer anyway, mostly because my mother would spend hours getting ready for one event, and it wasn't long before I realized that all of that took away from our time together, which wasn't much anyway. So I'd resented makeup my whole life, until a few years ago when I decided to try some lip gloss. Then I moved up to a little blush. And last year added mascara. But it was still nothing close to what my mother went through for an outing.

I dabbed on lip gloss, still amazed at how my heartbeat refused to step into a regular rhythm. And the only good thing about the afternoon's events was that they had erased the painful memory of the previous night.

The accident had only been a minor fender bender, but clearly my fault, said all the witnesses who came to the scene. Including Cinco.

He was nice enough to stand by me while everyone else stood by the little old lady, whose blue Mercedes I'd hit, instructing her on how to call her insurance company.

He asked if I was okay, helped me locate my insurance card in my glove box, and waited while I used my cell phone to call my insurance company. I kept wondering if Edward would look out and see the commotion, but if he did, he didn't come down to help.

When the little old lady finally drove off and the fifteen witnesses cleared, Cinco handed me his number on the paper. "Keep this. I saw what happened. It was minor, and she was not hurt in any way. But if her insurance company calls and claims otherwise, you have someone on your side."

I took it and folded it. It kind of seemed to burn against my fingers.

On my bathroom counter now, the piece of paper was a complete distraction, so I took it and put it in the bathroom drawer while I tried to finish getting ready for the dinner party and come up with believable excuses as to why Edward had not accompanied me.

Deciding on an outfit took me a while. For some reason, I wanted to make a good impression on this Dillan. Maybe he really was my sister's knight in shining armor. And if he was even a fraction of who she claimed he was, he was sure to be interested in what kind of family she came from. Maybe he was expecting a family of bohemians.

I knew it would take forty-five minutes or more to drive to Dillan's apartment, so I decided on a basic black number with strappy sandals. I switched handbags and gathered my things, including Dillan's address, and opened my apartment door.

"AHH!" I jumped back, startled at the presence of another human being in front of me. When I backed up and focused, I was even more startled to see it was Edward. He was dressed in a nice silk shirt and khaki pants and holding a bottle of wine.

"Hi." He tried to smooth his curly hair. "I'm glad I got here in time. You were just leaving."

"Yeah . . ." I wasn't sure what to say. I couldn't believe he'd decided to come after the way we'd left things. "I'm sorry about popping in unannounced today. I didn't realize it would upset you like that."

"You're forgiven," he said, grinning. He looked at my outfit. "You look really nice."

"Thanks."

"Listen, before we head out, I need to use the bathroom."

"No!" I said. Then I realized I had put Cinco's number away in the drawer. But I couldn't shake the fluster of what . . . and why . . . I'd just said what I'd said. "I'm sorry, of course you can. I was just trying to remember if I'd put a few . . . personal items away."

Edward nodded like he didn't care and went past me. I tried to nod back like I didn't care, but I knew, to my horror, that I really, really did care.

We were five blocks from Dillan's apartment building when I mentioned the accident.

"I was distracted for half a second, and the next thing I know, I've hit this blue Mercedes."

Edward glanced at me.

"I can't even tell you how embarrassed I was. All these students were gathered around, you know? I wanted to crawl into a hole." I tried *crawl into a hole* with a ring in my voice. This apparently didn't sound right, as Edward's face took on a strange look.

I continued. "And it didn't help that this old lady thought the world of herself. Her nose was so high in the air that had her airbags gone off, they might've saved her chin." I laughed at my own joke. Edward wasn't laughing.

"Everything's fine," I ventured. "We exchanged insurance names and numbers—"

"Did you give her your name?"

"Uh . . . yeah, of course. I wrote it on the piece of—"

"Your name only? Did you tell her why you were there?"

I paused. "It was a fender bender. No big deal." I looked from

Edward's worried face to the street. "Pull in there. Kate said we can park there."

Edward pulled in.

"Parking for visitors," I said. "Fancy."

"Did she ask you anything personal?" Edward said, turning off the car. He looked at me.

I wanted to ask if she was his mistress, but Edward didn't look in the mood for jokes.

"Why?"

Edward sighed, got out, went around and managed to open the door for me. Considering the great strain his facial muscles were under, I wasn't sure if there was enough strength left for his arm.

"Do me a favor, okay?" He moved a little closer, like he didn't want the parked cars around us to hear. "Just . . . if you happen to talk to this woman again, don't mention that . . ."

"That . . . ?"

"We know each other."

Maybe the mistress thing wasn't far off. My body language was crying foul and Edward knew it. He attempted a smile. His mouth cooperated. His eyes didn't.

"Why?"

"Light blue Mercedes. Probably hair to match, right?"

"You saw it happen? Why didn't you come down? Or didn't you want to admit we 'know each other.'"

Edward held out his hands. "I didn't see it. I know who she is. She's Dean Carter's wife."

It was taking me a moment to process this. In the meantime, Edward managed to ask, "Was she okay? You didn't hurt her, did you?"

"No. She was fine."

He directed me toward the parking lot exit. Dillan's apartment was across the street.

We walked for a few moments in silence, Edward cradling the wine like it was a newborn.

"Luckily," I said, a full minute after Edward thought the conversation was over, "there was a man who helped me through it all."

"Helped you through what?"

"The near-fatal assault on Mrs. Carter." I walked a little faster. "He gave me his name and number to be a witness in case I need it. Sounds like she's the kind of woman who might sue."

We crossed the street, Edward's full attention on me. "She wouldn't sue."

I was kind of hoping he would pick up on the fact that I had another man's phone number. Looked as if I could've left it out in plain sight after all.

At Dillan's building, we were greeted by a doorman, who politely asked our names and then opened the door for us.

I was filled with envy. I'd always wanted to live in an apartment with a doorman. Instead, my apartment had a universal access code.

We stepped onto the elevator, and I hit 12.

"I know him."

"Know who?" Edward asked.

"The man, who helped me."

"You know him now, or before?"

"Before. Just lucky that he was there."

I waited for Edward to ask where I knew him from, but he didn't. Instead, he said, "What's Kate's boyfriend's name again?"

"Dillan."

"Dillan the lawyer. Should make for an uninteresting evening. You owe me."

The elevator dinged right as my mouth opened, so instead of speaking I followed Edward out and to the left. Edward knocked and I could hear some laughing behind the door. Kate answered and I hardly recognized her. My mouth fell open as I took in a poet's blouse, a skirt that actually hit at the knee, and classy-looking shoes. Even her makeup was different. Overdone, but standing next to Mom, it was still understated.

"Hi," I said, smiling. "Great building. Love the doorman."

"Hi, Edward," Kate said, giving him a hug. Edward glanced to me for answers at the unexpected embrace. All I could do was shrug. "Come in, you two. I can't wait for you to meet him."

"Him" was busy charming the fake eyelashes right off my mother, who didn't even bother to greet us as we walked in. Instead, she was staring at Dillan and laughing . . . no, giggling. My mother was giggling.

Dillan was stir-frying something, but at least he managed to wipe his hands and shake ours.

"You must be Leah and Edward," he said, after my sister failed to introduce us.

"That's us." I smiled. Edward handed him the wine.

Dillan looked at it and said, "Wow. I'm not sure my cooking can live up to this kind of wine." My mom started giggling again.

"Thank you, Edward," he continued. "And thanks to you both for coming. It was really nice of you."

Polite fellow. "Where's Dad?" I asked.

Kate said, "Out on the balcony. Dillan has the most amazing view of the city. You've got to see it."

I followed Kate's gesture toward the balcony and went outside, where my dad was leaning on the railing. A breeze, the most perfect temperature it could be, swept through my hair.

"Bet it's cold up here in the winter," I said, joining Dad. I glanced back. Edward had decided to stay and giggle.

"Look at this view! Reminds me of the suite your mother and I had back in Washington. I could've stayed and looked out of that window forever. But then we had you two kids, and your mother thought we needed a backyard. Backyards are highly overrated."

I looked back again. I'd never seen Mother laughing so hard. Did she just toss her hair? "Dad, um, what do you think of Dillan?"

"Stunning."

Backyards might be overrated, but so was Dillan. "He seems to have it together, but—"

"What?"

"Dillan."

"I was talking about this view. I can't get over it."

Great. Mother was enraptured with Dillan, and Dad with the Boston skyscape. I felt a little left out. I excused myself back to the kitchen to make myself an impression. "So," I said, as the laughter lulled enough for me to get a word in, "Swadderly-Wade. That's quite an accomplishment for your age. How old are you?"

"Thirty-four."

"Your age," Mother pointed out with unnatural glee.

Dillan said, "Talk about accomplishment, I knew your work before I even knew your sister. I even went to see *The Twilight T-Zone* when it was off-Broadway. It was really great."

"Oh . . . wow . . . thanks." I glanced at Kate, who was grinning from ear clip to ear clip.

"What did I tell you?" Kate gushed. "Has this guy got good taste or what?"

That was a trick question, but I agreed. While Mom leaped back into the conversation, I tried to nonchalantly glance around the apartment to take in the decor.

Art. Lots of it. And originals, not prints, from the looks of it. Nobody likes prints. The lighting around the apartment was subdued—elegant, even. It wasn't exactly right for the old-world theme he had going, but at least it wasn't fluorescent.

"Smells great," Edward inserted into the conversation. I tuned back in to hear Dillan's history, including four years at Harvard Law

School, and how Swadderly-Wade had recruited him with a signing bonus to come work for them right after he graduated.

"Leah, do you want some wine?" he asked. I noticed everyone but me had a glass.

"No, I'm fine. Thanks." Maybe everyone else was seeing this guy through wine-colored glasses, but I wanted to see him under, well, a good set of fluorescents.

"Let me know if you change your mind." He smiled and patted my hand. Polite. Nice. Attractive.

Edward had wandered off to look at the skyscape that surely everyone in the city had seen a thousand times. The rest of us watched Dillan put the finishing touches on the dinner.

"Kate, I'm not sure you mentioned how you met Dillan," I said. She'd mentioned church before, but how would the story hold up now, with Dillan present?

"Church," Dillan said, smiling at her. "We sat by each other one Sunday." What was that in his eyes? *Adoration?* Surely not.

"I'll take that wine now," I said.

"Perfect. Because dinner is served!" He handed my mom and Kate each a bowl to take to the dining table. "Leah, will you grab the bread?"

"Sure," I said, taking the basket. He walked beside me toward the dining table.

"Your sister . . . she's so great," he said, watching her chat with Mother.

"How . . . long have you known Kate?"

"A couple of months. Seems longer."

"You can't really know someone in that amount of time, can you? I mean, really know someone?"

"I knew the first time I saw her in those horrific boots at church she was the one for me." He winked. "You know the ones."

Dad and Edward had managed to come in from Mount Perfect.

Everyone gathered around the table, which was impressive even without the meal on it.

Dillan offered my dad the chair at the end. *Good grief.* This guy knew exactly what to do and how to do it. Nothing was slipping by him. Dad looked terribly satisfied as he took his seat. As the rest of us gathered and sat, Dad said in his boisterous voice, "Now, Dillan, I recognize this is your place, but we always bless the food before we eat."

"I do too, sir," Dillan said.

"Good. Why don't you say the blessing then?"

"Thank you. I'd love to . . . Father, thank you for this day and for this fellowship with family and friends. And Lord, thank you for sending Kate into my life. In Christ's name, amen."

I quickly closed my eyes, realizing they'd been wide open the whole time. *That was overdoing a bit, wasn't it, Lord? C'mon.*

Strangely, the Lord wasn't answering. I opened my eyes, but nobody noticed my extended prayer because all eyes were on Dillan.

I couldn't quite identify from where my skepticism birthed. He looked completely normal. He acted completely normal. He was five times as normal as my sister. Maybe that was it. Surely there was a hidden side to him.

Edward inserted into the pause in conversation, "Leah had a car accident today."

That stopped all the chewing, including mine. I stared at Edward. He looked happy to have the attention on him.

"And get this. She actually hit the wife of the dean of my school."

The attention shifted to me. I was midchew, and as much as I wanted to respond, my manners forbade me.

But Edward's manners were running like wild horses. He chuckled. "It was Leah's fault, so she has a nice rate-increase to look forward to."

I swallowed most of my food whole, but before I could say anything, Mother said, "This happened at the university?" I nodded. "What were you doing there?"

"I went to see Edward."

Mother raised a disapproving eyebrow. "Edward, I didn't realize they let that sort of thing happen. Back when I was a professor, we weren't allowed any personal visits."

I stuffed another bite into my mouth to keep myself from making the puking signal with my pointer finger. Besides, I knew if I talked now, my voice would quiver with sheer embarrassment. And wouldn't you know it, I'd worn a low neckline.

"How bad did you dent her car?" Dad asked.

I made the "teeny-weeny" signal with my fingers and shook my head vigorously so there was no misunderstanding the situation . . . about the car. I tried to give Edward that look most couples of our tenure can give each other to shut the other one up. But he was still enjoying a good laugh.

"Did she know you're Edward's girlfriend?" Kate asked.

I shook my head again.

Dillan then said, "Leah, were you hurt? Are you okay?"

I looked across at Dillan. I managed to swallow again, and suddenly everyone seemed to want to know.

"She's fine," Edward answered. "It was just a fender bender."

"Right," I said. "Just a fender bender."

Everyone moved on to the next conversation.

Except me.

Well into the evening I found myself alone with Mother in the kitchen. She was pouring herself another glass of wine. "Edward has good taste in wine," she said.

I wanted to mention the strain our relationship had been under since the unfortunate dress incident. I wasn't sure what to do with it all, but things hadn't been right since. I didn't know how to make things right. Edward and I had never been not right. Our relationship was as dependable as Dillan's niceties.

"Edward and I have been fighting a little," I said.

Mother laughed. "Good one."

"Really. We had a fight."

"So you're human after all. And please, how big of a fight could it have been? Everything seems fine now." Mother looked at me. "You're not going to do something crazy tonight, are you? We have to make a good impression for Kate's sake."

I leaned on the counter. "Speaking of impressions, what's your impression of Dillan?"

"Leah, please, for once in your life don't be jealous."

"Jealous? What makes you say that?"

Mother lowered her voice. "I'll agree. He's a catch. I mean, an amazing catch. And look what he's done for Kate already. Did you notice she took her nose ring out?"

Yeah, I'd noticed.

"I'm not sure why, but he has fallen head over heels in love with Kate. Have you seen the way he looks at her?" Mother asked.

"I'm not jealous," I reiterated. "Truthfully, he's not my type at all. In fact, he gets on my nerves a little."

Mother's eyes narrowed. "Well, whatever you do, don't let on. Okay? This could be Kate's only shot at this kind of man. Nobody's going to blow it for her. Do you understand me?"

I stared past Mother toward the balcony, where everyone else had gathered. "What are they talking about out there, anyway?"

"Politics."

"That's a good way to blow it."

"No worries. He's a democrat. That was one of the first things Kate told us about him. Thank goodness she at least has the good sense to bring home a democrat."

Edward slipped up beside me suddenly, his eyes looking weary from all the socializing he was having to do. "It's getting late. About ready to go?"

I wasn't, really. I hadn't finished assessing Dillan. "Sure, we can go."

The rest of the crowd was tearing away from paradise. Dillan asked, "Are you two leaving already?"

"Oh, come on," Edward said, "you know you two lovebirds want time alone. Leah, remember those days?"

Edward was going to have to buy me a scarf if he didn't stop. I'd never seen him this uncharming. He wasn't excitement rolled into a ball, but usually he tended to keep his foot out of his mouth.

"We'd better go," I said.

Dillan shook my hand. "Leah, it was really great to meet you. Kate's lucky to have family like you. I hope you enjoyed dinner."

"You're a terrific cook." That was no lie. As annoying as this guy was, he could really cook.

We said another two rounds of good-byes, and then Edward and I took the elevator down. Outside I said, "Well, what'd you think?"

"About what?"

I paused. About *what*? "Dillan, of course."

"He's fine."

"You talked to him more than I did."

"Not really. Your dad did most of the talking, as usual. Somebody needs to get that guy a balcony."

"Right, but back to Dillan. You had to have had some sort of impression."

"Like I said, he was fine."

"You didn't find him annoying?"

"Annoying?"

"I can't put my finger on it, but there's something I don't like about the guy. I mean, he seems fine. He's nice, polite, seems to really like Kate. But I don't know; it's weird. He just gets on my nerves. I just don't think I could be around him very much."

"That's odd."

"You thought he was Mr. Perfect."

"No."

"Then what?"

Edward shrugged. "I don't know. I guess that, well, he . . ."

"He what?"

"Reminded me of you."

Me? Edward was out of his mind. I was nothing like that guy! Dillan seemed to be the biggest pushover, willing to say whatever he needed to make a good impression.

"And by the way," Edward said, "when are we going to tell your parents we're republicans?"

Chapter 12

[She feels unsteady.]

I actually faked the flu. Flu season was long over, but I did a good enough job of hacking into the telephone over the weekend that everyone wanted to leave me alone. I managed to graciously affirm Dillan to Kate, though. I couldn't deny how in love they appeared, and how Dillan's normalcy seemed to be drawing Kate back into reality.

I also couldn't deny how out-of-love Edward and I were. I mean, when was the last time we even exchanged an "I love you"? Though Jodie clearly thought those words weren't necessary to a relationship, I wasn't so sure. Then again, maybe I was fooling myself into thinking the dress incident had anything to do with the situation. And maybe I was fooling myself into thinking anything was different. Wasn't this how our lives had been for the past two years? Had our relationship really changed, or had I?

But the thing that had forced me into taking another sleep aid Friday night was realizing how much alike Dillan and I really were. It took me most of Saturday and Sunday to work through the idea that this genuinely nice man of predictability was my twin.

So I spent the better part of the weekend and into Tuesday afternoon sitting in my favorite oversized leather chair, drowsy and dumbfounded, hating the fact that I'd become a person I despised. And then I had to perform delicate and intricate surgery without the help of emotional anesthesia to try to figure out what exactly I was despising.

Maybe you are jealous.

I didn't have the strength to shut out Jodie, so I just closed my eyes and listened.

After all, how could a freaky, nonsensical person like your sister come away with such a nice, seemingly blind man like Dillan? How does that even begin to work? A person like Dillan, who has done everything right in his life and has the job to prove it, shouldn't be with a woman like Kate. That kind of romance doesn't make the world go around. It makes it come to a screeching halt.

First of all, Jodie would never use a word like *nonsensical*, but I let it pass. Jodie was coming from the perspective of a nonromantic, so her views were going to be slightly skewed. Of course I was happy for my sister, and of all people, I know opposites attract. Jodie was getting ready to learn that herself, because in about three pages, she was going to be introduced to Timothy.

I stood and marched over to my computer. That was one way to get Jodie to shut up . . . just give her some catchy lines in the play.

It took an hour to reach the scene where Jodie would meet Timothy for the first time. I'd been looking forward to this scene ever since I began. Jodie had lost a bet with a friend, and she had to pay up by letting her friend set her up on a blind date with anyone her friend wanted. The friend had chosen the most romantic restaurant in town, and here Jodie Bellarusa waited, drumming her fingers against a tablecloth more expensive than her entire outfit, staring at a centerpiece of five plump, dewy roses, complete with thorns.

I rubbed my hands together and cackled. J. R. wanted conflict? This was going to be conflict like she'd never seen before. I typed out the setting and then had Timothy enter from stage right.

Now, what in the world would Jodie say out loud that she shouldn't, when she first lays eyes on the man who could only be described as "dashing"?

"You must be Jodie."

"Yes."

"I'm Timothy."

I rubbed my hands together again. This was going to be good. Yesirree, brilliant. I watched the blinking cursor, waiting for that lightbulb moment. Don't rush it, I told myself. Don't panic. It will come. Clever, conflict-ridden dialogue doesn't always just flow down the mountain of literary genius like hot, bubbly lava. No, sometimes it spews. And spewing, while not as graceful, still gets the magma out of the earth.

A shiver of doubt swept through my body. Was I only capable of using *National Geographic* metaphors?

Maybe you've missed your calling.

"Jodie, why don't you use your energy to come up with a clever line for the play."

Huh. I'd talked back to Jodie. That was weird.

I think I had rubbed my hands together for the eighth time when it began to occur to me that I would be lucky to spew. In fact, I would be lucky to sputter.

I think I yelped. Some curse had come upon me! No thanks to Elisabeth. I stared at the screen and muttered to myself, "I am not a prophet. Nothing I have written or will write is going to come true. It's all a coincidence."

I carefully laid my hands across the keyboard and typed out:

"I've never been to dinner with a metrosexual."

The sigh of relief that rushed from my mouth could've blown out the Olympic torch. But as I studied the line, it wasn't really that funny. Too obvious. Timothy was a metrosexual, but stating it up front was overkill. I deleted it, but reminded myself that it was a start. At least I'd typed something.

"Come ON!" I yelled at the screen. *I need wit! I need a clever diatribe. I need snappy one-liners!*

For forty minutes I wandered around my apartment, hoping that elusive burst of brilliance would send me racing back to my computer. Then a thought struck me. Maybe, just maybe, I was trying too hard to create a scene that wasn't supposed to happen. *Maybe* to Jodie Bellarusa's everlasting surprise, they hit it off. Maybe that's why she couldn't come up with anything cleverly condescending.

"Aha!" I actually jabbed a finger toward the ceiling. As long as that clichéd gesture didn't make its way onto the page, I was going to be fine. "And before you say anything, Jodie, you should realize that sometimes you have to shake things up. I'm the playwright, and I know exactly what I'm doing." Jodie remained silent, thankfully.

Some writers put a body in a trunk. Some kill off a main character. It's called a plot twist, and more often than not, it's discovered by the writer after he or she has written him- or herself into a corner. There comes the belief in every story, with every writer, that it is the worst story ever written. This is not true, of course, and once a person other than the writer reads the story, a confirmation usually comes that the story is, in fact, good. But at the halfway point the writer will usually think the work is, as they say in the scientific world, "dormant."

After examining the many pages and pages of writing, she will come to the conclusion that the story is more boring than any other story that has ever been written in the history of the world. This thought causes even the most confident of writers to curl into a fetal position and suck the proverbial thumb.

But then days later, possibly on a dark and stormy night, after personal hygiene has become a distant memory and all hope is lost, the writer has a small, easily-described-as-crazy thought roll through her foggy mind. At first, she laughs it off as insane. But then, something convinces her that it's not so crazy after all, and if she reworks this and reworks that, she can sell it.

She rushes to her computer, and after several hours of nonstop typing, she realizes that all her story needed was a shake-up, and that one shake-up can carry the writer all the way to the end of her masterpiece.

"That's what everyone is expecting," I said. "They're expecting these two opposites to hate each other at first. That is what we, in the writing world, call preee-diiiic-tability." I rubbed my hands together for the ninth and final time and then wrote out a scene so shockingly unpredictable that it only took me fifteen minutes to create.

I smiled, laughed, and did a little dance that no one should ever see. Then I promptly sent the new scene to J. R.

I did the little dance again, but this time, I ended up with an audience, because my front door flew open and Elisabeth caught me just as I thrust my hip toward the kitchen and threw my hands in the air.

"Leah!" she screamed and rushed to my side.

My hands flopped to my sides. "What?"

"Are you okay?"

"Why?"

"You're okay?"

"Yes, I'm fine."

Elisabeth looked confused. "I thought you were having a seizure."

I rolled my eyes. "I'm dancing."

"You don't dance."

"I do too."

"Leah, no offense, but you're not the dancing type."

"How do you know?"

"I've known you for years. You've never danced."

"I dance all the time. Around here."

Elisabeth suppressed a smile. "That doesn't surprise me."

"What's that supposed to mean?"

"Leah, you already know this about yourself. You're just not really one to let loose, you know? You don't even throw caution to a soft, gentle breeze, much less the wind."

I wasn't going to let Elisabeth spoil my fun, so I did a little jig toward the kitchen, proving I could dance in front of other people. I did notice, however, that all that moved were my elbows as they sliced back and forth across my rib cage. "So, what brings you by?"

"You don't know?" she asked.

I thought for a moment. Creyton. That was the last time we'd spoken, and she'd nearly left upset. I'd managed to apologize, but we'd left up in the air what she was going to do about her life.

"Have you made any decisions?" I asked.

"Yeah. That's what I came over here to tell you." Her finger traced around the toast crumbs on my counter. "I'm going to take it to the next level."

"An affair?" I blurted.

"Call it what you want. I'll never know if I don't do this."

"You're willing to risk your family?"

"Henry won't know, Leah. He's never around to know. And I don't know if he would care anyway."

Here was another chance for me to tell her what I thought, but I wasn't sure what I could say. Last time I'd spoken up, Elisabeth had interpreted it as me taking Henry's side.

"You're quiet," she observed. "You think I'm making a mistake."

"I . . . think you should take more time to think about this. Obviously Henry isn't fulfilling your needs, but—"

"You're right. And he's not even trying." She took my hand. "I want you to meet him."

"Who? Creyton?"

"Of course Creyton."

"But . . . but why?"

"Why? You're my best friend. I want you two to know each other. He's home right now. You could come by and—"

"Elisabeth, I don't think that's a good—"

"You'd really like him, Leah, if you just gave him a chance."

I glanced at the microwave clock. "I'd love to meet him, really, I would, but I can't right now. I'm . . . I'm running late, actually."

"Late? You don't do anything on Tuesday nights."

I never thought the conflict resolution class would come in handy. But it was starting to provide a good excuse for a lot of things I didn't want to do.

Chapter 13

[She tries to stare out the window.]

"You're here," Cinco said when I stepped out of the elevator.

I simply nodded. I didn't want to have to explain my identity crisis to a man who didn't seem to need any help defining anything. I wanted to believe I came as an excuse not to have to meet Creyton. But in reality, part of me, deep down inside, knew there was a possibility I could use an overhaul . . . of some sort.

"Last time I saw you, you weren't doing so well."

"I'm fine," I said. "Turns out the woman I hit was somebody really important to my . . . brother. The dean's wife."

Cinco grimaced. "I thought you handled yourself nicely. Maybe this conflict resolution class is coming in handy after all." He smiled. "So what brought you back?"

"I didn't want to hurt my brother's feelings. He's . . . the overly sensitive type."

"And telling him you didn't want to attend would cause unneeded conflict." Luckily his radio-program listeners couldn't see the smug expression he often liked to wear. But I could.

"Marilyn's calling the group," I said, passing by him and heading directly for Carol. Carol greeted me by squeezing my arm and saying something that I couldn't quite understand. But I smiled and told her I was glad to see her. Surprisingly, even those who weren't ordered by the court had returned to class, and everyone was in attendance from the week before.

Nobody looked in the mood for casual greetings, though. I sat as still as possible and waited for everyone's full attention to shift to Marilyn.

"Good evening, class," she said. "Tonight we're going to be doing some unusual things, things that I don't think anyone in the class is going to like very much. But rest assured, passing this test will bring you closer to achieving your goal of being able to handle conflict."

My hand crept up to my neck, which was safely guarded by a summer-weight sleeveless turtleneck. I had one in every color.

"But first, I would like to go around the room and ask everyone to tell me who you would most hate being in conflict with and why. And people, let's be honest, okay? I know this is uncomfortable for many of you, but let me assure you, this will pale in comparison to what we'll be doing later on."

She laughed, then nodded for Glenda to begin.

"That's easy. Robert. Why? For fear he'd beat the living daylights out of me."

Everyone looked at Robert. Robert indeed looked like he wanted to beat the living daylights out of her. If ever there was an antagonist, Glenda was it.

Ernest was next. He thought for a minute and then said, "Stuart McDonald. He's the chairman of the committee at my church."

"And why him, Ernest?" Marilyn asked.

"Because every time we disagree, he threatens either to cut the budget, or my salary, or both. He doesn't say it directly, but he makes it clear in no uncertain terms that he's the one in control. And the fact of the matter is, that's true."

"Thanks, Ernest. Cinco?"

"My dad. No matter what, he always gets the upper hand in any argument. I've yet to win an argument with him. He's really good." Cinco said this with both frustration and delight.

"Thanks, Cinco. Robert?"

"Captain Huff. She's the meanest five-foot-two woman I've ever known."

I tried to imagine Robert arguing with a tiny lady. It made me laugh a little. Then it was my turn.

This was difficult because there were so many people in my life I hated being in conflict with. Edward was the easy choice, but I didn't want to complicate matters by trying to explain this in the context of his being a sibling. My sister was an easy one too, as we'd spent most of our lives in conflict. But with her new turnaround, I was holding out hope that those days were past. Mother was not an easy one to explain. Our relationship was plagued with plenty of unmentionable conflict, where words had alternative meanings, and we were just one badly construed sentence away from total estrangement. Elisabeth was a good one, but since I was sort of in the middle of a conflict with her already, I didn't really want to be scrutinized by the group. So I said, "My dad."

"Why your dad?" Marilyn asked.

"I guess because . . ." I hadn't really thought of it before. I paused to try to find the reason. "I don't want to disappoint him."

"Thank you. Carol, you're last."

I leaned in so I could hear Carol. When she was finished, everyone looked to me as her official interpreter. "Carol said her daughter, because she's afraid she might say something that will cause her never to talk to her again."

Marilyn slapped her hands together like she was a football coach. "All right, gang. It's time for our second task. Grab your things. We're going on a field trip."

Marilyn drove a passenger van filled with quiet participants.

Cinco had moved to the back, where I sat next to my ever-dependably-quiet friend Carol. He sat in the same seat as me, one row in front. Robert sat next to him and finished blocking my view. But then again, I wasn't sure I wanted to know where we were going.

"So," Cinco said to me, striking up conversation in the silence, "we both have issues with our fathers."

"For very different reasons," I pointed out.

"Maybe not. Sounds like we both respect our dads."

I nodded. I didn't really want to talk about this while everyone was listening.

"Your father must be very successful, in one way or the other," Cinco said.

"He is." I offered no further explanation.

"By the way you're not talking about him, am I to correctly guess he's a CIA covert operative?"

"Did you get your sense of humor from your dad?"

"As a matter of fact, yes I did."

"And what does he do?"

"He's in journalism."

"I would've thought you'd have followed in his footsteps."

"I did. I'm a journalist too. Just on the radio."

Oops. Unintended zinger. Oh well. One for the quiet team.

"So, Leah, I have to ask, I find it hard to imagine why a very attractive woman like you is so unsure of herself."

The van's occupants grew very still, and even the van's engine seemed to quiet down. While being mortified at the fact that he'd asked that question, I was at the same time distracted by the "very attractive" part.

"Why do you think I'm unsure of myself?" I said, cursing the fact that my voice chose to quiver at that very moment.

Cinco smiled. "I'm interested in people. What makes them tick."

That's why he hides behind a radio microphone. He can say what he wants, but he never has to say it to people's faces.

Jodie had a point.

C'mon, Leah! Zing him one!

"What makes them ticked off, from what I hear," Glenda piped in from the front row.

Cinco laughed. "Fair enough."

"How do you do it all day long?" I asked. "Engage in combat and enjoy it?"

"I don't always enjoy it. Sometimes we're tackling really tough issues that people are very passionate about."

"Besides, nice and sensitive radio doesn't make people want to listen. People want to hear people yelling and screaming at each other," Robert said. "My brother is addicted to your show, even though he almost always disagrees with you."

"I don't ever yell or scream, but guests and callers have been known to," Cinco said.

Glenda turned around in her seat. "Oh, give me a break. I've heard you raise your voice a time or two. I just think you're a pompous, arrogant, egotistical, self-centered jerk." Cinco must have been genuinely surprised by the attack, considering that he couldn't form a comeback. Glenda looked pleased.

"Ladies and gentlemen, it's a human thesaurus," Robert said.

I tugged at my turtleneck, which had gone from shielding my neck to strangling it.

I had to hand it to Glenda. She was as bold as they came. Of all the people to enter into verbal combat with, Cinco would be the one you'd want to avoid. He did this for a living. But apparently Glenda did it for a pastime.

"Tuesday, January 18, 2004," Glenda said.

Cinco shook his head, shrugged.

"The topic was the Big Dig," Glenda said, referring to the famously disastrous underground-tunnel project in Boston.

"Okay," Cinco said. "Still not following."

"You made a fool of me on the air, but it turns out I was right, wasn't I? It's become one of the biggest financial disasters of our city."

Cinco sighed. "Glenda, I talk to hundreds of people every week. I don't remember our conversation at all."

"Like I said. Pompous, arrogant, egotistical, and self-centered."

"If I'm self-centered, then what does that make the person who expects me to remember only her out of thousands of phone calls?"

Everyone's eyes shifted back and forth between Glenda and Cinco. But to my surprise, Glenda's attention suddenly honed in on me. "What are you looking at?"

Everyone looked at me and I tried to look away, but there was nowhere to look except out the window, and I knew that would only evoke more problems.

"I'm . . . I'm just . . . not . . . you're . . ." The properly structured sentence in my head seemed to have been shaken up like a martini in a tumbler, and now it poured out in the wrong order.

"Why are you picking on her?" Cinco asked. "She's not doing anything to you."

"Please," Glenda said. "I can see it all over her face. She's thinking all kinds of nasty thoughts about me. Little Miss Proper Manners, never rocking the boat." Her glare intensified. "Pegged you, didn't I? You've probably never raised your voice a day in your life."

The window drew me. I couldn't help it. It was the only safe place for me to look. But as I looked outside, I noticed something peculiar. "Stop and Shop?" I said aloud.

Everyone looked out the window as we pulled into the parking lot. Marilyn parked the van, turned around, and grinned. "Prepare yourselves. This one's going to be a doozy."

Once inside Stop and Shop, one of two main grocery chains in Boston, Marilyn gathered us near the frozen-food section to explain the task.

"With all the buzz about reality television, I thought it might be fun to add some competition. So we're going to break into teams of two, and whoever wins this task will earn a gift certificate to Mangalos." Everyone oohed. Mangalos was the newest and most talked about restaurant in Boston. But nobody aahed, because the next step was finding out what hideous thing we were going to have to do.

Marilyn numbered us off to six, and then she explained one and two were a team, as were three and four, and five and six. I whirled around, praying Carol was four. But smiling back at me was Cinco, who shrugged a little too innocently. Carol was paired with . . . Glenda, which left Ernest and Robert.

Marilyn appeared unconcerned as she continued. "Now, the point of this task is to become reconciled with the fact that in life there will be conflict, and there will be times that the conflict is played out in front of strangers. We're going to learn today how to handle ourselves gracefully when the heat is turned up.

"So the object of the task is to stall in line as long as you can. The pair that stalls the longest will win the restaurant certificates. In my hand is the scenario you will be playing out while in line." She handed each team a card. I read over Cinco's shoulder.

NUMBER THREE, YOU WILL HAGGLE THE CASHIER, CLAIMING SHE OWES YOU FIVE PENNIES. NUMBER FOUR, YOU WILL STAND BEHIND HIM/HER AND CAUSE A BIGGER

SCENE THAN HE/SHE IS CAUSING, CLAIMING YOU HAVE TO GET THROUGH THE LINE QUICKLY.

I glanced around at the other pairs. No one looked happy. Carol looked like she was about to cry. I felt the same way. I turned to Cinco and said, "I hope you're comfortable with losing, because I can already tell you I won't be any good at this."

Cinco gently took my elbow and led me a few steps away. "Come on, Leah. There's nothing like a good competition, right? And what a prize!"

I tried to smile. "I would eat dirt right now if it meant I didn't have to do this."

"You'll never see these people again."

"Can you assure me of that?" I whispered.

"Not really, but the chances that you will ever see one of these people again is very slim. Besides, who cares what they think about you? You don't even know them."

"Look, I understand your biological makeup makes these kinds of things pleasantly enjoyable for you. But for those of us who weren't ordered by the police to be here, this is kind of a nightmare."

He shocked me to the extreme by taking my hand. I glanced around, but everyone else was immersed in their own cue cards. "Leah, we can do this. I know there's a tiger in you waiting to roar."

"Okay, first of all, let's kill the clichés. If there's anything at all inside me waiting to roar, it would most definitely not be from the feline family. I'm deathly allergic to cats." I tried to say that string of sentences with a completely serious face. Cinco just looked amused. "Second of all, what makes you want to win so badly?"

Cinco took my shoulders and turned me around so I faced Glenda and Carol. Whispering in my ear he said, "I just don't want Glenda to win. Look at her. Already she's talking to Carol like she's a child."

I turned back to face Cinco. "Is that your entire motivation in life? Just to beat other people at your game or theirs?"

He smiled. "That's it! That's the kind of fire we need. Think you can transfer that over to the cashier who supposedly shorted you five pennies?"

I rolled my eyes. And then Marilyn said, "All right, everyone. It's time."

My knees actually went weak, but to my surprise, I felt Cinco's hand on my back, and strangely it reassured me. I realized if there was anyone in this crazy group meant to do a task like this, Cinco was the one. His unintended smugness was aggravating, but he was certainly the most balanced of the group.

Marilyn pointed to three long lines up front, where impatient patrons stood by their overfilled shopping carts. She handed us each something to buy. I got sunscreen. Cinco received a car magazine and a candy bar.

"I will be watching each of you. As soon as you step up to the cashier, your time will start. By working together and causing more conflict, you should be able to stay there for quite some time. Whoever stays there the longest wins." I glanced at Cinco. This guy could pitch a tent and stay all night. I was going to have to ambush his plans. I could live without Mangalos. I'm not sure I could live with knowing I'd intentionally made people late. If Cinco wanted to eat there so badly, heck, I'd buy him dinner. "All right, folks, pick a line."

I watched Glenda drag Carol toward one of the front cashiers. Robert and Ernest stepped to the left. Cinco motioned we should walk to the one in front of us. I stepped forward, clutching my sunscreen.

We stood silently. After all, we weren't supposed to know each other. I moved forward, inch by inch, as the cashier whizzed products by the scanner, throwing them into paper or plastic, all the while appearing to care about the person on the other side of the cash register. I was impressed with her ability to offer a genuine smile amid the chaos. My heart trembled and thumped as I tried to imagine myself haggling over five pennies. Once, I'd actually left a store five dollars short because I didn't want to hold up the line. On more than one occasion I've handed people money in line because they'd realized they were short and I didn't want them to be embarrassed. I once gave a man a twenty because he'd forgotten his wallet.

I closed my eyes, trying to figure out a few things I could say that would sound reasonable. Was there any good reason to hold up a line for five cents? I honestly couldn't think of one. So I decided I was just going to have to play a nut. I wondered what the other teams' tasks were. Poor Carol. The woman had to be dying a thousand deaths.

"Move it along, lady," I heard from behind me. I opened my eyes and noticed that I needed to step forward. After the woman in front of me, I was next. I glanced back at Cinco, who must've thought he'd landed a role on Broadway, what with how seriously he was playing his new character. I tried to smile at him. He didn't smile back.

Luckily, our line hadn't grown too much longer. There were only two people behind Cinco, and they looked to be together.

Every beep indicated I was one grocery item closer to being burned at the grocery store etiquette stake. I cleared my throat and balled my fists up, trying to get a grip. Cinco was right. I was never going to see any of these people again. They were all strangers, so why not pour my heart into this and see what happened?

The customer in front of me finished and the cashier, whose name tag read "Mindy," smiled appropriately at me. I handed her the sunscreen and then heard from behind me, "Oh, my heavens! Leah Grace Townsend, is that you?"

Chapter 14

[She digs for change.]

My forehead burst into a full-fledged sweat. I slowly turned my head and there, standing two people behind Cinco, in my line, was Renalda Musgrave, my mother's longtime Washington, D.C., friend. When Dad was senator, they'd done everything together, including raise children. Renalda's daughter, Castilla, was a year older than me.

"Mrs. Musgrave," I said. "What . . . what in the world are you doing here . . . in Boston?"

"We moved. Hadn't you heard? Your mother must not have told you. We've only been here about a month."

"Oh. That's nice."

"In fact, I'm having lunch with your mother next week!"

Mindy said, "Four dollars and eighteen cents."

I jammed my fist into my handbag, trying to find that floating five-dollar bill I knew was in there.

"How is everything in your world?" Renalda practically hollered. "Your mother said that the playwriting thing is working out for you."

"It's fine," I managed, finally finding the five-dollar bill. I realized I should've taken longer doing that. But right now, I wasn't exactly focused on the task. I handed it to Mindy. "I'm working on a new play right now."

"That's wonderful to hear."

I glanced at Cinco. He looked a little nervous himself, but it was probably only because I was distracted from the task.

"Well, Mrs. Musgrave, it was so nice to see you."

"Castilla's doing fine," she continued, stepping to one side so I could still see her. "She's at Harvard. Did you know that? She was always the smartest in the family. And Doug is working on Wall Street."

"Good. Great. That is wonderful to hear. Please say hello for me." I looked at Mindy, who was counting out the change. I cupped my hand and she handed it to me.

"Thanks." I smiled. I took the change and plunged my fist back into my handbag. I started to walk off. After all, what kind of insane task was this, anyway? But then, every reason I had for coming back to the stupid class washed away the good sense I wanted to hold on to. I pictured polite and courteous Dillan, smiling at all the right times, making sure everyone felt as comfortable as was humanly possible. The change, wet from the sweat on my hands, seemed to burn right through my fingers.

I felt for the nickel. I dropped it into my bag and my hand re-emerged with the rest of the change. Cinco handed over his merchandise, his eyes urging me to get on with it. "Excuse me," I said. I could sense Mrs. Musgrave and the others watching me.

"Yes?" Mindy asked.

"You shorted me five cents."

"No, I didn't."

"Yes, you did." I spread my hand and showed her the change. Out of the corner of my eye, near the front door, I could see Marilyn with her stopwatch. "You owe me five cents."

Mindy frowned and looked confused. "I just counted it out.

Maybe I dropped it." She stepped back and looked around her feet, then scratched her head. "Okay, well, if you can wait a moment, let me check this man out so I can open the register again."

"No!" I said. The people in line behind me all stopped moving, including Cinco. I tried a friendly smile toward Mrs. Musgrave, whose own smile became drenched with concern. "I, um, I don't have time to wait. I need that five cents right now."

"Lady," Cinco chimed in, "it's five cents. For pete's sake, let it go."

"I am owed five cents, and I am not going to let this store cheat me out of it."

"Ma'am," Mindy said, her pleasant demeanor fading by the second, "we were not trying to cheat you out of anything. I just can't open the register unless there's a transaction made, so if you'll let me check this guy—"

"I want to speak with the manager." I remembered my mom saying that once.

"Why?" asked Mindy, as genuinely confused as a person could be. I felt so sorry for her that I just wanted to rush around and hug her and tell her she was doing a great job handling the wicked witch of west Boston.

"You're insinuating I need to buy something to get my change back." I was on a roll now.

"Lady," Cinco said, "just let her check me out. You can get your five cents back then."

"No," I said. "I have a right to my change now."

The line had grown longer, and a couple of people near the back stepped away to find another one. Mrs. Musgrave's mouth was hanging open. I tried a reassuring smile again.

Mindy looked at the customer service desk, then checked her watch. "Ma'am, my supervisor is on break. She won't be back for another ten minutes."

"Then I'll . . . I'll . . ."

"Wait?" Cinco blurted out, throwing up his arms. "That's ridiculous! Nobody here wants to wait for you."

Suddenly, Mrs. Musgrave was rushing toward me, waving a nickel. "Here, darling. Let me just give you a nickel and this can all be resolved in a friendly manner."

I reached out to take the nickel, but Cinco swatted at my hand. "Ma'am," he said, addressing Mrs. Musgrave, "you are a very kind woman. But this lady doesn't deserve to be bailed out. She's acting like a completely spoiled brat. Who in her right mind would make all these nice people wait for a silly nickel?"

A large, disapproving groan came from the line, and I felt a small piece of me die. I tried to engage each angry gaze to show them I really was just a normal person like the rest of them, but nothing was reciprocated. I glanced to my right. Carol and Glenda were out, evident by the public tongue-lashing Glenda was giving Carol. Ernest and Robert, however, were hanging in there. Cinco noticed too, and though he maintained his accusatory expression, I could somehow see encouragement in his face.

So I did the only thing I knew to do.

I started crying.

Mindy's hand slapped her mouth. Mrs. Musgrave reached her hand out like that might help somehow. She never actually touched me, but at least she wasn't cowering away. And as for the rest of the line, they looked to be praying for a Prozac salesman to happen by.

"If you must know," I said directly to Cinco, "right before my favorite uncle died, he gave me a nickel, and to this day it signifies how much he loved me." I swiped at a tear.

The next thing I knew, in an amazing reversal of public support, everyone had pulled out a nickel and was handing it to me. When I opened my hand, six shiny silver nickels gleamed in the light. "Thank you." I sniffled. I dropped the nickels into my handbag and clasped it shut. Then, with a steady turn on my heel, I marched off in the direction of Marilyn. I noticed immediately that Ernest and Robert were still in line.

I didn't care. If that had gone on much longer, they could've certified me mental and locked me away.

"Ma'am?" I heard.

I could hardly make myself turn around. When I did, Mindy handed me a sack. "Your sunscreen."

"Oh. Thank you." I smiled ungracefully and continued on, until I reached Marilyn. I wanted to collapse into her arms.

Marilyn was writing something down on her clipboard. Glenda and Carol stood close by, clearly ignoring each other.

"And to think I did all that and won't even get free food," I growled, hoping never to have to see or touch another nickel for the rest of my life. Cinco was behind me soon enough. He patted me on the shoulder.

"You did good, kid."

I shook my head. "That was the most horrible thing I've ever been through in my life." We all watched as Ernest and Robert left the line. Robert was grinning like he'd won the lottery. Ernest was trying to look enthusiastic, but his skin was pale and he looked like I felt.

"Hand it over," Robert said, opening his hand up right in front of Marilyn. "That was way too easy, if you ask me."

Marilyn was jotting something on her board, but she said, "Robert, some of these tasks will be easy for some and harder for others. But rest assured, you will be stretched at some point."

"Sure, whatever. Just give me my prize."

Marilyn said, "Actually, I hate to break it to you, but Cinco and Leah won."

"What?" Robert looked ready to make a spectacular spectacle of us. I wanted to crawl inside Marilyn's tunic and hide my face.

"Sorry"—she shrugged—"but even though you finished last,

Cinco and Leah win. They started before you and beat you by eighteen seconds."

Cinco encircled me in a bear hug. I didn't know what to say. Carol's shaking hand reached to pat me on the shoulder. I felt like I'd won the Ironman Embarrassment Marathon. Marilyn handed a certificate to Cinco, then another to me.

Then she began going down her list of observations for each team, what everyone did right and what everyone did wrong. I hadn't realized there was a right way and a wrong way. It all just seemed freakishly unnatural.

I listened quietly until Marilyn finished and we headed back toward the van. Suddenly Cinco sidled up beside me and said under his breath, "What do you say we go celebrate our victory together?"

As I rode the elevator to my floor, I was still trembling from head to toe. In the car on the way home, I'd tried listening to classical. I counted backward from twenty-five, one hundred, one thousand. I did deep-breathing exercises. But my chest hurt and my mind reeled.

I'd actually said yes.

I'd said yes.

"You said yes."

Yes.

Unbelievable. We'd set a time. We would meet at Mangalos tomorrow night between seven and seven fifteen. I thought that was funny. I'd never had a fifteen-minute window for dinner before.

"It's just a celebration for winning . . . winning . . ." Whatever it was we won tonight. I still couldn't believe I'd actually done it.

I also realized that I had started talking out loud to myself, which was extremely scary. That was something I never did, because I was completely aware that if I said out loud what was in my head,

I would probably be locked up. It wasn't an insecurity. After all, I'm a writer. My characters are birthed out of fantasy and imagination. But I always knew that whatever the process was, it should be kept inside my head.

As I unlocked the door to my apartment, I mumbled to myself about what an idiot I was to accept Cinco's invitation. A ringing phone interrupted me. I raced to the closer phone—in the kitchen—to answer.

"Hello?" I said, catching my breath. Why was I out of breath? It must've been all the mumbling I was doing.

"Leah?"

Edward? I checked my watch. It was almost ten. He should be in bed. "Edward, what are you doing up?"

I could hear him sigh. "I couldn't sleep. I'm worried."

"About what?"

"You."

I set my stuff on the counter and moved into the living room where I clicked on a light and sat down. "Why?"

"Something's different about you, Leah. I don't know what it is. But I'm worried." Edward sounded genuinely concerned.

I closed my eyes and tried to concentrate. "I'm fine. Why do you think something's wrong?"

"I don't know," he said. "You've just been acting a little differently lately."

"How so?"

"You seem . . . restless."

Restless. That was the spice. Restlessness. It made all the other flavors disappear.

Edward continued. "I just want to make sure you're okay."

"I'm fine."

"What about work? How's the new play going?" It was the first time Edward had even inquired about it with any real seriousness.

"The play . . . well . . ." Be honest, be truthful. "It has had its ups and downs, but I think we're up again. I wrote a great scene today. It was a very unexpected scene." Was that today? It seemed like ages ago.

"I know you're feeling a lot of pressure about this play, Leah. Maybe it's getting to you. And you know what, I don't think that agent of yours helps matters."

Edward had never liked J. R. And granted, most people didn't like J. R. But I reminded myself that I was fortunate to have her. Most playwrights of my stature didn't have agents. She picked me up after *Twilight T-Zone,* and she had a long and distinguished track record of making young playwrights overnight stars. That track record, thanks to me, was in jeopardy.

"It's been a struggle," I said. "But sometimes it is. It doesn't mean anything. Maybe struggling and wrestling with it make it better. I don't know."

"That's probably it," Edward said. "That explains the funk you're in."

"Edward, what funk are you talking about?" I didn't want to mention the dress, but I was curious if that's what he was referring to.

"Leah," Edward said, his tone lowering as if he were about to give a classroom lecture, "you can't tell me that you haven't seen some changes lately."

"Between us?"

"Okay."

"Sure, Edward. I've noticed."

"So what's wrong with you? Why all of a sudden are things different with you?"

I bit my lip and stared at the carpet. Was I sure enough about it even to say it out loud? Had the grocery store incident brought about a boldness I would soon regret?

I paused, hoping Edward would fill in the silence. But he didn't.

So I said, "Look, Edward, maybe I am in a funk, you know? I mean, I'm thirty-four. And yes, I've accomplished a lot, but somehow that isn't filling me up. And if I'm being honest, maybe it's not the external things in life that are bothering me. Maybe it's internal. Maybe I'm unhappy with who I've become. Maybe nobody really knows me. Edward, sometimes I think I'm two different people, you know? I'm the person everyone knows, and then I'm the person I know, and the person I know isn't the same person everyone else knows. Maybe I want to be one whole person. That's what I'm trying to say. I just want to be the same person as I am."

I could hear him breathing. I tried to rewind and mentally go through what I'd just said, because the words had escaped like a surprising string of drool.

"Edward?"

"I'm here," he said. Then he didn't say anything else. I squeezed my eyes shut. What had I done now? Why not slip on the pink dress and go platinum blonde? Piece by piece I seemed to be wrecking my carefully constructed life.

I started to apologize, but Edward interrupted. "Let's talk about this over dinner Thursday night," he said.

Thursday night? "Sure. That's fine," I said. But I hopped out of my chair, knowing that wasn't fine. Pacing the floor and knocking my knuckles against my forehead, I added, "Actually, I can't."

"You can't?"

"I've got that . . . that . . . thing."

"What thing?"

He didn't even remember. Great. I was going to have to say it out loud. "The conflict resolution class you enrolled me in."

"Oh." His voice came alive. "You're going to that?"

"Yeah."

"I thought you quit."

"No."

"Huh." I could actually hear Edward scratching his scalp. "Okay, well, let's go out tomorrow."

"Tomorrow?"

"You don't have anything on Wednesdays. And I don't on the fourth week of the month."

I closed my eyes and fell back, my couch catching me like I'd just fainted. "That's not going to work."

"Why?"

"I'm busy." How could I explain this? Was this even explainable? And why shouldn't I be able to explain this . . . unless I was feeling guilty.

"Busy doing what?"

"It's the class I'm taking," I said. "We were split into groups for a challenge, and my group won, so we're going out to celebrate." I took a breath. That wasn't a lie, if you define a group as two or more people. Granted, most people define it as three or more, but I wasn't going to get into technicalities.

"I didn't realize I'd signed you up for *Survivor*."

"You have no idea," I said, laughing hard enough for two people.

"Well," Edward said, "why don't I just come with you?"

My collapsing heart begged for mercy from me. It had been through a lot tonight.

"Oh, how I wish you could," I said, "but it's reservations only. It's some new, hot restaurant. Besides, if we're going to talk, I don't want it to be around other people."

Then there was silence again.

"Maybe Friday?" I asked.

"Restaurants are too crowded on Fridays."

"We could make reservations."

"No. In general, it's really not a good idea to go out on Fridays."

I closed my eyes. By turning his Wednesday gesture down, I might've just missed the only opportunity to see Edward be spontaneous. "Right. Bad idea."

"I'll see you sometime this weekend. We can talk then."

What were we doing now? I'd just spilled my guts and Edward wanted to wait until the weekend to discuss it? I felt myself growing angry.

"So have you learned anything from this class?" he asked.

"A few things. It's pretty boring. A lot of lectures."

"Leah, look, you don't have to go to that thing to make me happy. I thought it might change your life, but if it's boring, why waste your time?"

I wondered to myself how, exactly, Edward wanted my life changed.

"Anyway," Edward continued, "I guess I'll plan on seeing you this weekend. Maybe we can go to the beach or something."

"Sounds good," I said.

"All right. I'll call you tomorrow. Oh, what time's your dinner?"

"Between seven and seven fifteen." Why did I feel the need to add the extra detail? "When you're working with a large group it's hard to get everyone there at the same time. Real hard." I wanted to slap myself. This was getting more disgusting by the second.

"Okay, well, call me when you're finished, okay?"

"Okay, sure."

Edward said good-bye, and I went to my bedroom, crashing onto the mattress. My body ached with fatigue. I wanted to close my eyes and make all the bad things go away. Then my phone rang again. I reached for it on the bedside table, figuring the caller was Edward, and with my new, bold attitude, I answered, "You missed me already?"

"What? Leah?"

I gasped. "Mother?"

"Leah, oh, thank goodness I got a hold of you."

"What's wrong?"

"You must come to the hospital. Now. Hurry."

Chapter 15

[She smiles.]

On an uncomfortable padded bench stained with years of spilled drinks and who knew what else, Mother and I sat. The hallway leading to the operating room was so white it hurt my eyes. Elevator music played through the intercom so softly that it was more irritating than it was soothing. I had been with her for forty-five minutes.

The doctor had explained that the surgery on Dad's heart could take more than four hours. Mother explained in less than a minute when I arrived that he had complained of chest pains but had been too stubborn to go to the hospital. He collapsed at home, and Mother had called the ambulance.

Here we were, sitting in stunned silence. Mother looked awful. The rosy circles on her cheeks that she took such great care in applying had faded into her now-sallow skin, and her mouth drew downward like two strings were pulling at the edges. It was the first time in my whole life I'd felt sorry for her.

"It's going to be okay," I finally said, reaching over to pat her knee. She startled, as if she hadn't even noticed I was sitting there. But when she looked at me, tears filled her eyes and she nodded.

"We brought him here in time," she said. "The ambulance was

passing near our neighborhood when they got the call. That saved him. They were at our house in less than three minutes."

"That's good. And now they're opening up his arteries to make sure this doesn't happen again."

"It's hard for me to imagine him lying on the table, his chest open, his heart stopped." She covered her mouth. "It doesn't seem real."

"You want some coffee?" I asked.

She nodded, so I went down the hall to try to find a fresh pot, with no luck. I had to go two floors down to the urology floor, but finally found some. When I returned, a nurse was just walking away from Mother. I handed her the cup and asked, "Is there an update?"

"She said he's holding his own in there, and there haven't been any complications thus far. But he does have three out of four arteries blocked." She glanced at me. "And some reporters caught wind of it. She said a few have gathered downstairs, wanting a comment."

"Really?" I couldn't believe it. Dad was a well-known and loved ex-senator, but he was from the South. They had decided to retire to Boston because Dad loved Massachusetts so much. I wasn't aware his health was even newsworthy, but then again, with twenty-four-hour cable news, I figured they often needed something to fill in the gaps.

"I can go talk to them," I told Mother as we sat back down.

"No."

"No?"

She shook her head and returned the pat on the knee. "Honey, it's okay. They'll leave soon enough."

"Mother, they're probably not going to leave until they get some sort of statement. If I go down and give them a brief one, maybe that will hold them off for a while. I don't have to give any details. Just enough for them to have something to write down."

She pressed her lips together like she was thinking about it, but then she waved her hand. "No offense, Leah, but you've never been that good in front of a microphone."

"What? What are you talking about?"

"You probably don't remember. You were only eight. But a reporter asked how you liked Washington, D.C., and you said something about how gross the homeless people were."

How could I forget that? Both Mother and Dad had been completely upset by my answer, and when we returned home, I was sent to my room. Mother had me practicing for weeks after that on how to answer any question posed to me with either a yes or a no. I never really understood what I'd done wrong. I did think the homeless people were gross. And where I came from, there weren't that many homeless people, at least right there on the street where you had to look at them.

I leaned my back against the wall, sipping the weakest coffee I'd ever put to my lips, wondering how something I did as an eight-year-old could still haunt me as a thirty-four-year-old. Obviously I was capable of handling a few reporters' questions. But then again, Mother had never had much confidence in me in general. I'd once stumbled on the steps of the West Wing as we were following the president out. I was around eleven. Mother wouldn't let me wear even the slightest heel again until I was fourteen.

And to this day, I prefer flats.

"So have you and Edward mended things?" Mother asked, setting the coffee aside with a pointedly disgusted look, as if I'd made it myself.

"We're, you know, we're fine."

Mother eyed me. "It's not necessarily a bad thing to fight. Every once in a while. Your father and I certainly had our share of scuffles. Of course, it was always behind closed doors, the only proper place to have a disagreement."

Mother wasn't usually so generous with personal advice, so I heeded the moment. "What do you think about Edward, Mother? Do you think we're a good match? Do you think he's good for me?"

She looked a little overwhelmed by the questions and grabbed that wretchedly disgusting coffee again. She took a moment to think about the question, and then she said with one of the most sincere faces I'd ever seen on her, "Dear, considering the limited fishing rod you have, I would say he's a pretty good catch."

I returned home just as the sun was waking up the rest of the city. I wasn't much of a morning person, and as I walked into my apartment, I couldn't help but notice how beautifully it glowed with soft, hazy light. I made a mental note to myself to start praying to become a morning person. Surely morning people had better self-esteem, for the simple reason that they were able to fight off the beast of sleep with such ease.

I went straight to my coffeemaker and turned it on, dumping scoops and water in without measuring. I leaned on my counter, holding my head in my hands. Morning light was overrated.

Dad had come out of surgery at around 4:00 a.m. The surgery took two hours longer than expected, which made Mother a ball of nerves. She elected not to call Kate at that late hour. I knew the real reason was that she didn't want to call Kate at her house, get the answering machine, and then have to call Dillan's. Mother and Dad raised us to be churchgoers and, among other rules, not to engage in premarital sex. Mother always had her suspicions, of course, but with her husband in heart surgery, she didn't need any confirmations.

She asked me to call Kate in the morning.

I gulped down one cup of coffee while holding my pounding head. It was 6:00 a.m. I couldn't remember the last time I'd seen morning this early. I stumbled to the living room and picked up the phone, trying to focus on the keypad. Blinking through watery eyes, I dialed Kate's home number and crumpled into my leather chair.

After four rings, I almost hung up, but then she finally answered. "Hello?" It was obvious she wasn't a morning person either.

"Kate, it's Leah."

"Leah?" I could hear the sheets rustle. She was probably giving Dillan the "hush" sign. "Why are you calling this early?"

I paused. This was going to be hard to say. "I've been at the hospital all night with Mother."

"What's wrong with her?"

"It's not her, it's Dad—"

"Well, tell me." Her tone was tense.

"Just listen. He's going to be fine. He had a heart attack—"

"A heart attack?" She was wide awake with panic now.

"Kate, he's fine. He went through surgery last night and early this morning. They unblocked three arteries."

"Are you saying he had triple-bypass surgery?"

"He's out now, and resting comfortably."

"Why didn't you call me?" I could hear the hurt and anger in her voice. This would take some finesse. Mother had called me because, as of now, I was still the more reliable sister, though these days Kate was gaining on me.

"We talked about it," I lied, "and realized we were going to have to work this thing in shifts. Mother is going to need help. I stayed the night. Mother's okay now, but she's going to need you to come up sometime this morning. Can you do that?"

"Yes, of course!" I could hear her feet padding against the wood floors of her apartment. "I can't believe this," she mumbled. "He's going to be okay?"

"Looks really good. The surgery took longer than expected, but the doctors said he should make a full recovery."

"Okay, okay," she said, over and over. It sounded like she was trying to pull on some clothes.

"Kate, you've got to calm down. It's going to be fine. We just need to be there for them."

"I know." She sniffled. "I'd better go. I need to call Dillan before he leaves for work."

A single eyebrow popped up on my head. Dillan wasn't there? That was suspicious. Was she just saying that for my benefit?

"Right. Call Dillan." I shook my head. "Want me to call him?" Okay, that was mean. But Kate had shacked up with every boyfriend she'd ever had. I was finding it hard to believe Dillan was any different. "So you can get to the hospital."

She paused. Then said, "Yeah, Leah. That would be great. I don't know if I can handle talking to him right now." She told me Dillan's home and cell numbers, and I jotted them down using a pen and a piece of paper from the end table. "Thanks, Leah. Explain what's happened and tell him I'll call him later."

"Sure," I said, feeling heavy with guilt. "No problem."

Her voice was higher when she asked, "Is he really going to be okay?"

"Kate, you need to go see him. It'll make you feel better. He looks a little pale, but he's just been through major surgery. He even woke up sooner than the doctors had expected. You know Dad; he's a fighter."

"Yeah," she said, managing a chuckle. "That he is."

"Go on. He's in room 5772. I'll call Dillan for you. And I'll probably see you up at the hospital later. I've got to get some sleep."

"Okay. Thanks, Leah." She hung up the phone.

I stared at the number I'd written down. I decided to go back for another cup of coffee before calling Dillan. Maybe more caffeine would make him more likable. Maybe it would make me more likable. Why I didn't care for Dillan was still a mystery to me. I didn't want to accept Edward's theory that we were twins separated at birth. Besides the obvious ick factor that came with the idea of Kate dating someone who could be her brother, I figured the more likely reason was that my sisterly instincts kicked in. There was something about Dillan that I just couldn't put my finger on. I intended to find out what it was, though.

I looked at the clock and realized this was the perfect opportunity to call. People were more likely to be their real selves when woken out of a dead sleep.

I made the call from the kitchen while sipping on my second cup. Dillan's phone rang twice and then I heard, "Hello?" His voice was more chipper than I'd expected.

"Hi, Dillan, this is Leah, Kate's sister. Did I wake you?"

"That's okay," he said, his voice smiling through the phone. "I was about to get up anyway. Is everything okay?"

"Kate wanted me to call you. Our father had a heart attack last night."

"Oh, no! Is he okay?"

"He was in surgery all night, but it looks like he's going to be okay. He's recovering now, and Kate just left to see him."

"What can I do to help?"

I crossed my arms and cradled the phone with my chin. The guy had this down to a science. "Nothing, really. Just wanted you to know."

"Okay."

"Kate will probably call you later."

"Leah, please let me know if there's anything I can do to help, okay?"

"Yeah. Sure."

"All right. I'll be praying for you and your family." He hung up and I dropped the phone into the receiver. *Praying for us.* How nice. But with slumped shoulders, I realized I hadn't even prayed about this. Shouldn't that have been my first instinct?

I went to sit down on the couch, where I buried my face in my hands. I wanted to cry, but I wasn't sure I had the strength. I fell sideways into the pillows, closed my eyes, and began to pray.

My prayer stopped. God had to answer another call. Why wasn't he answering the phone? I was witnessing what most people had suspected for thousands of years . . . God didn't answer every prayer.

"Aren't you going to answer it?" I asked. There was no reply. Just more ringing.

Suddenly I sat up, my face hot and sweaty from where it had lain for . . . how many hours? I looked at my desk and my phone was lighting up . . . ringing. I blinked away the odd dream and bright sun that flooded my apartment, jumped to my feet, and snatched up the phone.

"Hello?" I half expected God to be on the other end. I'd fallen asleep while praying this morning. Now, I prayed it wasn't late afternoon.

"Good morning, Leah. It's J. R." I breathed a sigh of relief. I hadn't slept the day away. I glanced around to see if I could make out the microwave clock. Looked like eight something.

"J. R. Hi. How are you?"

"I'm fine. You sound a little . . . tired."

"No. Just a head cold. I'm fine."

"Okay, well, the reason I'm calling—"

A knock at the door interrupted my concentration. Who was knocking this early? Was it even early?

"Um, J. R.," I interrupted.

"Yes?" She sounded irritated.

"Hold on for a second. Someone's at my door."

She sighed.

I walked over, peeked out, and opened the door. Edward stood there, perfectly groomed, holding a present. "Hi." He grinned.

My eyes bulged as I combed my hair with my fingers. "Hi." I pointed to the phone and mouthed "J.R." to him. He nodded that he understood and followed me quietly back to the living room.

"Okay, I'm back. Sorry about that. What were you saying?"

She sighed again. This time heavier. "Look, Leah, I don't know how else to say this. I've read through the pages you've sent me so far. In fact, I've read them three times. And Leah, it's just . . . well, I hate it."

Did she just say *hate it*? I glanced at Edward, who was watching me, still grinning. Why was he grinning? He was not a grinner. My fingers continued to push through the tangles in my hair. I smiled back at him and tried to focus on J.R. "You . . . you did?"

"*Hate* is really too nice of a word. When I was reading through it, it made me angry."

My knees grew weak. I smiled at Edward again, who looked like he was about to burst with eagerness. "I'm sorry," I said.

"Sorry? Leah, are you listening to me? This play is wretched. *Wretched.* It has one thing going for it. A strong character. Her monologues are great, but you can't carry a three-act play on monologues. Last night I reread the scene where Jodie meets Timothy, and if there was ever a polar opposite of sexual tension, that was it. The dialogue fell flat. I mean, here are two people, completely different from each other, agreeing on everything from politics to religion."

"I . . . I know. I was trying to write the unexpected—"

"I'll say. Leah, surely by now you're an experienced enough writer to know that the audience is going to want to see certain things. They're not coming to see a play where everyone gets along. There's got to be some fire, you know? At least a spark. Something! I felt like I was floating through a literary utopia! It put me to sleep!"

A large ball swelled in my throat, but I managed to wink at Edward and mouth *one more minute* to him. He could not suspect my world was crumbling by way of phone call.

"I understand."

"Is that all you can say? You understand? Leah, I just called your play wretched. I'm questioning your abilities as a playwright. Your entire future hinges on whether or not you're going to be able to do this. How can you sit back, as docile as a petting zoo animal, and take this?"

"I'm—I'm not. I . . . I . . ."

"Leah, if you're going to make it in this business, you're going to have to get tough. That's all there is to it. Meek and mild ain't gonna cut it. I'm normally not one for a scene, but something makes me want to beg you to stand up and fight."

Edward was growing a little bored. His grin had fallen into a placating smile. I didn't want to lose this moment with him. A grin was like a gold nugget with this guy.

I shifted my attention back to J. R. "I understand what you're saying."

She laughed, ridicule in her voice. "You understand. Right. Okay, well, I guess the next move is yours. I don't know what I'm going to tell Peter. He's anxious for this script. It may be time to let him know he should look elsewhere."

"That won't be necessary," I said quickly.

"Won't be necessary. Leah, I wish you could hear yourself. You sound as polite as a Mormon boy knocking on my door. We'll speak about this later. Maybe you need some time to think." The phone went dead.

I swallowed, trying to keep my cool. "Okay . . . all right . . . yes, you too, J. R. And thanks for calling with the good news. Okay, bye."

I hung up the phone, and Edward perked back to life. "Good news?"

"Nothing big. J. R. was just calling to . . . tell me how much she liked my latest play."

"Well," Edward said, with unnatural gusto that made me take a step back, "that's the reason I'm here."

"My play?"

"Sort of." He handed me the box that he'd brought in. It was wrapped in red-and-white-striped paper and tied with a big red silk bow.

"What's this?" It was very heavy, so I set it on the coffee table and sat down.

"Unwrap it!" I looked up at him. He appeared ready to jump up and down and slap his hands together. He didn't seem to notice that I'd barely had two hours of sleep. And by the hour that he'd arrived at my apartment, I guessed he thought I was always up at this time. My hands were shaking. Was it the coffee? The conversation? The fact that my dad had almost died? I realized I needed to tell Edward about Dad, but this didn't seem the time. He was staring at the package like it might explode.

I pulled the ribbon and it fell off. I unstuck the tape and tore the paper away. "Do you like it?" Edward asked.

It was a white box, about three inches tall and three feet wide. "What is it?"

He rushed to sit beside me and slid his fingernail under the single piece of tape that closed the box. He opened it up and there, lying between foam cushioning, was a laptop computer. He pulled it out. "It's very lightweight. Everything you could ever need is on here. It's wireless, so you can check your e-mail or connect to the Internet wherever you want. I also had them add all your favorite programs on there. And look, it comes with its own carrying case!"

I could not close my mouth. Edward had bought me a laptop computer? I'd never owned one. My mentor, Charles Teallu, had always insisted that real writers stay at home and write in the shadows. He said he'd never once written outside the home, because he already felt exposed enough when he wrote.

"I think this will help," Edward was saying as I blinked back into reality. "I mean, how great will it be when you can go to Starbucks or wherever, even the park, and write. You can get out of this gloomy apartment, Leah. I think that's half your problem. You just need a little more contact with the outside world."

"My problem . . . ?"

"Yeah. You've been talking about how you're in this funk, right? This is the perfect solution! You can go get yourself a latte, sit at Starbucks, and get some fresh air. You never know what will inspire you when you're out amongst the world." He was grinning again.

I stretched an amiable smile across my face. "Wow."

"I knew you'd be speechless. I don't usually do things like this, I know. But it really did seem like the perfect solution." He actually dusted his hands off, like he was ridding himself of the crumbs of my pity-evoking life.

But all I could say was, "Thank you, Edward." He looked at me, as if waiting for more, so I added, "What a kind thing for you to do."

He smiled, completely unaware of how stilted I sounded. He looked at his watch. "Okay, well, I have to get to the university. Glad you're already up and dressed. I thought it might be a tad too early, but I wanted to get this to you today so you could start using it right away." He hopped off the couch and bounded to the door. "Call me later this evening and let me know how you like it."

"Sure." I walked to the door. I hadn't even told him about Dad yet. "Edward?" I called after him as he made his way toward the elevator.

He turned, but first made an obvious glance at his watch. "Yes?"

"Never mind. I can talk to you later."

Chapter 16

[She ducks into the shadows.]

After cleaning myself up and grabbing my stuff, including my new laptop, I arrived back at the hospital at 11:00 a.m. Dad had been moved to a room with a nice view. Kate and Mother sat on opposite sides of the bed, staring at a man who lay perfectly motionless, breathing shallow but steady. Neither noticed when I walked in.

"Hey."

They turned. I tried not to let my jaw fall open when I saw Mother. I'd seen her look this terrible only one other time in our whole lives. Kate had started her rebellious streak and had disappeared. Mother was certain she'd been kidnapped. Turned out she'd just skipped town for the weekend with friends, but that was the longest weekend of my mother's life, and the only time I saw her stay in her pajamas all day without a stitch of makeup on.

To this day, Mother still talks about it like it was a kidnapping. And when Elizabeth Smart was kidnapped, my mother's only comment about it was how pulled together Lois Smart looked every day. "How can she get up and do her hair and face?" my mother remarked. "When Kate was missing, I could hardly get out of bed."

I went to Dad's bedside. "How's he doing?"

"He's mostly slept," Mother said. "The doctors said that's normal, and that they don't expect him to be awake much until tomorrow, or possibly this evening."

Kate added, "He woke up one time, smiled at Mom and tried to give the thumbs-up, then went back to sleep."

I watched him for any movement. Then I looked at Mother. "Kate, why don't you take Mother home to get changed and take a rest—"

"No, no. I'm staying here," Mother said firmly. "He needs me."

"Mother, I'll stay here. Go home for an hour or two, change clothes, take a shower. Get a little bit of rest while he's resting. You're going to need your energy once he starts recovering. You know he's not going to want to take it slow. You're going to have to make him."

Mother glanced at Kate, who I noticed looked particularly sophisticated with her hair tied up in a messy French twist. She was even wearing close-toed shoes and a blouse that you couldn't see through. I made myself stop staring. "I'm not sure," Mother said to Kate. Why was she asking Kate?

But Kate nodded authoritatively and reached across the bed for Mother's hand. "It's okay, Mom. Let Leah sit here for a while. You need to go home and get a bag packed for you both anyway. I'll come and help you. Leah's right."

I tried to smile, but it was hard hearing that line come out of Kate's mouth. *Leah's right.* Of course I was right. Why did that need to be stated by the daughter who had suddenly decided to act her age?

Mother looked at Dad, then slumped in resignation. And my mother never slumped. She was a total mess. "All right. But Leah, you can't leave. I want someone here with him the entire time."

"I understand. He'll be in good hands."

"Mom, why don't you tell the front desk you're leaving, and I'll gather your things and meet you out there."

Mother walked out the door and Kate whispered, "He looks like he's on his deathbed!"

"Kate, he's been through major surgery. Of course he's going to look that way."

"I don't know. I think the doctors aren't telling us everything." She looked at him like he was already dead. Tears formed in her eyes.

"You're going to have to pull yourself together. Mother doesn't need either of us falling apart."

"I know," she said, placing a finger under her nostrils. "I know. Did you call Dillan?"

"Yes."

"And?"

"He offered to help, said he'd pray for us, but I told him to wait until you called."

"Okay. I guess I'll go. It should be pretty quiet here for a while. And I gave the press a statement earlier this morning, so they should leave you alone too."

"The . . . the press?"

"A group of reporters with nothing better to do was lingering downstairs. Mom asked me to go take care of them."

"Oh."

Kate walked to the door but then turned back and asked, "In case I can get Mom to go to sleep, is there a certain time I need to be back here?"

"Back here?"

"I mean, do you have anything going this afternoon or this evening?"

"No . . ." I stopped, realizing that tonight was my celebration dinner with Cinco.

Kate waited as I hesitated. "Is there something?" she finally asked.

I glanced at Dad and closed my eyes, tightening my grip around the handle of my laptop case. Then I shook my head. "No, nothing."

"Okay. Don't know when we'll get back. I'll try to call you."

I nodded and took a seat. I hadn't brought Cinco's number with me. It was still in my bathroom drawer. I didn't even know what radio station he worked for. But Mangalos was only about ten blocks away from the hospital.

I decided not to think about it for now. Perhaps this was God's way of saying I shouldn't be anywhere near Cinco Dublin. Poor Dad, having to suffer a heart attack just to keep my social life straight.

I decided Dad wasn't going to wake up anytime soon, so I opened up my new laptop. I had to hand it to Edward—the computer was really nice. He'd even bought me a flash drive, and I'd had the presence of mind to transfer my play onto it before leaving for the hospital. Of course, *presence of mind* was up for debate, as I was really trying to recover from J. R.'s emotional tongue-lashing.

I hated it kept echoing from the four corners of my mind. Just days ago she'd liked it. Now she hated it. How could things have changed so quickly?

I uploaded my file and scanned the play as if I could assess where exactly I'd gone wrong by paging down at lightning speed.

I was a rational person, and so as diplomatically as I could, I retraced our conversation and tried to convince myself that I'd misinterpreted what J. R. had said. But fifteen minutes later, I realized there was really no misinterpreting *I hate it*. That said it all.

So with nurses coming in and out and my father oblivious to the world around him, I worked feverishly, trying to pinpoint the problem areas. Obviously, there was the small issue with lack of conflict, but it was done intentionally, and eventually the conflict would come. Maybe my literary experiment wasn't working. Or maybe I was fooling myself, and Elisabeth's speculation that I was a prophet had jarred my common sense.

"I'm not a prophet, I'm not a prophet, I'm not a prophet," I whispered to myself.

"Leah?"

I jumped in my chair, just catching the laptop before sending it crashing to the ground. I whipped around to see Kate standing over me. "Oh, hi."

Kate glanced over at Dad, then behind her, then said, "What were you saying?"

I clamped my laptop shut and stood. "It's nothing, just a writing exercise. You're back so soon?"

"Soon? We've been gone for four hours. I was worried it was too long."

Four hours? I looked at the wall clock. I couldn't believe the time had slipped away like that.

"How's Dad?"

"The nurses said he's doing fine. He hasn't woken up, but he stirred once or twice. How's Mother?"

"Much better now that she's had a chance to rest and apply rouge. She went to get some coffee. Look, why don't you take a break. You really look pretty awful."

"Oh. Really?"

"Yeah. Go home, maybe come back after dinner."

Dinner. Cinco. My heart fluttered with indecision.

"Okay. Tell Mother I'll be back after dinner. But call me if anything happens."

"I will." Kate smiled, and for the first time in years, it was the smile I remembered from our youth. I felt tears strike my eyes and I turned away. Maybe it was the fatigue and the stress of the last few hours talking.

"I'll see you," I said, walking out the door. I'd seen a flash of Kate's old self, and maybe, just maybe, I had Dillan to thank for that.

I went home, agonizing over what to wear, then agonizing over the fact that I was agonizing over what to wear. After the fourth application of eyedrops, I realized my eyes were just going to have to look tired. I was, after all, tired. I couldn't shake the excitement that kept buzzing through my body as I waited at Mangalos, a full fifteen minutes before we'd agreed to meet.

I stood outside the door and watched the attractive people enter the attractive restaurant. There were two voices going off in my head as I waited. The first was guilt. I was having dinner with a man and hadn't told Edward. I'd tried to tell Edward, but Edward seemed very uninterested in my life. But maybe that wasn't fair. After all, he'd dropped a couple of thousand dollars to buy me a laptop computer, which was supposed to solve the apparent pre-midlife crisis I was enduring.

I argued with guilt, defending my position. If not for Edward, I wouldn't be in this position in the first place. Edward had been the one insisting that I go to the stupid class. So I went. I conquered. Now I was celebrating. And that was all it was. A celebration dinner.

Guilt, however, was no match for Jodie Bellarusa, who was the second voice, and in a particularly foul mood following this morning's conversation with J.R. She'd been snappy and sarcastic all day. She was often fond of playing the devil's advocate. She took a completely opposite stance of guilt, and as I stood quietly in the shadows, she got pushy.

Edward doesn't deserve to know about your escapades.

"Escapades!" I whispered. A few people glanced in my direction. I stepped deeper into the shadow of the building, until my back was against the wall.

All right. Maybe that's too harsh of a word. I meant "escapades" in a completely non-sinful sense. But if Edward thinks the solution to all of your problems is that you need to drink coffee that costs ten times as much as it does to make it at home, maybe Edward needs a wake-up call. That's all I'm saying.

It wasn't often Jodie took my side. Mostly she ridiculed me, so I stayed silent to see what else she might have to say. But then I noticed him. He was taking long strides down the sidewalk, combing his hair with his hands.

He walked under the awning toward the front door, and as I stepped away from the building and into the soft light that illuminated the front of the restaurant, he spotted me.

His face looked both distressed and relieved. "Hi."

"Hi there."

"I thought I was running late." He checked his watch. "I'm sorry."

"You're not late," I said. "I'm early. I was nearby, so it wasn't far for me to get here." Lie number one. I'd gone home and I knew it. Who was I trying to fool? Actually, that was lie number two, because lie number one was that I didn't care what I was wearing.

He placed his hand on the small of my back and guided me in the door. I could smell his cologne. It made my knees weak. And the fact that my knees went weak made my heart flutter. And my heart fluttering made my cheeks flush. I tried to get a grip.

We were taken to our table, which had a nice window view, on the second floor of the restaurant. The room was filled with dusky light, and the candles were already lit. This was much more of a romantic setting than I had imagined.

Cinco pulled my chair out, waited for me to sit, then took his own chair. He smiled, and for the first time I noticed how straight and white his teeth were. They weren't overly white like they'd seen a bleaching tray. They just looked natural and clean.

He tilted his head. "You look a little tired. You okay?"

I blinked away my observations and focused. "It has been a long day. I'm . . . wrestling with the play I'm writing."

"You write plays?" His face lit up with complete interest. It had become so much my toil and labor that I'd actually forgotten it was kind of an interesting aspect of my life. Maybe the most interesting aspect of my life. I was not all that interesting of a person apart from that.

"Yeah," I said. "I had one that took off, but I've been struggling ever since."

"What is your play about?"

It was a question writers loathe. Most people ask the question because it seems to be the one that should be asked of a writer. But most people's eyes glaze over as you begin to answer, because they really don't want to know. It's kind of like the literary form of "How are you?" Except there's no way to answer, "Fine."

I waved my hand. "I'm not really sure yet. All I know is my character is named Jodie and she's an antiromantic."

Cinco laughed. "An antiromantic. That sounds interesting."

"You would think, but my agent doesn't really agree." The waiter brought us water and menus. "So, I've been wanting to ask you about your name. Every time I say it, I feel like I need to throw a fiesta and eat guacamole. Where did the nickname come from?"

"I insisted on a nickname when I turned ten, and it was actually my buddy who named me. He happened to be taking Spanish classes at the time. We thought it was pretty funny. My parents never liked it, and they still call me Rupert."

"What does a string of Rupert Dublins do all their lives?"

"We've all been in journalism of some sort. My great-great-grandfather started a printing press, my great-grandfather took over the business, my grandfather started a newspaper from that printing press, and then my father became a journalist."

"Then there's you."

"Then there's me." He smiled. "And my parents are still getting over the shock of me moving to radio. But they also see the importance. I'm lucky that they're supportive."

"I've tried to listen to your show before."

"Tried?"

"It gets pretty intense, and I usually turn on the radio when I'm trying to wind down."

He nodded. "Yeah, it gets intense. But I love passion. I'm a passionate person and I love talking about passionate topics. I just need to work on keeping my cool when people are really pushing my buttons."

I nodded, but all I could focus on was the flutter in my stomach every time he used the word *passion*. There was no mistaking the fire in his eyes. I'd seen it the first time we met. It was what made me squirm when I was around him. That and the way he didn't seem capable of mincing his words. Plus, he had gorgeous eyes.

He looked down at his menu. "So, we get to experience a new restaurant. I love trying new things. Do you?"

Flaming pancakes came to mind. "Sometimes."

We took a moment to read over the menu, and then he said, "Let's try something crazy. What do you say? To celebrate our victory."

Try something crazy. I already was.

Chapter 17

[She turns, addressing him.]

My choice wasn't out-of-this-world experimental, but I tried the Caribbean fish with fruit I'd never even heard of. Cinco ordered mahimahi, and we each agreed to taste the other's dish. While waiting for our dinner, Cinco asked, "So, I've always wondered where the word *playwright* comes from. I have to admit, I don't go to the theater much, but I do find it interesting."

Now, that was a good question. "Well, *wright* comes from the word *wrought,* meaning to craft or work into shape. I love one definition of *wrought*—'to beat into shape by tools.' That's what I do. I beat my story into shape with my tools."

"And your tools are your words."

I couldn't help the smile that came. "That's right. It's been said that poems and novels are written, but plays are built."

"I've never known a playwright before."

"Our jobs aren't all that different, are they? You, after all, beat *people* into shape with your words."

Cinco laughed. "You know, I didn't realize you were so funny. You're very reserved at the group."

"It's uncomfortable; what can I say?"

"I noticed. You're really uncomfortable every time you're there."

"Thanks for pointing that out. It makes me feel more comfortable."

"Sorry. But it does interest me. You're an attractive, bright, obviously successful woman. Why is it hard for you to assert yourself?"

I could feel my ears burn, and I was thankful my hair was down to cover them. I tried to smile and pretend I was unaffected by the fact that we were talking about my greatest weakness.

"I'm making you uncomfortable. I'm sorry."

"No, I'm not . . . I'm just trying to . . . to . . ." My words hung in the air. What excuse could I make? I glanced at him, and he looked like the kindest person in the world. He had the darkest brown eyes I'd ever seen, lined with dark lashes and topped off with unruly eyebrows. Something made me want to be vulnerable. The skin on my neck was begging me not to, but before I knew it, I said, "Yeah, okay. It makes me uncomfortable. I don't like talking about myself, and I don't like the attention on me. That's why this class is—"

"Good for you."

I smiled and looked down. "Right. Good for me."

"And good for me. I need to learn to stop saying everything that comes to mind. Maybe it's okay on the air, but sometimes it leaks into my personal life too. It's how I was raised. My father taught me to speak my mind, so I always have."

"My parents taught me not to, so I don't."

"That can be a good thing. Because my father taught me to speak my mind, I did, and for a while in my twenties, we didn't have anything to do with each other. But we're okay now. I regret it, because I missed learning a lot from him. At the time I didn't want anything to do with him or what he did. I think I could've learned so much from him during those years."

This man spoke calmly and quietly, as if he knew that all the sounds around him would settle down, as if his words were important enough to strain a little to hear. A gentle, genuine peace filled his eyes, and he didn't seem at all uncomfortable with telling me about his past, estrangements and all.

I reminded myself this was not a date, but if it were a date, this would be the part where the two individuals normally paint the very best pictures of themselves. Date or not, Cinco didn't seem the least bit concerned about what I thought of him. He shared openly about his life—his fears, his weaknesses, his misguided attempts at fame and fortune. I listened intently, unaware that time was passing.

"So," he said, smiling, "now I'm here. I have my face on a billboard, and it makes about a million people cringe when they drive by."

I laughed. "Does it make you cringe seeing your head that big?"

"From my perspective, it looks a little small."

I cracked up. "Sorry, but you're not really selling me on the idea that you have a big head."

"Better luck next time." He smiled. "So, why don't you tell me about Leah Townsend."

"But I'm really enjoying hearing you talk about yourself."

"I know. I can tell. You could let that go on all night. But I'm starting to bore myself, so you better start talking."

"I'm afraid you may still be bored. I live a pretty uninteresting life."

"Uninteresting life? You're a playwright. That's a dream job."

"It's very interesting when you've written a blockbuster and you're the It writer of the moment. But that goes away, and then you're just part of the daily grind like everyone else." I looked into his shining eyes. "Except you don't look like you know what I mean. Your job is never a daily grind?"

"What can I say? I love it."

"Except when you punched out that reporter in front of your home."

"Yeah." He smiled sheepishly. "Except that. I'll pay the consequences, but sometimes the consequences are worth it. That guy needed a beating. Period."

I shook my head. I couldn't relate. I felt guilty about most everything in my life. If I ever punched out someone, no matter how much they deserved it, I would probably eventually punch myself out too, just to make sure everything was fair.

"What are you learning from the class?" I asked him.

"That a diverse group of people can all come together for the same reason."

"So, who is your polar opposite?"

He thought for a moment, then said, "You."

"Me?" I laughed, spewing a little water. I blotted my mouth, eying him. "How is that? Surely we're not that different."

"I guess we'll find out." His eyes engaged mine, and without any reservation, he held them, a small smile perched on his steady expression. Luckily for me, I'd worn a mock turtleneck. But I was feeling the heat. "So," he continued, "how's your brother doing?"

I couldn't help but look away. I wasn't good at lying, even though I seemed to be doing it all the time lately. "Fine. Why do you ask?"

"Well, he's been through a lot."

"He's fine."

"And what about you? You're recovering from losing a kidney?"

"It's hardest on the recipient."

"Feel any different with just one kidney?"

"How do I turn you off?" I finally asked.

He grinned, then threw up his hands. "Okay, okay. What can I say? I'm curious."

"I'll say."

"You want to switch topics, then?"

"That would be nice. I'm not one for dinnertime discussions of bodily organs."

He laughed hard. "Good point."

"So, yes, let's change the topic."

"Okay. Are you dating anyone?"

My jaw dropped open, and I couldn't hold in the shocked laugh that always escaped whenever I was feeling uncomfortable or vulnerable. He sat there, obviously fully aware that the sudden silence was doing a great deal of explaining.

Thankfully, the waiter saved me. He brought our food to the table and was asking if there was anything else we needed. I was about to make a bold move and preorder dessert. But in that moment I was struck by the realization that this was not truly a celebration dinner, and I wasn't here just because I had nothing better to do. My father was lying ill in a hospital bed, my boyfriend was at home believing I was out with my class, and I was here with Rupert Dublin V—Cinco. And I was enjoying every uncomfortable moment of it. I didn't need Jodie to tell me that. My fluttering heart was doing a fine job on its own.

Then enjoy it. Let everything else around you go, and enjoy it.

One of Jodie's stronger qualities was not compassion, but on occasion she would drop her facade and actually show a bit of wisdom.

My head was spinning, and yet there was only one image that kept showing itself front and center: baked cod in a Piperade sauce. I loathed baked cod. Why had I ordered it? Because Edward suggested it? Why didn't I just order flaming pancakes? I wanted flaming pancakes. There was nothing wrong with flaming pancakes. I looked at Cinco across the table, who smiled gently, confidently, like he assumed there would be no other place in the world I'd rather be. Maybe this was the spice. And when you find a good spice, you should use it a lot. That's what Mother always said—one year we could taste Beau Monde in everything she cooked.

Let everything around you go. That was Jodie's advice. And why not? Here I was, uptight and worried about what other people would think. Why not throw caution to the wind? Why not—

I gasped. Cinco looked up at me. There, three booths away on the opposite side, was Dillan. And another woman! Cinco was asking for more water, so I managed to steal glimpses. He was smiling! Flirting? Was he flirting with this woman? I couldn't see her face, but she had long blonde shiny hair and delicate shoulders. Dillan was definitely enjoying himself.

I tried to focus back on Cinco and concentrate on my own . . . escapade. *Is that what this is?*

Yes. Because I knew that if Dillan saw me, I'd have as much explaining to do as he did. But we were talking about *my sister.* The one he'd rescued from the depths of her multicolored hair and eight-too-many body piercings.

Cinco noticed I was distracted. "You okay?" he asked.

I looked at him. I wanted to stay here as long as possible. I smiled. "I'm fine."

It was nine thirty by the time I arrived back at the hospital. I had walked faster than usual. Maybe it was because I felt like I needed to be back with Dad. Maybe it was because I was running from the experience I'd just had. I didn't know, but I was out of breath.

On the elevator, crowded for this late in the evening, I stood near the back and thought about Cinco. I wondered if there was ever a chance I could be like him. I had already learned a lot about myself in the conflict resolution class and had proved that I could haggle for pennies in front of a crowd. But how did that translate into real life? How did that make a difference? I still couldn't say what I wanted to say to people. I still couldn't just speak my mind. Maybe it was going to take some practice, some time. I mentally went over the acronym that Marilyn said could change my life. It was a long list of unparallel attributes to remember when dealing with conflict. I could only be so lucky that an acronym, any acronym, would change my life.

C-ontrol (Keep yourself calm, no matter what the other person does.)
O-penness (Don't hide your feelings, because you're not fooling anybody.)
N-egotiable (Realize that there may be some negotiation needed.)
F-airness (Don't make overblown statements; only state the facts.)
L-ove (Remember, the person with whom you're engaged has feelings too.)
I-nvaluable (This class, so don't forget what you're taught.)
C-haracter (Keep your character; don't stoop to below-the-belt tactics.)
T-ruth (Telling the truth is the only way to resolve conflict, no matter how hard it is to hear.)

I wasn't sure, but I think this was everything I'd learned in kindergarten.

My floor arrived and I apologized as I scooted through the crowd. The floor was quiet and the windows were dark. A few nurses milled about, looking as tired as I felt. I found Dad's room. The door was cracked open, so I knocked softly.

"Come in," I heard. I opened the door, and there was Dad, sitting up a little.

"Hi!" I beamed, rushing to his bed. "You're awake."

"I'd feel better if I were dead," he grumbled.

"The first few days will be difficult," I said, patting his barely clad shoulder.

Dad huffed and tried to sip the water in front of him. "It tastes like dirt."

"Have you eaten?"

"I don't have any appetite. Every part of my body hurts. I'd be better off dead, I tell you."

I pulled up a chair. "Dad, you're going to be okay. This is the rough stretch. You had your chest cracked open and three out of four arteries worked on. I wouldn't expect you to be feeling good."

Dad glared at me. "You're a doctor now, huh?"

"I'm just relaying what the nurses told me." I felt a little sting in my throat. Dad wasn't normally this combative, and it was throwing me.

"The nurses." He laughed joylessly. "What a joke. They've got all these initials after their names, but I swear they don't know a thing. I'm getting mixed messages about what I am and what I am not supposed to be doing. With every shift change comes a different set of instructions and a new nightmare. If my heart doesn't kill me, one of these nurses will!"

I took a breath to try to settle myself. Dad wasn't ever down and incapable that I could remember, so maybe it was pain that was making him moody. I'd never seen such a fierce scowl on his face, though.

"Where's Mother?"

"Down getting something to eat," he growled. "I had to send her away. She was fussing over me, about to drive me insane. I told her if she didn't take a break, I'd have to be transferred to McLean."

I sighed. McLean was a mental hospital in Belmont. Now Dad was getting downright obstinate.

The door to the room opened, and as I turned a young man walked in, wearing light blue scrubs and a dreary expression. He didn't look a day over twenty-five.

"Good evening, Senator Townsend," he said. I was glad the doctor was here. I planned to pull him aside after he was finished and ask him if Dad's attitude was normal. "I'm Jeff." He picked up my father's chart and scrutinized it.

Jeff? Since when did doctors use their first names?

Dad eyed him. "Jeff?"

"I'm the nurse on duty," he said without looking up.

"Does that mean Jane is gone?" Dad asked.

"She just got off her shift, so I'll be taking care of you now."

"Good. She was the stupidest person I've ever met."

That got Jeff's attention. He looked up, and his eyelids lowered like a menacing cat's.

"Dad!" I gasped.

"What?" Dad shrugged. "It's true. She couldn't answer a few simple questions."

"I'm sorry," I said to Jeff, who was clearly not in the mood for this kind of harassment. "My dad didn't mean that."

"Yes I did!" Dad barked. "I'm telling you, Jane is an idiot."

I put my hand to my forehead, trying to find a graceful way out of this.

"Sir," Jeff said, "Jane is as capable as anyone here. She might've been tired. She just pulled her third twelve-hour shift in three days."

"Son, you're not going to get any sympathy from me. I worked sixteen-hour days seven days a week. Long hours aren't an excuse, especially when it's someone's life you're talking about. And speaking of life, what in the world are you doing choosing nursing as an occupation? I know I'm old school, but this is woman's work, son."

"Dad!" I couldn't believe what my dad was saying. I'd never seen him act this way before. "Nursing is a perfectly legitimate occupation for a man or a woman." I tried to smile at Jeff for his approval. He wasn't approving of anything.

"You know," Dad growled, "this is the reason our country is going to pot. It's because men want to be nurses and women want to play professional basketball."

I knew the mock turtleneck wasn't going to cut it: I was splotching clear up to my chin. Jeff took one look at me, did a double take, and raised an eyebrow. "I'm fine," I mumbled, placing my hand around my throat.

Jeff returned his attention to my dad. "If you're finished, sir, I need to take your vitals."

"Do you think you can do it without killing me?"

"Dad," I urged, giving him a stern look.

Dad shook his head, ignoring me. "Used to be the only good thing about being in the hospital was getting felt up by a nurse."

"DAD!"

"But even that's ruined now."

Jeff looked like he wanted to break something. I stepped closer to the bed. "Dad, you owe Jeff an apology right now!" My voice was stern, and Dad's eyes cut to me with unexpected anger.

"What did you say to me?" he asked, his nostrils flaring. I noticed Jeff was looking at the heart monitor, which was suddenly beeping faster.

I swallowed and lifted my chin. Dad was wrong, and I wasn't going to stand for it. Not after all I'd learned in my conflict resolution class. That acronym was coming in handy after all. I lowered my voice a little. "You owe Jeff an apology."

But Jeff wasn't even paying attention anymore. He was punching buttons on the monitor. He turned to me and said, "You need to back off."

Jeff's words tickled my ears, then left and flew into the middle of my stomach with a hard right hook. I opened my mouth, but I couldn't breathe. "What?" I squeaked.

"This isn't the time or place for this," Jeff said. He glanced back at the monitor. "Your father needs to stay calm and rest."

A self-satisfied smirk covered Dad's face.

"I . . . I just felt that . . . that was . . . inappropriate." My words were tangled in my shock that this man I was defending, a man a good decade younger than I, was now rebuking me.

"It's not necessary," Jeff said drily. He took Dad's pulse, wrote something down on a chart, and left quickly.

I stood there at the side of Dad's bed, trying to decide what to say. Dad wasn't even looking at me, but instead had found something interesting on the wall to stare at.

I couldn't stand it any longer. Jeff was right. Dad didn't need this right now. What was I thinking? I looked down and my hands were shaking. I wanted to cry.

"Look, Dad, I'm sorry. I just thought—"

"Just leave, okay, Leah?"

"But Dad, I—"

"Get out of my room."

I stared at him. I couldn't believe what I was hearing. Dad had never asked me to leave his presence. Not once. I waited, hoping he would change his mind, but he stared forward, his face stony.

I picked up my bag off the chair and placed it gently on my shoulder, stalling, hoping he would stop me before I walked out the door. Then I paused at the door, waiting to hear his voice, but the only sound that filled the room was the steady, pulsing beep that monitored his cold heart.

I shut the door, and as it clicked, a rush of tears fell down my face. I stared at the carpet, hoping none of the hospital staff would notice. I glanced up. Jeff was at the nurses' station, oblivious to me, writing something down. Swiping my tears, I headed quickly toward the elevators.

I punched the down arrow, trying to hold back more tears until I got to my car, but they were brimming and pushing their way forward again, and it was all I could do not to break. The light *dinged* and the doors slid open. Without looking up I tried to rush in but knocked into someone stepping out. It was Mother.

"Leah, look where you're going!" she harped. Kate stood next to her. They both carried boxes of food in their arms.

"You're leaving?" Kate asked. "I thought you were going to pull the night shift."

I shook my head. I was afraid if I opened my mouth, I would start wailing. And I didn't want to admit to Kate that Dad was mad at me. He'd never been mad at me. She was always the one who was the recipient of his anger, and for good reason.

"You can both go home. I'll be fine," Mother said. Kate stepped out of the way of the doors, and they closed before I could get on. I glanced up at Mother, and she looked drained. Thankfully, she seemed not to notice my despair. Kate, however, was studying me intensely.

"How's he doing?" Kate asked me.

"Fine," I answered. "A little tired, I think."

"It's been a bad few hours," Mother said. "This nurse we had was a real piece of work. I think she just arrived from nursing school. Your father had to have a new IV, and it took her three tries. Plus she couldn't answer a single question for us! I think her name was Jane. Yes, that's right. Jane. Because your father said it rhymed with insane."

My hand automatically went to my face, where it slid from my forehead down to my chin. I'd admonished Dad, and it turned out he had legitimate reasons for feeling the way he did.

Kate was still looking at me. "Are you okay?"

"Tired," I mumbled.

"Go home. Both of you," Mother said. "Dad needs to rest, and you know how he doesn't like to be fussed over."

Kate said, "If you think that's best. I need to go get my stuff from the room, though."

Mother patted her on the back and they walked down the hallway together. I stood there, watching them. They looked so ordinary, like this was the way things had always been. And I felt like an outsider, gazing on a snow globe that encased the life I wanted.

I shook my head and punched the down button for the second time, an ironic reminder of how this day was ending.

This is what happens when you speak your mind, I thought, scolding myself as I repeated the sentence over and over in my head. I got onto the elevator. Thankfully, it was empty. As I rode it down, Jodie interrupted me.

You could've finished strong and told Kate about Dillan.

"Shut up, Jodie."

Shut up? I couldn't recall ever telling Jodie to shut up.

I needed a new acronym.

Chapter 18

[She tries to explain.]

It was 5:00 p.m. I'd been up since 4:00 a.m. I'd come home from the hospital and crashed into my bed. Sleep swallowed up all my worries until four, when my eyes flew open and I stared into the darkness, realizing the events of the evening hadn't been a dream.

Then sleep would not come again, so I rose and decided to be proactive. My problems weren't going to go away on their own. I overrode my coffee timer, made a big pot, and had been working on my play ever since. Well, at least I was sitting in front of my computer.

Inspiration was hard to find. I knew what separated a hobby writer from a professional writer was that a professional writer would write whether or not she felt inspired. Yet, the turmoil that boiled around me made it hard to focus.

I kept hearing J. R.'s smoldering words: *I hate it.* So there was no part of the story on which I could focus. I would try to tackle a scene, only to wonder if I should scratch the entire thing.

This went on for hours, and between those moments of non-inspiration, I would replay the scene with my dad the night before. And every time, it would break my heart.

Then, if my mind continued to be idle for too long, I would see

Dillan and the back of that woman's blonde head. How could I tell Kate this? But I would want to know. Of course I would want to know, even if it hurt at the time. Besides, I reminded myself, there could be an easy explanation for it. Maybe she was a client. A co-worker. But it was the way he leaned in, engaged her eyes, oblivious to anything else around him. I knew it wasn't an innocent dinner.

I knew it, because I was doing the same thing. Realizing I would have to go talk to Edward, I closed my eyes, temporarily shutting out the computer screen. I didn't even know what to say. But sitting there with Cinco made me realize there was something missing in our relationship. I wanted more; I couldn't help it. I would've been perfectly content to leave out the special spice if I hadn't known about it. After all, you don't know it's missing unless you've tasted it.

Somehow, I had tasted it. I didn't know when, or where, but I had.

So between feelings of failure, indecision, and guilt, there'd been plenty to keep my mind busy on this Thursday. By evening, I knew one thing for certain: I wasn't going to tonight's conflict resolution class. I wouldn't be able to handle it, no matter what the task. And I knew there was a good chance I would burst into tears without a moment's notice.

I had picked up the phone twice, just to make sure it was working. I don't know who I expected to call. Dad wasn't talking to me. Cinco, maybe? I laughed to myself, but it wasn't a laugh of joy. It was a laugh of pity. I was pitiful.

It wasn't always so. I'd held my life together for a long time. But things were slipping, more rapidly than I could've ever imagined. The relationship that I'd always depended on to be so dependable was making me crazy. The thing that my mother and I had always based our relationship on, the fact that I was the reliable, good daughter who would never let her down, now had competition. The idea that I had a grave weakness, the inability to handle conflict well, continued to draw my attention and was becoming more and more of a distraction. This was what kept me from telling Kate I saw Dillan, from telling Elisabeth she'd gone crazy, from telling my father he was being a jerk, from telling Mother I always just wanted to call her Mom.

I finally left my computer, realizing there wasn't anything I could do there. I was convinced Elisabeth had put a curse on me. Or maybe I'd cursed myself. Either way, I was sure that the more conflict I put in my story, the more conflict I'd see in my own life. It was happening already! With each page of the play I wrote, the more crazy my life became.

I took a moment to enjoy a cup of decaffeinated tea. I didn't need to shake any more. The adrenaline that had awakened me out of a dead sleep was still working overtime in my body. Finally, I decided I had to do something.

I dialed the hospital and asked for Dad's room. Mother would most likely pick up the phone. I wasn't even sure what I would say, or how much Dad told Mother.

"Hello?"

I froze. It was Dad's voice. He still sounded irritated.

"Hello?"

"Dad?" I said. It came out barely a whisper.

"I can't hear you. Speak up."

Speak up. Dad and I had never had a fight. Ever. In the back of my mind, Jodie piped up with, *Why not?*

"It's Leah."

"Oh."

I closed my eyes and tried to breathe deeply. My voice would quiver, but I couldn't control that. "Dad, I just wanted to say I'm sorry. Mother explained how terrible the nurse had been. I just thought you were being irritable."

There was a pause. Then Dad said, "When have you ever known me to be irritable, Leah?"

It was true. My dad was not one for unsteady moods. Why hadn't I taken that into consideration before I opened my stupid mouth? Maybe this conflict resolution class was doing more harm than good. My life before had been a tidy arrangement of carefully crafted and thought-out words. What had it become?

"I know, Dad. I'm really sorry. I'm just horrified at myself."

I could hear him sigh, and then his voice was softer. "Thank you for the apology." Part of me just wanted to start crying, to tell him everything I was going through, to try to explain why I had done what I had.

Instead, I said, "How's Mother holding up?"

He lowered his voice. "I finally got her to get out of here and take your sister. I'm so sick of people hovering over me. Leah, please, talk some sense into them!"

I couldn't help but laugh. "I'll try."

"Okay. I've got to go. They're getting ready to take me for some test."

"I'll be by to see you later."

"Oh, okay."

"Dad, I promise. I won't yell at you."

"Okay," he said, and offered a small laugh. I closed my eyes in relief. Things were going back to normal. At least in this part of my life. There were so many other areas falling apart, though.

I grabbed my handbag and keys. One by one, I was going to straighten everything out and make it all normal again.

The look on Edward's face was a grim reminder of where my problems arose. Here I was, arriving unannounced again. And even after more than two years of dating, he reacted like my visit might send him running.

"What are you doing here?" was his greeting.

"I wanted to talk."

"Is my phone not working?" The poor man asked this in all seriousness.

"In person, Edward."

He took several long seconds to process this. Then he said, "Oh. Okay." He opened the door and walked to the living room, leaving me to shut it. I joined him and we each sat down on opposite couches. He clasped his hands together and waited.

"First, I want to thank you for the laptop. It came in really useful yesterday."

"Good."

"Before we start, I want to tell you that Dad has had a heart attack, and they did triple-bypass surgery on him."

Edward's eyes grew round. "Is he okay?"

"He will be. He'll be in the hospital a few more days for sure."

Edward shook his head. "That's so hard to believe. Your father is so thin and looks in good shape."

"Well," I said carefully, "sometimes things that look to be perfectly fine on the outside aren't fine on the inside."

"I'll say," Edward replied. I realized speaking in metaphors was not going to cut it. Edward was a very logical person. I was going to have to present this in well-thought-out formula.

"Edward," I began, as gently as I knew how, "I know I'm going through a funky thing in my life. I realize that. And I take full responsibility for it. But one of the things that is continuing to trouble me is . . . is . . ."

"Is what?"

"I just need us to be . . . spontaneous, you know?"

Edward looked completely lost.

"Like, eat at restaurants we don't usually eat at. See each other on days we don't usually see each other. Go do things we don't usually do."

Edward looked down, and I wondered if I needed to explain more or let him process it. I tried to stay quiet, though everything in me wanted to keep on rambling.

"Why?" he finally asked.

I shook my head. "Honestly, I don't know. I'm just feeling restless, I guess. And I'm feeling like every part of my life is completely predictable. I'm not really a spontaneous person, you know? Maybe it's because I'm getting older. Or maybe it's because I'm going to have to choose a new career pretty soon. I don't know."

Edward sat up a little. "Well, the laptop is perfect, then. That's why I bought it. So you could go write wherever you wanted. *Whenever* you wanted. You could actually write in a different location every single day if you wanted! I'm telling you, you don't know what you're missing by not writing at Starbucks." His face was bright with enthusiasm. I smiled, throwing him a bone. But he was completely missing what I was trying to say.

"Yeah, so maybe some of that can spill over into our relationship."

Edward cocked an eyebrow. "You're saying you want to meet at Starbucks?"

Why did everything in the last twenty-four hours have to be so *hard*? "Edward, I'm just trying to say that . . . I need"—how was I going to say this?—"*more* out of our relationship."

Edward didn't blink. He didn't move. He just sat. So I said what I always say. "Look, I'm sorry. I—"

But to my surprise, Edward held up his hands. I froze, my mouth open in an *O* shape. He clasped his hands together, looked at me and said, "You're right."

I slowly closed my mouth.

"You know, you get into a routine," he said. "It's human nature. But why not? We can change things up a little, Leah. What harm is there in that? If that's what you want, we can do it. I want you to be happy."

I could hardly breathe. "Really?"

"Let's go to lunch on Saturday!" He threw out his hands. I'd never seen him throw any extremity. It startled me.

"O . . . kay."

"Yes! Lunch it is. I normally jog on Saturday afternoons and do laundry, but what the dickens. Laundry can easily be moved to Saturday night. And I can try to fit my jog in on Sunday . . . though Sundays I have lunch with my mother and grandmother, as you know. Well, maybe I can get up early and jog. Except then I'll be tired come Monday." He glanced at me and waved his hands. "I'll work it out." He stood and opened his arms for a hug. I accepted, and we pounded each other on the back like we'd just won the first stage of the Tour de France.

"Thank you for understanding," I said.

"Sure." He walked me to the door. "I'll see you for lunch. On Saturday!" He was getting a real kick out of himself. And then he said, "You even pick the place, okay?"

"I'll put a lot of thought into it," I assured him and then left.

I was putting out the fires, one by one.

I never skipped classes in college. I hardly ever skip a Sunday at church, unless I'm desperately ill. I can't even manage to skip a meal. But the conflict resolution class came and went, and I stayed home.

I struggled with doing it. I wasn't one for shirking commitments. But then again, who exactly was I doing this for, anyway? It was Edward's idea in the first place, and he didn't seem exceptionally desirous that I go.

I closed my eyes and tried to focus on the real reason. The truth was, I had to stay home. I had a play to write. To rewrite. I was having a hard time with it, because truthfully, I didn't see it as flawed as J.R. did. Sure, there were holes. But I didn't hate it.

It was a little past nine when the large pepperoni-and-olive pizza I ordered arrived. I threw my hair into a ponytail and slung a piece of pizza onto a paper plate. I had hours and hours of work ahead of me, so I figured I was entitled to a little bit of greasy cheese. I chomped, chewed, and typed for a good fifteen minutes, by then well into my fourth piece of pizza.

But the Dillan incident continued to distract me. I couldn't get over the picture in my head of him and that other woman. It didn't seem like a business dinner. Or a family dinner. Yet, how would I break this news to my sister? Mom was right. She was more radiant than ever, more normal than ever. This man had totally changed her life. If he was the kind of man who cheated, shouldn't she know it now before she got in deeper?

But what if you're wrong? You'd drop another eight notches down the popularity pole, you know.

Jodie had a bad habit of stating the obvious. But the situation certainly wasn't black and white. There was a lot at stake here, and it went beyond my feelings.

I snatched up the phone, trying to make myself dial Kate's number. But my fingers couldn't get past the first digit. Then I remembered something. In the kitchen, I found the pad of paper that I'd written Dillan's phone numbers down on. There was his cell number. It seemed to glow against the white pages.

Could I do it? Did I really have the guts to call Dillan and confront him? All I could think about was my sister, deceived into thinking Dillan's whole life revolved around her. If everything was a misunderstanding, then Dillan would have no problem explaining himself.

I started to dial and was two digits from completing the phone call when a knock came at my door. I held the phone in my hand, unsure what to do. Whoever it was knocked again. I turned the phone off, wishing (for the thousandth time) they would fix the intercom security system downstairs. Holding the phone in hand, I walked quietly to the door so as not to alert the stranger outside that anyone was home.

I peeked through the hole and nearly dropped the phone from my greasy pizza fingers. Without any hesitation, I swung open the door.

"Hi," Cinco said, smiling that wonderful smile.

"Hi."

"You, um . . ." He dusted his fingers against his left cheek.

"Oh . . ." I whirled around to grab a napkin off the counter. Smashing it against my face, I prayed I got it all, then quickly scrubbed at my hands. When I turned back around, Cinco was still standing at the door. "Hi. Um, what are you doing here?"

"I came to check on you. Can I come in?"

"Check on me?" I had the sudden realization I was in the most ragged clothes I owned, with hair like a rat's nest. "I'm . . . I'm just working." I pointed toward my computer screen as if I needed to prove it.

With a bashfulness I wasn't accustomed to seeing in Cinco, he said, "I sort of glanced at your address when I was holding your car-insurance card. Anyway, we—the class—were a little worried that maybe it was all getting to you."

I waved my hand, which he took as an invitation to step in. He closed the door and waited for a reply. "No. Not at all. I just had a lot of work to do. And . . . my dad, he had a heart attack."

"Is he okay?" Cinco asked, deep concern flashing over his expression.

"He will be. Triple bypass, but he's going to make it."

Cinco nodded and didn't seem to have anything else to say. I wasn't sure what I was supposed to be saying, but not one to let silence linger, I asked, "Would you like a piece of pizza?" I glanced at the box, a little embarrassed by the fact that half the pizza was gone.

"No, thanks. In fact, I ate at class tonight."

"Oh?"

"You would've hated tonight's task. We actually had to go to a restaurant and complain about the food."

"You probably breezed by."

"You know, Leah, I don't go looking for conflict. Sometimes it comes for me, and sometimes I don't handle it all that well. I don't like it any more than the next guy."

"Then why is it so easy for you?"

"It's not easy, but it's part of life, you know? I just learned a long time ago that I wasn't going to get along with everybody."

I offered him a seat in the leather chair and he took it. I sat in the middle of the couch, not ready to get cozy and comfortable. I'd already done that once this week. I couldn't let my guard down twice. So I was truly dismayed to hear myself say, "I want to know what makes you tick."

Chapter 19

[She peeks through the hole to the other side.]

I glanced at the clock and nearly gasped. It was eleven thirty! Two hours had gone by and it seemed like an instant. I had scooted to the end of the couch close to Cinco and made myself cozy with the pillows.

Not a moment of silence, or awkwardness for that matter, had gone by. We'd talked like old friends who needed to catch up on the last ten years. In fact, the only thing that made me remotely aware of the time was the fact that someone else was now knocking on my door.

Cinco said, "Expecting anyone?"

I shook my head. "Not at this time. Or anytime, for that matter." I rose, my knees crackling like my grandmother's used to. I walked to the door, peeking out the hole for the second time this evening.

"Oh . . . no."

"What's the matter?" Cinco asked.

I glanced over my shoulder. "It's my best friend."

Cinco stood. "I can leave. It's late anyway."

"No, please. I"—I looked to the ceiling for help—"don't want you to."

I could feel him smiling behind me. I slowly opened the door.

What I hadn't seen when I peeked through the door was Elisabeth's three children, who were now all gathered up by her legs. She looked horrible, and I'm no parenting expert, but I was pretty sure small children were normally not out this late. They all had dark circles under their eyes. Elisabeth looked as unkempt as I'd ever seen her.

"Are you okay?" I asked.

She moved forward into my apartment, dragging the children in with her. The angle of the wall must've hidden Cinco, as she didn't notice him. "I need your help," she said.

"Oh . . . what for?"

Tears shimmered in her eyes. "I need you to keep the kids for me tonight."

I looked down at their dirty faces. Danny was the oldest, at five. Then Cedric. Then Amelia. Amelia had two lines of snot trailing from her nostrils down to each point of her lip. "Wh-why?" I glanced around her at Cinco, who was watching.

Elisabeth didn't catch the clue someone else was in the room, even as Cedric and Danny saw him and stared like he'd grown a third eye.

"Henry and I had a fight." She sniffled. "I took your advice and tried to tell him how I felt. Well, a few things slipped out."

"He . . . knows about Creyton?" I whispered.

"Look, it's too emotional right now. I don't want to talk about it in front of the kids. Can they stay here tonight? They've already seen and heard enough."

This time Elisabeth saw me glance at Cinco. Her face spasmed with mortified expressions as her voice climbed several octaves. "Who is he?"

"A friend," I said quickly. "Cinco Dublin, meet Elisabeth Bates."

"Hi," Cinco said simply. Then he smiled at the kids. Danny smiled back. Cedric stuck his tongue out. Amelia's tongue busied itself with her snot.

Elisabeth's eyebrows rose. I couldn't help but feel my neck heat up. "I'm sorry," she said, her tone accusatory. "I didn't realize you had company."

"I know Cinco from a class I attend." I redirected her back to her own problems. "Look, Elisabeth, the children have never stayed with me. I'm not sure they'd be comfortable here."

"It's just for one night. Kids adapt. Besides, I wouldn't ask if I wasn't desperate."

Cinco stood and walked to the door. "Leah, I'd better get going. It was great talking with you. I'll see you at class."

I didn't want him to leave. I felt the urge to reach out and grab him, but instead I just nodded and let him go. Anger crept to the surface, but I stifled it, not without some difficulty. Elisabeth held up a sack. "Everything they need is here."

"But . . . what do I feed them?"

"They're fed. In the morning, whatever you have is fine. I'll pick them up by ten, okay?" She bent down and hugged each of them, then left. The door shut and six cranky-looking eyes stared up at me.

I clapped my hands together. "All right. A sleepover at Auntie Leah's!" Cedric belched, Danny rolled his eyes, and Amelia started crying. I wanted to do the same.

It was 2:00 a.m. and the apartment was finally quiet. But not dark. I'd had to leave the hallway light on for the boys, who I put in my bed. They insisted the three of them could sleep together, but I wasn't sure what was appropriate, and after Cedric gave his sister the third wedgie, I figured she would be thankful for the opportunity to sleep away from the boys. But at age three, sleeping on the couch was like a death sentence. She kept insisting she would roll off, and I kept insisting the two-foot drop wouldn't kill her. Finally I made a bed for her on the floor near the couch. (It was only after this that I realized I would've been without a place to sleep if she'd taken the couch.) Then she wanted her stuffed animal that her mother had apparently forgotten to pack. The only thing that I had remotely resembling a stuffed animal was my overly padded bra. She cuddled it in her arms and fell asleep immediately. I just prayed she wouldn't get too attached and want to take it home.

I laid on the couch. My eyes were shut, but my mind was jumping like a live wire. After absorbing the shock that I had three small children sleeping over because my best friend had apparently been caught having an affair, my mind settled into a review of my evening with Cinco.

Every word that poured out of the man's mouth was like the best wine I'd ever tasted. I felt myself be more real with him than anyone I'd ever known. He drew it out of me. He wouldn't sit by and let me be passive. He dug deeper, wanted to know more.

We'd talked a lot about what made him tick. He described what he called the spiritual awakening of his twenties and how it made him fiercely loyal to the causes of Christ. And that, he shared, was where his passion came from, as well as his fervent drive to help people know the truth about God. He made sure I understood that this passion was what made him a magnet for controversy.

I sat and listened, and with each word realized how different we were in so many aspects of our lives. I sat remembering my own spiritual awakening. Church had been a private matter for my parents. Church didn't really come home with us, and saying grace before dinner was the extent of our religious activities there. But one day the words I heard in church stopped being boring and started taking on meaning. They tantalized me with something more. I sensed it was something that could change my life. When I chose to believe in Jesus, my family smothered the budding flame by dismissing my enthusiasm as a fanatical phase—one that would soon pass. When Dad compared me to Kate one evening, I decided to keep that side of my life to myself.

So what made someone like Cinco declare it to the world, and someone like me keep it concealed so as not to rock anyone's boat? I mean, my dad still didn't know I'd become a republican. I was too scared to tell him, yet my political values had never lined up with his. I could remember as early as eight disagreeing with him about the environment.

I rose to go check on the boys. Their arms and legs were tangled with each other and the covers, but they were sleeping soundly. Amelia hadn't moved an inch. My eyes were burning like two matches, and the last thing I remembered was climbing back onto the couch, rolling over, and thinking more about Cinco.

I jumped off the couch, my heart thumping against the wall of my chest. I tripped over the pillows on the floor and yelped. Amelia wasn't there! And then I realized what woke me was the phone ringing. I lurched to my desk to check the caller ID. It was Elisabeth.

"H-hello?" I choked, racing into the bedroom. The boys were just waking up. No Amelia.

"It's me," Elisabeth said with a tired voice.

"Hi. Uh, how are you?"

"The kids okay?"

"Fine," I said, running back into the kitchen. Amelia wasn't there either. I glanced at the lock on the front door, and it was bolted. I looked at the windows in the living room, and they were still locked. She had to be here somewhere.

"They sleep okay?"

"Yes." I ran to the bathroom, but the lights were off and it was empty. I wanted to collapse, but amazing myself, I kept the chipper ring in my voice. "So, how are you?"

"I need you to keep the kids a little longer, if you could."

I stopped in my hallway. "Longer? How much longer?"

"I don't know. Things are bad here, though."

"How bad?"

"Bad."

I closed my eyes. I had so much work to do on my play. How was I going to work with three kids here?

"Elisabeth, it's just that—"

"Henry has left. He packed a suitcase last night."

My eyes flew open. Amelia. Where was she? I checked the coat closet. "I'm sorry, Elisabeth."

"I just need to sort through some things, okay? I can't do that with the kids. They're going to ask where their dad is, and I need to just . . . I just need some time."

I sighed. Should I break it to her now or later that I'd lost her daughter? "Okay, sure. Whatever you need."

"Thank you!" Elisabeth said.

I leaned against the wall. This was going to be great. Just great.

"I'll call you later," she said, "to check on how everything is going. Oh, and Leah?"

"Yeah?"

"Just FYI, Amelia has a tendency to hide under beds, so if you think you've lost her, look under there."

I laughed as if that were the most absurd thought imaginable. "Okay. I'll talk to you later." I hung up the phone and rushed to the bedroom, dropping to my knees like a soldier at boot camp. I lifted up the covers and there, peering back at me, were two big brown eyes. I rolled to my back and tried to catch my breath. When I looked up, another set of brown eyes hung over the top of my bed, looking at me. It was Cedric, and he simply declared, "I'm hungry."

After futile attempts to feed them oatmeal, biscuits, and eggs, I finally gave them each a Snicker's Bar and was done with it. I turned on cartoons and ate cold pizza, chewing through the tough crust like it represented every problem I had in life.

Today was Friday. Tomorrow I would have lunch with Edward. I couldn't believe I was even thinking it, but I was. I was thinking of breaking up with him. The thought had never entered my mind once in the past two years. We never fought. I was never unhappy. He was never unhappy. Life was predictably good.

And then something happened, and I still couldn't identify exactly what it was. But I could definitely blame flaming pancakes.

In all honesty, though, I couldn't imagine saying the words. How could I sit there and explain to him that I needed more flaming pancakes in our relationship when he was agreeing to have lunch on a Saturday?

My thoughts were interrupted by Danny bellowing from the living room, "I'm bored!"

I had not one clue what to do. I loved children. The concept of children. I supported children being born and I never stared at one throwing a fit at the supermarket. My parents never let me babysit when I was growing up because Mother feared I'd gossip about family secrets.

I honestly didn't know what to do with them. And I hadn't been one for praying about trivial problems in my life. My theory was that if I had time to pray about trivial problems, I wasn't doing enough to help God. Though that philosophy appealed to me, it somehow didn't seem healthy. I hadn't taken the time to find out for sure.

And I didn't have time now, either, because there was a knock at my door. The kids jumped up, yelling, "Mommy!" and Danny opened the door before I could get there. The "mommy" chant stopped and their jaws hung open. I didn't do much better with my jaw.

There, standing in my doorway, was Cinco. Holding two huge sacks of toys.

"Hey guys," he said, looking down at the kids. "Leah asked me to pick up a few things for you." He walked in and set the sacks in the middle of the living room. The kids scrambled to their knees. I laughed out of sheer astonishment and gratitude.

"I can't . . . I can't even speak!" I said.

"It sounded like you were caught off guard last night. I thought these might come in handy."

"You went to the toy store?"

"Nope. Grocery store. Those sacks are filled with all those toys they have on the cereal aisle. Don't you remember begging your mother for those stupid two-dollar toys? She'd never let you have 'em, and yeah, they're stupid toys, but we always want what we can't have."

I glanced over at the kids, who were holding up Slinkys, plastic baby dolls, cars, toy guns, and more.

"You have literally just saved my life. How can I ever repay you?"

"Coffee would be nice."

"For you and me both," I said. He followed me into the kitchen. I switched on the coffeepot and then turned to face him. I couldn't stop smiling at him, and he couldn't stop smiling at me.

This went on for the next hour.

Chapter 20

[She gasps.]

It was Saturday morning and I wanted to cry. Not just whimper. And a simple weeping would understate the problem. I wanted to cry that kind of cry that comes from deep in the throat and makes you sound like the girl from *The Exorcist.*

The Slinky had ended up tangled in Amelia's hair. The car lost three out of its four wheels. The baby doll lost its head, which made Amelia freak out and the boys die with laughter. And all the other toys were now being used for things toys aren't supposed to be used for.

Yesterday I'd agreed to another day. I didn't know why. I was going absolutely bonkers as it was. But Elisabeth had sounded so desperate. In the midst of it all, Edward had called. "Let's meet at Billy's."

"Billy's? I've never heard of it before."

"It's at Twelfth and Darcy."

I was trying to keep the kids hushed so I wouldn't have to explain myself. There was no time for protest. Billy's it was.

I managed to trick the kids into distraction by claiming they couldn't touch a bowl of junk I had on the kitchen counter. Danny insisted he would be careful, and pretty soon all the kids were curious about the bowl. I took advantage of the situation and decided to give them a speech about trust. Before I knew it, they were on the floor digging through the bowl of odds and ends that I would have never thought could come in so handy. The junk gave me an hour of peace.

So I took the hour to write. J.R.'s words continued to torment me, and I decided once and for all I would write in a conflict scene. A *big* conflict scene. How corny was it to believe that my plays had some strange prophetic power. I'd been writing my own demise by believing in that nonsense. Did I really think I could write a play without conflict? Sure, it was a little daunting since the play was more personal than my other plays, but once and for all I decided it was time I got over this ridiculous omen and wrote a good old-fashioned conflict scene.

That precious hour passed and I had built up to the conflict. The kids were getting restless, but luckily it was almost time to go drop them off with Elisabeth and meet Edward.

Elisabeth had called and agreed to make the exchange at Sixteenth and Darcy, since it was about halfway between our residences. While trying to get the kids ready and make sure that Amelia didn't have an "accident" (Danny had explained one to me in vivid detail), my mind continued to ricochet between thoughts of Edward and thoughts of Cinco. I tried to think as logically as I could through every implication. For instance, how exactly would I bring home to my senator father a man that had to be introduced by a Spanish numeral? Then again, how exactly could I go on for the rest of my life in such a predictable state? My mind bounced from one question to the next, and I zoned out long enough for the kids to "redo" my hair in a way that would've guaranteed me a makeover on any morning show.

When it was time to leave, I wiped their dirty mouths and hands, put on a little makeup, and then managed to get them to the subway station. The ride took fifteen minutes, and those kids took every second they had to cause some kind of strife. They fiddled and bickered and rubbed everyone the wrong way. I had people give me the evil eye, as if they were my own children and I'd done them a horrible disservice by being their mother.

Finally we got off the T and walked two blocks to Sixteenth and Darcy. I bought the kids each a large sucker and waited near the convenience store for Elisabeth, hoping I wouldn't accidentally run into Edward. He wasn't fond of Elisabeth, and I knew that if he found out I had kept her kids for two days because of her indiscretions, I wouldn't hear the end of it.

As I leaned against the building, waiting, I watched their three tiny faces become stickier and stickier. Did they have any idea why they'd been passed off to Auntie Leah for two days? Did they understand their lives would never be the same? That Daddy was probably never going to come home and live with them again? It broke my heart, and I had to hold back the tears.

This made me think about Edward and his predictability. Was it that bad? Sure, life was destined to be one long and boring schedule, but at least I knew he would be there. Didn't I?

Still, I couldn't shake the feeling I got from Cinco, the buzz that caused me to stop thinking straight.

"Hey."

I looked up and Elisabeth was stepping on the curb. She hugged me, and when she stepped back, I couldn't believe it. She looked like she'd aged ten years. I swore I could even see gray hairs. She glanced at the kids. "They okay?"

"Yeah." I smiled. "They were a delight."

"Good."

"How are you? And Henry?"

She shook her head, tears blocking words. Finally she managed, "I don't know. I don't know what's going to happen." She stared at the ground. "How could I have done this? How could I have been so stupid?"

I took her hand. "It's going to be okay."

She wiped away her tears and then looked at me. "Thanks for doing this for me. You're the best friend I could ever have." She embraced me, then said, "I shouldn't keep you waiting. You're meeting Edward, right?"

I nodded, and before I knew it, I was confessing, "I think I might break up with him."

"What?"

"I know, it sounds crazy. Maybe it is crazy! I don't know."

"I can't even imagine that, Leah. You really might break up with him?"

"I'm not happy. I don't think. Maybe I am happy and don't know it." I covered my face with my hands and took a breath. "I don't even know what I'm going to say when I step into Billy's."

"Billy's?"

"The restaurant."

"I know the place. Are you sure you're meeting there?"

"Yeah . . . why?"

"Oh . . . um, no reason."

"What?"

She shrugged. "It just doesn't seem like the kind of place Edward frequents."

"What kind of place is it?"

She patted me on the shoulder. "I'll let you be surprised. Now, let me get these kids out of your hair."

"Do you want some help?"

"No. I parked just around the corner. You go and enjoy . . . Billy's."

The air became thicker and greasier the closer I got to Billy's. The neighborhood indicated I wasn't here for the fine dining. I was so bewildered I could hardly think about what I would say to Edward. He was going a little overboard on the spontaneity, wasn't he? As I stared up at the big glowing sign that announced Billy's as a "diner," along with the smaller sign below it that announced they were having a double onion rings special, I couldn't shake the feeling that maybe Edward had lost his mind. And come to think of it, I hadn't ever seen Edward eat a hamburger. He wasn't fond of eating things that didn't require utensils.

I opened the wooden door, which creaked and led me into darkness for a few steps until I rounded the corner. At least there was someone there to help me to my seat. "I'm meeting someone," I told the hostess as she grabbed a laminated menu from beneath her stand.

"Edward is waiting for you over here," she said, motioning to her left. I looked and there Edward sat, waving at me. I walked over and the hostess put the menu in front of me and asked me if I wanted a Coke. Edward, to my astonishment, was having a Coke. I had never seen him drink Coke.

"Sure," I said. My hands were trembling underneath the table, but I tried to act as calm as I could. "Hi."

"Hi."

"This is . . . quite a place."

He looked around. "Yeah. A different kind of atmosphere, right?"

I nodded. "How did you hear about it?"

"I asked around. Wasn't sure what a good place for lunch would be."

"Ah."

He held up the menu and looked it over. "Hope you like hamburgers."

"Actually, I do," I said. "And onion rings."

"Really?"

"It's the Southerner in me."

"I thought Southerners liked fried chicken and fried okra."

"That too. Maybe we can save that for next weekend."

He went back to reading his menu. I tried to look over mine, but I didn't have an appetite. I had no idea how I would . . . how I could . . . broach the subject. After the waitress came and took our orders—hamburgers for both of us—I decided I had to at least get my feet wet.

"Edward," I began, "I want you to know how much I appreciate your trying to be spontaneous." And then I noticed Edward's hands were shaking. They were folded on the table in front of him, but they were shaking like he was on a caffeine high. It sidetracked me, because I couldn't for the life of me figure out why he was shaking so badly. Was it because he'd ordered a hamburger? Was this what spontaneity did to him?

I started to say something, but before any words could actually come out, Edward said, "Leah, I need to say something."

I couldn't stop looking at his hands. "What?"

He sighed, and now we were both looking at his hands. "I'm sorry, give me a second." He wiped his mouth. What was happening?

"What is it, Edward?"

He finally met my gaze. "Look . . . I can't keep dating you."

Now my entire insides were shaking. I couldn't believe what I was hearing. "You . . . you can't . . . keep . . ." My eyes blinked at an absurd rate. I took a breath. "Is this because I want you to be more spontaneous?" I asked, my voice rising. "This is about spontaneity?"

"Sort of," he said with a shrug. I wasn't sure I'd ever seen him so flippant as when he said that. He seemed distracted, like there was something more important than breaking my heart. But . . . was he breaking my heart? Wasn't there, deep inside me, a little bit of relief? I tried to search at the same time I tried to decode the man in front of me.

He looked at me. "Leah, I brought you here because I didn't want to do this at one of our usual places."

I fell back into my chair, stunned. He didn't want to do this at one of our usual places? Like have to spend a lot of money on dinner just to break up with me? I felt my eyebrows crashing down with force. Even with a lot of sleep, this was probably more than I could take, but after the two nights I'd had, this was close to unbearable. "This is unbelievable," I breathed. "Why . . . why didn't you want to do this at one of our usual places?" It was the only question I could think to ask. I couldn't imagine there was even a reasonable answer.

"You wanted me to be spontaneous," he said.

I slapped my hand to my forehead. It was throbbing like I'd been hit with an ax handle. I didn't know what to say. I wanted to cry. I wanted to laugh. Instead, my entire body went numb. But when I looked up at Edward, to my confusion, he was smiling.

And then I saw him reach into his pocket. He pulled out a tiny black box. It was like I was watching someone else's life. He opened the black box and there, sitting in the middle of it, was the most beautiful diamond ring I'd ever seen. I gasped and threw my hands to cover my mouth.

"How's that for spontaneous?" he asked. And then I watched as he stood up and took my hand in his. We were both shaking so badly it was hard to hold on. I felt tears rolling down my face as I looked up at him. "I can't go on dating you, Leah. It's time that we secure our future together. It's the right time." He smiled and said, "Will you join me in this new journey of our life by entering into wedlock with me?"

"I . . . I . . . ?" I stared at the ring. Was that Edward's way of asking me to marry him? I assumed he wasn't down on one knee because of the filthy floor beneath us. I glanced around. The entire diner had hushed. And for the first time in my life I felt like I might pass out.

I looked at Edward, who was patiently waiting. I wasn't sure if a full minute had passed or only ten seconds. I'd lost all sense of reality. Edward squeezed my hand as a reminder that he'd just asked me a very important question, which prompted me to do the only thing I could.

"Yes," I squeaked.

Edward nodded approvingly and slid the ring onto my finger. He pulled me to my feet. And he kissed me. Then he hugged me. Then he said, "Look out there." He pointed through a window at the side of the restaurant to a horse-drawn carriage. "That's for us. Come on!"

He pulled me through the restaurant and through the front door. "But . . . but what about . . ." I was pitching my thumb backward. What about the hamburgers? And why was I thinking of hamburgers at this moment?

He laughed and whispered, "That was all part of the ruse. We're going by horse-drawn carriage to a real restaurant."

He helped me into the carriage, which was sprinkled with pink and red rose petals. We were the main attraction on Twelfth Street. I tried my best to enjoy the moment. But deep inside, I was so scared I could hardly speak.

And oddly, still craving onion rings.

Chapter 21

[She lifts her glass.]

The carriage took us three miles to a posh new restaurant we'd never been to before. It was very . . . clubby, and Edward seemed particularly proud of himself. The entire day was a complete shock to me, and at the end of it all I was so numb I could barely feel the kiss Edward planted on my lips.

He took me back to my car, which he'd paid someone in the restaurant to keep metered, and took my left hand into his. "Do you like the ring?"

"I really do." And I did. It was gorgeous.

He couldn't stop smiling. I'd never seen Edward like this. He was actually giddy. Of course, why not? He was engaged. So why wasn't I giddy? I was forcing every smile that appeared on my face.

"You look really tired."

"I am a little. I haven't been sleeping well. I'm, um, behind on my play."

He batted his hand in the air. "Who can think about work at a time like this?"

"Not me," I said, stretching yet another smile across my face.

"So when do you want to get married?"

"We want plenty of time to plan the wedding," I said quickly.

"I can't wait too long," he said with a wink.

"We've got the rest of our lives."

"Right. We do. We do!"

He kissed me again, this time on the cheek, lingering there like we were starring in a romantic movie. Then he stepped back. "I'll let you go for now. But we've got big plans to make. I want this to be the most amazing wedding. We've both waited long enough. We deserve the best."

Deserve the best. Even once I got home, that phrase was all that kept going through my head. Was Edward the best for me? I couldn't look at the beautiful ring without a lump forming in my throat. Surely that was enough of a red flag. But there was a part of me that was happy. I couldn't deny it. I wanted to be married.

It was late afternoon and I had done nothing but pace my apartment. I'd decided not to tell my family about the engagement. Not yet. There would be a right time, but not now. I wasn't sure if there was actually going to be an engagement.

The phone rang. I looked at the caller ID and hesitated. It was Cinco. I held the cordless phone in my trembling hand. Should I answer it? I was now an engaged wom—

"Hello?" I said.

"Leah? Are you okay?" Cinco's voice flooded my ear. I loved his voice. Then I squeezed my eyes shut, hating that I loved it.

"Hi. How . . . how are you?"

"I'm fine. Worried about you, though. How'd it go with the kids?"

"The toys made it bearable." I laughed, pinning the phone between my shoulder and chin and twisting the ring around my finger. It was good to hear from him. Somehow I knew Cinco would have wise words for me if I could only tell him what was going on, but that would mean explaining how I'd somehow become engaged to my brother. "Hey, I'm running out the door. Maybe I can call you later?"

"Sure."

"Okay, thanks. And thanks again for bringing by the toys."

"You're welcome."

I lay on the couch, phone in hand, and drifted into a deep sleep about two onion rings getting married.

I called Edward in the morning to say I'd come down with a cold and couldn't make church. It was a lame excuse, but I couldn't face him. Not yet. I knew I couldn't marry this man. I loved Edward. Or at least I had. But there was more of me that said no than yes. After all, I'd had full intentions of breaking up with him, and now I wore a ring promising to marry him. If I let Jodie speak, she would have a lot of things to say about the transpiring events. But I kept her locked away for now.

I knew Edward wanted to see me this evening, and I'd agreed. But I also knew it would be one of the most painful experiences of my life. I was going to have to give the ring back and tell him I couldn't marry him . . . and that I didn't want to be with him anymore.

I cried a hundred times that afternoon. I knew there was a very real part of me that loved Edward. The relationship hadn't been a fake all these years. I'd just . . . evolved. I wanted more and I realized Edward couldn't give it to me. It seemed silly, but maybe it all really did boil down to flaming pancakes and a show-stopping pink dress.

I'd taken my eighth Advil of the day when a knock came at my door. I prayed it wasn't Elisabeth needing a babysitter. I prayed it wasn't Cinco. I couldn't face him right now. I prayed it was just a figment of my imagination.

But as I peered out the peephole, I saw my sister. I opened the door and she threw her hands up into the air like a cheerleader, jumped up and down and squealed. Then she threw her arms around me and pulled me into a lung-deflating hug. When I brushed her hair out of my eyes, I saw Dillan, standing a few feet behind her, looking at me and smiling. It startled me. I felt like I was looking into the face of the devil. He had that same gentle, engaging expression that had won my entire family over in an instant.

Kate grabbed my shoulders and held me two feet away from her and looked me up and down, then grabbed my left hand and pulled it up to her face. "It's beautiful! Congratulations!"

"Congratulations?" I whispered. Tears were pooling in my eyes and Kate mistook it for sheer happiness. "How did you know?"

"Edward has called the whole world!" she said. "I think he's called every relative we have, Leah. He is out-of-this-world happy. And I am soooo happy for you. This is perfect timing. I'm in love, too, so I can fully appreciate what a great joy this is." She embraced me again.

"Mother . . . Mother and Dad know?"

"Yes! And Mom is actually meeting us at the restaurant. She's leaving Dad for a few hours, if you can believe that."

"What restaurant?"

"We're all going out to celebrate the engagement. Dillan and I are buying. Edward's meeting us there." She scooted me into the apartment. "Go change and get ready. We're meeting them in thirty minutes."

My head started pounding so hard I was only hearing about every fourth word. Kate's hand pressed against my back and pushed me toward my bedroom. I glanced back to see Dillan stepping gingerly toward the couch, apparently avoiding all the toys strewn everywhere.

"But . . . but Kate, listen, I don't think—"

"Look, Leah, I know in the past I haven't been in the position to pay for meals, but things are different now, and—"

"No, it's not that. It's that . . . it's . . ."

I watched Kate rummage through my closet, mumbling that she had to find me something exciting to wear. She finally emerged, and in her hand hung a dress. A pink dress. The pink dress. "This is perfect!"

I waved my hands in front of me and shook my head. "Noooooo, no, no. That's not appropriate." I tried to laugh so I wouldn't burst into tears. "That's too fancy, isn't it? Where are we going again?"

"Dillan recommended this great new restaurant called Mangalos!"

It was over Caesar salads that Dillan finally made eye contact with me. He was sitting across the table, two chairs down, oblivious to the fact that for thirty minutes I'd been staring him down. He was too busy coddling Kate, and it was beginning to irritate me so much that even Edward noticed.

"You okay?" he whispered, leaning into me.

"Fine. How are you?"

"Fine. Perfect." He put his arm around me. I tried to act snuggly, but I couldn't, so instead I pretended I needed to go to the bathroom. Inside the stall, I tried to get a grip. There was too much at stake. My life was tangling more and more into a web, one strand at a time. My conflict resolution class would've demanded I stand up at dinner, declare I wasn't marrying Edward, and enlighten Kate to her boyfriend's indiscretions.

I wasn't quite ready for that, so what would change my dilemma? I was still engaged to a man I was pretty sure I didn't love, and my sister was falling hard for a man who obviously didn't love her. What could I do?

I leaned against the door of the stall and prayed. It was all I could do. I'd spent many years of my religious life following all the rules and being a good and faithful parishioner. But I'd spent little time on my knees, implementing everything I'd learned. Why should I? I'd managed to keep the conflict in my life to such a minimum that I really never needed much divine help.

I was apparently making up for lost time.

I stepped out of the stall, washed my hands to kill more time, dried them twice, then returned to the table. I couldn't solve either of these problems overnight, or over dinner for that matter, but maybe I could make a little headway.

As I took my seat, I noticed that Dillan wasn't engaged in conversation at the moment. I seized the opportunity.

"So, Dillan," I began, and he shifted his attention from his salad to me, "this is a great restaurant. How'd you hear about it?"

"Glad you like it." His smile dripped with innocence, but he avoided the question and stabbed a bite of salad.

"How'd you hear about it?"

He'd managed to stuff his mouth and held up a polite finger as he chewed. *Yeah, you chew. Think up a lie, you . . . you chewer.* Finally he finished and said, "My brother told me."

"Your brother. I didn't realize you had a brother."

He nodded. "Darren."

"Darren."

"My twin."

I almost laughed. His twin. He had a twin. Of course! He had a twin. Kate had mentioned him, but I'd forgotten.

Okay, please. That is so contrived. His twin. That would never fly in a play of yours.

I wanted to tell Jodie to shut up again, but that would've stopped the huge grin from stretching across my face. My intense gaze must've perplexed Dillan. He tried to smile back, but he cleared his throat and shifted in his seat. I wanted to leap across the table and squeeze him, and he seemed to sense that because he pretended to be interested in something on the side of his drinking glass. Maybe his explanation was contrived, but at least it was an answer!

Before I could think too much more about it, I heard a clanging sound and Edward stood up. As elated as I was about the news of Dillan's brother, my heart sank. Edward was going to make an official toast. I glanced at Mother, who had clasped her hands together and looked as proud as she ever had. This was what she wanted for me . . . a happy home, married to a wonderful, reliable man. With Dad's health, this was probably the one thing that was helping her get through the week.

"Leah," Edward said, towering above me as he held his champagne, "I am so excited that you have accepted my proposal. I know this was a long time coming, and you were wonderful to wait patiently for the right time. I realize we're just engaged and haven't even discussed a wedding date yet . . ."

I nodded. That would be the only saving grace, a long engagement so I could wiggle my way out of this in a very planned and prepared way.

But suddenly Edward's face turned very somber. Everyone at the table noticed, and even the restaurant seemed to grow still. His head hung, and I thought for a moment he was going to change his mind about this marriage. And then I realized how humiliated I would be. But before I could continue with my worry, he said, "Leah, you know my dear grandmother, Gammie."

I knew Gammie. She was ninety-seven years old, and looked every day of it. Her skin was deeply wrinkled, with flaps of skin where skin normally doesn't flap. She was bent over like a sunflower too heavy for its seeds, and was known for carrying a different-colored cane every day of the week.

"What about her?"

Edward's hand was now on his heart. "Gammie's health is failing," he said. I thought that was an odd statement, because according to Edward, her health had been failing since she was seventy. Nobody knew how she'd made it this long. "The doctors have told my parents she has only a couple of months to live."

Well, she's ninety-seven. What do they expect?

My thoughts exactly. I was looking up at Edward, wondering how in the world he was going to tie this into a toast about our engagement. Then he said, "Leah, you know how much Gammie means to me. And it would mean the world to me to have Gammie at my wedding. As you know, she paid for my entire education, so it would only be right to allow her this final pleasure and happiness before passing to the other side."

I was nodding, but I was having a hard time figuring out what education had to do with wedding plans and Gammie's happiness.

"So," he said, raising his glass, "I propose that we marry in three weeks!"

"Three weeks!" I gasped. I couldn't even begin to pretend properness.

He smiled. "I know, I know. It sounds impossible. But I've thought of everything, even hiring a wedding planner to help us get everything in order. In fact, all we have to do is tell her what we want, and she'll take care of the rest."

I knew my jaw had dropped in just the way that horrified my mother when I was a child, and an adult for that matter, but I couldn't help it. What was I going to do? I looked at Mother, and she had an eager expression on her face, the likes of which I hadn't seen since the day Dad won the election. She tapped her chin to remind me to close my mouth.

Dad . . . yes, that was it! "Edward, I don't think three weeks will be possible considering my dad's health. Right, Mother?" I tried not to look too desperate as I glanced at her.

She batted the air. "It will be the perfect thing to get him back on his feet!"

I had never felt this sick in my life. Couldn't everybody tell the color was draining out of my face? By the happy looks on their faces, nobody noticed or nobody cared. Edward, still standing, thrust his glass into the air. "May 23 it is!"

I heard the clanging of glasses, one of which was mine. It was the sound of my future shattering.

Chapter 22

[She browses, trying to decide.]

Monday was the longest day of my life. There were twenty-two messages on my answering machine, twenty-one congratulating me on the engagement. I didn't even know I had that many friends. And I had no idea how the news was spreading so quickly.

The twenty-second message was from J.R., wondering about my play. There was a nasty impatience in her voice, and I knew I was in jeopardy of losing her as my agent if I didn't send her something soon. She mentioned twice in her thirty-second message how Peter was calling and calling, asking to see something, and then she stated how she couldn't possibly show him what she had. She hung up with a curt salutation.

So I spent most of the day trying to rework what I had, trying to add as much conflict as my nauseous stomach could tolerate. It wasn't much.

I felt trapped by the reality of my life, but I couldn't escape into my fantasy world the way I usually did.

By Tuesday afternoon, I was a wreck. I had spent as much time on my play as I had plotting my way out of the engagement. I made little progress on either. My tortured thoughts were undone by the ringing of the phone, the first time on this day.

"Hello?"

"Hello, my bride-to-be."

"Hi."

"Surprised I'm calling this time of day?"

I glanced at the clock. "Yes. Aren't you in class?"

"I let class go early today."

"You did?"

"I did."

I had never known Edward to do that before, but there wasn't too much left to shock me now.

"Do you want to know why?" he asked.

"Sure."

"Because you and I are going to go pick out a cake today."

Now, if that's not the icing on the moral dilemma.

No thanks to Gammie, I was now meeting Edward in an hour and a half to pick out a cake for a wedding that was supposed to take place in three weeks. I stopped by Elisabeth's house for help. I had to talk to someone about this. I thought about talking to Father Harper, but I already knew what he would tell me to do. I didn't need guidance on what the right thing was to do; I needed help coming up with underhanded tactics to get there.

"You could fake schizophrenia," Elisabeth said, and not glibly, either, after we sat down at her kitchen table. She was totally serious. Little did she know about Jodie, but I kept my mouth shut. "Cynthia can make an appearance every once in a while, real subtly."

"Who is Cynthia?"

"Your split personality."

I rolled my eyes. "Elisabeth, right now Edward is so giddy and Cupid-afflicted that if I introduced him to Cynthia, Jan, and Carol, he'd think the more the merrier. Honestly, I've never seen Edward like this. Ever. It's an entirely new side of him that's just now coming out. Maybe it's always been there; maybe marriage is doing something to him—I don't know."

Amelia tugged on Elisabeth's pant leg. She wiped Amelia's nose with her thumb and forefinger. "Maybe you should give this new-and-improved Edward a shot."

"It's not . . . it's not a new-and-improved Edward. It's just Edward on a temporary high."

"You don't know that. Maybe this is the real Edward." She sighed and sent Amelia off to play in the backyard where she could see her. "Look, Leah, I wish I'd known the side of Henry I saw last week."

"What side?"

"The side that showed some passion in life, you know? Some passion about me. When Henry found out about, you know, he got so upset and started ranting and raving about family and love and trust. I didn't even know the guy had it in him. I didn't think he cared that much. What I'm trying to say is that maybe this is bringing out a better side of Edward, a side you didn't even know existed before now."

"But if that's true, it scares me that it takes such extreme measures to bring this side out. You know that pink dress I bought for the party I went to with Edward?" She nodded. "He hated it. He was embarrassed to see me in it. And nothing has been the same since."

"Why didn't you tell me?"

I sighed. "You helped me pick it out. Plus, you've had . . . a lot going on. And truthfully, I wasn't even sure I was right about the whole thing. Maybe the pink dress was too much."

"You looked beautiful in it, Leah. Absolutely stunning."

"At the end of the night, I felt like an idiot."

"If that's how Edward made you feel, then you're right to question this."

"You think so?"

"Yeah. I think so."

I stared at the tile. It all seemed so unbearably real sitting in Elisabeth's kitchen, talking about it.

"I feel like I've written my own doom," I finally said.

"What do you mean?"

I shook my head and shrugged off the comment. I looked at my watch. "I've got to go. I'm meeting Edward in twenty minutes."

"You're going to break it off?"

"Yeah. I've got to."

I stood and Elisabeth hugged me. Then she said, "If things go badly, don't forget, Cynthia is just one creepy voice away from a sure victory in this situation."

Spring sunshine warmed my shoulders as I walked down the sidewalk. Freshly sprouted leaves adorned the trees lining the boulevard. Birds twittered and rustled. The afternoon was perfect. Perfect for people in love. I was in desperate need of a barf bag.

I stopped in front of David and Shelley's, a quaint corner shop with a gold awning perched above arched glass windows that framed beautiful displays of three-, four-, and five-tiered wedding cakes. I looked at them through the windows. One boasted golden yellow frosting with slightly lighter-hued roses stacked on each tier of the cake. Shimmering glitter gave the appearance of soft dew resting on each petal. I had hoped Edward would be waiting outside for me, but when I glanced beyond the cake, I could see him browsing inside.

I stayed there and watched him. He looked like a stranger to me, and it made me unbearably sad. But this man that I'd dated for more than two years seemed at best like a distant relative. I knew what I had to do. I stood there for a full minute, praying for strength. When I looked up, Edward was watching me, and he waved me in with a bright smile on his face.

I clutched my handbag and headed inside, rehearsing exactly how I would approach Edward. I needed to be kind but firm. *Kind but firm. Kind but firm.*

Immediately a lusciously sweet aroma filled my nostrils and swept me into a momentary state of sugary delusion. I pictured myself in a gorgeous wedding dress, taking a huge bite of something cream-filled and moist and—

"Hi," he said, taking my hand. "I see sugarplums dancing in your eyes."

I couldn't help but smile. There was definitely something sugary dancing in my eyes.

Kind but firm? You're already melting like chocolate under a heat lamp.

"They've got the most amazing samples," Edward said, guiding me toward the counter where two women waited to help us. "I've already tried the buttercream, and I swear it is the best cake I've ever had in my life. Maybe we could go all out and choose a different flavor for each tier!"

"How many tiers do we need?" I said with a nervous laugh.

A sloppy, goofy grin covered his face. I'd never seen anything sloppy on Edward. He was the most pulled-together man I'd ever known. "Maybe eight!" He laughed.

I managed a jolly chuckle that I knew made Jodie roll her eyes. I wished she would stop pressuring me. It was all about the timing. I had to wait for the right time to segue from wedding cakes to permanent breakup. It was not going to be easy.

Edward pulled me from one display to the next, talking with so much excitement I felt like he'd just discovered a new . . . well, whatever it is physicists discover. I found myself not just looking at the cakes, but looking at him. I'd never seen him smile this much, at least with teeth showing. He was a very reserved person. So every time he looked at me with that silly grin, my heart pitter-pattered, and I hadn't felt that since the third week we were dating.

I tried to ignore my heart by focusing on the wedding cakes. A woman named Della was now accompanying us around the room, pointing out cake features like we were in the market for a Volvo. I didn't know there were so many different options when it came to wedding cakes.

I knew I would never get the chance I needed with Della streaming behind us. After a few minutes, I said to her, "Maybe you could give us a moment to think some of these wonderful options through."

"Of course," Della said, stepping back and returning to her spot behind the counter. Edward was still grinning.

"I love the one with the three tiny tiers on top," he said, pointing to a cake in the corner. "But I also love the one that is covered with roses, where they look like a waterfall cascading down the side." He squeezed my hand. "Speaking of waterfalls, I think you're really going to enjoy our honeymoon."

A nervous wheeze crept into my chest. "Honeymoon?" I hadn't even thought of a honeymoon. How could he do all of this in three weeks?

"We'll talk about that later. After we're finished here, we're going to meet Cynthia."

Cynthia? A flush of heat strangled my neck. How did he know about Cynthia? Maybe I was going crazy. Maybe I was the only one who didn't really know I had a split personality.

I could hardly get the question out, but I managed to ask who Cynthia was, bracing myself for an answer I didn't want to hear.

"The wedding planner," he said. "You'll love her. She's really emotional and high-strung like you are." He slapped his hands together. "So, if you could have any cake in the world, what kind of cake would you want?"

Steady. *Steady.* I looked into his dream-filled eyes and tried to remind myself that as charming as Edward was being inside this glorious house of sugar, there was another side of him, a side I had known much longer than this one . . . a side that functioned from day to day with a passionless, predictable determination to structure every single element of his life.

"I have to say," Edward continued, "I'm very partial to the buttercream. I want you to taste it, and the chocolate marble too. I know how much you like chocolate, and—"

"Edward . . . Edward, wait."

He slowed his rambling to a crawl and glanced down as I took his hands in mine.

"What? What's wrong? You don't like buttercream?"

"It's not that."

"Then what?"

Kind but firm. A part of me wanted to scrunch up my hair and slip into something more Sybil, but instead I simply gathered up as much courage as I could. "Edward," I said, as assuredly as possible considering my neck was hot enough to warm a small office building, "we need to talk."

Chapter 23

[She clutches the blouse.]

I stood at the counter of Olivia's, one of the nicest clothing stores for men and women in the district, a two-hundred-dollar purple silk blouse in my clutches. The woman behind the counter, hardly wide enough to cast a shadow, glared at me with severe eyes made worse by how tightly her hair was pulled on top of her head.

And I hadn't even said a word yet.

But "Greta," as her gold-plated name tag read, sensed I didn't belong. I found it amazing how easily this could be sensed. Belonging in this world wasn't just about the expensive clothes. It was an attitude.

I didn't let Greta's glare distract me, though. I slapped the blouse on top of the counter with such force that Greta took a step backward. I looked behind me. The class, mingling among the clothing racks as Marilyn had instructed, was stealing glances, watching and waiting to see what I would do, to see if I would pass the test.

Over at the men's counter, there was Robert, also trying to complete his task, which was to argue that the backside of a new pair of slacks was cut too small and that he'd blown it out not because he had a big butt, but because the slacks were too small. The man behind the counter had such an astonished look on his face that I almost laughed.

I focused back on Greta.

"What is the problem, again?" she asked in her prissy accent.

"I decided this blouse is too expensive." That was my task. To return a high-priced item to a high-priced store, claiming I couldn't afford it.

Greta looked down at the blouse, her neatly trimmed and lined eyebrow arching with immediate disapproval. "You decided this is too expensive," she said slowly, eying the price tag.

"I want my money back."

"Ma'am, returning a blouse because it is damaged is appropriate, but returning it because it's too expensive is simply not acceptable. Obviously," she said, raising her hands and gesturing toward the store, "this is an expensive store."

"I realize that. But I want my money back. I made the mistake of believing I could afford this, and I can't. Here's the receipt."

The woman surveyed the receipt, and I glanced over at Marilyn, who looked surprised at how forthright I was being. I returned my gaze to Greta.

"And you want to know something else?" I asked her.

Greta looked like she did not want to know something else.

"This blouse is not worth two hundred dollars."

"It's a designer blouse," Greta retorted.

"I don't care if it's made of gold; it's just a stupid blouse. I can get this same kind of blouse at Wal-Mart for fourteen dollars. Did you know that? In purple too."

"Let me assure you," Greta said, "that you cannot. This is silk. Real silk."

"Synthetic silk actually feels better. Maybe it's just me. Plus you can wash it." I pointed to the receipt. "And I'd like cash back, if you don't mind." I realized my voice was very loud, because when I glanced around the room again, everyone, including the class and the other customers, was watching me.

"I'm going to need to talk to the manager," Greta said.

"You can't think for yourself?" I asked.

Greta's eyes narrowed. "Fine." She opened the cashier's drawer. "But let me just ask, ma'am, that you don't shop here anymore until you can afford the clothing."

The muscles in my jaw protruded as Greta counted back one hundred and eighty-two dollars to me, with some change.

"Wait a minute!" I snapped. I could feel the entire store grow still and quiet. "You shorted me!"

I felt something brush against my arm. Marilyn had stepped up beside me, but I ignored her. I was handling this just fine. I certainly wasn't going to be ripped off by a snooty, overpriced store like this.

"Ma'am," the woman said, becoming flustered as she, too, realized everyone was looking at her, "there is a ten percent restocking fee on all returned items."

"A restocking fee?" My voice climbed. Marilyn touched my arm, but I shrugged her off. "A restocking fee? Are you kidding me?" I grabbed the blouse off the counter.

"Ma'am!" the woman snipped. I whirled around, found an empty hanger on the holding bar at the end of the counter, put the blouse on it, and marched to the back wall, where I hung it with the rest of the overpriced purple blouses.

"There!" I shouted. "I've restocked it for you. So you can give me all my money back!"

Marilyn was touching my arm again. "Leah, you've really done just fine. We don't need all the money back. This was just an exercise in—"

"I want the rest of my money back," I said, staring directly into Greta's smoky-lined eyes.

"A restocking fee covers more than just hanging up the blouse," Greta replied sternly.

"Like what?" I crossed my arms. This was going to be good. "Does a restocking fee cover the number of footsteps it takes you to cross the floor to go hang it up? Does it cover the number of keystrokes it takes your fingers to reenter it into the system? I can see how that could cost well over fifteen dollars."

"Ma'am, you're extremely out of line here," Greta said, looking at Marilyn as if she could help. Didn't she wonder why Marilyn, who was dressed this evening like she might be an extra from the movie *Flashdance,* was standing there with me? I looked over at the men's counter where Robert had finished up and started to walk out. I spotted Cinco, who was standing by the ties, watching me.

"I'm an unhappy customer," I said, my jaw thrust forward. "Since when is an unhappy customer out of line?"

"You're unhappy because you don't make enough to shop here," Greta said, her words as cold as her eyes. "So why don't you try Wal-Mart next time? You can probably get a good two-for-one deal, all right?"

I stomped my foot, causing both Marilyn and Greta to jump. "I am *not* leaving this store until you refund my entire money to me!"

Marilyn took my arm. "Come on, Leah; it's time to go."

"What?" I asked as Marilyn swiftly removed me from the store by way of firm grip on my biceps. "I'm solving a problem here. And her name is Greta!"

Marilyn stopped once we got to the corner, and the entire class followed closely behind. Marilyn looked like she'd just witnessed a horrific crime. The rest of the class stood still and quiet, encircling us.

"I was on a roll in there," I complained. The class looked at me with wide eyes. "What? You're all acting like I wasn't solving the problem. I was solving the problem."

"Addressing conflict isn't always just about solving the problem, Leah," Marilyn said. "Robert was able to get his money back while remaining calm and collected."

"I was calm and collected!" I said, realizing in a detached way that I was shouting. "I just didn't think it was fair that they charge a restocking fee! Robert blew his britches out! Now, that's worth a restocking fee!"

"The idea of the exercise was to confront an embarrassing situation with grace and dignity," Marilyn said.

"What did you think I was doing back there?" I asked, throwing up my arms.

"Leah, you don't really seem like yourself tonight," Marilyn tried. "Are you okay?"

"I'm fine. And I would like to take issue with your claim that I did not handle myself with grace and dignity. It takes a lot of grace and dignity to point out that Wal-Mart sells purple blouses too." I shot each class member a confident smile.

"Now," I said, "if you would like a prime example of how not to handle oneself with grace and dignity, I would be more than happy to provide an example."

Marilyn opened her mouth to say something, but I cut her off by thrusting my left hand out into the middle of the crowd. I waved my fingers to help them notice the ring. Several oohs and aahs indicated everyone had taken full notice.

"A prime example of not handling yourself with grace and dignity would be to tell your boyfriend of two years you want to marry him when in fact you really don't want to marry him. Now, that is neither graceful nor dignified. Especially when you continue with the lie well into wedding cake plans and picking out invitations." I twiddled my hand again, just for effect. "Yes, that's right. As you can see, I've learned a great deal in my conflict resolution class, so much so that I'm going to end up marrying a man I don't love simply because I can't stand to hurt his feelings." I raised a finger. "But, I did pick out a fabulous cake! Oh, you can't even imagine it. As far as unique goes, this, well, this takes the cake. It's hot pink. I didn't even know they made hot pink. Sure, my fiancé was a little worried it might be too much, but I don't think anyone's even going to notice the color due to the Olympic event-like ring of fire that will be surrounding each tier."

I looked around. Everyone was staring at their feet, humiliated for me, I was sure. Everyone except Cinco. He was staring at the ring, and then he looked me in the eye. Shame overwhelmed me. I could tell he was hurt.

With my voice cracking, I said, "Now, if you'll excuse me, I've got to go decide what kind of wedding dress I want to wear to the wedding of my nightmares. Good evening." And with that, I strolled past the class, past Olivia's, and to my car, where I locked myself in and had myself a good cry.

I had not been able to do it. I wimped out. And not only that, I was so horrified at myself that when it came time to pick out the cake, I totally lost my mind. Edward wondered out loud if the cake was too much, but I told him modern wedding cakes were an expression of creativity. So that's what we ordered. A hot pink cake set aflame. It looked like a Las Vegas sideshow.

But to Edward's credit, he just seemed happy to be picking out a cake. Deep inside, I knew I'd tried to ambush the whole thing by ordering the most repulsive cake I could find. And I knew Edward had a strong aversion to hot pink.

My plan had backfired, though. Edward thought the fire was cool, even though he didn't catch my joke about my finally getting my flaming pancakes. I'd told the joke on the way to Cynthia's. She'd already drawn up our wedding invitation and was just missing our guest list, which Edward promised to pull off the spreadsheet he'd created the year we sent out joint Christmas cards.

Cynthia had even planned out the ceremony, including the music, reassuring us that of course anything could be changed to our liking, that her plan was just a starting point.

A starting point?

All I could think was that it was an ending point . . . to life as I knew it.

But how could I complain? I wasn't a strong enough person to stop all the nonsense. Every time I would dredge up an ounce of courage, Edward would mention Gammie and how all of her dreams for him were getting ready to come true.

After an excruciating half hour with Cynthia, I couldn't stand to hear about wedding plans anymore and made the excuse that I needed to leave for the conflict resolution class. Why I thought that would be a good place for me to go, I couldn't understand. Maybe I needed to prove something to myself.

I only proved I was a royal idiot.

As I drove home on this clear night, I turned on my windshield wipers. The sound drowned out all the sniveling I was doing, and the squeaking noise distracted me from thinking about anything hot pink.

When I returned home, there was a message from my dad, congratulating me and telling me he was sorry he missed the dinner, but that he would be coming home from the hospital Thursday.

I fell onto the couch, more ashamed of myself than I'd ever been. I was picking out cakes and designing wedding invitations like a woman in love. How could I do this to Edward? To myself? How could I have become this big of a coward in life? Was I willing to throw away my life's happiness because I was scared of confronting the truth?

I curled my knees to my chest, hoping Cinco would call, but he didn't. I prayed Edward wouldn't call, and thankfully he seemed to have had his fill of me. The phone was silent, my apartment was silent, and the whole city seemed silent. But inside my mind, one horrible scenario chased another. I rolled onto my back and stared at the ceiling, tears dropping down both of my temples and wetting the couch on either side of my head.

"God," I whispered through the quiet night. But that's all that came out. What else could I say? I needed his help, but did I really want it? Didn't God have a history of shaking things up? Really shaking things up? I'd tried so hard in my life to make sure nothing was shaken or stirred or rocked or messed up. With one prayer, God could undo it all.

You know, you're doing a pretty good job of stirring and shaking all by yourself. If you're not careful, you're going to end up with one funky martini.

I knew I couldn't shut Jodie up. Not tonight. So I just let her talk. And she did. Rambled until daybreak, when I finally opened my eyes. I looked at the clock. It was 7:00 a.m., which was strange since I hardly ever woke that early. I sat up, and immediately noticed how refreshed I felt. I thrust my arms to the ceiling and stretched until my back popped. My first instinct was to go turn on the coffee. After all, this wasn't really my time of morning. But surprisingly, I didn't even feel groggy, nor did I feel particularly depressed.

I felt normal.

I sat there for a moment, wondering why. I was still engaged to Edward. I still had a crush on Cinco. Nothing had changed from just a few hours before.

I decided to make coffee anyway. My body was probably just in shock. I was pouring the water into the coffeemaker when the phone rang. I didn't look at the caller ID.

"Hello?" I hoped it was Cinco. Mother's voice dashed that hope.

"Hi, Leah. How is my newly engaged daughter?"

The reality of my crisis began to come back. "Hi, Mother. I'm fine." I glanced at the clock. Why was she calling this early? "Is everything okay?"

"Wonderful! They're releasing your father today, thank the good Lord."

Today? "A day early! That is fantastic."

"A day early? No. This is when they'd planned to."

"On Wednesday?" Maybe I'd misunderstood Dad's message.

"I woke you up, didn't I?"

For once, no. "No, why?"

"Well, honey, you seem a little groggy."

"Groggy? Why do you say that?"

"Well, dear, because it's Thursday."

I dropped the phone. *Thursday?* I'd slept through Wednesday? I slumped onto the counter, trying to make sense of it. That meant I'd lost an entire day! A day of writing! Of . . . of . . . I glanced at my answering machine. It was blinking. People had called!

I remembered the phone and quickly picked it up.

"Dear, are you there?"

"I'm here," I said, squeezing my eyes shut. I would have to work doubly hard today to catch up on my play.

"Anyway, the reason I'm calling is to see if you could meet us at the hospital and drive my car back to the house. I'm calling for a driver today so I don't have to worry about anything, but I don't want the car stuck at the hospital."

No . . . no . . . Not today, of all days!

"Leah?"

"Sure, Mother, no problem. I'd be happy to."

"All right. Meet us at the hospital at eleven, all right?"

"I'll be there."

I hung up the phone and listened to the coffeemaker gurgle. Then I punched my answering machine.

"Hey, Leah, it's Edward. Wanted to just touch base with you about a couple of things concerning the wedding. Call me around six; I should be home. Thanks. Love you." *Beep.* "Leah, it's J.R. I need you to call me as soon as you get this message. Thank you." *Beep.* "Leah . . . it's me. Where are you? Maybe out shopping for that wedding dress, huh? Can't wait to see you in it. Well, if you get in before eight thirty, call me. If not, call me tomorrow before I leave for work, okay?"

I glanced at the clock. I had just enough time to call him. But I hesitated. I was getting so tired of playing the game. I'd just slept through an entire day. Hadn't I had enough? I dialed his number, praying for a miracle, like God speaking through me. No, *for* me. That would be convenient.

"Hello?"

"Hi."

"Hey, you," he said in his new gushy voice. "You got my message?"

"Yeah, sorry I'm just now calling."

"Well, I figured you were out shopping for your wedding dress."

I gulped loud enough that he was sure to have heard it. "Edward, listen, about that—"

"Cynthia can help you with that too. I don't know if women want help with that or not, but she can help. I'd be happy if you came down the aisle in blue jeans and a T-shirt . . . well, not really. People say that, you know, but it's more a figure of speech for the idea that I'm just happy to marry you. But what can I say? I'm a traditionalist about that sort of thing. Other than being white with lace, though, I really don't care."

I held my face in one hand as I held the receiver in the other. I hated lace, for one thing. But I couldn't focus on that right now.

"Edward, don't you think . . . ," I hedged, and I could hear him breathing. I imagined him glancing up at his wall clock, realizing he was getting ready to be late. It was exactly 3.2 minutes before he had to leave. How could I break off an engagement that quickly? Or maybe I was fooling myself. Maybe it would take less than thirty seconds. Could I bear that? Edward hanging up on me and never talking to me again?

"What is it? I've got about three minutes before I need to leave for work."

I smiled. There was something to be said for this kind of predictability. "It's nothing. We can talk later. I've got to go help Dad home from the hospital."

"Is he doing better?"

"Yeah. Expected to fully recover," I said, closing my eyes at that statement. I was afraid this relationship was not destined for the same optimistic outcome.

"Okay, well, listen, maybe we can get together tonight and—"

"I've got the class," I blurted. Yeah, like I really intended on going.

"You're really still going to that. Amazing."

"It was your idea."

"I know, I know," he said lightheartedly. "I just didn't think you'd be this . . . excited about it."

"It's not exciting. Only helpful."

"Helpful in what way?"

"You better go. You've got .8 minutes before you're running late."

"Oh, right. I'll talk to you later on, okay?"

"Bye."

I stared at my coffee. I needed something stronger than coffee but not as threatening as alcohol.

I grabbed my keys and headed for the Godiva outlet. It didn't matter that I would have to wait two hours before it opened.

Chapter 24

[She starts out whispering.]

I was crying. Hard. I was sobbing goo and liquid out of all the orifices in my face, but I didn't care. I had to let some things out, and surprisingly, the class, sitting in a neat circle with Marilyn at the helm, looked as if this was fully expected and they were exactly the right people on whom to unload. I even spilled the beans that the mysterious kidney-disease-stricken brother of mine was actually Edward, my fiancé. Getting the lie off my shoulders felt good, even though I noticed that Cinco didn't look too happy. But he also didn't look surprised.

I could feel myself splotching, but I never made a move to cover my neck. After all, my face was doing plenty to keep their attention.

I threw up my hands. "So I don't know what to do. I feel like I'm in an impossible situation. I'm going to hurt so many people, but my life's happiness is at stake here!"

Marilyn moved into the empty seat next to me, put a packet of tissues in my lap, and patted me on the shoulder. "First of all, Leah, it's good to let this all out. Obviously you've been holding in a lot of emotion for a long time."

I tried to see her through my teary eyes, fumbling to extract a tissue. "You have no idea. I've never felt I had the right to express emotion. I might hurt someone's feelings."

"That's been your entire concern all these years? Others' feelings?" Carol asked, the loudest she'd ever spoken before. "That's truly beautiful."

But Marilyn said, "I disagree. I don't think it's quite as noble as that. No insult intended, but I think the person you've been protecting is you."

I didn't know what to say. I didn't know if it was true. I would've liked to think my intentions were motivated by others.

"But it *is* natural," Marilyn added. "We all have an instinct inside of us that makes us want to protect ourselves. But it's impossible to do. You can do it for so long, maybe, but eventually it will all catch up to you."

Glenda said, "It's not only caught up with her; it's beaten her to a bloody pulp."

I took that as Glenda's attempt at sympathy.

Marilyn returned to her seat. "We're going to scratch the lesson plan today and work out this problem. Leah, I think what you need is practice. You've never stood up for yourself, you've never voiced your opinion . . . you simply need to practice. So that's what we're going to do. Practice. And we're all going to help you through it."

"How are you going to do that?" I blew my nose and set the tissue packet on top of my handbag.

"Well, we're going to do a little role-playing. Now, we need someone to play Edward."

My eyes widened as I glanced around the circle. I looked at Cinco and he said, "I'll do it."

Before I had a chance to argue, someone brought a chair and set it in front of me. Cinco quickly plopped down in it, his eyes focused and steady. *Confident. Always so stinking confident.*

I cut my eyes to Marilyn. "You know, I think Carol might be a better pick for Edward. She has blonde hair and . . . and the same color eyes and—"

"I think Cinco will be just fine," Marilyn said knowingly. I looked at Cinco, blushing my way through an apologetic smile. He smiled back. Sort of.

"Now, Leah, where would you feel most comfortable breaking off this engagement to Edward?"

"In a morgue. I'd be dead, so that would make it pretty easy." I sighed when no one laughed. "His apartment."

"Okay. Why?"

"Well, it's isolated. Nobody else around, plus I could leave on my own terms, and I wouldn't have to wait for him to leave."

"All right. Then we're going to set this in a crowded restaurant."

"What?"

"It's a neutral place. That way if things go unexpectedly when you really break off the engagement, you'll be prepared for anything."

I swallowed and looked at Cinco, who looked eager to get started. Marilyn assigned Glenda, of all people, to be the waitress, and then gathered the rest of the class to the side.

I searched my feelings for a moment, trying to identify the exact place humiliation was hiding. But to my surprise, I didn't really feel humiliated. I felt relief. If I could just say the words, even in pretend, maybe I'd find the courage to really do this thing.

I swept the hair out of my face and sat up tall, ready for my new role in a performance that was sure to be Oscar-worthy. From the side, Marilyn actually said, "Action!" I had to laugh. But Cinco was taking his role a little too seriously. Concern now plagued his normally placid expression. I tried to settle into the role-play.

"Edward," I began, "I wanted to tell you why I brought you here, to this restaurant."

"I assumed it's to celebrate our upcoming wedding," Cinco said, a little too cynically for my taste.

I took in a breath. This was more nerve-racking than I thought it would be. "It is to talk about that."

"Good. Because my whole life revolves around this marriage now. It's all I think about, all I dream about."

I tried not to roll my eyes. Edward wasn't quite that pathetic. Cinco reached out and took my trembling hands, startling me, then distracting me. I suddenly knew what it felt like to have my hands in Cinco's. It felt . . . right. But then again, he wasn't Cinco. He was Edward . . . or playing Edward.

Concentrate, will you? Let's get on with this thing. It's actually pretty entertaining.

I gritted my teeth and tried to offer a casual smile. "Anyway, what I'm trying to say is that . . . well . . ." The words were on the tip of my tongue. Just one hefty push of courage, and I would say them out loud.

"May I take your order?" I whipped my gaze upward, and there Glenda stood, with an imaginary pad of paper in her hand, smiling and pretending to chew gum.

Cinco let go of my hands. He said, "I'll have the"—he looked at me—"chicken."

I narrowed my eyes at him. "I'll have the bull," I said.

Glenda raised an eyebrow. "I realize you're from the South, but we don't serve bull here."

"Oh, that's too bad," I said, avoiding Cinco's amused face by pretending to look over the menu. "Okay, then I suppose I'll have the . . . triple-garlic medallions."

Everyone looked disgusted, but what could I say? The garlic might help my cause. Glenda walked off and Cinco said, "So, there's something on your mind, besides making me the happiest man on earth?"

I wiped my mouth with my pretend napkin, which ended up

just being the back of my hand, and with all the strength I ever had in me, I looked Cinco—Edward—right in the eyes and said, "I don't want to marry you."

The room grew completely silent, but all I could do was laugh. I actually said it! I said it out loud! "I don't want to marry you," I said again, holding my breath to contain my wildly beating heart. This was like riding a roller coaster. I engaged Cinco's eyes. "I can't marry you."

"Why not?" Cinco asked, feigning a wounded expression.

"You're not right for me, Edward," I said, the words rolling off my tongue as easily as if I were making weekend plans.

"You've been with me over two years, and you're just now figuring this out?" Cinco said, his voice growing angry. It didn't deter me.

"Yes. And I'm sorry. I am. But Edward, sometimes you don't realize that a person isn't right for you until you start thinking about the rest of your life. I need someone who is . . ." I looked into Cinco's eyes, and we connected so strongly for a moment that I lost all concentration. I couldn't even remember what I was saying.

"You need someone who is what?" Cinco asked softly.

I wanted to reach across our imaginary table and take his hands again, but instead I simply said all I knew to be true. "Someone who will make me the best person I can be."

Now, wasn't that poignant. It almost sounded like a line from a movie. I couldn't help the self-satisfied smile that I knew was spreading across my face. Everyone commented on the good job I did. I looked up at Cinco, expecting to be met with a congratulatory expression from him. Instead, he said, "Speaking of that . . ."

"Of what?"

"The best person you can be."

"What about it?" There was something odd in his tone.

"You lied to me."

I cut my gaze sideways. Everyone was still watching, so I tried to keep the mood light. But Cinco's brow was heavy across his dark eyes.

"Lied to you?" I noticed I had that same ring in my voice that my mother used to indicate a mood change was in order.

"You told me Edward was your brother. But he wasn't. Just wondered if you wanted to address that now or later?"

All the applause and "good jobs" that lingered in the air fell to the ground with a thud. I wanted to glance around the crowd and smile as I normally would when assuring people that despite the humiliating situation, I was "perfectly fine." But I knew this crowd wouldn't buy it. So I cleared my throat, ignored Cinco, looked at Marilyn, and said, "I'm not quite over the hump yet. Can we have two people play my parents?"

I called Mother after class to see if she and Dad were still up, and asked if I could come by. Mother seemed to want me to. With Lola's untimely vacation, she sounded nervous about being all by herself to take care of Dad. I'd helped them home from the hospital earlier that day, but Dad had pretty much just gone to bed. Mother told me on the phone that he'd slept nearly seven hours, but now he was awake and propped up on the couch.

As I drove to my parents' house, I was still reeling from class. I couldn't believe Cinco had humiliated me like that. What he did was at the very least inappropriate. But Marilyn had talked a lot about keeping conflict in its place, not allowing it room to grow inside my head. So I did my best not to think about it.

When I got there, I went in the back door, through the kitchen. Mother was standing near the stove. "Hi," she whispered. "I'm just making your father some tea. Want some?" I could barely make out what she was saying, but I gathered from the teakettle in her hand that she was offering me a hot beverage.

"Sure," I said, joining her at the stove. "Why are you whispering?" I whispered back.

"Your father. He's very fragile."

"Do you have to whisper?"

She nodded. "Yes. And I'm keeping all the lights low, so don't go flipping switches all the way through the house." She handed me a large mug. "This is chicken broth. Why don't you take it to him. I'll bring the tea in a little bit. You want sugar?"

I nodded, a little taken aback by the lengths Mother was going to. "What, exactly, did the doctor tell you to do once he got home?"

"He said absolutely no excitement."

"So he was referring to things like golf and lap dancers, right?"

Mother didn't find that funny. I wiped the smile off my face. "Seriously, Leah, he's still in a frail state. I have to do everything within my power to make sure he stays calm and collected. I'm forbidding him to take any phone calls until next week, at the earliest." She waved me on into the family room with the chicken broth.

There was Dad, propped up by fluffy pillows, staring blankly at the television. He still looked pale, but when he saw me he smiled that familiar, easy smile I'd convinced myself he reserved just for me.

"Hi, honey, I didn't even hear you come in." He tried to sit up. "What you got there?"

"Chicken broth," I said apologetically.

He groaned. "I have no appetite, and your mom is trying to force-feed me." I set the chicken broth on the table next to him and joined him on the couch. He didn't look frail or feeble. He just looked tired.

I'd performed perfectly at class when telling my parents that I was not going to marry Edward. Of course, Mother was played by Carol, who sympathetically nodded her head the entire time. And Pastor Ernest played Dad. He just hugged and consoled me, even though I didn't shed a tear and actually became pretty invigorated by how I handled the situation.

But it was from practicing with Cinco that I gained a confidence

I never knew I had. And after all, wouldn't my parents want me to be happy? That's what Marilyn said. She told me I was being played by "fear and scenario," as she called it, where I allowed a fear to play scenario after scenario in my head. It was true. I'd spent hours doing it with Edward and my parents, and Jodie, I realized, was not helping the situation by adding her unwanted commentary.

Dad patted my knee. "So, any new wedding news?"

I smiled. "I just saw you a few hours ago."

"I wasn't in too talkative of a mood, though," he said. "I want you to know I really am happy about this wedding, though I've never heard of one being planned this quickly. But, Edward has assured me that this wedding will be worthy of a senator's daughter and that this wedding planner has even done celebrity weddings before. He assures me you'll be well taken care of."

"Um . . . how many times have you talked to Edward?"

"A couple, I guess. He called your mother to get phone numbers of all our relatives. He's really over-the-top happy."

Mother entered the room, bringing the tea. She served Dad his, but not before blowing on it and reminding him in a whisper to be careful because it was hot. Dad shot me a look. I tried to hide how nervous I was becoming. I was losing my confidence. Yet this was not going to be as hard as telling Edward, and in fact Marilyn had said it would be a good practice run to tell them first.

Mother turned down the volume of the television, reminding Dad that he was not supposed to get excited.

"I'm watching C-SPAN," Dad complained, "not NASCAR."

"Don't be glib with me," Mother said. "I won't put up with it like those nurses."

Dad rolled his eyes and decided to try some of his tea. His hands were shaking badly as he picked it up, and I watched nervously, but he brought it to his lips and set it down without incident.

I was about to broach my subject when Mother said, "Well, Kate sure seems in love. She can't stop talking about Dillan. We may have two weddings this year!"

"Dillan's been good for her," Dad said, like that wasn't the understatement of the year. Dad never liked to be overly obvious.

"And Dillan and Edward seem to get along," Mother added. "It'll be nice to have two sons. Daughters are nice, but I always thought I'd be more suited toward sons myself." She looked at me. "But God knows best, I suppose." She sipped her tea.

I took a sip of tea. I knew it was time. I had to do this or I would completely lose my nerve. I looked at the television, focusing on the gray-haired man droning on and on about natural gas.

"Mother, Dad," I said, and I could feel them both look at me, the mugs in their hands halfway to their mouths, "I'm not going to marry Edward." I said it directly, just like Marilyn had taught me, with my emotions in check. It was very matter-of-fact. I kept staring at the television, waiting for a response. I didn't hear anything. Finally, I looked at Mother.

She had grown pale. "What did you say?" she asked, still whispering.

She was going to make me repeat it. *Great.* "I'm not going to marry Edward."

Dad looked frozen. I couldn't make out any expression on his face. A different expression, on the other hand, passed across Mother's face every second. "What are you talking about?" she asked in that demeaning tone she was so fond of using with me. "We've just been sitting here talking about the wedding."

"Edward's not the right person for me."

"You couldn't have figured that out before?" Mother set down her tea. She wasn't whispering anymore.

"It's . . . something I'm just now realizing, Mother. The engagement came as a complete surprise. I was talking to Edward about how maybe we weren't right for each other, and the next thing I know I've got a ring on my finger."

"It just slipped right on there, did it? Without you knowing?" Mother's usually well-hidden small-town Southern accent was starting to show.

I bit my lip and looked at Dad. He was still holding the mug just inches from his lips. "I know you are both disappointed. I'm disappointed too, but—"

"Disappointed? Only the entire world knows about this engagement, Leah. I even had a *Times* reporter call me about it! It's no small thing when a senator's daughter gets married, you know. It's an important matter. The wedding is two weeks away, for goodness' sake! You can't just call off a wedding that's two weeks away. I've already had Sylvia start designing a dress for me!"

I clawed the armrest of the couch, trying to hold back the anger that wanted to come out. "Mother," I said, "all of that aside, doesn't it matter to you that I don't want to marry Edward? What if it was the day before? So what?"

"That would be so like you," Mother said. "It would certainly fit your propensity for the dramatic. At least you didn't do *that*."

Dad finally put his mug down and spoke. "Leah, why don't you want to marry Edward? Maybe this is just a case of cold feet."

"I don't think it is," I said. "I've given this a great deal of thought, Dad. Just like you told me to do in life. Give everything thought. That's all I've been doing." I shook my head, trying to explain myself. "It's just that Edward is a very scheduled, predictable man. And I'm starting to understand about myself that I need more spontaneity. I need someone in my life who is going to challenge me. Edward doesn't challenge me. Everything about Edward is very safe and . . . and I need more . . . and I didn't know this until I met this guy who is everything that I'm not . . . everything that I fear, really, but when I'm with him, I feel alive and—"

"Wait a minute!" Mother screeched. I jumped. "Are you saying you *cheated* on Edward?"

"Cheated on him? No!" I said. "Well, no, not really. I mean, I didn't cheat, but I did meet this other man that—"

"Heavens!" Mother declared. She looked like she was going to faint. I turned to Dad for help, but he looked concerned about Mother.

"Mother, don't get the wrong idea. I'm not with this man. I just realized that Edward wasn't the right person for me and—"

"Leah," Mother said sternly, "there is always something to make us think the grass is greener on the other side. Don't you understand that Edward really is a nice find? I've known Edward for as long as you have, and he's a decent, caring, dependable man, Leah. Dependable. Not everyone can say that. Don't take that attribute for granted. Why do you need all this other stuff you're talking about? A man who brings excitement to your life? There are a lot of people who just wish their husbands would come home with a decent paycheck! And Edward makes a very good living. He always will. He's respected, he's intelligent, and he's willing to marry you, Leah. Are you going to throw all that away?"

I felt like a knife had sliced right through my heart. My mother's words stung as much as anything had in my life. Edward was "willing" to marry me. Did she think so little of me that she didn't believe I could find another man to love me? I felt my face turn red.

"How can you say that?" I said, tears rolling down my face.

"I just want you to be happy, Leah, and you have a tendency to not want to be happy."

"What does that mean?"

"It means you're just one of those people in life—and maybe it's because you're the artsy type, I don't know—who want to be downtrodden. It's like you're always waiting for the other shoe to drop, and when it doesn't, you take off your boring navy flat and throw it to the ground, just for good measure!"

I couldn't believe what I was hearing. I wanted to scream and cry and slap my mother. I actually wanted to slap her. But I could see in her eyes that she wanted to slap me just as much.

Out of the corner of my eye, I saw Dad move. It was about time he came to my defense. He never was good at standing up to Mother. He could lead a filibuster but could hardly win an argument with his wife.

Mother glanced at him, as if ready to smack down any remark he was about to make. And then we both noticed at the same time. Dad had spilled his broth, and it was dripping down across the pillows and onto the floor. And he was grabbing his chest. And wincing. Mother screamed.

"Go get the phone!" she ordered me, and I ran into the other room, trying to find the cordless phone. I got it and ran back into the room. Dad was slumping to the side, still grabbing his chest. "Call 911!"

I quickly dialed and told the operator what was happening. My entire body trembled as I watched my mother cope with the situation in front of her. Dad was still conscious, but he looked like he was in a lot of pain.

"They're coming, Mother, they're coming," I said as she glanced at me, her eyes filled with terror.

"This is all your fault!" she yelled at me, and with that she began crying. I'd never, not once, seen my mother cry.

Chapter 25

[She tears the page.]

On the same dirty padded bench in the same stale hallway, Mother and I sat, waiting, at the hospital. She stared forward, indicating she did not want to talk, so I didn't push it. The doctor had informed us that Dad would be fine, and in fact was probably experiencing non-life-threatening muscle spasms, but they were checking him out anyway.

Waiting gave me a good forty-five minutes to assess my own mental state of being. I had always taken pride in the fact that I was able to self-assess, and so this seemed as good a time as any to do it.

I tried to step outside myself and figure out if I was insane. This was not an easy task, because most insane people don't know they're insane, but I talked myself into the fact that being the extremely self-aware person that I am, I would probably notice at least a few red flags before others started to intervene.

So, was my parents' reaction to the news their weird and freaky quirk, or was the very fact that I was calling off the engagement a sign of my own weird and freaky quirk? I asked myself the tough questions, like: Was I really that lucky Edward was marrying me? Did I really not have that much of a chance to find true love and happiness after he was gone?

I tried to gauge whether or not my conflict resolution class was the problem. Perhaps it was trying to render me into a person I wasn't capable of being. Maybe there were people in life who were meant to be peacemakers, the ones who always said yes when they meant no, the ones who always agreed when they disagreed, the ones who always put others' feelings in front of their own.

I stared at the squeaky-clean white tile underneath my feet. That's how my life used to be. Squeaky clean. Problems, sure. But still, nice and tidy. A tad on the antiseptic side. I felt numb and wondered whether I would snap out of it any time soon. I knew there was a very good chance I could walk down that aisle, family and friends on either side of me, smiling broadly as they do at weddings, and I could feel nothing. Oh, sure, I would nod and gesture as if I did, but I knew there was a real possibility that I might not feel a single thing.

Either way, insane or sane, I had definitely hit the lowest point of my life. And it seemed that no matter what choice I made, the outcome was not going to be good.

My thoughts turned to Cinco, and I wondered if there was really a chance for two people who were so different to be together. I wondered if my infatuation with him was only because he was my antithesis. Was it silly to throw away a two-year relationship because of one that had spanned only a few weeks, if that? Besides, it looked as if the relationship was already doomed. He'd called me on lying. Who would want to be with a liar?

And then, to my utter surprise, Mother spoke. She didn't look at me, and at first I wondered if she was really talking to me or just talking out loud. But I sat very still and listened.

"It was a year before I met your father, 1967. I was working on my master's and there was a . . . a . . ."

I leaned forward, anticipating.

She glanced at me before continuing in a much more hushed voice. "Well, a freshman," she finally said. "His name was Howard.

He preferred Howie, but I called him Howard because it just sounded more dignified. Anyway, he was studying . . ."

I rocked forward again, trying to help pull the words out of her mouth.

". . . opera. Yes, that's right, opera, of all things. He had this voice . . . this unbelievable voice. I can still hear it in my head after all these years. I was smitten with him, and he with me. We were an odd couple, that was for certain. My goodness, I was six years older than he. But nevertheless, we dated for almost a year, before I met your father."

I tried not to breathe. I didn't want to distract Mother in any way. She'd never opened up like this, and I didn't want to stop it now. I figured I knew what was coming, a lecture about how although she liked Howie, my father was the better man for her, but I listened anyway, just for kicks.

"Of course, your father was any woman's dream, as you know. He was studying law, but anyone who knew him knew he had a future in politics. His entire family served in politics, and he was expected to do the same. Not only that, but he had a charisma for it, you understand. Everyone knew he would do great things. I was captivated with him from the moment we met, and my family was too. Pretty soon I knew that I would not marry Howard, but that I would marry your father." She paused, and I sighed. Then she said, "But I never stopped thinking about Howard."

I turned to her. "What?"

She looked at me. "It's true. I never have, actually. From time to time I think about him and wonder what he's doing, wonder if his life took him the way that he dreamed. He was a dreamer, oh, what a dreamer. He lived his life in the clouds most of the time. But we really had such a good time together. I never have felt like that before or since." She cleared her throat. "Your father is a good man, and he's done great things. His greatest pride and joy, of course, is you girls. And he's been a good father; there's no disputing that." A *but* hanging in the air was never spoken. It didn't need to be. I could see it in my mother's eyes. She regretted losing Howard. My stomach churned at the thought, but my thoughts were interrupted by the white doors swinging open and a blue-clad doctor walking toward us.

Mother stood, and any hint of the conversation vanished from the air.

But not from my heart.

They wanted to keep Dad overnight, and Mother sent me home, telling me I had better things to do with my time than sit in a hospital room. I wasn't sure what she meant by that, but it was certainly true on more than one level. I managed to get four hours of sleep, but was awoken once again by the phone ringing. I couldn't manage to get myself out of bed, but J.R.'s voice came through loud and clear.

"Leah, you really must call me back. This is the second message I've left, and that's one more than I'm accustomed to. Thank you."

I rolled my eyes and groaned, praying sleep would find me again. But underneath the heavy pile of covers, all I could do was listen to myself breathe, so I finally got up.

And I marched straight to my computer. I was going to finish this play if it killed me.

It was three o'clock in the afternoon. Immersed in my play, I barely heard the phone ring. The answering machine picked up. It was Edward. "Hey you." That was his newly engaged phrase. Hey you. He'd never used a phrase like that in his life. I guess it was the closest I would get to a pet name with him. It made me smile a little. "Just wanted to check in. Cynthia said you hadn't called her, so I wanted to make sure I gave you the right number and everything. I'll be home at 5:30. Call me then."

I grasped in my hand one hundred and three pieces of paper that held my play. I'd been working all morning and all afternoon. But there was nothing to show for it. The play was a mess. It had gone from what I thought was a pretty decent play about an unromantic woman to a jumbled collection of scenes that now made no sense.

At precisely 4:32 p.m. I burst into tears. I sat in my chair, my shoulders popping up and down, and cried harder than I'd cried in my entire life. I was a failure. In every sense of the word, I was a failure.

And before I could stop myself, I was ripping up the first ten pages of my play, listening to the sound of tearing paper with complete detachment.

Whoa, now. Wait just a minute, lady. What do you think you're doing?

I rarely conversed with Jodie, except to tell her to shut up, and that was only a recent behavior I'd acquired. She liked head time, but never stuck around much for an answer; plus, I knew it would be considered ultraweird if I was ever found talking out loud to her. Speaking aloud to your characters might be an endearing trait only if you're a very rich playwright, but it's probably endearing only if you're dead and people find it out after the fact.

Seriously, you've lost your mind. You're actually ripping up the play?

"Yeah."

Let's just stop and think about this for a second, okay? Before you do something really irrational. Understandably, you're under a lot of pressure. Anyone can plainly see that. But let's not get carried away, all right?

"I know what I'm doing."

You know what you're doing? Think this through. You're destroying something you've worked months to create and cultivate.

"I'm destroying a relationship that took two years to cultivate. Frankly, this seems kind of mild." I heard silence for a long time and then . . .

You realize what this means for me.

"Yes." I ripped up another ten pages.

Listen, please. Think about this. You're going to regret it. You're going to rip up the pages, and then you're going to smack yourself on the head and be horrified at what you did.

I ripped up another stack and another, letting the tiny shreds fall to the ground. It looked like a blanket of snow around my feet. It took another three or four minutes, but soon, every page I had was torn to pieces. I sat in my chair, hardly breathing.

Okay, fine, you've proved your point. I know that probably felt good. You know it did. It made you feel a little powerful, didn't it? We all need to feel a bit of a power surge now and then. But who are you kidding? Obviously, there's an electronic copy on your computer and a backup copy on the CD in your laptop. So stop kidding yourself and get on with the business of finishing this play like the good, dependable playwright that you are.

I rose and calmly went to the laptop. I turned it on, ejected the CD, and snapped it in half. I heard Jodie gasp. Then I went back to my computer and pulled up the file.

Wait! What are you doing? Have you lost your mind! You're actually going to delete the last copy of your play? That's insane, Leah. I mean, really whacked out. Certifiable. Begging for Prozac. Seriously, go get a prescription. It will make all the difference in the world.

My finger hovered over the Delete key.

Listen, go dump Edward. Really. If that's what it's going to take to keep this play alive, go dump the fellow. I mean, you at least got a nice laptop out of the deal, right? You know me, I'm the last unromantic left on the earth, so I'm going to have no problem with it. If you're going to delete something, delete him, not me. Not me.

"At the end of the day, you're just a string of words," I said.

I couldn't believe I was going to do it. I was going to delete the file. And I knew how to delete it permanently too. A computer tech showed me how once when I thought I'd accidentally deleted a file. Now my finger rested on top of the key, ready to push it down. One inadvertent twitch, and the file would be gone.

Leah! Do you realize that if you delete this play, I'll be gone. Forever! I'll be gone, Leah. Jodie Bellarusa will be gone. You need me. You can't just throw me in the trash! I'm too important.

"I don't need you," I said.

You don't need me? You're such a fool. Don't you get it? I am you.

I raised my finger a half inch, still letting it hover. But maybe she was right. Jodie Bellarusa was me . . . maybe a part of me that I'd kept hidden for a long time. Maybe she was just a part of me, but if I deleted her . . .

File deleted.

I rolled my chair back, panting like a dog in need of water. I couldn't believe it. I'd done it. I'd deleted my entire play. There was no going back. But in a way, I felt relief too. The play didn't hold any more power over me. Yeah, sure, I would probably have to get a real job, and maybe waitress for a while, or maybe teach writing courses at a local community college, but the burden was gone. I realized I was actually smiling. I was smiling. Really smiling, for the first time in a week.

I realized, too, that I was biting the back of one of my fingers. I released it from the grasp of my teeth and knew what I had to do. I had to call J. R. I dialed her number, hoping she'd still be in the office.

"Yes?"

"J. R., it's Leah."

"Leah," she said, sounding both annoyed and relieved. "I thought you might have fallen off the face of the earth."

"I could be so lucky," I sighed.

"I'm assuming you got my message? My *messages*."

"Yes. That's why I'm calling. J. R., I've . . . I've got to tell you something."

"I'm sure you do, Leah, but before you begin, I . . . I, well, I owe you an"—she sounded like she was gasping for breath—"apology."

I clamped down on the back of my finger again. I didn't realize J. R. was even capable of an apology, and then I wondered what in the world she would be apologizing for. She'd never shied away from criticism.

"Oh . . . um, what for?"

"What for? You are a sweet little nincompoop, aren't you? The fact of the matter is that when I'm wrong I say I'm wrong. I reread your play."

"You reread my play?"

"I'm certain I didn't stutter. I realized I was particularly harsh. And the truth of the matter is that, well, I stopped smoking. And unfortunately it was the week you sent me those pages. I was very grumpy and not myself, and nothing could make me happy. But since then, I got on the patch, and things are looking much brighter. So I reread your play with the help of the patch, and frankly, Leah, it's quite good. I see glimpses of genius, really. I think it's ahead of its time, and I'm not sure everyone will understand it, but someone will get it, and whoever does will make us all a lot of money." She paused, and I felt like I might faint. "I've called Peter about it, and he's excited. I was hoping I could count on a few more pages from you. You know how Peter likes a nice, lengthy example. And also . . . " Her voice went on, but I couldn't decipher anything else she said. It was as if she spoke from a long, dark tunnel, and the next thing I knew, I'd hung up the phone and slid down the wall, crumpled into a tiny ball.

I listened carefully.

But Jodie was silent.

Chapter 26

[Rounding the corner, she looks for him.]

I knew I looked a wreck. I'd attempted to brush my hair, but even that seemed to take too much energy. My face, a display of bright, splotchy patches stained with tears, drew startled expressions from the people I passed. I slipped on a pair of dark sunglasses, but that did little to make me invisible. Sunglasses worn indoors were reserved for celebrities and important people, and I was neither.

I made my way up the stairwell so I wouldn't be stuck on an elevator ride with curious people and managed to reach the fifth floor without collapsing from exhaustion. I opened the door and entered a long corridor lined on both sides with tons of candid pictures from past radio days, framed neatly in black, and hung in exact rows.

Ahead of me was a reception area, and I immediately noticed a security guard standing nearby. I don't know why I was surprised. Of course he needed protection. Protection from crazies like me.

I tried to hold my head high as I approached the receptionist, who looked hip, blonde, and stunningly beautiful. I removed my glasses, and she was kind enough to mask her reaction to my puffy eyes. I glanced at my watch.

"Hi. I'm here to see Cinco Dublin."

She smiled politely. She surely got that line all day long. "Is he expecting you?"

"No. I'm a . . . friend."

"A friend." She smiled again, but this time not politely. "I'm sorry, but Cinco's on the air right now."

"He just got off, didn't he?" I looked at my watch again.

She sighed. "He doesn't take visitors without appointments."

"I understand. If you could just tell him Leah Townsend is here to see him . . ."

She dialed a number and turned away from me as she spoke on the phone. I could hear her mumbling something about a distraught-looking woman. She turned back around and pointed. "He'll see you. Through those doors and to the left. You'll see his office."

"Thank you." I walked past the guard and opened the door. As I rounded the corner, I saw an office straight ahead, with a nice view and plenty of space. My heart pounded so hard in my chest that it hurt, but I kept walking forward.

When I entered the office, no one was there. But evidence of Cinco was all around, including a gold-plated radio microphone, Cinco posing with celebrities and politicians, including the president, and all kinds of books and awards. Plus there was a huge American flag hanging against one wall, and a gold cross on the other. I noticed a Bible was open on his desk, and I felt strange for being there, like I was intruding.

"Leah."

I whipped around to see Cinco stride into the room. He took one look at me and quietly shut the door. "Hi," I said, taking off my glasses. I shoved them into my bag and tried to act like this was a casual visit. But we both knew better.

"Hi. This is unexpected. What are you doing here?"

"I came to talk to you. I'm sorry to drop by, um, unexpectedly. It's just that . . ." I felt myself choking up.

He took me by the shoulder and guided me to a soft leather chair. "Here, sit down," he said. He handed me a tissue then sat in the chair on the other side of his desk. He leaned forward. "Leah, you look awful. What happened? Did you . . . Did things not go well with Edward?"

I couldn't even look at him. I stared at my feet and said, "I haven't told him yet. I know how pathetic that is, but I just haven't yet. I told my parents, and that didn't go well. My dad ended up in the emergency room with chest pains, and my mother told me I was lucky to get a man like Edward, that I shouldn't blow the chance." I blotted my eyes and then said, "And then I destroyed my play because my agent thought it was awful, and I couldn't ever get it to be what I thought I wanted it to be, only to find out my agent really liked the play, but her sensibilities were temporarily rendered useless due to her sudden decision to stop smoking." I finally looked at Cinco. He seemed to feel every part of my pain.

"Leah, I'm so sorry," he said.

I leaned forward, putting my hands on his desk, forgetting the tears running down my face. "The thing is, Cinco, the reason that I'm here is because . . . I want to know . . . if you have feelings for me." I couldn't believe those words had come out so easily.

He didn't answer immediately, so I quickly filled the silence. "Because, I think I've got some feelings for you. I know it sounds crazy. Really, we hardly know each other. But there's just something there. I can't describe it, but I feel it, you know? And I'm about to throw my whole life away. I've pretty much thrown most of it away already, and now there's this final piece that's just hanging there, suspended, waiting for me to either yank it down or put it back in its former place. But I just can't . . . I can't stop thinking about you. You're nothing I ever imagined in a man that I would want in my life, and none of this is making any sense, I know, but something tells me this is right and . . ." I paused to take a breath, but I realized

I didn't have anything else to say. I'd pretty much just spilled every inch of gut I had.

Cinco was looking at his hands. I slumped back into the chair. He did not have the look of a man who had the same feelings. He stood suddenly and walked to my side of the desk. He stayed a good three feet away from me as he leaned against the desk and crossed his arms in front of his chest.

"Leah, you still haven't told Edward you don't want to marry him, right?"

I nodded.

"And what I'm hearing is that you're wondering if we've got a chance. You want to know that before you break it off with Edward."

I looked down. Maybe that was what I was saying. It just sounded so harsh summed up like that. There was an awkward silence, and I wanted to crawl into a hole. This wasn't how I imagined the conversation going. I thought Cinco would tell me he had feelings for me, but why was I surprised? Nothing in the last twenty-four hours had gone the way I'd planned it. My life was officially spiraling out of control, and there was nothing I could do to stop it. It was the first time I'd felt so totally . . . helpless.

"You know what I've been reading lately?" he asked.

I looked at the Bible on his desk. "Your Bible."

"Yeah, but what in my Bible?"

"It's a big book. I have no idea."

"I've been reading about the prodigal son."

I didn't want to listen to this. I didn't need a sermon, and I didn't need to be compared to the prodigal son. I'd spent my whole life doing all the right things. Slipping up doesn't assign one to prodigal status.

"I've read the story many times," Cinco continued, "but something stuck out to me this time. It was the other brother."

"What about him?" I asked, nearly sneering. I couldn't recall much about him except that he was unhappy about a fatted calf.

"Well, his whole life he'd done everything right. His brother was the mischievous one, always doing the wrong thing, always demanding things he didn't deserve. One thing that really stuck out to me this time was that the good brother seemed to be the one missing out on so much in life."

"How do you figure that?"

"Well, it seems to me that his entire life he'd worked hard to make sure there were no mistakes, no falling from grace, no unneeded conflict in his life. But because of that, he was never able to understand or feel what his brother understood and felt."

I tore my gaze off the carpet and looked at Cinco. What was he trying to say?

"The brother that made the most mistakes felt the deeper love. He understood what it meant to be forgiven. He understood and experienced mercy. He was the reason grace was created."

"He was also a pain in everyone's behind."

Cinco smiled. "Yeah. But the conflict he created by his own poor choices led to an understanding of his father's love that his brother could never get. The father's love was the same, no different from one brother to the other. But it's just that the prodigal brother, he needed the love more. He'd lived with pigs—he understood how low life could get. The other brother was pretty self-sustaining. All his t's were crossed, and all his i's were dotted. He didn't need anyone because he always had himself. And he was the most reliable thing he had."

"I'm not sure what you're getting at, Cinco. I just confessed feelings for you and you're talking about pig slop." The humiliation of our public face-off in class last night resurfaced.

"I'm saying that you're looking at all your life falling apart and feeling like you're failing. But maybe you're succeeding at something else. Maybe for once in your life you're having to depend on someone other than yourself."

"So I'm the un-prodigal daughter. That's what you're saying?"

"It's not a bad thing. It just has different challenges. It's a different experience."

My eyes teared up again. "I've always taken a lot of pride in being the good daughter."

"I know. And there's nothing wrong with that. You've been a source of pride for your parents, I'm sure." He moved a little closer to me and lowered his voice, talking so softly I had to strain to hear what he was saying. "I'm not going to tell you how I feel about you."

"Why?"

"Because you've got to do what you need to with Edward for your own reasons. Not because of me. You've got to decide if Edward is right or wrong for you, regardless of what else does or doesn't wait on the horizon for you."

"So no safety net."

"No safety net." He touched my arm. "But maybe this time, you'll feel what it's like to fall toward your doom, only to be caught by arms of love." He patted his Bible.

Anger surged in me again. "My whole life I've been everybody's doormat, I guess you could say. I've never stood up for myself. But I haven't been completely weak, have I? Because I've taken great pride in the fact that all my ducks are in a row."

"So kick your ducks out of line and stop being a doormat."

Alrighty then. I stood and started for the door, but before I left, Cinco said, "Leah, you have great worth in your Father's eyes. And whether all your ducks are in a row or whether you're rolling in pig slop, you're worthy, and you always will be."

Maybe it was the vision of myself rolling in pig slop. I don't know. But words I definitely hadn't planned came rushing from my mouth. "I came here to see how you feel about me. But let me tell you how I'm feeling instead." My voice was harsh, and I could see surprise in Cinco's expression. I didn't care. "I'm not one of your radio callers."

"What?"

"That's how you treated me at class. Like a radio caller. Like the particular issue of lying was fair game for everyone, and that it could make for some lively entertainment if I'd given you the chance to debate it."

"Leah, I didn't—"

"You embarrassed me." He tried to say something else, but I held up my index finger. "And if we're going to talk about people's imperfections, you want to explain what good reason you could possibly have for punching out a reporter? Want to explain that?" Cinco's mouth actually fell open. "Didn't think so!"

I slipped my sunglasses back onto my face, turned, and left. Cinco's opinion was that I needed to wallow in some pig slop? I was one rotten corncob away from it.

Even though I was raised in church, I couldn't remember ever actually kneeling to pray. Or going to the altar. Or being in church any time other than on a Sunday morning. I knew they kept the doors open, and so here I was, alone in the church sanctuary, kneeling.

I felt weak.

And by coming here in the "off-season" to pray, I was admitting that. Yet I still couldn't get over the irony of it all. This truth had played through my mind for the rest of the afternoon and evening.

I was a doormat. I always had been. A self-sustaining doormat, maybe, but a doormat nevertheless.

Cinco telling me I was worthy struck me. *Worthy* had never been a word I would've used in the same sentence with my name. The idea that I was worthy haunted me, because I knew that not an ounce of me felt it.

The only worth I felt was when I was being an acceptable addition to people's lives. So in every way I knew how, I would try to be what they wanted me to be for them, whether that was the straight-and-narrow daughter, the dependable girlfriend/fiancée, the always available friend, the up-and-coming playwright, the uncomplaining tenant . . . the list went on and on.

I wondered if I was the only doormat in the world that didn't know I was a doormat. I thought of myself more as . . . compliant. A complement, if you will, like a good Syrah is for a filet mignon. Or, well, maybe the house wine for the chopped sirloin. Whatever the case, I was a complement.

It was a tough thing to swallow, a tough thing to accept—that I didn't need to be all those things to be me. I needed just to be me. And I now understood this not to be selfish, but in fact to be just the opposite—unselfish. The selfish thing to do was to play to everyone's needs to feel accepted. The unselfish thing to do was to be the person God created me to be, to serve him and people, to speak the truth, even when the truth wasn't going to make me popular. And the truth was, I hadn't been doing any of these things.

Was I a perfectly likable human being, even when I didn't fulfill people's expectations?

All these things came to me as I prayed. I felt refreshed deep inside my soul, where I hadn't even bothered to look in a long time. I wasn't even sure what was in there. My soul was like one of those cabinets you have in your house, the one you've been meaning to clean out for years, but you don't bother because you're sure no one's going to look in there anyway. But then, one day, somebody mistakenly opens it, and your mess is exposed.

I prayed for strength and wisdom for what I needed to do. Things were bound to get messier. I would have to call my entire family and tell them the wedding was off. For Edward's sake, I would have to offer to leave this church that Edward and I had attended together for two years, and find a new one. The fallout might last for weeks or even months. There was nothing neat and tidy about what I was doing.

In fact, it was starting to look a little like a pigsty.

As if I'd adopted a new mantra for making sure that whatever I was doing was the worst it could be, I arrived at Edward's at 9:45 p.m. I buzzed his apartment, and by the full minute it took for him to answer, I knew he'd been asleep for well over an hour and a half. He groggily answered, and when I told him I needed to come up, he unlocked the main door and grumbled something inaudible.

When I arrived at his door, he opened it for me. All the lights were off inside except a single lamp in the living room, which he'd probably clicked on while stumbling to answer the intercom. His hair was mashed on one side of his head, but remarkably his pin-striped pajamas looked like they had just been pressed and starched.

"Hi," I said.

"Is everything okay? Is something wrong? Did something happen to your dad?"

I shook my head. "No, I just need to talk."

He was still squinting. "It's kind of late."

"I know. But it's important."

He opened the door wider and swung his arm in the direction of the living room. "You want something to drink?" he asked. "I can make tea."

"No, that's okay."

He sat down in the chair next to the couch I came to sit on. He appeared to be waking up a little more. The grim look on his face indicated his awareness that the visit was rare, and if rare, probably serious.

"What's going on?" he finally asked. I was having a hard time starting the conversation. I'd taken the T, instead of my car, to

Edward's. Doing so had given me enough time to think through thirty different ways to break the awful news to him. Now, sitting there, I couldn't think of a single one.

"Edward," I began, already choking up, "this is probably going to make no sense to you. And that will be completely understandable. But . . . well, it all started at the French restaurant. And maybe it didn't start there; obviously it didn't start there, but anyway, one night I wanted to order flaming pancakes, and that totally threw you. You couldn't imagine why I would want to order flaming pancakes, because they're kind of a spectacle. And so you suggested I order cod, which really is the anti–flaming pancake, if you will. So I ordered the cod because I didn't want to make a scene over dinner choices. And we were eating, and you mentioned there was an odd spice in the food.

"Your comment got me to thinking about spices and life, and somehow I ended up at your work party in that pink dress. I kind of liked the pink dress. I thought I looked pretty decent in it. But you were embarrassed. And ever since then, I've just kept thinking there was this spice missing in my life, you know? And I've tried to compensate for it. I ordered a hot pink wedding cake, for crying out loud, with flames around it. But what I'm realizing is that . . . I liked the dress. I liked wearing the pink dress. And I want to order flaming pancakes. Not every meal. But every once in a while, just to stir things up. I don't want to eat at the same restaurant at the same time every week. Sometimes I want you to be running late, be harried . . ."

Edward looked so confused. He was genuinely trying to keep up and understand, but I knew he was lost by the way he was nodding at appropriate times, by how his eyes were kind of blank.

I could hardly fathom saying the words, and as I drew them out of my mouth, one by one, they sounded like an echo, like someone else was saying them, and I was just an observer.

"Edward, I'm so sorry, but I can't marry you . . . and I can't be with you."

The words hung out there, and for several long moments I thought Edward had not heard what I said. He did not move a muscle or show any amount of emotion. His eyes didn't register that anything I said was extraordinary. I was about to repeat myself when Edward stood. His expression had morphed into a complex mixture of anger and pain.

My hand went over my mouth, and my eyes brimmed with tears. I couldn't believe I'd said it. And now I couldn't believe the look on Edward's face. I wanted to take it all back, tell him I was sorry, that I'd temporarily lost my mind, and that I would never wear pink again.

But I didn't. I simply sat still and waited. I'd also, on the way over, envisioned a nice selection of scenarios for how Edward would react. Yet, this very predictable man, the one for whom spontaneity was as challenging as athletics, did something I could not have predicted.

He didn't say a word, and instead, he turned and padded quietly down the small hallway of his apartment, closing the door to his bedroom with a single, solitary click.

I gave the engagement ring one last look, twisted it off my finger, and placed it gently on Edward's coffee table. The tears finally jumped off the cliff. I grabbed my bag and hurried out of his apartment. Outside, I found a quiet place in the shadows and cried into my hands.

Inside, I felt more pain than I thought I was capable of feeling. I'd never felt this much pain for myself. I didn't think I was capable of it. But to know that I'd hurt someone I cared deeply for was nearly unbearable.

It was official. Everything in my life was now undone.

Chapter 27

[Quietly, she closes the door.]

I knew one person for which the hour of the evening was considered early. I called Kate on my way home and asked her to meet me back at my apartment. I gave her no details, but she could tell by the strain in my voice that it was important.

When I arrived, she was waiting outside my door. She took one look at me and formed an expression that most people reserve for funeral attendance. It made me want to burst into tears again. I unlocked my door and she followed me in. As soon as she shut the door, she blurted, "*What* happened to you?"

I threw my things on the floor and fell onto the couch. Kate sat beside me, eagerly leaning forward to hear the details. I could hardly get myself to say it out loud. That meant it was real.

"I called off the wedding."

"What?" Kate nearly fell off the couch.

While I nodded, Kate shook her head in disbelief.

"Why?" she asked.

My hands fell open. It was so hard to explain.

"I'm making tea," she announced, going into my kitchen. "A few months ago, I would've made us Bloody Marys." She laughed. "Times have changed . . . for us both." She put the kettle on and returned to the living room. I could see compassion in her eyes, and before I knew it, I stood and we were embracing, crying together, and being like sisters should be. It was quite possibly the only thing that was right in my life.

"I sent Dad to the hospital with the news," I said, wiping my nose. "I tore up my play and deleted it from existence. And I broke up with the only man Mother thinks is capable of loving me."

She pushed the hair back from my eyes. "But Leah, you look . . . peaceful."

"I do?"

"Yeah. Something in your eyes. I've noticed lately how strained you've been. The smiles and jokes can't cover the window to the soul." She studied me. "You definitely look better. Except the splotching."

"I wish there were a cure for that." I sighed. But that was the least of my concerns right now.

"So what did Edward say?"

"Nothing. Absolutely nothing. He stood there like it took him a few seconds to register what I'd just said, and then he walked into his bedroom and shut the door. He didn't utter a word."

"It must've come as such a shock. You guys have like, what, half the wedding planned?"

I started crying again and Kate embraced me. "Oh, I'm sorry. I didn't mean to—"

I waved my hand. "It's not you. It's all of it. And poor Gammie. Poor, poor Gammie."

"Gammie's going to be dead in a few weeks, so don't worry about her."

I laughed and blew a snot bubble. Kate grabbed a tissue for me from the box on my desk. I was a wreck. An utter wreck. But when I stopped crying long enough, I realized Kate might be right. Something was different inside me. A sense of empowerment in the midst of complete loss of control.

"You know what Dillan's always telling me?" I shook my head. "That you have to do what feels right, deep inside yourself. And nobody can go that deep except you."

I smiled. It wasn't Francis Bacon, but there was certainly truth to it. And if I was going to get that picky, I should consider the ironic way Bacon died . . . from pneumonia after packing a chicken with ice to see if that would preserve it. So maybe Dillan was the next great philosopher.

"Dillan's a smart guy," I replied.

"Leah, you're going to find the right man for you, just like I have. And if Edward's not the right man, then you were right to let him go, no matter how long you two had been together. If you're not going to be happy until eternity, then you should move on."

I nodded. All things I knew. But what nobody realized—what I hadn't realized until now—was the fact that I didn't take into account my own happiness much. I watched Kate walk back into the kitchen to get the whistling kettle. She'd been happy dressing bohemian. At the end of the day, she was who she was supposed to be, and not what anybody wanted her to be. Even her new transformation was on her terms, not anybody else's. Sure, she'd made really bad choices in her life. But she'd certainly faced the consequences.

And maybe, just maybe, that was why she called our mother Mom instead of Mother.

"Here you go," she said, bringing me a mug of steaming tea. I tasted it. It was loaded with sugar, just the way we used to drink it as kids. We used to have to attend so many stuffy political receptions that doctoring our hot tea with this kind of flavor was our only saving grace.

"You know," Kate said, "sometimes things don't make sense until after they're over. Hindsight, you know? Sometimes what you see—what's right there in front of you— isn't always the truth. And it isn't always real."

That was the truest thing I'd heard all day.

"Speaking of that," I said, laughing, "I have a funny story to tell you."

"Yeah?"

"Last week I was at dinner with a . . . friend, at Mangalos actually, and I looked up and saw Dillan."

"Really?"

"Yeah. But I was pretty ticked, because he was with this blonde girl, and they were laughing it up and having a good ol' time. When I left I was really bothered by it because I thought Dillan was cheating on you." I kept chuckling.

"So what's the funny part?" Kate looked concerned.

I waved my hand. "Turns out the guy was Dillan's twin! I'd forgotten he'd mentioned having a twin until dinner the other night. I was fretting about how to tell you, you know? It was awful. But then Dillan mentioned his twin, thank goodness." I laughed. But Kate didn't even smile. She stared at her tea. "What's wrong?" I asked. "It was his twin. What's his twin's name?"

But Kate didn't answer. She looked angry.

"Kate?"

She looked up at me.

"What? Dillan does have a twin, does he not?"

"Yes. But he's blond and about a foot shorter. They don't even look like brothers."

Any words I was about to say screeched to a stop inside my mouth. Kate looked exactly like I felt.

"You say a blonde woman?" she asked.

I nodded.

She cursed and flew to her feet, pounding her fist into the air. "Brandi!"

"Brandi?"

"She works with him. I've seen her at a couple of dinner parties.

They went out a few times, but Dillan told me it was totally over between them."

I stood and said, "Maybe it was innocent. I mean, I didn't see them kiss or anything."

"No." Her eyes had the fierceness of an athlete in the final seconds of a tied game. "No. No!"

I reached out to her. "Kate, I'm so sorry. I honestly didn't mean to . . . I didn't know. I thought I was telling a funny story. I had no idea Dillan was really . . ."

"He's the first man I've loved in a really long time. But you already knew that, didn't you?" Her eyes cut to me momentarily, and she sat back down.

"Maybe you can work it out."

"He's not who I thought he was. It's not the first red flag, actually. I noticed that at dinner one night he was giving the impression to others in our group that he was a devout churchgoer. That is how we met. But he was at church for the first time, following an ex to see who she was dating." Staring at the carpet, Kate added, "And it wasn't love at first sight, like he presented it. He wasn't really that interested in me until he found out who Dad was. How else would a girl like me get a guy like him?"

Kate, who'd always been a picture of confidence, had used Dad to get a date? I couldn't believe it. Maybe I wasn't the only person in the world whose confidence had been compromised a time or ten thousand.

"What are you going to do?" I asked. But before she could answer, there was a knock at my door. It was after eleven. Who would come by at that time?

Maybe it was Cinco. I prayed it was Cinco. I also prayed once again that the security system downstairs would be fixed. I was tired of people making it all the way to my door before I knew who was coming.

I stepped up to the door, peered through the hole, and gasped. "It's Edward!" What was Edward doing here? I stumbled backward as another persistent knock rattled the door. Kate grabbed her purse.

"Wait, Kate. You don't have to leave. I don't know why Edward's here, but—"

She held up a hand. "I have to go. I've got to think through some things."

The insistent knock came a third time.

Kate passed by me and opened the door. Edward looked like the wreck I'd been for most of the day. My heart melted with pity. Seeing Kate startled him. His gaze wandered until it found me.

"I'm sorry. I thought you would be alone."

"I was just leaving," Kate said, brushing by Edward.

"Kate . . . " I reached out for a hug, but she was gone. I prayed she wouldn't take this out on me, but that steely look in her eyes made me unsure.

Edward came in, and I closed the door behind him. He didn't even make it to a couch. He turned and looked at me with such intensity that I stood very still at the door, my back flat against it, and held my breath. I couldn't imagine what he was getting ready to say. I braced myself for a tongue-lashing.

But instead, as quietly as a shy boy, he said, "Come back to me." He stepped closer, his hands nervously playing with each other, tears at the corner of each eye. "Leah, please. Marry me. Please marry me. You're the only thing that I want. Everything else can leave." He looked down, searching for words when I offered only silence in response. "I'll change, Leah. I'll be more—what do you call it—spontaneous. I'll let you wear pink. I didn't know," he said, each new word choking with emotion. "I didn't know it meant so much to you. I thought you were trying to be someone you weren't. But I'm realizing now I never gave you a chance to be who you really are. I grew comfortable . . . I like predictability, Leah. It's what my whole life revolves around. But I can change. I will change. If you will please, please come back to me. Don't do this. Don't leave me. Please."

I'd never once heard desperation in Edward's voice. He'd always taken a great deal of pride in his poise: straight shoulders, a confident expression, verbiage dripping with intellect. Now, his hair was disheveled, his shoulders slumped, and his body language oozed neediness. I couldn't help but feel regret, because I'd always wanted to see this side of Edward that I hadn't thought existed.

"Say something," Edward finally said, his pleading eyes locked onto mine.

But I could hardly look at him any longer. "I don't know what to say," I admitted, and without much emotion, I noticed. Maybe I'd had my fill of crying.

"You've got to say something. I need you to say something. Don't you understand how this came out of left field? We were picking out wedding cakes, and now you don't want to marry me."

I prayed for the right words. "Edward, everything wasn't all right. You just couldn't see it. I've been trying ever since the pink-dress incident to tell you something wasn't right. But you didn't have the time or the patience to listen to me. You didn't want to deal with it."

He sighed. "That's true. I thought it was a passing phase. I realize that was a mistake." He took three steps toward me. With my back still against the door, he took my hands as tenderly as he ever had, and looked into my eyes with more passion than I ever thought he was capable of. "Leah, please, will you reconsider your position in this matter?"

It was such a simple, small word, but so heavy on the tongue, so difficult to push out. It was one word, but it had so many implications.

"No."

He let go of my hands, his brow falling over his narrowing eyes. He stepped back and studied me. Dull disappointment washed over his bright eyes. "What am I supposed to tell my family?" he blurted.

He gestured toward me. "And what about your family? I cannot see your family being okay with this. Have you told them?"

"Yes."

He shook his head. "This is unbelievable. Maybe I never really knew you, Leah. Maybe that's the problem. Because the Leah I knew was not capable of doing this."

There was never a truer statement.

"I'm sorry, Edward. This isn't meant to hurt you. But I know it does."

"I don't even know you!" He backed away from me like I had some disease.

"You do know me," I said calmly. "It's just who I've never had the courage to be."

"I liked the old Leah better." He pointed to the door. "Do you mind? I'd like to leave now."

I wanted to hold out my hands, talk this through, try to make Edward not hate me so much. But even though I knew I was completely breaking his heart, I also knew this was exactly what I wanted. I didn't love Edward enough to marry him.

I stepped aside and opened the door for him. He stared at me as though even that simple gesture was beyond his comprehension. He hesitated, obviously expecting me to say something. I didn't, and with a swift stride he was out the door, which I closed without looking after him.

I went to my bathroom, washed my face, put on my favorite cozy pajamas, crawled into bed, and slept as if my world were not falling to pieces.

Chapter 28

[She aims her gun.]

Millions of stories have been told through the centuries, but stories, no matter how they're told or why, seem to have the same basic structure. There is the beginning, where the protagonist's life is in a state of *equilibria*. Life is balanced, for the time being. Of course, it cannot stay that way. Every good story has built into it the rising action—the *desis*. This is where the protagonist's life becomes unbalanced, where complication is introduced, which leads ultimately to the moment of crisis, the climax—*peripeteia*. The way the protagonist deals with peripeteia is what brings sympathy to the character. He must deal with it. The climax is the point of no return. But then, when the heat is turned up as hot as it can go, the *denouement* arrives. The falling action, the unraveling of it all, where the consequences of the character's decisions must be dealt with, good or bad.

Then, resolution.

That was the part, two weeks later, that had not arrived for me. I'd always referred to resolution as the story's "deep breath." But in my own life, during more conflict than I would've dared put my own characters through, I still had no resolution.

I had not spoken to Cinco, nor had I returned to the conflict resolution class. I figured if I hadn't learned how to resolve conflict by now, there was no hope for me. But not seeing Cinco was difficult. I had to take his absence as a sign that he was never really that interested in me, or that our fight had undone an already fragile beginning.

Dad was still at home recovering. Mother had suggested I not come see him for a while. She told me she didn't want him stressed. I talked to him twice over the phone, but we never mentioned the abandoned wedding plans, only his improving health.

Kate broke up with Dillan, but she was refusing to talk with anyone about it. Mother's snippy words, which tiptoed around the subject about as delicately as a gorilla, reminded me that she blamed me for that too.

I heard the rumor through the few friends I had in the theater industry that J. R. was telling everyone I'd gone mental. To have that particular rumor spread wasn't as bad as it might seem, for an artist anyway. Just such a thing could make a playwright's work very popular, and themes inferred but never implied could become a touchstone for the artist's every play. For all I knew, J. R. was still trying to resurrect my career.

And as if those things weren't enough, I missed Jodie too. I was never sure how much of her identity was really me. But nevertheless, she provided a lot of entertaining thoughts, which I could've used during the long and lonely days. She wasn't the most optimistic presence in my life, but at least she was something.

I sat in solitary confinement in my apartment on this Saturday, as I had for many days. Today would've been the wedding. I hadn't cried once about Edward. I knew beyond a shadow of a doubt I'd made the right decision.

But I couldn't resist imagining myself walking down the aisle. In my daydream, there was nobody at the end waiting for me. It didn't matter. I could still see myself in a white dress, the titanic version of a veil hanging off the back of my perfectly coifed hair, and guests smiling widely as I passed.

I sat in my quiet living room at three o'clock in the afternoon flipping through a Pottery Barn catalog. Each picture reminded me of how discombobulated my life was. I stared at each engaging page, with the matching comforters, crisp, colored window treatments, expensive-looking furniture, storage space beyond your dreams—all arranged to look as enticing as possible.

In contrast, my life looked like a garage sale.

And then there was a knock. I raced to the door, hoping they wouldn't leave in the half second it took me to get there. I didn't care who it was, I just wanted some company. I didn't even bother looking through the peephole.

"Hi!" I shouted with glee.

Cinco laughed. "Hi. You look . . . happy."

I pulled it in a notch. "I am. I'm fine. Surprised to see you. But glad to see you. Come in."

"Thanks." He stuck his hands casually in his pockets as he walked in. He surveyed the room, probably for any surprise guests.

"How about something to drink?" I asked. I was trying to play the perfect hostess, but my efforts were really an attempt to direct my energy away from the urge to jump up and down and shout.

"Sure. It's starting to get hot outside."

I poured him iced tea that, thankfully, I'd made up the night before. I perched a lemon slice on the rim and carried it into the living room, where he'd sat down on the leather ottoman.

"Thanks." He watched me as I sat across from him. "You look really good."

I looked away. "Anything's an improvement from the last time you saw me."

"True," he said. "But you still look really good."

"I feel good," I said. "A lot has happened in my life lately. More than I could even explain. But I feel good."

His gaze found my hand. I kept it steady on my knee so he could take all the time he wanted. "So it's over?"

I nodded.

"How do you feel about that?"

"Like it was the best thing I've ever done for myself."

His finger traced lines in the sweat of the glass. "I wanted to give you some space. You needed time to work through some things."

"Was it that obvious?" I laughed.

"It meant a lot that you came to me to talk about it."

"Really?"

"Yeah. Really. And I hated how things ended." He set his tea down on the end table and leaned forward, propping his elbows on his knees and clasping his hands together. "I came by to apologize."

I came by to apologize. Before now, that was my key phrase. I used it all the time, even when the conflict wasn't my fault. I always said I was sorry, just to diffuse a strenuous situation, or even one that had that potential. Yet, here I sat, being apologized to. Nobody else knew it, but this was a monumental occasion.

Cinco continued, "You were right. I should've never brought all that up in front of the class. I'm used to dealing with conflict publicly, but that doesn't mean it's always appropriate. I'm really sorry, Leah. I would've never intentionally embarrassed you."

I prayed the tears in my eyes wouldn't fall. "Cinco, it's okay."

"No, it's not okay. But will you forgive me?"

I nodded. And then I said, "I'm sorry that I lied to you about Edward. Or that I kept lying to you. The night we had dinner I should've told you he wasn't my brother." I laughed a little. "You already knew it, but I should've said it."

"You're forgiven. And just for the record, I don't normally go around hitting people. This reporter had promised to do a story on my father's accomplished and respected career in journalism, but it ended up basically being part of a smear campaign. He attacked my father's integrity, spread as many lies as possible, and then had the gall to tell me to my face that everything he said was the truth. And to top it all off, he used a long-lens camera and took a picture of my mother in her bathrobe. I gave him a chance to apologize to my family, to my father, but he said he'd rather eat dirt. So I smashed his face into the ground. The bathrobe thing was just the last straw." He threw his hands out. "What can I say? My family's honor was at stake." He paused, then said, "So is two weeks enough time?"

I wasn't exactly following the subject change. I was trying to absorb what Cinco had told me, meld his actions with what I knew so far about who he was. "Enough time for what?"

"For you to feel comfortable if I asked you out."

I laughed that laugh that always blurted out when I was nervous. It wasn't even really a laugh as much as it was a cleverly disguised shout. I thought I might not ever be able to shake it. Cinco didn't seem the least bit deterred. A small smile curled the edges of his lips, and he stared at me like he wouldn't blink until I answered him.

I, on the other hand, couldn't stop blinking. "I would feel . . . feel, well, that would be just fine . . . . and completely appropriate, and sure. That's not problem. A. A problem. It's not."

"Good, Yoda." He leaned back as he picked up his iced tea again. "So when is a good time for you?"

"Oh, well, you know. I'd have to check my—"

"How about now?"

The laugh again. Oh, how I wish I could drive a stake through it. "Now?"

"Are you busy?" He raised an eyebrow, indicating he knew perfectly well that I was not.

However, I was in cotton sweats and an old T-shirt. "I'm not really dressed."

"Now, that would be embarrassing if it were true. And by the way, you're dressed perfectly for what I have planned."

"Run!" Cinco shouted. "Hurry up! You're going to die!"

Thick, dirty, oily sweat covered my face and dripped down my chin as I stumbled along the small path lined with trees and shrubs and sticks. As we entered a denser part of the woods, the sun nearly vanished from view. But it was still hot. Especially as we hadn't officially hit summer yet. Cinco pulled me into the shadow of a large tree trunk. He put a finger to his mouth to indicate I should be very quiet.

I could hardly breathe, and though I tried not to gasp for breath, it was nearly impossible. But equally impossible was ignoring the fact that Cinco kept grabbing my hand, pulling me from hideout to hideout. As our backs pressed against the tree and Cinco listened for any movement, two of his fingers intertwined with two of mine. The fact that we were in grave danger was not making my heart pound nearly as much as this small detail.

I tried not to let it distract me. Suddenly Cinco ripped his hand from mine and fired his gun through the woods. "Come on!" he shouted, and we ran the opposite direction. And then I saw a man, twenty-five yards away, hiding behind a cluster of bushes. He peeked out and then ducked back again. Cinco apparently didn't see him.

I stopped, and Cinco sensed it. He turned and I beckoned him behind a nearby tree. "Stay here," I whispered.

"Where are you going?"

"Trust me." I smiled. I then worked my way around another small grouping of trees. Cinco hadn't followed my instructions, and was following close behind me.

Then I saw the man, still squatted down, trying to get a glimpse of where we might've gone. I aimed my gun and shot.

Splat! Right on target! The man groaned as a patch of blue spread itself over the middle of his back.

"Yes!" Cinco said, slapping me on the shoulder. "Good job! You're a natural."

"You can thank all the hunting trips I was forced to participate in growing up. Imagine a bunch of stuffy politicians walking around trying to shoot quail. It was a ridiculous sight. Trust me. Paintball is much more exciting."

He laughed, but then he pulled me behind a tree again. "There's one more out there, and he's not going to let up until he gets us."

"Are you sure this isn't personal for this guy? Maybe he recognizes you from your radio show or something?"

This really made Cinco laugh. "I do get recognized, but typically not in this kind of setting." He pointed to his protective eyewear. I knew we both looked like complete idiots in our getups, but for once, I didn't care. I was having way too much fun.

"Where is he now?" I whispered.

"I'm not sure, but if I had to guess, I'd say he went up that hill to try to get a better angle on us. It's two against one, though, so we definitely have the advantage." Cinco checked his watch. "We've got three minutes to find him, or it's a tie. And I always like to win."

Cinco grabbed my hand again, and we wound our way through the woods to the edge, where we could see the small hill. A made-to-look-dilapidated shack rested on top, and at that second we both saw a small movement.

"He's there!" Cinco said, and just then, we heard the guy's gun fire. Paint splattered right above my shoulder on the tree behind me. "Duck!"

We squatted down and Cinco said, "You've got to cover me." I tried not to laugh. He said it as seriously as the star of some intense cop show. I nodded stoically. "Fire on him. I'm going to try to move up the hill to get closer."

"Gotcha."

He raced toward a group of trees ahead. I fired, hoping I wouldn't accidentally hit him. The guy in the shack fired back at me, so I fired again, allowing Cinco to move forward even farther. I fired two more shots and then noticed I couldn't see Cinco anymore. He'd disappeared.

The guy inched his head out the window, trying to get a location on Cinco, so I fired again, and he fired back. This went on for a few more seconds until I saw Cinco again. This time he was coming from the back of the shack. Somehow he'd made it around to the other side of the hill. I fired, trying to distract the guy so he wouldn't see Cinco. A paint pellet whizzed by my head and hit the ground behind me. And then I heard gunfire up on the hill, followed by Cinco's shout. "Game over!"

I slowly rose and could see the other man coming out of the shack. The two were laughing. They shook hands. Then Cinco trotted down the hill toward me, a self-satisfied grin on his face. "Good job!" I said.

"Couldn't have done it without you. You fired at just the right time so I could get into the shack. If you hadn't, he definitely would've seen me."

"How'd you get around there so fast?"

"It wasn't hard. He said he was expecting me to move up the front by using the trees and rocks. But when he ducked, I ran to the side of the hill, fell on my belly, and scrambled up the back. His attention stayed on you."

"What draws you to this?" I asked, gesturing the paintball field.

"It's a safe place to take out my aggression, rather than on the radio."

"Or on ruthless reporters."

He laughed. "That too."

"Maybe I'm mistaken, but it seems like your entire radio program is aggressive. Don't you kind of obliterate people?"

"No," he said smoothly, "I just argue with them until they admit they're wrong."

Suddenly, several places on my body were beginning to ache where I'd been hit with paint pellets.

"So what did we win?"

"A great deal of satisfaction and a hundred bucks."

"Cinco?"

"Yeah."

"Promise me we'll never, ever play paintball again."

He laughed. "You didn't like it?"

"It was entertaining. But the only thing I liked was that it was with you." I smiled to myself. Never in a million years would I have protested a date activity in the past. I would've pretended to like it so I wouldn't make the other person feel bad.

He brushed a sweaty piece of hair out of my face. "I promise. And the good news is that we now have plenty of money to go out on the town tonight." And then he took my sweaty cheeks into his hands and kissed me.

Chapter 29

[She takes in the view.]

I couldn't get enough of Cinco. We spent every moment available together for four solid weeks. During that time I spoke to my family only occasionally on the phone, basically just so we could reassure one another we were still alive. I didn't hear from J. R., nor did I care to.

My absence perplexed Elisabeth. "You're always home," she complained one day on my answering machine. "That's one thing I love about you. I know where you'll be."

But I didn't care. I was with Cinco, and falling madly in love with him. This man, whose sense of adventure might have terrified me once upon a time, was everything I ever wanted. And not once, since we'd been together, had I splotched.

I celebrated by buying a nice V-neck cotton top for the next time we went out. When I returned home from shopping, the phone was ringing. It was Mother.

"Leah, we're having Sunday dinner. Tonight. I insist everyone be there. There's been enough of this nonsense. We are family, and we are going to spend time together if it kills us, which it might, but at least we'll be together."

Another remark indicating she still blamed me for almost killing Dad with my news about Edward.

"I don't know if I can," I said, closing my eyes. "I might have plans."

"Plans? What could you possibly be doing that's more important than a family dinner?" Mother asked. "Your father is getting stronger each day, but it would still do him some good to get things back to normal."

As far as I was concerned, things would never be back to normal, but I wasn't sure Mother would ever acknowledge that. I sighed into the phone, loudly enough for Mother to hear. I didn't have plans with Cinco, so I had no excuse.

"What time?"

"Seven o'clock. Lola has the night off, so I'm cooking rosemary chicken, our favorite."

I laughed. Mother always referred to that dish as the family's favorite, but really the only person who liked it was Mother.

"Okay. I'll be there."

A satisfied acknowledgment came through the receiver, but Mother didn't know how dangerously close she was to hearing that I couldn't come. I recognized, however, that I needed a nice slap of reality. I'd been living and breathing Cinco Dublin for weeks, and everything else had been set aside, including my work. I'd accepted some editing jobs for money until I knew what else I would do.

"I'll see you tonight," Mother said and hung up the phone, just as I started to ask if Cinco could come.

The rosemary chicken was providing the only real conversation at the table. Kate was still sulking, but, unlike Mother, she didn't seem to be blaming me. Mother kept asking if the rosemary was too overbearing. *It's not the rosemary,* I kept wanting to reply. But the new and bold Leah didn't include unnecessary insults. And truthfully, the rosemary chicken would've been exceptional if Dad hadn't kept using it to illustrate how his surgery was performed.

I slumped against the straight-backed chair. I wanted to be with Cinco, where things were comfortable and good and I felt accepted for who I was. But then something occurred to me, something that Cinco had told me on one of our dates. I had asked him how he was capable of being hated by so many people simply because of what he stood for. He said, "I try to love everyone but I serve only One."

I try to love everyone. I knew it to be true. As combative as Cinco's show sounded, his words were almost always filled with love. Other people said hateful things, while Cinco tried to offer them love. But his words definitely drew out the worst in people. I'd learned first-hand that he was a persuasive and sometimes pushy debater. But people mostly hated hearing what he had to say about God and about truth. Amazingly, their reactions never deterred him from saying it. Or from loving them.

And within those few seconds, I suddenly felt free to love my family. Because I realized loving them didn't mean they made choices for me or had power over me. Maybe that was why I'd been so reluctant to fully love them all these years. Maybe it was because I thought loving them meant giving up control of my life to them.

Cinco was saying that I *did* have to give up control . . . just not to them.

"I love you," I said. All eyes shifted to me. With utter horror, I realized I'd said it out loud. There had been a lull in the conversation, and my remark hung out there like a lonely tree ornament.

I focused on my plate. I couldn't believe I'd said it out loud. What was I thinking? It's one thing to feel it, but to be an idiot and say it?

"I love you too." Kate smiled at me from across the table.

And Dad said, "Well, you know I love you. I raised you and spent half my life's fortune on you." He grinned. I could hardly smile back because of the great big lump that was forming in my throat.

I looked at Mother, who looked as horrified as if she'd served Spam at a senators' wives brunch. When she realized she was the only one who hadn't responded, she cleared her throat and said, "Well, of course we love each other. We're family. The sky's blue too, if you haven't noticed." I guessed that was the best she could do.

Then Kate said, "You know, Leah, I've got to hand it to you. I didn't think you had the guts to do it."

"Do what?"

"Hello? Break off your engagement. I mean, sis, that was one gutsy move. You'd already picked out the cake, everyone in the family knew, and it was practically Gammie's lifeline. But you stuck by your convictions. It was an amazing thing to witness."

Dad said, "Honey, it was shocking. But I would never want you to marry someone you didn't love."

I looked at Mother. She smiled a little and nodded, then sliced another thin piece off the quarter breast she'd served herself. She never had been a big eater. I remember her being horrified at how much food I would pile onto my plate at certain events. "Three cucumber slices' worth," she would say, forming her index finger and thumb into a circle. That was our appetizer limit. And as for dinner, we were instructed to leave at least a third on our plate. I always had trouble doing that, especially when they served lobster.

"How have you been doing? Have you talked to Edward?" my sister asked. This was shocking coming from her, because until now she hadn't acknowledged anyone's pain but her own.

I decided this was the right time to mention Cinco. "I haven't talked to Edward," I said. "It's officially over. There's no reason for us to talk anymore."

Mother shook her head, like that was the saddest thing she'd ever heard.

"But I am seeing someone."

It seemed even the chicken carcass looked up at that statement.

"So soon?" was Mother's predictable reply.

"Is this the same gentleman you mentioned before?" Dad asked.

I nodded. "We've been seeing a lot of each other. I really like him." I looked around the table. "No. I love him. I'm in love with him."

"It's not a rebound?" Kate asked. "Because I've had two dates with the copier serviceman at work, and I have no idea why."

"No," I said. "This is the real thing."

"Pass the chicken," Mother said. She hadn't even eaten half of what was on her plate, but she obviously needed to slice into something. I was thankful it wasn't going to be me.

For a few moments we all listened to Mother try to slice through a stubborn tendon. Finally it snapped loose and a leg fell off. Mother stabbed the leg with her fork and dropped it onto her plate.

"Well," Mother said, "the good news is that you should have plenty of ideas for your next wedding. That's half the battle." She smiled, all the while stabbing food items on her plate, but not putting anything in her mouth. Finally, a green bean made its way in.

Dad set his fork down and gave me his full attention. "Why don't you tell us a little bit about this new man. He seems very important to you, and if so, I'd like to know more about him."

I wanted to reach out and hug Dad. But instead I said, "His name is Cinco."

Mother thought I was joking, so she laughed lightheartedly like she did when she didn't understand the jokes told by other senators at parties.

"Cinco? Like the number four?" Kate asked.

"Five, actually. And yes. It's a nickname."

"A nickname for what? A character on *Sesame Street*?" Mother quipped. She'd always hated that show, even though Dad spent lots of time as a senator fighting for public-television funding.

"Think of it as a nickname, like Howie is for Howard." That shut Mother up, so I continued. "His real name, actually, is Rupert."

"*Rupert*?" Dad said as though I'd just leaked top secret information.

"Yes, Rupert."

"Then I'm glad he goes by Cinco," Dad said. "I'm not fond of the name Rupert."

I wanted to sigh loudly. Really loudly. Everyone was so caught up with his name I hadn't even had a chance to describe what a wonderful human being he was, what he had already done for my life so far. And I couldn't imagine why Dad wouldn't like the name Rupert. It sounded as old-Washington as they came.

"Anyway," I continued, "he has a political radio talk show that you may have heard of. He's a Christian. And he thinks I hung the moon."

"So he's into politics," Dad said, slowly rubbing his hands together.

"Yes. He's very intelligent. You two would have a lot to talk about."

Dad raised an eyebrow. "Well, I suppose it would be nice to talk politics with somebody in this family, since I'm the only one who seems interested in it." Dad looked distracted. He took a bite of food, then pointed his fork at me like he was about to say something, but a full minute went by without anything being said. Then, "What'd you say his name was again?"

"Rupert," I said carefully. Maybe the heart attack had damaged his brain.

"His other name."

"Cinco."

"No, his *other* name."

"His last name?"

"Yes."

"Dublin."

"No!" Dad shouted and slammed down his fork. "No! No!"

I dropped my own fork, and all three of us women had our

backs straight against our chairs and our fingers clinging to the edge of the table.

Dad pointed to me. "No! I forbid you!"

"Why?" I asked meekly. I had never seen my father's face so bloodred.

"Calm down," Mother instructed him in a voice that Dumbo would've struggled to hear. "This isn't good for your—"

Dad's hand slammed onto the top of the table as he stood. I was shaking all over. "I don't ever want to hear that name spoken in this house again. Do you understand me? You will break off this relationship and never see him again." Dad threw his napkin onto his plate and stomped out of the room.

"What is going on?" I asked Mother, though my lungs were so depleted of air that I could hardly get the question out.

Mother blotted her mouth as if dinner had gone just as planned. "Rupert Dublin the Fourth is your father's greatest enemy."

"Enemy? What kind of enemy?"

"He was the reporter for the *Globe,* the one that dogged your father during his entire political career. You two were mere children at the time. He was relentless, always calling your father unreliable, and I believe he even used the term 'pigheaded' a time or two."

"Well, I'm not dating the *Fourth,* I'm dating the *Fifth,*" I said. I heard Kate quietly counting *uno, dos, tres, cuatro . . .*

"It doesn't matter to your father. Mr. Dublin is a sworn enemy. He always will be."

I stood, startling both my sister and my mother.

"What are you doing?" Mother asked.

"I'm going to talk to him."

"Not a good idea," Mother said, standing as well. "I've hardly ever seen your father that angry. He needs to calm down." I started to move to the door and she said, "For his health, Leah."

I took one look at her, a long look that made her squirm in her hosiery, and walked straight to the back patio, where I'd heard my father slam the French doors.

The evening breeze caught my breath as I walked toward Dad, who stood against the concrete railing that overlooked the gardens. He heard me walk out but didn't turn to acknowledge me. My armpits were reminding me that as bold as I wanted to be, I was never going to be like Cinco. This kind of confrontation was not in my blood. But if I didn't stand up for this, what else was there to stand up for? I had to fight for the man I loved. The man who loved me like I'd never been loved.

I started to say something, but Dad whirled around to face me, a stern expression catching my words and flattening them like a bug under his shoe.

"You will not see him anymore," Dad said. "I cannot even imagine having that man's own flesh and blood under my roof."

"You are not being fair!" I said, and I could tell my outburst surprised him, but he didn't pause long.

"Leah, you are a member of this family, and that requires your loyalty. I have raised you to be my daughter, and up until a few weeks ago, you were everything a father could want in a daughter. Nobody has been more reliable in my life than you. I understand that right now you're going through some emotional turmoil. You've called off your marriage to Edward, and you think this Roman numeral is the answer to all your problems. But I am telling you that you will not date him anymore. Call it off. It can't be that serious. It's only been a few weeks since you called it off with Edward. Tell this man you're sorry, but that you can't see him anymore because, unfortunately, his father is a cockroach."

Surprisingly, tears didn't rush to my eyes. I kept expecting them to come, but they didn't. And my neck didn't feel hot either. All I said, as calmly as if I were talking about rosemary chicken, was, "I won't."

"What did you say?"

"I won't."

"You won't."

"I'm sorry you have your disagreements with Mr. Dublin, but that's not my problem. Cinco is a fine man that you would adore if you gave him the chance."

"Ha! Nothing fine or good could come from that man. Do you realize he almost ended my political career? Do you realize that?"

"I do now. You've made it pretty clear that if given a chance, you'd allow him that kind of power over you again."

"What is that supposed to mean?" Dad was nearly shouting now, but I tried to keep my voice low, reminding myself how much I loved my dad.

"It means that Rupert Dublin the *Fourth* apparently still holds his power over you. You can't even say his name without trembling with rage, Dad. Don't you see? You could let go of all that and embrace Cinco and let it be done with."

Dad's voice boomed. "What's come over you? You've changed."

"No. I just want to date a man named Cinco, who is good and decent, and who, if he had any other last name, would be a person you could like too."

"What are you saying? You're going to defy me?"

"Defy you? I'm thirty-four. It's called having my own life."

"So you've made your decision."

"I want to date him, Dad. That's all I'm saying. And I'd like you to give him a chance."

Dad turned back toward the gardens, his knuckles flat against the railing as he leaned on it and lowered his head, not unlike the famous picture of President Kennedy during the Cuban Missile Crisis. "Then so be it. If it's that important to you, then date him. I can see where your priorities are. But know this. As long as you are with him, you are not allowed in my house."

My heart was shattering with each harsh word that he spoke.

Dad turned and brushed by me, through the doors and out of sight. I couldn't believe what I'd just heard. Was he disowning me? If ever there was the equivalent of a missile crisis in my life, this was it. Dad had never been this angry with me that I could remember.

Suddenly, I heard someone behind me. I turned, hoping it was Dad with immediate regrets. But it was Kate. She slid beside me and looked toward the garden as she plopped her hand around my shoulder and pulled me close.

"Thanks for taking over my old job in this family," she said. "I can show you where to get your nose pierced." We smiled at each other, but as we stood there, I wondered if this would be the last time I would ever see this beautiful view.

Chapter 30

[She twirls, then gazes at herself.]

The full-length mirror on the back side of my closet door framed me standing there, my shoulders slumping a little. *Stand tall,* I reminded myself, and I thrust my shoulders back and lifted my chin. I brushed my hair out of my face and tried to smile.

Smile. Come on, smile.

I couldn't. I wanted to. I felt . . . beautiful. But something kept me from enjoying the moment.

Twirl. Yes, twirl, like when you were a child.

So I did. I twirled. The bottom of the dress filled with air. I twirled again. And again. And finally I laughed.

Pink *was* a good color for me. It made my cheeks flush and my eyes light up with excitement.

Cinco had told me to wear something really nice, formal even. He enjoyed surprising me from day to day. I had originally put on my ever-reliable black knee-length dress, the sleeveless one with the turtleneck. I wasn't a fan of showing off my shoulders, but I was usually willing to make the sacrifice to have my neck covered up. Splotching, though infrequent these days, was still a possibility.

The pink dress, though, with its spaghetti straps and square neckline that showcased splotching, won me over. It was still as bold a move as I was capable of making. But I imagined myself sitting across from Cinco, and I trusted I would be as comfortable as if I were wearing my favorite sweater. He would make sure of that.

He told me a car would be waiting for me at seven sharp. I looked out my window and there it was, waiting down below, a shiny black Cadillac. I grabbed my handbag, took one more look in the mirror, and went downstairs.

The driver opened the door for me, and when I asked him where we were going he laughed and said, "He told me you would ask, and he told me not to tell you!"

We rode in silence. I couldn't imagine where we were headed, but I felt like Cinderella. Thirty minutes passed, and we drove into the South End district. The driver pulled up to a beautiful building, boasting a large sign that read "The Boston Center for the Arts" and below it, in curvy lettering, "*Welcome to the Cyclorama.*" Tons of people streamed up the stairs into the building, all dressed like they were going to a . . .

The door clicked open and I gasped. The driver laughed. A man in a tuxedo was standing where the door had once been, and he reached out his hand. I couldn't get myself to take it, even though I knew, attached to that tuxedo was Cinco. Finally he bent down so I could see his face.

"Hi there," he said. I took his hand and he helped me out of the car. He shut the door and took a step back from me, examining the dress. "You look so . . ."

I held my breath.

"Perfect."

I exhaled, and Cinco took notice. "You okay?"

I nodded. "I just don't . . . dress up much. Occupational hazard. I live and work in sweats."

"Hey, I'm in radio. I've got the same problem. As long as my voice sounds good, who cares what I look like, right?"

"You look really nice," I said, returning the compliment. "You clean up well."

"Thanks."

"So . . . what are we doing here?"

"Having fun and enjoying each other," he said, taking my hand and leading me into line with all the other dressed-up people.

"Well," I said, not letting him off that easy, "we can do that without getting all dressed up."

"True." He smiled. "But I don't want you to grow bored with me."

"I don't think that's possible."

"Good," he said. We entered the building, where a stunning display of red and blue lights hung from the ceiling, waiters greeted us with cocktails and appetizers, and important-looking people swarmed around one another like bees on a honeycomb.

"Oh, my gosh," I said. "Are we . . . Is this . . . This is! It's the Boston Charity Gala!"

He smiled. "You figured that out pretty quickly."

"My father used to come to this and then talk about it for days. It's one of the biggest events in Boston!"

"That's right."

"And there's always a ton of famous people here!"

He laughed. "See? You're already enjoying yourself."

Any hang-ups I'd had about wearing the pink dress vanished. Cinco led me to the dance floor, and as my guide, made me look like a professional. All I had to do was hold on to him, and I danced as gracefully as I could've imagined. Which still wasn't that graceful, but I enjoyed myself.

The evening had just begun, and already, I was completely enchanted. As we danced, a thought popped into my head. I still didn't have a pet name.

But I didn't care.

Dinner was served at 8:30 p.m., and the main course was lobster. I couldn't believe it. We sat at a round table with six other people, several of whom Cinco knew and one lady who had worked in my father's office in Washington. She went on and on about how nice Dad was, which made my heart ache a little. I missed him. I hadn't told Cinco about the incident with Dad. This relationship was too precious to spoil with the news that our fathers were archenemies.

I shook off the bleak thoughts. "My favorite!" I told Cinco as the waiter placed the lobster in front of me.

"I know." He smiled.

"Really? I told you that?"

"Yes."

"Is there anything you don't know about me?"

"Probably, but I intend to find out everything."

"And how do you intend on doing that?"

"The same way my grandparents did it."

"They had a secret way?" I asked, laughing.

"My grandparents were married for seventy-five years and died within two weeks of each other."

"Wow. What a nice life."

"Yes. Their marriage survived my grandfather serving in two wars and my grandmother surviving cancer three times and losing a child at birth and another as an adult, just to name a few things."

"But it sounds like they were madly in love. How'd they meet?"

"My grandfather saw my grandmother in a park one day. She was sitting under a tree, reading. He went over to introduce himself, and they started talking."

"That's so sweet," I said. "Sometimes I really long for the days when things were so much simpler."

"Two weeks after he met her in the park, he married her."

"Wow," I said. "And they were married for seventy-five years."

Cinco leaned toward me, his mouth near my ear so I could hear him over the crowd. "I believe in that kind of love."

I looked into his eyes, completely forgetting about the lobster tail sitting in front of me.

"I believe love is a choice, and that's why their love worked. They didn't know everything about the other person in two weeks' time. But they chose to love each other no matter what. I don't believe there's such a thing as the perfect mate. I think there's only perfect love. And it casts out all fear. And it's patient and kind. It's not jealous or rude or boastful or proud. It doesn't demand its own way. It doesn't get irritated or keep records of wrong. It hates injustice and rejoices when the truth prevails. Love is always hopeful, it never loses faith, it never gives up, and it endures through every conflict."

I couldn't take my eyes off him. Every word set my heart into a spasm. His fingers touched mine and he said, "I'm thirty-nine years old, and all my life I've been searching."

"For what?" I asked.

"You." He pulled a small pink velvet box out of his pocket, and his normally confident eyes betrayed him. He could hardly look at me. "I know it's only been a few weeks, Leah, but I love you. And if you'll let me, I want to love you for the rest of our lives."

All around us, the tables hushed, and when I looked back at Cinco, he was on one knee, taking my hand. "Will you let me? Will you marry me?"

Every fear I'd ever had in my life was, in an instant, gone.

Chapter 31

[She unlatches the gate.]

"You're shaking," Cinco said. He took my hand in his. "Are you sure you want to do this? Now?"

It was a beautiful, breezy day. The sun winked as clouds passed in front of it. But I couldn't enjoy it. We sat in my car on the concrete circular driveway of my parents' enormous home. Visiting my parents seemed like such a good idea at the time, but now that I was here, all I could hear was my father's angry voice and hurt-filled eyes.

"You don't have to do this today," Cinco said.

I studied the ring on my finger. It looked stunning and felt warm.

"I want to. You are the man I love, and I want Dad to know." When Cinco proposed, I did not hesitate to say yes, and later on, as we were basking in the joy of the evening, I broke the news about our fathers. But Cinco already knew. He said he hadn't given it a second thought, and that his father would deal with it one way or the other.

I turned to him. "Cinco, I don't know if I can be like you. I want to be strong in every way possible, but I don't think I am. I don't think I can always stand up for the weak guy, you know? I *am* the weak guy."

Cinco chuckled and touched my face. "You're not weak, Leah. You have a beautiful, sensitive heart. You feel deeply for people because that's how God made you. Nothing can change that, especially when you know who you are. And now you know who you are. You are a woman in love with me!"

I laughed. "That is true. So true. And I will do anything to protect that." I looked up at the house and gathered my nerves. "You don't mind waiting in the car for a few minutes?"

"Not at all. Whatever you want."

"Okay. I'll be back in a few minutes." I touched his hand. "It's Dad's heart condition. I don't want to startle him."

Cinco laughed. "Don't make excuses. Go do what you need to do. I'll be here when you need me."

I got out of the car, clenching my hands in fists as I walked toward the house. Seeing some lawn bags near the fence, I realized Mother was probably in the back tending to the roses. I opened the gate, which was always unlocked, and followed the path around the house, glancing back at Cinco, who had unfolded a newspaper and was reading. I laughed. Was the man capable of being nervous about anything?

I was still on a high, hardly able to believe that in just a few short weeks, the life that was in shambles at my feet had been resurrected in the most unexpected way. I tried not to let my urge to turn and run distract me from how great it felt to be engaged to a man I truly loved.

Mother had her back to me while clipping roses, a big floppy hat perched on her head, and white gloves dirtied only at the fingertips. Mother was rarely caught in pants, but she made an exception for gardening.

"Mother," I said.

She startled and turned, dropping her clippers. "Leah," she said, patting her heart. "I wasn't expecting you."

"I know," I said and hid my hand behind my back. "I wasn't sure if my call would be answered."

"What brings you by?" she asked.

With a deep breath in, I swung my arm around and placed my hand directly in front of her. Her face lit up. "Oh, how beautiful!"

"Thank you," I said, relieved she wasn't throwing something.

She looked at me. "It's what I've been praying for."

"It is?"

She nodded. "I always thought you and Edward were meant to be together."

I closed my eyes and wanted to kick something.

"What?" Mother asked.

"I'm not marrying Edward. I'm marrying Cinco Dublin."

Mother looked down at the ring again. "You are."

"Yes."

"I came to tell you and Dad. And . . . introduce you to him."

Mother's eyes widened. "He's . . . here?"

"Waiting in the car."

"You brought him here?" Mother looked down at herself. "I'm a mess!"

"Mother, you look fine. Take off the gloves and you look like you're on your way to a Cape Cod luncheon."

Mother relaxed a little. "Really?"

I nodded, then looked toward the house. "Is Dad here?"

"In his office," she said.

"I'm going to tell him. I'm sorry if that upsets you, Mother, but this is what I want, and I can't pretend that it's not. I can only pray that Dad will accept it."

"Poor follow-through."

"Excuse me?"

"That's what Mr. Dublin always used to say about your father. He would write about how many promises and threats your father would make, but how when push came to shove, he had poor follow-through." Mother had pulled off her gloves and was looking at her own ring. "It's true."

"It is?"

"Sure. Everyone has their weaknesses, Leah. I know you think your father is near-perfect, and as fathers go, he's certainly the cream of the crop. But as a senator, he was always trying to please everyone. He wanted to make everyone happy, but he just ended up making people unhappy. And the person he was most unhappy with was himself." She straightened her posture and said very matter-of-factly, "So that's what made him mad all these years. Mr. Dublin continued to point it out, and your father knew it was true. But," she said, with the ring in her voice that indicated a mood change, "that can work to your advantage in this situation."

"How so?"

"He's a lot of bark, but little bite. He would never disown you, Leah. He hates Mr. Dublin, but he loves you more."

Tears streamed down my face. "Really?"

"Of course. I've been furious with him for doing this. He's acting like a child. So you march in there and give him a piece of your mind, do you hear me? Tell him to grow up. Tell him you're a grown-up, for crying out loud, and you can marry who you want to!"

My mouth fell open. Mother had never spoken to me like I had any sense. Now she was giving me permission to read Dad the riot act. "Mother, why haven't you ever encouraged me to speak my mind before?" I hated to ruin a decent moment between us, but I had to know.

"I never thought you were capable of it." She took my hand in hers and looked at the ring. "It's exquisite. Just exquisite. Now go on, go tell your father what's on your mind. Tell him the news, and make sure that he understands it's *good* news." She smiled.

Butterflies tickled my stomach as I looked up toward the house, toward Dad's office window.

"Leah," Mother said, "love is worth the risk."

I nodded. "Okay. Can you . . . can you go bring Cinco inside? He's out in the car, and—"

"Oh! We can't have guests sitting out in the car! I'm a complete mess, but I can invite him in and make some good Southern tea."

"Okay." I walked up the steps toward the back patio. Every possible scenario rolled through my head, but I kept walking. Then I stopped and turned around.

She was messing with her hat.

"Hey," I said, and she looked up at me.

"Yes?"

"Thanks. Mom."

I walked through the house to Dad's study, which was a large room with two huge windows looking out over the gardens. Dad had his feet propped up on his desk and was watching a small television mounted in one of the bookcases.

"Would you look at that!" he said, without turning around, as he gestured toward the television. "Bob Wolmat is an idiot! He has no television presence. None. He's as dry as a bone, I tell you."

Dad liked to relive the glory days. He was a favorite on morning news shows and had a good rapport with the anchors. He still made appearances from time to time, which would make his month, especially when he was invited onto *Meet the Press,* which was his favorite.

"Bob!" Dad shouted at the television. "Stop scowling! You're trying to sell this thing, and you can't even manage to look pleasant." Dad laughed. "And to think this guy was going to be a VP candid—" He turned in his chair and saw me. "I thought you were . . . no matter. What are you doing here?"

"I came to talk to you."

He put his battle face on, and with little expression pointed to the chair across his desk. He locked his fingers together and rocked slightly in his chair, saying nothing.

"It's about Cinco."

"What about him? Have you dumped the spawn of—"

"Dad," I said. "That's not necessary."

Dad didn't look pleased that I'd called him down. "Then why are you here?"

"To tell you that Cinco has asked me to marry him, and that I've accepted his proposal."

I expected rage. And shouting. And lots of insults using the word *spawn*. But instead, he seemed to freeze to his seat, and his eyes became like ice. "So you've come to tell me you've made your choice. You would rather be in his family than mine."

"I'd rather be in my family and have you act like the decent man I know you are."

Dad looked at me like I'd lost my mind. So I looked at him like he'd lost his. We stared at each other for a long time, and something flashed through my father's eyes that I'd never seen before, at least when he was looking at me. I'd about convinced myself I hadn't seen it when it flickered again.

Respect. That's what I saw. Respect.

He held a good poker face, though. And then he sneered and said, "Old Dublin know his son's a democrat? That's probably really got his goat." Dad chuckled, like that might be the only good thing that could come out of the situation.

"Cinco's not a democrat. He's a republican. And so am I. I have been for years."

I bit my lower lip, nearly chewed through it. I couldn't believe I'd finally spilled the long and closely guarded secret. I'd set up my own guillotine and willingly placed my head in it. At least death would come quick.

But Dad stood, walked around the desk, and folded his arms like a math teacher about to spout off a pop quiz. "So this is what you want."

I nodded.

Dad groaned and mumbled something about God having a sense of humor. Then he said, "Fine, Leah. Fine. If this is what you want. Don't expect me to attend the wedding. I could never pretend to be cordial to Rupert Dublin, but his son, well . . . he's welcome in my house."

I stood and gave Dad a gigantic hug. "That's good! Because he's out in the living room with Mom right now, waiting to meet you."

"Oh, good heavens," Dad said. "This is a lot for a guy who just had a heart attack."

"Don't pull that heart-attack card with me. And you know, I think your heart could stand a break from some of the resentment and bitterness you're holding against Cinco's father."

"Leah, you've brought enough change here today to last a lifetime. I don't need you to start lecturing me too."

I smiled. "Fair enough."

He nodded and straightened his shirt. "This isn't going to be easy."

"Dad," I said, wrapping my arm around his back, "you've been in politics for years. I'm sure you can manage an insincere smile at the very least."

He glanced at me. "Well, let's give it a shot. Come on. Let's go see what evil incarnate's only son looks like." Then he mumbled some things about my being a republican.

I laughed.

Chapter 32

[She dances.]

I opened my apartment door. Cinco stood with a small bouquet of flowers, his eyes peeking over the top. "Hi." I loved how he said it. After four months of knowing him, it still made my skin tingle with delight.

"Hi."

He kissed me and came in, putting the flowers on the counter. "So, I'm not used to being away from you this long."

"You're not used to me working."

"True. Since I've known you, you've pretty much been an out-of-work playwright."

"I still am. But this new play, I think it's going to be good. Really good. I haven't been this excited about a project since my first play."

"That's good. I haven't been this excited about a woman since . . . well, never."

I pecked him on the cheek. "Two more months and we'll be Mr. and Mrs. Rupert Dublin V. I can't wait to wear the dress I found. It's so beautiful."

"I can't wait to see you in it."

I went to the kitchen to put the flowers in water and to take a moment to marvel at how much my life had changed in just a matter of months. For once in my life, I felt like I was who I was supposed to be. I was a kind, sensitive person, but a woman who knew how to stand up for not only herself but for truth, even if it meant things would get ugly. I was by no means at Cinco's level, but I had certainly come into my own.

"Have you asked Elisabeth to be your matron of honor?"

"Yeah. She said she would love to. She just asked that I pick a dress with her 'situation' in mind." Elisabeth continued to be a constant reminder of what tragedy can result when you don't stand up for the truth. Two days after Cinco and I were engaged, Elisabeth told me she was pregnant with the mechanic's baby.

She and her husband had decided to try to work things out, although they still weren't sure what to do about the child she was carrying. Elisabeth wanted to keep her, but Henry was insisting they give her up for adoption.

I would never know for sure if standing up for what was right would've made any difference in Elisabeth's life, but I vowed never again to let another person's influence decide what I would do. If I had it to do over again, I would grab Elisabeth by the arm and tell it to her straight.

There are few chances in life to do things over again. But I felt like I got a second chance to be the person God first created me to be. I finally felt worthy. I finally felt free.

"So," Cinco said, coming to stand behind me in the kitchen and entwining his fingers with mine, "are you going to tell me?"

"Tell you what?"

"What your play is about. I'm dying to know, and you're keeping it so top secret that I'm about to decide you're not really a playwright; you're a spy!"

I smiled and turned around in his arms. "Okay. But you can tell no one."

He put his hand to his mouth and said, "I pwomise."

I laughed. "Okay, it's an ensemble cast, about a group of people in an anger management class."

"What kind of people?"

"Oh, there are all sorts involved. A literary agent with a nasty personality. Two former politicians who used to hate each other. A popular television personality with some heavy political views. To name a few." I winked at him.

"No! That's pretty bold."

"Well, you know what they say. Never tick off a writer. You may find yourself immortalized in ways you never expected."

He laughed. "Is there a love story?"

"I can't give you any more details. If I did, I'd have to kill you."

"That would be inconvenient for the wedding."

"True."

The phone rang, and the caller ID announced it was J.R. I hadn't spoken to her in ages. She'd left a message recently, wondering aloud on my machine whether I'd checked myself in somewhere. She didn't know about the new play I was working on. So this morning I'd called and left a message at her office for her to call me back.

"Excuse me, Cinco," I said. "I've got a bit of unfinished business." I answered the phone. "Hello?"

"You live and breathe," J. R. said. "What do they have you on, Prozac?"

"I'm not on Prozac, J. R. I'm perfectly fine."

"Well, that's the excuse I gave Peter. However, I told him that some of the best playwrights around are mental cases, that it's just a sign of genius. So if you wouldn't mind keeping up that facade, it might just sell this next play of yours. And by the way, what is it about and when will it be finished?"

"J. R., I want to thank you for everything you've been for me. Because of you, I've realized some very important things about myself. I just wanted you to know that."

"Leah, this is no time to be sentimental. I hated sentiment even when I was a smoker, so you can only imagine how it rubs me now. Let's just get down to business."

"Fine," I said, smiling. "J. R., you're fired."

Welcome to my new life. Don't bother wiping your feet.

Acknowledgments

I want to thank Ami McConnell, Allen Arnold, and Amanda Bostic for believing in me as a writer and believing in this project. I'm thankful to have worked with such exceptionally talented people with great vision and love for what they do. I'd also like to give special thanks to Erin Healy and Laura Wright, whose editorial contributions to this book have made it better than I ever dreamed it could be. I count it a privilege to have your fingerprints within the pages of this manuscript. Thanks to Janet Kobobel Grant, my agent, for always supporting me and guiding me to the books I should be writing. Thanks to my family, Sean, John Caleb, and Cate, for loving me so much, and to my Lord, for allowing me this extraordinary journey.

ALSO AVAILABLE FROM